INDELIBLE

Indelible

A NOVEL

Adelia Saunders

BLOOMSBURY

NEW YORK · LONDON · OXFORD · NEW DELHI · SYDNEY

Bloomsbury USA
An imprint of Bloomsbury Publishing Plc

1385 Broadway	50 Bedford Square
New York	London
NY 10018	WC1B 3DP
USA	UK

www.bloomsbury.com

BLOOMSBURY and the Diana logo are trademarks of Bloomsbury Publishing Plc

First published 2017

ISBN: HB: 978-1-63286-394-2
         TPB: 978-1-63286-999-9
         ePub: 978-1-63286-396-6

LIBRARY OF CONGRESS CATALOGING-IN-PUBLICATION DATA
Names: Saunders, Adelia, author.
Title: Indelible : a novel / Adelia Saunders.
Description: New York : Bloomsbury, 2017.
Identifiers: LCCN 2016001367 | ISBN 978-1-63286-394-2 (hardcover)
Classification: LCC PS3619.A82337 I53 2017 | DDC 813/.6—dc23
LC record available at http://lccn.loc.gov/2016001367.

2 4 6 8 10 9 7 5 3

Typeset by RefineCatch Limited, Bungay, Suffolk
Printed and bound in U.S.A. by Berryville Graphics., Berryville, Virginia

To find out more about our authors and books visit www.bloomsbury.com.
Here you will find extracts, author interviews, details of forthcoming events and
the option to sign up for our newsletters.

Bloomsbury books may be purchased for business or promotional use.
For information on bulk purchases please contact Macmillan Corporate and
Premium Sales Department at specialmarkets@macmillan.com.

For Nick

{MAGDALENA}

Vilnius, 1991

IN THE OLD days when a child was born, Luck would stand outside the house and whisper at the window. *He will be rich. He will be tall. He will have his share.* After the baby was washed and wrapped the midwife would sit by the window and listen. *He will live only as long as the little fire burns,* Luck might say. And the midwife, if she were clever, would tell the family that they must never let the fire in the stove go out. The mother would spend her days feeding twigs into the flames and the son would grow up with the kitchen always warm until—this is how it happened in the stories—he married a rich girl who didn't care about the old ways, who probably wasn't very good in the kitchen and had no use for her mother-in-law's advice, and he would fall stone-dead the moment she let the stove get cold.

That was a story Magdalena's mother used to tell her, until one day, when Magdalena was just beginning to learn to read but before she knew that anything was wrong, she asked her mother why the midwife hadn't stopped Luck from coming through the window with her pen.

"What pen?" her mother said.

"To write her name."

"What name?"

"On the baby."

"What are you talking about?" her mother said.

"Like here." Magdalena ran her fingers over the words that were written across her mother's neck and down her arms, looking for *Luck,* which in Lithuanian was a word that also meant *Happiness,* and sometimes meant something that was not exactly either. Almost everyone had it on them somewhere, and she found it at the bend inside her mother's wrist, where the soft skin folded the letters. "Here," she said. The letters moved a little with the beat of her mother's pulse. Magdalena traced her fingers over the word, wondering how Luck had learned to write her name so neatly, considering she was nothing but a fairy and had never gone to school.

But her mother pulled her hand away. "You're making jokes," she said, not laughing. She felt Magdalena's forehead for a fever and made her go to bed, and after that she didn't tell the story of Luck outside the window anymore.

2008

Paris, June

INGA BEART LOST so many things in Paris that her biographers hardly get around to mentioning the shoes. At the time, several newspapers reported that she was barefoot when she boarded the ship back to New York, refusing the arm of the ship's doctor and feeling along the deck with her toes. Yet to the best of my knowledge no one has ever tried to explain what exactly happened to her shoes. They were red, with a high delicate heel, and historians say that throughout her career she was rarely seen in public without them. By the time she left France in 1954 those shoes would have been as familiar to a generation of readers as the pale eyes and ink-stained lips in her dust jacket photograph, or the way she had of bullying something fine and lyrical out of a plain phrase.

I don't blame the biographers for giving so little attention to the subject of her feet. In the wake of the most violent episode of Inga Beart's quick life, the fact that her shoes were gone must seem like a minor detail, and scholars have focused instead on the last lines she wrote on the ship back to America—a confession, though no one believed it, scratched into the paint on the side of her berth with the stub of a pencil she had kept hidden under her tongue. Because by then, of course, they'd taken everything else away.

But of all the questions that remain about Inga Beart's final months, it's the disappearance of her red shoes that matters most to me. I'd thought for years about going to Paris to see if I couldn't find out for myself what happened to them, though of course I knew it was next to impossible that any evidence of their fate still existed some fifty years on. I'd asked a few of the historians about them, but they only gave me a shrug or raised an eyebrow at an old man's interest in a pair of ladies' high heels long since gone to dust. They must have gotten left behind in Paris, they told me. Those shoes wouldn't have been any use to her by the time the nurses packed her things and sent her home.

...now much more about Inga

...my mother once, and I never

...and the rest of the family flatly

...know is that I couldn't have been

...use by my fourth birthday she was

...ey never would have let a child see her

...he returned.

...she came to visit have gotten so mixed up

...ies and bits I must have taken out of her biog-

rap... ...o be sure what actually took place that day and what m... ...n filled in later. The memory is too detailed for someone so... ...I'll be the first to admit it, but I've read that at that age a child's retention of a single piece of seemingly random information is sometimes remarkably accurate. And though it's rare, that must have been the case with me, because I remember my mother's shoes so clearly that I can see them even now if I close my eyes.

The memory is framed by a bit of what looks like lace but what must have been the corner of Aunt Cat's vinyl tablecloth, leading me to imagine that I spent my mother's visit hiding under the kitchen table. The rest of the memory—a blue door, a teacup smashing—doesn't quite belong to Aunt Cat's kitchen; it may have been spliced in later. But the image of those shoes is mine alone. In the hours or minutes I spent there under the table, while she and Aunt Cat must have been talking, I came to possess a bit of Inga Beart that the publishers and academics and fans and reporters and even Aunt Cat and the doctors missed. Nowhere in all the literature, in all the minute details of her life that have been written down, is there a record of her shoes in the vivid detail I remember. I tried to tell a couple of the biographers that I got an up-close look at them, but they didn't seem too interested and wrote in their books the same thing Aunt Cat said, that Inga Beart never came to see me.

But one can only really be certain of a few things in one's life, and I'll bet those biographers and university professors have used up their share of certainties on other things. I saw her once, I know that, and through the years as I lay awake at night I learned the memory of my mother's feet by heart. I saw the way the bones in her ankle twitched like there were little birds caught under the skin. I knew the soft leather and the exact shade of red of those shoes and I saw the places where they were scuffed and mended. To me the homophone was never a coincidence: I saw that her sole was broken before anyone else did—it was the left one, split across the ball of her foot as if she'd been standing on tiptoe for a long, long time.

I suppose it makes the most sense to begin this account with the morning I arrived in Paris. I've tried to think back over my first moments in the city: Was there a sound that brushed just right against a memory? Or a smell that was in some distant way familiar? But the fact is that after all those hours on the plane, everything felt so new and odd to me. When I finally stepped off the airport shuttle bus and onto the boulevard de Sébastopol, the only thing I remember noticing was that it was very early in the morning.

At that hour there was a hush that country people don't expect of a city. The loose spokes of a bicycle's wheel made a musical sound across a cobbled alleyway, and the sun was just beginning to light up the rows of buildings, all done in the same milk-washed stone. But I didn't stop to appreciate the quiet. I was worried about my Aunt Cat's old suitcase. The clasps had given way and I'd found the suitcase on the baggage carousel in its own plastic tub, wound in tape with a sticker explaining that my luggage had been damaged during the flight.

I should have known that the suitcase wouldn't stand the trip, I'd thought, but I didn't dare undo the tape and open it there at the airport—I wasn't sure I'd be able to get it closed again. In any case, all my notes and the important documents were safe in my carry-on; the suitcase only had my clothes and a few books in it, I told myself, and it wasn't until I was already on the shuttle leaving the airport that I remembered that among those books was the latest biography of my mother, published just a few months ago. I needed to have it with me for my appointment at the French National Archives the next day, and I had no idea if I would be able to buy another copy in Paris.

So, as soon as the shuttle driver handed me my luggage I got down on one knee on the sidewalk and started unwrapping the baggage handlers' tape. I'd put the book in last, right at the top of my suitcase, not thinking about how old those clasps were or how a heavy book would be the first thing to fall out.

I got the suitcase open. The undershirts I'd packed were rumpled, like they'd fallen out and been stuffed back inside, but the book was there. It had a smear of grease across the cover, and I took out my hand-kerchief to try to clean it. It wasn't that I cared at all for the book itself: another sensationalized retelling of my mother's life by a British professor named Carter Bristol. Bristol has written a number of revi-sionist biographies, and if he's come to tasteless conclusions about several household names, it has only made him more successful. The cover of the book, with Bristol's name superimposed over a photograph of my mother, particularly annoys me, but I wiped the grease off anyway. It's a lovely picture, one of the few I've ever seen in which she is looking directly at the camera. Against the shadows her pale eyes have an eerie quality, and I was reminded of a description I once read in a magazine article: Inga Beart looked out at the world through a pair of blank spaces, it said. Her eyes were two small gaps in creation that had never been inked in.

I got the book cleaned up as best I could and wrapped it in a shirt. After all, I owe Bristol a debt of sorts. It had taken me most of a lifetime to work up the nerve to come all the way to Paris, and it might have taken me the rest of one if it hadn't been for him. Because even as Bristol twists the facts of my mother's private life to fit his purposes, in his chapter on Inga Beart's final years in Paris he does seem to have made a genuine discovery: a handful of letters and unpublished photo-graphs that Bristol claims were taken of my mother during the summer of 1954. The footnote says, "*Fonds Labat-Poussin, Archives nationales de France.*" If it's true, then this is the first new material anyone has found on her in years.

My Aunt Cat's suitcase was not the kind that rolled. It was heavy, and with the broken clasps I had to carry it carefully. I'd chosen a hotel near the National Archives, not realizing how hard it would be to find. First I turned down a narrow passage that ended in a high stone wall, then found myself on a number of little streets that weren't included on my map, all of them ending at odd angles to where they'd begun.

Of course I started right off wondering if maybe Inga Beart had walked down one of those same streets some early morning a good half-century ago. If she might have left a party as the streetlamps blinked out, leaning for a moment against one of them to steady the same patch of lightening sky. I've seen photographs from those Paris soirées: Inga Beart is usually at the edge of the frame, drifting toward unconsciousness on somebody's arm or turning away from the lens— which in any case was no longer focused on her, but on the new writers and artists and the day's fresher beauties. They wouldn't have noticed my mother as she slipped away, unsteady on her feet, stumbling, perhaps, as the heel of one shoe caught a gap in the stones and tore free.

I happened to be passing a shoe repair shop just then, and I stopped for a moment to look in the window. I set my luggage down to give my arms a rest and peered in through the glass at the dusty back shelves. It wasn't that I actually expected to see a pair of red high heels that might have been left for repairs some fifty years ago in among the galoshes and summer sandals that customers had forgotten to reclaim. But I looked for them anyway, just to be sure.

I hadn't noticed that I was taking up most of the narrow sidewalk, bending down to look in the window. A young woman with a suitcase of her own stepped into the street to go around me. Her suitcase bumped off the curb and rolled over. I turned to apologize and the girl stopped short, saying something I didn't understand.

"I'm sorry," I said, and when she looked confused, "I'm sorry, I don't speak—"

"Ah, no, okay. It's okay," the girl said in English. No point in asking her for directions, I thought. She spoke with an accent I was sure couldn't be French.

"Let me help you with that," I said. I picked up her suitcase and set it back on the sidewalk. "I'm afraid you've lost a wheel." I looked to see if it had gone down into the gutter.

"It is missing from before," she said.

She must have mistaken me for someone else because she was looking at me intently, squinting her eyes a little as if she were trying to place a particular detail of my face. I looked away, and without meaning to I started counting to myself, *one-one-thousand two.* It was a habit I'd gotten into during my trouble with the school board, when for most of my last semester teaching I stopped meeting the eyes of the girls in my classes and looked instead at the parts of their hair, counting to myself, *one-one-thousand two,* then shifting my gaze, careful that no one would think a glance had lingered too long. The girl had a high, even hairline, plain brown at the roots. *One-one-thousand two,* I thought, and directed my eyes down at our two suitcases, *one-one-thousand two,* then at a rose in a cheap plastic cone that the girl was carrying. Along with the rose I noticed that she had a shoebox under her arm.

"Let me get the door for you," I said. When she looked at me blankly I nodded to the shoe repair shop. "Are you going in?" I asked.

"No," the girl said. Seeing that I was looking at the shoebox she was carrying, she said, "Ah, no, not this. It isn't shoes."

"Oh," I said, and to myself, *one-one-thousand two.*

It was only then it occurred to me that there was something half-familiar about her too. I looked again, trying to place the curve of her chin or the tilt of her head.

"Do you know what street is for the station Montparnasse?" the girl asked.

"No idea," I said. "I'm sorry. I don't know Paris."

One-one-thousand two, I thought, and when I looked at the girl again I realized what it was I recognized. It wasn't that I'd seen her face before—at least not exactly. But I'd just been looking at the cover of Bristol's book, where the photograph of Inga Beart captures the uncommon lightness of her eyes. The girl with the suitcase didn't look like my mother except that her eyes were also very pale, and they gave her face the same distant expression—she was looking at me, but her eyes might have been tracking dust motes, or they might have been focused on something very far away.

The girl said something again in her own language. She was still looking at me; I could see the minuscule adjustments of her pupils, spreading like drops of ink in still water. I remembered too late to shift my attention to the girl's forehead. Then, not knowing what else to do, I looked back in at the window of the shop.

There's something they say about my mother: For all she saw in people, she never once looked at me. At the moment of my birth, according to the biographers, Inga Beart turned her head away. One of the biographies quotes a nurse who claimed she was present at my delivery, saying that she remembered it out of the thousands because even the girls who got their babies in the professional way would try to get a peek before the sisters carried them off. But Inga Beart shut her eyes, as the nurse remembered it, and wouldn't open them again until I had been weighed and footprinted and bundled off into the care of the state, and they told her it was time to sign the papers.

It took some time for the hospital staff to sort out where my relatives were, and a while more before Aunt Cat and Uncle Walt could arrange to come and get me. It was no easy thing for them, taking on another baby with Pearl still in diapers and Eddie barely six months old, and I spent my first weeks of life in an orphanage.

Of course, when my own son was born I was determined that for him everything would be different. He lay in his hospital bassinet and gripped my finger with fierce newborn strength, too new to the world to do anything by half measures, and I told him that so long as I had anything to do with it, he was never going to feel alone. I was lucky enough not to know back then the thousand ways a promise like that would be impossible to keep, and I stayed all through the night at the window of the nursery. I wanted to be sure my son had his father there, a face to see through the glass when he opened his eyes.

But if my mother ever worried that I was lonely or afraid, there's no record of it. In fact, in all her novels and stories, her volumes of correspondence and the hours of interviews she gave over the years, my mother never once mentioned me. All the scholars have noted this, and even the more restrained of her biographers can't help but put it rather painfully. As one of them said, "*For Beart, who refused to believe in anybody until she had them written down, her own child simply did not exist.*"

Perhaps. I am willing to admit that it is possible that Inga Beart and I never came face to face—that on the day she came back to the ranch to see us I stayed hidden under my Aunt Cat's kitchen table. But she did come back. However much she might have tried, my mother did not leave me behind entirely. It's the one thing I've been sure of all these years. Because when I close my eyes I see a double stitch just below her anklebone, then three stitches more and the straps begin, crossing left over right on the right foot and right over left on the other. They buckle on the outside and cinch at the fourth hole, but there is a crease just below the third, a little light wearing to show that she must have worn her red shoes a little looser for a while. It's a detail I never thought about when I was young. But later when I heard a pregnant woman tell her friend her feet were swollen, I started wondering if those little creases in the leather hadn't been my addition to my mother's life, my mark on her.

I was surprised to find that the girl with the suitcase was still standing there on the sidewalk. I had the sense that she was waiting for me to say something, though I couldn't remember exactly what we'd been talking about.

Most of the other stores on the street weren't open yet, but at the back of the shoe repair shop I could see the shopkeeper already at work, threading an old hiking boot with new laces. Beside him a pair of red shoes had been polished and tagged for pick-up. They had an old-fashioned look to them, but the color was too bright and the straps were wrong.

The girl was still studying me, as if she wasn't entirely satisfied that we were strangers to each other. She was about the same age as my son. I kept looking in the window of the shop, trying to think of something to say.

On a ledge above the sewing machine was a collection of figurines, clever little things all done out of pieces of shoes. The owner of the shop had clearly made them himself as a way to show his skill with a bit of leather and thread. Crusaders carried lances tipped with cobblers' tacks, and a child's insole had been fashioned into a tiny boat, with shoelaces for rigging and a buffing cloth for a sail.

I turned to the girl. "Aren't these something?" I said.

"What?" she said.

"Here," I pointed to them. "These figurines in the window. See how they have the little suits of armor? My son would get a kick out of that."

"Kick?" she said.

"I mean he'd like them."

"Yah," she said. "They are cute."

Her eyes were on the tiny Crusaders in the window. The rose in its plastic cone had begun to droop.

"We used to make things like this when he was little. Castles and knights, and I remember a catapult—do you know what that is? We built one out of Popsicle sticks and a wooden spoon."

"Yah?" the girl said.

"That was a long time ago," I said. "My son is in college now. But he's studying history." I nodded to the knights. "Just this sort of thing."

In fact, I'd had the idea that this trip to Paris might be something my son and I would do together. With his high school French I could have used his help and he would have liked the research—we could have made an adventure out of it. I'd imagined that he'd be the one to find it: a picture of my mother hidden away in the Paris archives all these years. A photograph Carter Bristol never looked too closely at because her face was blurry while her feet were clear. Or maybe a snapshot from a garden party at someone's chateau: a country brook, a dark-haired woman with eyes like flecks on the negative, the flash a second too late to catch her smile as she leans and dips one toe. Her arms held out for balance, in one hand a pair of shoes with straps that cross, two creases each where the buckle bit the leather, one deep, one only faintly there. And my son, *Wow, Dad. Just like you said.*

The girl was looking at me again, closely. Then she smiled. "So you are here together?"

"My son? No, no, he's not here with me. I'm afraid I'm on my own," I said.

"Ah, okay, I'm sorry," she said. She didn't quite meet my eyes. After a moment she said, "So you come for—reunion?" and she put a slight emphasis on the last word, stretching the syllables and mispronouncing the *u*.

"A reunion? No, did I say that?"

The girl half-laughed to apologize. "Yeah, I have thought you said something. Like something about reunion with the family."

"Well, I probably did," I said. It wasn't the first time I've caught myself thinking out loud. I hadn't meant to embarrass her, so I said, "It's funny how those things slip out."

"Sorry?" she said.

"It's just that you're right, actually." The long flight or the sudden switch of hemispheres must have jostled my subconscious, because, though I couldn't remember ever calling it that, even inside my own head, a reunion was exactly what I'd pictured: my son and I searching through old documents for a glimpse of his grandmother. Finishing a day's work at the archives, comparing our notes on Inga Beart's life in Paris over a glass of beer as evening set in. The three of us, reunited, somehow, across time.

The girl was still looking at me, so I said, "I've come to do some research. Family research. And my son, he likes all that. I thought—a trip to Paris. It was going to be a present. For his birthday."

"Yah, that can be nice," the girl said.

Of course, when I called my son to suggest the trip, the conversation didn't go at all as I had planned. "Be reasonable, Dad," was what he really said when I started to explain about Carter Bristol's footnote and the possibility of finally finding a photo that includes her shoes. "Memories are wrong all the time," he told me. In the end I never got around to asking if he'd like to come with me to Paris.

"But you know, these things," I said to the girl. "Sometimes they don't work out."

"Yah," she said. "Things usually can be like this."

The girl's expression, which a moment before had seemed so intently focused on the details of my face, was all politeness now—after all, she'd simply asked me for directions. I was probably making her uncomfortable going on like that.

"Here," I said. I took out the map I'd bought at the airport and gave it to her, flustered. "Maybe you can ask someone else about the station."

She gave me a brief smile. "For me?" she said. "Okay, thanks."

She glanced down at the map, then tucked it under her arm and turned to look in the window of the shoe repair shop, cupping her hands to block the glare as if something inside had caught her eye.

I picked up Aunt Cat's suitcase but I hesitated a moment before going on. There was something indescribably non-American about the girl's cadence, and the particular way she'd said *yah* and *okay* reminded me of someone, an Eastern European lady named Diana who used to come help out around the house. I wished I'd thought to ask the girl where she was from, though I realized how ignorant I would seem to her. We get so few foreigners out our way, I suppose to me most of them sound about the same.

Still, the thought took me back to certain afternoons after Diana finished the housework, when I'd drive her back to town and we'd get to talking. Sometimes I'd take her out to lunch. I stopped calling her after Uncle Walt passed away last fall, because to be honest I didn't like the idea of her cleaning up after me alone. I thought of asking her over socially, except, of course, the house was a mess, and pretty soon her visa was up. Before the holidays she called to tell me she was going home and we made a rather elaborate plan to exchange gifts anyway— our kids are both over in England and Diana thought it would be a shame not to have them meet. But Christmas came, then spring, then summer, and by the time I left for Paris I still hadn't heard whether she'd received the little things I'd sent for my son to pass along—and no package to me from Diana ever arrived.

The girl with the suitcase was still looking in the shop window. She'd clearly forgotten all about me. I didn't want to startle her by continuing our conversation, and it would have embarrassed us both if I'd tried to explain the little pang I felt at the sibilance of her *t*'s. But just then all I could remember was the way Diana's laughter had its own accent, so that even when she was laughing you could tell she was a foreigner. I wished I had something funny to say to the girl, something that would make her turn around and laugh out loud, just to hear if hers was the same.

Instead I counted to myself again, *one-one-thousand two,* to clear my head. I got a better grip on Aunt Cat's suitcase and nodded toward the girl, who was still intent on the window, and I walked on down the street a little more quickly than I needed to.

It wasn't long before I regretted giving the girl my map. I had the instructions for how to get to my hotel, but I couldn't seem to find the street. I took another wrong turn onto a busy avenue. Traffic was heavier now; young people on scooters raced their engines at traffic lights—or at me—as I hurried across.

I thought I'd better head back toward the spot where the shuttle bus had dropped me off, to see if I couldn't start all over. But I'd gotten turned around, and on top of that the street names kept changing, even when I was sure I'd been going straight in one direction. My arms ached with the weight of the notebooks and papers I'd packed and suddenly I felt tired and very far from home. I turned down another street, then another; I didn't have the heart to stop and take stock of where I was, much less try to find an English speaker and ask for directions.

I was on my way to being truly lost when I remembered an old cowboy trick from my childhood. It was probably something I read in a Louis L'Amour novel: Look back as you ride and memorize your land-marks from the return direction. Somehow the thought of those dimestore Westerns made me feel better. The jog in the sidewalk was a bend in a riverbed—I remembered that—and the shops and restaurants that all looked the same were just another kind of sagebrush wilderness.

I retraced my steps until I found my first wrong turn down the walled-off street, then continued on through narrow canyons of expensive-looking shops, enjoying the thought of my lost cowboy teth-ering his mount and ducking inside one of them to buy a packet of macaroons. Soon the canyons opened into a construction site around an old church tower. The shape of the tower under its layers of scaffolding was familiar; it might have been the core of an extinct volcano rising from the plains.

Sure enough, in a block or two I was back to where I'd started on the boulevard de Sébastopol. Another airport shuttle bus was coming down the street. I even recognized a stained spot on the sidewalk near where I'd knelt to open up my suitcase. Again I found myself wishing that my son was there with me. He could have groaned in forbearance at an English teacher's sort of joke: so many lost tourists in Paris, walking in circles, certain they've seen the place before. No wonder we borrow from the French when we say *déjà vu.*

(NEIL}

London, May

BY THE TIME Neil bought a bus ticket to Swindon the Christmas presents he was supposed to be delivering were already five months late. On the morning he was supposed to go he woke up on the couch. He'd been dreaming that he was eating the baling twine that used to sit in a pile in front of Nan and Pop's barn. If dreams meant anything, this one foretold a hangover. So did the empty glasses and cartons of discount wine that covered the kitchen table and part of the floor. Someone, possibly Neil, had started cleaning up the night before and there were bottles filling the sink. Neil took out a few to get to the faucet; he could feel the dream-fibers still stuck to his tongue. He turned on the water and drank some out of his hands.

From the kitchen he could hear Veejay, his roommate, turning in his sleep and mumbling. Under the mumble was a beeping sound, because Neil hadn't turned off his alarm. He stepped carefully between the glasses to get to their room. It smelled like feet. Veejay, who had been all over a girl from the film school the night before, was now, mercifully, sleeping alone, with only Neil to see the way his eyes didn't close completely, leaving little white crescents in the gap between his eyelids. It was spooky, and if Neil weren't feeling so like the undead himself, he might have gotten out his camera. For some reason Veejay denied that he slept with his eyes open, like he denied that he got a huge Indian accent when he was on the phone with his parents. Neil switched off the alarm.

Back in the kitchen he started putting the bottles in plastic bags, as quietly as possible. Nothing would wake Veejay up, and Alex's door, like always, was closed, but the clink of the glass gave Neil a bruised feeling behind his eyes. No more parties at their flat, he thought, not for the first time. No more wine and cheese parties with the girls next door that started out with the girls bringing over bottles of something bubbly and ended up with Neil and Veejay running to Tesco for cartons of wine and everyone sitting around watching Arsenal play on TV. Neil was a lousy drinker. Starting now there would be no more pretending otherwise. He didn't even like football, and he was tired of trying to remember to call it that in front of the girls, who thought Americans were boorish if they didn't take a frenzied interest in a sport where the score was almost always tied at zero.

It was on mornings like this that he envied Alex, who never went out—not even when going out meant joining the party in the kitchen. Alex, their vampire roommate without any friends. Who knew what kind of dreams Alex had, but right then Neil would have given anything to be asleep with a clear head on the black sheets that Alex washed twice a week, a habit that caused their shitty British washing machine to inch its way out from under the counter and across the kitchen floor during the spin cycle. Sometimes he and Veejay placed bets on where the washer would end up, and there were pencil marks on the floor, recording its various journeys.

Neil wondered, dully, why he was awake, but it wasn't until he was out on the street, wincing with each crash of broken glass as he pushed the bottles one by one through the rubber flaps of the big recycling container by the park, that he remembered the bus ticket. Which explained why he'd set his alarm for today, which was a Sunday, and was normally reserved for rehydrating and finishing the reading he should have done on Saturday. Swindon. Fuck, he thought. He'd have to call what's-her-name again and go next week. This was the third time he'd canceled on her, and it was starting to get embarrassing, although it wasn't like what's-her-name ever volunteered to come to London. And why should she? The whole thing was ridiculous.

The exchange of presents must have been what's-her-name's mother's idea. Neil's father barely even remembered Christmas, he would never think of doing something like this. If he had wanted to send a present, he would have put it in the mail like a normal person. It wasn't like her country didn't have a postal service. No, this was some sinister plan by what's-her-name's mother. Probably the daughter was supposed to try to seduce Neil to get a green card. It was going to be embarrassing.

Neil pushed the last bottle into the recycling container. Swindon. His father almost never asked him to do things, but he had sent Neil a package back in November, saying that his friend's daughter was also living in the UK, so he and his friend had decided to swap presents through them. *It'll be a way for you to meet someone new,* Neil's father had said. He always wanted to know if Neil was meeting new people, which was sort of funny, because Neil was pretty sure it was a heredi-tary awkwardness passed on to him through his father that *kept* him from meeting new people, and that, when he did, kept him from saying the interesting things that would make them want to be his friends.

From the shape of the gift, Neil could tell that it was one of the minia-ture handcrafted bow-and-arrow sets his father liked to buy from the Ute ladies, who sold them for surprisingly high prices outside the Conoco at Christmastime. The present had sat under Neil's bed since then, and every time he planned to take the bus to Swindon—which it turned out was a *long way* from London—something came up or he forgot, and he had to call what's-her-name (what *was* her name?) and make up some excuse. *Okay, iss okay,* she would say. *You come next week okay?*

One of the bottles hadn't been entirely empty, and Neil's hands were sticky with wine. He wiped them on his jeans. It would be nice not to have his father's package under his bed anymore, reminding Neil of home every time he looked for his sneakers. It was wrapped in the same Santa Claus paper Nan and Pop had always used. Nan used to tuck a dollar bill, new from the bank, into the paper as an incentive not to tear it, and each Christmas Neil and his cousins dissected their gifts, slicing Scotch tape with their thumbnails and sliding out whatever was inside. Nan would scoop up the paper and smooth the creases out of Santa's beard to use again next year—it became a family joke, since obviously she could have just saved those dollar bills and bought more wrapping paper. Neil had put his father's present under his bed in the first place because it was depressing. When he turned the package over he could see that one edge of the Santa Claus paper was cut in a sawtooth pattern and there was a bit of yellowed tape where it had been attached to the cardboard cylinder, showing that his father had finally used up the last of the roll. Nan had died when Neil was about to start high school and now Pop was gone too, but somehow Neil hadn't imagined that even the Santa Claus wrapping paper would come to an end.

The clock was just striking ten. If he hurried, he could probably make the bus. After he'd delivered the Christmas present he would call his father and tell him that Professor Piot had picked Neil to be one of his research assistants for the summer. Neil had found out two weeks earlier and it was a big deal—Professor Piot was practically famous. Plus he got to go to Paris for the summer. Neil had almost called his father with the news a couple of times already, but didn't. Neither of them was very good on the phone, and the last time they'd talked, back in January, they'd had what was almost an argument and Neil had said some unnecessary things. He knew he should have called his father back and apologized, even if it wasn't really his fault. But with the present still under his bed he'd put it off, knowing his dad was sure to ask whether he'd made it out to Swindon.

On the bus Neil's hangover really got going. His stomach felt empty, but also like it wanted to be emptier; he took a few deep breaths. As they bounced along the little streets leading out of London he felt each dip and speed hump add to the disorder of his gut. He wished he'd bought a bag of the curry crisps Veejay swore by. He wished he were at home in bed. He caught sight of a homeless person asleep in a doorway and would have pawned whatever social privilege he'd been born into if it meant trading the jostling bus for the sidewalk, which moved only very slowly as the earth spun on its axis, the planets rotated around the sun, tectonic plates shifted and—

Neil's stomach gave a small, terrible hiccup, its contents apparently seeking a more stable environment. He looked around. The door to the lavatory was taped shut, the bus windows weren't the kind that opened. The seat beside him was empty, but across the aisle there was a woman and a little girl. The girl was sleeping the determined sleep of a child on a bus and the woman's eyes were closed. Her hair was twisted on top of her head in an African cloth and the weight of it made her chin dip down onto her chest. Each time her chin touched down, her eyes opened. Nothing would spoil her bus ride like watching Neil throw up all over his seat.

Now the speed humps were gone and they were stuck in traffic.

The bus lurched into an intersection and stopped. The light was green but no one moved. It turned red, then green again. Next to them a truck's engine stalled and started up with a puff of bluish smoke. The light turned red, and the cloud of truck exhaust floated up and made it purple.

In his lecture on the Second Industrial Revolution, Professor Piot had brought blackened, half-eroded bricks to class to show the effects of air pollution in London at the turn of the century. Umbrellas are black even today, he told them, because they first came into fashion when that was the color of the rain, and in the late Victorian era silver tarnished so quickly that people stopped eating off it—although it could have been due to socioeconomic factors as well. As factory jobs became more plentiful and the price of labor rose it would have been more expensive to hire servants to polish all those cool heavy plates . . . They were moving again. Neil leaned against the cool glass of the window, imagining Victorians pressing their aching heads to gravy bowls. The bus picked up speed, the suburbs passed by behind a smudge on the glass. Letting his thoughts smudge with them, Neil fell asleep.

Professor Piot believed in what he called *observed knowledge*, and he was always telling his students about all the things one could learn about the past by noticing the details of the present. In France, for example, where Professor Piot was from, you could tell if a town had had monarchical or republican political leanings, say, a hundred and fifty years ago, by whether or not the trains stopped there. If the town had a train station, and you had to bet, you'd better bet it had been republican, because the towns in good standing with the new République were the ones that got the rail lines to the capital. And Professor Piot told them you could go to little towns and look at where the World War One monument had been placed in relation to the church to see how religious the people were by the time the war was over and the town's young men were dead. There was actually a statistically significant relationship between the number of local boys who had died in battle and the distance between the church and the town's memorial to the soldiers that were lost. The more dead soldiers, the less inclined the townspeople were to build a monument in the churchyard.

They'd put it up in front of city hall instead. There were some villages, Professor Piot had told them, where the World War One monuments included broken crosses—broken on purpose, maybe even carved that way, to show that the people of such and such a little town knew what was up, up there.

As Neil slept, the drone of the bus motor gave way to the nasal patter of Professor Piot's voice. Neil hoped it was an indication of his future greatness as an academic rather than of extreme nerdiness that during restless sleep his dreams tended to center on the history department, and that Professor Piot's voice in particular seemed to stick in his head, maybe because he had two classes with him that semester. Neil had even started thinking his own thoughts in Professor Piot's accent, which was definitely weird, and during their meetings—Professor Piot was also Neil's faculty advisor—he had to concentrate very hard to make sure he didn't accidentally gargle his *r*'s.

Neil felt something move against his foot. He opened his eyes. The little girl across the aisle had crawled under her mother's legs and was reaching for Neil's father's present. "It's okay," Neil said, as her mother hauled her back into her seat. "I'd let her open it, just—it's not really mine."

He settled his head against a new, cooler spot on the window. They were well out of London now. Something bright and yellow was blooming in the fields in all directions. The color rose and fell over little hills, like someone had taken a highlighter to the entire landscape.

Professor Piot would be able to learn something from the view out the bus window. Neil looked at the unbroken expanse of yellow flowers, but all he could think of was that there weren't sprinkler systems in England. The Colorado prairie might have seemed endless to the pioneers, but every patch of green back home now had a dotted line running through it, wheels and pipes and bursts of high-powered water making frets in the landscape. When Neil was a kid he and his cousins used to run through Pop's sprinklers on summer afternoons, and the water felt like the smack of a two-by-four when it hit them across the back. But in England there was rain, and Neil wondered if British farmers led a fundamentally sweeter existence, not always fixing broken irrigation pumps and wondering who upstream was taking more than their share. The yellow of the fields was so bright it hurt his eyes, so Neil looked out through his eyelashes for the rest of the trip, thinking about Nan and Pop's ranch and wondering how his dad was doing now that he was running it all on his own.

The girls in the flat next door thought it was cute that Neil's father was a farmer—actually his dad had been an English teacher, but Neil left that part out. During halftime the night before Neil had told the girls about the first time Neil's dad brought Neil's mom home to meet the family, which happened to be on a day Pop was castrating bull calves. Nan had served Rocky Mountain oysters for supper—the marriage was obviously doomed from the start—and Amanda thought the idea of breaded testicles was so funny that she sort of fell against Neil's shoulder while she was laughing and stayed there through the penalty kicks. Neil made a mental note to ask his father if anything interesting had been happening at the ranch in the months since they'd talked. It was too bad the cows had been sold after Pop died; it would have been great to have some stories about calving chains or coyote problems to tell the girls.

Now that he was finally delivering the Christmas present, Neil was honestly looking forward to talking to his father, and he figured that with the time difference it would work out perfectly to give him a call when he got back to London that night. He'd tell his dad about Professor Piot's class trip to East Sussex, where they'd tramped through privately owned meadows looking for the famous and possibly nonexistent ditch where the English made their last stand during the Battle of Hastings. He would save the news about getting picked to go to Paris for last, knowing that when his father was proud of him for something he tended to choke up and get awkward and would probably end up hanging up before Neil was actually done talking. Unlike Neil's mother, who didn't see why Neil wouldn't want to spend one last summer at home, working at the movie theater and saving money for school, Neil's father would understand that it was a big deal to be the only under-classman on Professor Piot's research team.

The bus station in Swindon wasn't much of a station, just a place for buses to turn around and a covered waiting area. The bus stopped and

Neil peeled his face off the window. His cheek felt flattened and cold from the glass, like a refrigerator cookie stuck to wax paper. His mouth had the briny, nutty taste of terrible breath. He searched for a piece of gum in his jacket pockets and forgot his father's package under the seat, then had to fight the getting-off crowd to go back and get it. In the bottom of his pocket he found a restaurant mint, long since unwrapped and fuzzy from his jacket lining. At first it stuck to his tongue, then began to dissolve slowly, turning one half of his mouth sticky and cool. Neil's headache had concentrated itself into a single jab down his spine and his stomach felt gritty and hollow. He needed a Coke and a cheese-burger and a nap and a toothbrush. With his father's present under his arm—the real-feather fletch of an arrow now sticking almost completely out of a hole in Santa's chin—Neil was the last person to get off the bus.

Most people headed toward the city bus stop. A couple of cabs stood by but no one took them. Neil looked around for someone who could be the daughter of a mail-order girlfriend of his father's—he was pretty sure that was the situation. But aside from a lot of blue eye shadow or something, he didn't know exactly what such a person would look like, and anyway, it was hardly fair. He could only imagine what the friend's daughter would be expecting of him. So Neil looked around again for a normal female person. A youngish woman sat at the city bus stop, but she was talking on her phone with a serious British accent. A bus came and she got on. Nobody got off. Neil crossed the street to the ticket-buying area. There was a girl smoking a cigarette outside. Neil smiled but she didn't. She ground out her cigarette and didn't seem to notice as he passed. Neil went inside the ticket office. A guy with no shoes was asleep across the chairs, despite the armrests. Behind the ticket window a woman ate a vending machine sandwich, avoiding the crusts.

Neil went back outside. He checked his phone, but no one had called. Maybe she forgot. In a few minutes he would call Veejay and probably wake him up and get him to dig through the stuff on Neil's dresser to find the notebook where he'd written her number, which he had forgotten to put into his phone and which was going to be embar-rassing, because Neil was pretty sure he'd written a couple of incrimi-nating lines of poetry in that notebook about Amanda. Neil was no poet, but Amanda had a way of tracing her fingertips along the edges of her clothing while you talked to her. It was *literary*, or so Neil had thought the night before, when he was supposed to be watching Arsenal but was really watching her, and when he was likely to have already been slightly drunk. Maybe it was better to leave Veejay sleeping, his notebook safely buried under pizza boxes, and just go home.

Another city bus came and went. Neil stood with the now only mostly wrapped souvenir bow and arrow under his arm. He was suddenly sick with the thought of the stupid things he'd said to Amanda last night, combined with the thought of her fingers brushing along the edges of the shirt she'd been wearing. His breath mint was almost totally gone, and he felt his hangover gathering strength for a last assault before burying itself in the patient recesses of his liver.

"Ni-yell?" It was the girl with the cigarette, who had apparently decided to notice him.

"Oh hi," he said. "I didn't know it was you."

"I am waiting for you on the other side," she said.

"Yeah, I know," Neil said. "I guess you didn't see me." She seemed distracted, like something interesting was going on behind him. Maybe she'd expected someone better looking.

"We should walk?"

"Okay," Neil said, and they started up the street. "Cool town."

"London is more cool," she said.

She was about Neil's age, or maybe a little older. She didn't seem to have on eye make-up of any color, and Neil felt like a jerk for expecting her to look like a hooker or something, though she did have an accent like the hot robot in Warcraft Reloaded. Jesus, what was her name? Had she said? He couldn't remember.

"How's your mom?" Neil asked.

"She's good," she said.

"She went back home?" Neil asked.

"Yeah. She's having one restaurant now in Vilnius," she said.

"Oh, wow. What kind of restaurant?" Henry IV had spent a lot of money trying to invade Vilnius before he turned his attention to deposing Richard II, but Neil couldn't remember what modern country it was in. Belarus?

"Pizza," she said. They crossed through a mostly deserted shopping center, then a little park. A fountain dribbled over mossy tiles. It made Neil have to pee. He wished he could remember where Vilnius was. Being a European History major, it was pretty bad that he didn't know.

"Pizza is new big thing in Lithuania," she said. *Lithuania*, Neil thought. *Lithuania, Lithuania, Lithuania.*

"Oh, yeah, I bet," Neil said.

"And your dad?" she asked.

"Oh, yeah, he's good," Neil said. "You know." Which was a stupid thing to say, she didn't know his father, and if her mom had told her anything it was just that he'd been all alone in a big house since Pop died. They walked quietly for a little while, and Neil looked hard at the patchy flowerbeds, trying to think of something to say.

"So, what do you do?" Neil asked, just as she was starting to say something too. Their words got jumbled up in the air and they had to start again. "You first," Neil said.

"No, it's okay," she said. "I am only asking it is okay to go to my house?"

"Sure," Neil said. He really had to pee.

"So, what do you do?" he asked again.

"I work at one club," she said. "Like giving drinks and things. It's okay job, but, you know. And you?"

"I'm in school," Neil said.

"At university?"

"Yeah. It's like an exchange program with my school in America. They let you spend a year studying in London if you want to." *Studying in London*. Jesus. She probably thought his dad was really rich. "See, usually you have to be a junior, but I'm trying to finish in three years to, you know, save money"—which was true enough, though with all his AP credits he was practically forced to graduate early—"so they're letting me do it a year ahead of time. See, they have this program here, for what I'm studying—it's actually better to learn about it here, because it's European History, and this is Europe. I mean, I thought this was Europe until I got here and heard all the British people talk about *Europeans* like they were an alien race or something." That was something the American kids in the history department joked about, and obviously she didn't care, it might even be offensive, since she *was* a European. Her gaze kept flicking up past his shoulder, like she was trying not to look at him. He wondered if he had something on his face.

Her purse began to ring, and she dug around for her phone, which gave Neil a chance to do an all-over exploration of his face with his fingertips. He smoothed his eyebrows and wiped the sides of his mouth and the corners of his eyes. Since he hadn't eaten anything, he could hardly have food stuck in his teeth. When he was done she was still on the phone, saying, "Yeah, it is plugged in by the wall? You are sure?" and he had a chance to really look at her for the first time. She had a very round face and hair that was intentionally cut at different lengths so that it wisped out at the slightest bit of wind, and she had on high-heeled boots like no one ever wore back home. American women in high heels always looked apologetic, like they knew they were crushing the dreams of their suffragist grandmothers or giving themselves varicose veins, and women in London wore heels with such grim awareness of how good they looked that Neil no longer found them attractive. But on what's-her-name the boots had the effect that only Eastern European women could pull off. She didn't look comfortable, exactly, but she walked like it was no big deal—and that in itself did something nice to her hips.

She finished the phone call, saying something in another language and then, "No, I am not talking to you when you're calling me this . . . yeah, I know this, yeah okay good-bye." She threw the phone back into her bag, which was large with a lot of buckles and fringe.

"Everything okay?" Neil asked, though it wasn't his business.

"Well, everything is shit," she said. She had one grayish tooth, like Neil had had when he was a kid and the roots of one of his baby teeth died after he got hit in the face with a swing.

They had turned onto a residential street—rows of houses with pale curtains across the windows and gardens in the back filled with hollyhocks and pieces of tricycles. She didn't say anything more, but Neil felt like he couldn't just leave it at that.

"What happened?" he asked.

She was still looking past his head in a way that made Neil want to give his face another once-over, thinking there must be something nasty on his cheek. Suddenly she leaned in, looking right at him with strange intensity. Either he had something on his face or she was going to kiss him. Neil thought he might pass out. But instead she smiled, like something there had pleased her.

"It's nothing," she said.

They stopped in front of a largish house. Neatly clipped hedges made it look businesslike, like a dentist's office. She stood on the sidewalk, digging for her keys. "Wow, this is your place?" Neil said. It even had a garage.

"It's my friend's," she said.

They went around to the back door and left their shoes in the hallway. Without her heels she was the same height as Neil. She put on some slippers and Neil followed her down the hall, clenching his toes to hide a hole in his sock.

The house was warm. It had a carpety smell and the soft floors seemed to absorb any sound. "My friend, he's a little bit crazy today, so, you know, sometimes he says some stupid things."

"Was that him on the phone?" Neil asked.

"Yeah, he's always calling like this. He has some small problems with his computer, I don't know what."

"We can go someplace else," Neil said.

"No, no, it's okay. I think I must show him how to make it working again." She led Neil through a living room into a sort of study. At first Neil didn't see anybody, just lots of cardboard boxes, some of them open and filled with plastic spools of photo negatives. Books with titles in various languages stood on a bookcase with World War Two army helmets acting as bookends. There was a large photograph of a naked girl on the wall. Something about it made Neil feel that it was only polite to look away. Which was when he saw a man sitting in the blue glow of the computer monitor, watching him.

"She's beautiful, yeah?" the man said, and Neil thought for an awful second that he was talking about what's-her-name. "Picked her up at an auction in Leeds. Fucking five hundred quid, but she's worth it, yeah?"

"Yeah," Neil said, looking at the photograph in what he hoped was a mature and thoughtful way. "Oh yeah, wow," he said. "I'm Neil."

"Barry," the man said. He wasn't British; he sounded Australian. His chair was the rolling office type and he scooted it on well-worn furrows in the carpet toward Neil to shake his hand. "Magdute said something about you coming. American, eh?"

"Yep," Neil said. "I'm studying in London." *Magdute*, he thought to himself, trying to print it into his brain. *Mag-doo-tay*.

"London's a great town," Barry said.

"Oh yeah," Neil said. "Yeah, definitely."

Magdute shifted behind him.

"You made it working?" she asked.

"Hardly. Get me out of this blue screen, okay?" Barry said, and added something in another language. The sound of it was so different from Barry's Australian accent that it took Neil a moment to realize that the words, whatever they were, were coming from him.

"Yeah, okay," Magdute said. She clicked on a couple of things on Barry's computer.

"So you're studying—" Barry tipped his head back to look at Neil. "Economics?"

"History, actually," Neil said.

"Ah-hah!" Barry said. "Bit of a history buff myself. What's your area?"

"I haven't totally decided," Neil said. "I have a professor who's an expert on medieval France, and, I mean, I think that's pretty interesting."

"Mm," Barry said. "I go in for the more recent events myself. See those casings there?" Barry pointed to a glass jar of what looked like bullets sitting like a paperweight on his desk. "Dug those myself out of the Ponary forest, just outside Magdute's hometown. A hundred thousand executed from 1941 to '44. Give or take."

"Okay, Barry, don't start with this now, okay?" Magdute said. She dug the router out from under some papers and unplugged it.

"You get east of Berlin and they're fucking allergic to history," Barry said. "Lits are the worst. Couple of skeletons in that closet, *ja Liebchen?*"

"You have Explorer like from 2002," she said, not looking up. "I am getting you new, okay?" She plugged the router back in and got Barry's computer downloading, then turned to Neil and said, "So you will wait please? I am going to get you those things." She went out and Neil tried to think of something to say. He could still see the naked photograph out of the corner of his eye. It was making him uncomfortable, but when he turned his head he saw there were others. He didn't want Magdute to come back and see him looking at them, so he focused on a dusty case filled with old army canteens and a gas mask that stared back at him with black apocalyptic eyes. It gave him the creeps, but he was running out of places to look.

Barry jiggled the mouse, then shouted something in the direction Magdute had gone. Neil knew he ought to know what language it was. He took a guess.

"Gosh you can speak Russian?" he asked.

"Lithuanian," Barry said. "Roots in ancient Livonian. Don't let her hear you call it Russian—too long under the Soviet boot, yeah?"

"Oh, right," Neil said. Some history major he was. "So, did you live there or something?" He was glad to have a reason to stop looking at the walls.

Barry laughed. "God no. It's a hobby of mine, languages." Magdute came back in with a shopping bag and a chair for Neil. "Magdute helps me," he said.

She said something in Lithuanian to him, and then to Neil, "He does the endings no good."

"Poorly," Barry said to her. "I make my declensions poorly." He turned to Neil and said, "Estonian is easier."

"You know Estonian?" Neil said.

"And six or eight others. Bulgarian, Latvian, Polish—a hobby. I've been trying to learn Ukrainian, but I can't find a girl, and the tapes are shit, you can't do it with the tapes." He said something else to Magdute. She rolled her eyes and left again, and there was the sound of banging from another room. Barry shouted something that made Neil jump. It was incongruous, the switch to those strange-sounding words from Barry's big-voweled accent.

"Always banging into things, that one," Barry said. "Blind as a bat."

Magdute came back in with lemonade. She said something to Barry and he said something back. It was a language that sounded like sticks rubbing together, occasionally making a spark. As she bent to give him a glass of lemonade Barry brushed his hand over her cheek, like there was an eyelash there.

Neil wanted to leave. He tried to drink his lemonade quickly, but it only made him remember that he needed the bathroom. He wondered how soon he could ask for it without seeming rude.

"You must be really good at languages," Neil said.

"The girls help. You've got to use the words, you know. You've got to speak. A new language, a new girl, sometimes the other way around. Take Lithuanian. Filthy language, but I just had to have little Magdute here."

Barry chuckled. Neil wasn't sure, but he might have chuckled too. His hangover was making him sweat.

"For Polish I have Zosia, for Bulgarian there's Desislava, Veronika for Czech, but for Ukrainian, nobody. Little Galya lied to me, didn't she?"

"She was Russian," Magdute said.

"Stupid cunt," Barry said. "But what can you do? Some of these girls'll put on a real show for a place like this, eh? Rent-free. And I have such a hard time saying no." Another wink. "You know, that Baltic charm. *Ees veery nice, yah?*" he said, in perfect imitation of Magdute's accent. Neil's mouth tasted vinegary. He was sweating a lot. "Am I right?" Barry asked.

"Oh yeah," Neil said. He wasn't exactly sure what they were talking about.

"Just no Russians. I have a rule against Russians. Germans too. Goddamn Bolsheviks and Nazis, yeah?"

Neil really needed some gum. His mouth tasted like something had died in there. He finished his lemonade.

"I have to go to work," Magdute said.

She left the room, and Neil looked at his watch—which actually wasn't there, he'd forgotten to put it on that morning—and said, "I'd better be going too."

"Right-oh," Barry said. Then, with Magdute out of the room, he scooted his chair toward Neil again and said, "Listen here. Wouldn't you like to stay a bit? For a historian—I've got a few things that might be of interest."

"I can't," Neil said. "The bus, it's at three, I think, three fifteen . . ." Barry was nodding.

"But there's another bus you know. Tomorrow."

"Yeah, but I've got to get back." A warm drop of sweat broke free of Neil's armpit and rolled down his side. It hesitated for a moment on his ribs, then gathered momentum and rolled purposefully down into his underwear.

"I've got a bit of footage from the Kriegsberichter film crews— official cameramen for the Waffen SS. Himmler at the horseraces, a burlesque show in Minsk—that one hardly for official purposes. Real collector's items."

"Wow, I'm sure," Neil said.

"Spend the night," Barry suggested. "We can set up the projector."

"Gosh, thanks," Neil said. "But I've got a paper to write." Which was possible, even likely, but at that moment he couldn't remember whether or not it was true.

"I'm only joking," Barry said, thumping Neil on the arm and leaning back in his chair. "Only ladies welcome here, yeah?"

Neil could feel his thoughts banging along behind what was actually happening, like a kid pulling a tin can on a string.

"Can I use your bathroom?" Neil asked.

"Left and left again," Barry said, pointing toward the hallway.

The house was strangely noiseless. Neil's socks left footprints in the thick carpet, but his steps didn't make a sound. In the silence, Neil could almost hear his breathing reverberate against his bladder, stretched tight like a drum.

Neil flushed, then stood at the sink, letting the cold water run over his hands. Finally he had a chance to look at himself in the mirror.

Nothing out of the ordinary about his face, although it was hard to tell; the mirror was more like a plate of tinted glass than a real mirror, as if it hadn't been intended for actual use. Like the rest of the house, the bathroom had an impersonal feeling. It was clean enough, but clean in a way that left a film over everything. Soaps shaped like sea horses sat unwetted in a dish and there was a little silver padlock on the medicine cabinet. Only an eye pencil without a cap that had been left beside the sink gave any sign that the bathroom had been used.

Neil splashed some water on his face and cupped his hands to drink. The water had the same plasticky taste as the water in London and it left his tongue feeling chalky. He needed some mouthwash or a dab of toothpaste, anything to cut the taste in his mouth, a sign of what was surely inexcusable breath. He looked closely at the padlock on the medicine cabinet and saw that it wasn't entirely closed. He opened the cabinet.

It could have been a TV commercial, Neil thought. The medicine cabinet was empty, except for a tin of Altoids sitting like the Holy Grail on the middle shelf. *Curiously Strong Peppermints when you need them most.* The box had obviously been there for a long time, it was stuck to the shelf. But Altoids don't go bad, and when the lid wouldn't open Neil worked his fingernails under the lip, which was a little rusty. It always bothered Neil when people groped around in Altoids tins and ended up touching every one of them. He got the lid open and looked inside. There were no little white candies. Just a bundle of black wire cinched with a red elastic hair band. Neil nudged the wire with his fingernail. One end led out through a little hole drilled in the back of the Altoids tin and disappeared through another hole cut into the wall. The other end of the wire attached to what Neil thought at first was the cap of a black magic marker, wedged sideways into the box. Another little hole had been cut out of the front of the tin, and when Neil leaned in to look at it he saw the glass eye of a tiny camera lens staring back at him. It was pointed in the direction of the shower, and Neil noticed that what he'd thought was a mirror on the outside of the medicine cabinet was actually translucent from the inside. There was a bit of paper stuck to the underside of the shelf.

усмихни се
naerata
uśmiechnij się
pasmaidiet
šypsokis
smile

it said.

There was one more thing Neil saw before he slipped his shoes back on without even tying them and hurried after Magdute out onto the street. Back in London, when he tried to make Veejay understand why a house full of Eastern European girls with cameras in the walls was not cool, it was creepy, and Veejay looked at him with his I-don't-get-it eyebrow raised, it was the thing Neil couldn't quite explain, the image that would stay with him forever, labeled "The House in Swindon" in the archives of his mind.

As Neil left the bathroom, a door in the hallway closed quickly—he hadn't even noticed it was open. But before it closed he saw a girl with blonde hair wearing a going-out dress. Her makeup was smudged and she was carrying her shoes—Neil had the sense that she'd been tiptoeing. The girl turned quickly, her eyes flicked up and two fingers pressed against her lips, as if keeping them shut. For an instant they stared at each other. And as they did, an unwelcome flash of a memory came into Neil's head: someone he'd known when he was a kid, her eyes red from crying, glancing up, startled, looking at Neil with the same sudden panic in her eyes. Some complicated psychological process was responsible for bringing her face to mind at just that moment, and Neil intended not to think too much about it. But he knew it meant one thing for sure: He was not going to call his father when he got back to London. He was not going to say that he'd finally delivered the Christmas present, or that he'd been chosen to go to Paris for the summer—which meant that the entire day had been a waste. But with that particular memory in his head, Neil knew there was no way he was going to be able to tell his dad about Barry and Magdute and the other girls all living in that house.

*

Magdute walked him to the bus station. They were quiet and Neil imagined the things he might say, how he might take charge of the situation
and calmly, carefully tell her what he'd seen, downplaying things a little
bit so she wouldn't freak out. But each time he made up his mind to tell
her about the camera, he wasn't sure exactly how to start, or, when he'd
decided on a way to begin, what had seemed simple became suddenly
much more complex and nothing came out. So they kept walking and
Neil said nothing, feeling the moment passing him by when, for a
second or two, he had the chance to really *be* someone and life could tip
like a seesaw toward—well, who knew what? That was the point. A life
as a person with guts, the kind of person who, at the right historical
moment, would be raising a peasant army or hurling paving stones at
the Bastille, the kind of person Neil never quite managed to be.

"Barry's really into that World War Two stuff, huh?" Neil said,
because he had to start somewhere.

"Oh yeah," Magdute said. "He's totally obsession for this. He is
going over all country for buying cigarette lighters of German army
and such."

"That's weird," Neil said.

"Yeah, totally," Magdute said. The heels of her boots tick-tocked
against the sidewalk, reminding Neil that time was running out. He
took a breath.

"That's a really beautiful church," Neil said. Why was he talking
about churches? Anyway, it was a lie. The church had the studied
boringness of the interwar style.

Magdute looked up and squinted her eyes. The church was made
of yellow bricks, squat and intent in its ugliness. God, he was such a
moron. *I think you're being spied on in the shower*, Neil said inside his
head.

"Yes?" Magdute said. "I am not so much looking at this church
before."

They were a few blocks from the station, and Neil could see the
bus was waiting. Magdute was standing, looking at the church sort of
vacantly, like she was thinking of something else.

"There's my bus," Neil said. "I'd better run." Magdute looked up the street.

"No, I think it will come only at three o'clock," she said.

"Oh," Neil said. It looked like his bus, but he didn't argue. They walked slowly up the street.

"You know, I have really liked churches when I was young," Magdute said. "I am thinking about becoming some kind of nun, how about that?" She laughed. "But now we are all fuckshit heathens, yes?"

"I guess so," Neil said.

"This is what Barry says. This land is full of fuckshit heathens still praying on rocks and things. And when he says this I was looking all over for rocks and crazy English praying on them, but I'm not finding it so much."

Speaking of Barry, Neil said in his head.

"Well, there's Stonehenge," Neil said. The line to get on the bus was getting shorter. He was starting to be certain that the little sign in the windshield had LONDON written on it. "I really think that's my bus."

"Is here?" Magdute said.

"Yeah, it's right there," Neil said. "Shoot, I'm really sorry, I have to run." The door to the bus was closing. "It was really nice to meet you," he said.

"Okay, good-bye," Magdute said, and Neil waved over his shoulder as he sprinted up the street. The driver opened the door, and Neil dug in his pockets for his ticket. Coins and gum wrappers fell out.

"Hey," the driver said. "You with her?" He nodded out the window. Magdute was waving her arms. She started up the street toward the bus, then hesitated, looking confused. She turned and went the other direction, but she was still waving and calling his name, like she hadn't seen where he'd gone.

"Hang on just a second," Neil said to the driver. He got off the bus and ran toward Magdute, who had an odd look on her face, like a kid lost at a shopping mall, hollering "Niii-yell!"

"Yeah?" he said. Her head turned toward him and the lost look disappeared.

"You are forgetting the present!" she said. Sure enough, Neil's father's package was still under his arm. He'd been holding onto it so tightly that there was a little imprint of an arrowhead on his wrist.

Magdute took a paper bag out of her purse and gave it to him, and Neil handed her the package. The bus driver honked the horn.

"Gosh, thanks," Neil said. "Merry Christmas."

"Okay, bye," Magdute said.

Neil waved to her as the bus pulled away, but she didn't seem to see.

{MAGDALENA}

Swindon, May

T HE SHAPE OF Neil disappeared into the layer of permanent fog
that was all that was left of Magdalena's vision beyond an arm's
length. The colors he had been melted their membranes and
Magdalena was turning to go, when she remembered that her mother's
package was still in her bag.

She almost didn't call him back—Magdalena hadn't decided
whether or not she ever wanted to see Neil's face again. On the one
hand it was unnerving. No one, not her mother or Lina or Ivan, as far
as she could tell, had Magdalena's name written on their skin. It didn't
say anything else about her, or give any explanation of how those
particular letters had ended up under the eye of an American she'd
never met before.

It was possible that the letters were a reference to another
Magdalena Bikauskaitė, although even back home it wasn't such a
common name. Maybe there was more to it and the name came at the
end of a sentence that began under his hair. Magdalena squinted toward
the bus stop and waved her arms.

In a moment a shape detached itself from the bus and hurried
toward her, colors resorting themselves as he got nearer until Neil's
jeans became distinct from his sweatshirt and a smudge of orange
became his hair. The edges of him sharpened and then, when he got
near enough, panting a little, the words on his face came into focus.
There it was: *Magdalena Bikauskaitė*, just above his cheekbone. She
handed him the package.

"Gosh, thanks," Neil said, and he was running back to the bus
before Magdalena had a chance to ask him to lift up the hair by his ear
so she could see if the name followed other words across his temple.

Magdalena waited until she heard the bus leave, and then she
looked around, wondering which side of the bus station she was on.
But the streets were nothing more than wedges cut into a wash of tan

and gray. Out of habit she took her glasses out and started to put them on, just to get her bearings, but she stopped. A crowd of little shapes was coming toward her in twos.

In another moment they were all around her, bobbing at the edges of her sight in smears of green uniforms. "Sixty degrees north-northwest!" an adult voice called out. The little shapes pivoted in their pairs, bumping into Magdalena.

"*North* northwest!" the leader said. "Kimberly! Emily! What do we say?"

"Sorry, Miss."

"Sorry, Miss," and they circled what she now saw was a compass held like a fiddler crab on the palm of one of their hands. Magdalena took out her phone and pretended to check the time to avoid seeing their faces.

"Ours's stuck."

"Ours's too."

"Follow Becky," the leader said. "Right. Forty paces north-northwest. Careful as you cross the street. Careful! *Kimberly!*" and the little shapes ducked back into the haze.

Then the street was empty, but Magdalena put her glasses back in her bag just to be safe. It was bad enough when she accidentally got too close to an old person and it said *inflammatory heart disease* or *lung infection* or *regret* across their face. Nobody wanted to see something like that on a child. There would be other things written there too: *Lives at No. 12 Hollbury Mews. Air stewardess. Marries Ronald. Finds a sea anemone.* But sometimes a face that said *loved* across the lips when it smiled would have a *never* hidden in the dimple, and Magdalena had learned a long time ago that it was better not to look at all. Old people could have whole sentences disappear in their wrinkles, but Magdalena did not like looking at children, with their skin so smooth across their faces that it was hard to ignore what it said.

For as long as Magdalena could remember the words had always been there, although she didn't used to think of them as words. At first she didn't think of them as anything, they were just extensions of a person's skin, like eyebrows or the chicken pox or the long brown birthmark on the back of her mother's knee—which her mother told her was a footprint left there many years ago by fairies, who sometimes walked over children as they slept. So for a while when she was very young Magdalena thought that the other kind of marks had also been left by fairies, who were known for making trouble and who must have walked up and down each person's body with ink on their shoes.

But the marks turned into letters when Magdalena started school. "Who can show us the letter *A*?" the teacher said. The class pointed to the chalkboard, and Magdalena pointed to the chin of Tomas Kukauskas sitting next to her.

Pretty soon the letters came together into words and each person's body became a puzzle. Once when her teacher bent over to correct her exercises, Magdalena looked at the marks that curled out of her teacher's nose and disappeared into her ear and found that she could read them.

"Magdalena, if you have a question say it out loud so we all can hear," her teacher said as Magdalena tried to fit her mouth around the letters. The first word was long, but when she made each sound and then made them all together she realized it was somebody's name: *MY-KO-LAS*.

"*MYKOLAS*," she said. She followed the letters along her teacher's cheek, stringing the sounds together like they had been taught to do. The second word was even longer: "*ISN'T-COMING-BACK*," Magdalena said. It was all one word in Lithuanian. Her teacher stood up so sharply that her pen made a mark across Magdalena's paper, as if she'd gotten all the answers wrong.

"What did you say?" her teacher asked. Magdalena said it again. She stacked the sounds of the letters on top of one another, and when they came out of her mouth they were words.

"Who told you that?" her teacher said. The class was quiet.

"I read it," Magdalena said.

"Where did you read it?" her teacher asked.

"There." Magdalena pointed to the place beside her teacher's nose. Her teacher brought her hands up to her face and Magdalena thought she was going to wipe away the writing. But she only rested her fingers against her lips for a moment.

"Finish your work," she said.

When the teacher passed her again, Magdalena took another look. It was hard to keep all the sounds in her head and remember where she'd started, but if she said them aloud and listened to her own voice, then the shapes became sounds and the sounds became words. *"MYKOLAS-ISN'T-COMING-BACK."*

Magdalena's teacher put her hands to her face again, then reached for the chalkboard rag and looked for a clean part. Magdalena craned her neck to read the words one more time before her teacher wiped them away. *"MYKOLAS-ISN'T-COMING-BACK."*

"Stop saying that!" her teacher said. The class looked up. The teacher pressed her face into the chalkboard rag and the chalk dust powdered her cheeks. Magdalena wanted to say the words just one more time, but she stayed quiet. And as it turned out, these words weren't like the ones on the chalkboard. Even though tears ran down her teacher's face, they did not get washed away.

Sometimes Magdalena wondered what would have happened to her if the world hadn't started going blurry when she was six or seven years old, when she was still sounding out people's foreheads like other kids sounded out street signs, when she had cried because she was the only one in her class who had to wear glasses, not knowing that nearsightedness had been given to her like a blessing. Perfect vision and she might have ended up like her father in the bathtub, wrists open like books.

By the time she was ten or eleven Magdalena had stopped wearing her glasses, and she passed her adolescence in a fog. When she and Lina first moved to London she put them on again, and even let Lina talk her into getting contact lenses because they looked better. In London only Lina's skin had words she understood without even trying—and those she already knew by heart—so Magdalena made an appointment with an optometrist and then walked around the city marveling at the mortar that suddenly appeared between bricks. But now that she'd learned English well enough to find herself accidentally understanding most of what was written there at the hairline or over an eyebrow, she preferred to leave her glasses off and let the world melt around her.

The haze was not ideal. Magdalena had permanent bruises on her shins from bumping into things, and at times like this it would be nice to know where buildings stopped and streets began. She was at the bus station, she knew that much, but she seemed to have gotten turned around. Colors and shapes smeared together and nothing looked familiar.

Magdalena tried to think back to her first day in Swindon, when she'd gotten off the bus from London with Barry's address written on a scrap of paper. Which way had she gone? Probably in the other direction. She had been trying to balance Lina's old suitcase on its one good wheel while she held the shoebox with the ashes in the other hand. She'd dropped the box and a fine dust puffed out; she remembered kneeling to pick up the shoebox and watching the dust settle between cobblestones, which meant she must have been on the other side of the bus station because this street was paved.

Nearly a year had gone by since that first day in Swindon and the shoebox was still under her bed, waiting to go home. But that wasn't what Magdalena wanted to think about. She kept her glasses in her bag, chose a direction, and started walking.

If Lina were there they would walk together, arm in arm like old women. They would make it halfway across town and then suddenly, dramatically, Lina would be too exhausted to go on. Or she would decide that the other direction was better after all and she'd wave down some man in a nice car and get him to give them a ride. Magdalena would read *three children* or something she didn't understand, like *pneumonectomy* across his forehead—things that were easy to ignore. And when he let them off they'd have to find another ride back into town. Lina was like that, always getting them into places they shouldn't be. She never thought things through—it said so across the arches of her feet.

A car honked at her, and Magdalena realized she'd ended up in the middle of the street. Without her glasses, the curb a few feet away melted into the fuzzy gray of the gutter and she had to feel with her toes to find the sidewalk. She did this expertly, with no sudden falterings, because it was better to whack her shins sometimes than to look like a blind person and have somebody come up close to give her their arm.

Off to her right there was a shape taller than the rest. That would be the church she and Neil had passed on their way to the bus stop. She pressed her fingertips against the sides of her eyes. Sometimes that made her vision sharper, though she had to be careful to avoid looking at a woman who was passing. The woman was already close enough that Magdalena could see dark patches of text across her cheeks.

Magdalena always told Barry that she had to be at work at quarter to three, a lie that gave her three hours to meet Ivan, or, lately, to call Ivan and walk around waiting for him to call her back. It often didn't happen, and Magdalena would get all the way to the Sainsbury's on the edge of town before she had to turn back if she wanted to make it to her shift on time, with her feet already hurting.

Having Ivan for a boyfriend had seemed like a good idea at the time, when Magdalena first came to Swindon and needed a reason to get out of Barry's house. It was Zosia, the Polish girl's, advice to her. "Get a boyfriend," Zosia said when Magdalena first moved into the bedroom next to Barry's study. "He'll call you a whore but he'll leave you alone." Barry hated boyfriends, but he was a little scared of them too. So when Ivan asked her to get a drink with him one night after the bar closed, Magdalena didn't say no.

Ivan was different from the men Lina used to try to get Magdalena to go out with when they were in London. After a while Lina gave up on her, but there was a time when she was always arranging double dates for them, choosing for Magdalena some older guy who'd made money on the stock market and invested it collecting photographs of circus freaks or old-time jazz records, things Magdalena learned she had better not pretend the slightest interest in; if she did, the men would call her for a second date and she'd have to grab her phone quick to keep Lina from answering it for her and saying yes.

But Ivan had no investments besides an old Vespa he'd fixed up himself, with red flame decals pasted on the sides. Magdalena was pretty sure Ivan was seeing other girls, but she liked to ride with him on the Vespa on weekends, when he'd pick her up in front of Barry's house and they'd go out past the brown edges of town until they got to fields of yellow rapeseed, the little engine, which wasn't made to be taken on the motorway, sputtering under the weight of the two of them.

But the thing she liked best about Ivan was his skin. Magdalena knew some Russian but she couldn't read it, and Ivan's body remained a mystery because even though he claimed to be one hundred percent British now that he'd been in Swindon for most of his life, there wasn't a single word in English on him anywhere, Magdalena had made sure of that. So even though he was the kind of boyfriend Lina would have said they'd outgrown before they were even in high school, Magdalena didn't like the thought of leaving him and his incomprehensible skin and finding somebody new, steeling herself to look closely at a body that would most likely tell her all sorts of things she would rather not know. It was easier to keep filling her afternoons walking around Swindon, waiting for her phone to ring.

Lina used to say men had a kind of radar. They never called if you were waiting for them. The trick was to do something that sent a signal out into the universe showing that you didn't care. Lina used to throw away jewelry or other things that she'd been given and sure enough, as soon as she'd flushed a pair of earrings down the toilet, the phone would ring. Magdalena didn't believe in those kinds of things, but even so, not for the first time, she erased Ivan's number from her phone. But still he didn't call.

Magdalena first heard Lina's theory of men and their radar on the day many years earlier when Lina climbed down onto the balcony of Magdalena's mother's apartment in Vilnius to the sound of glass breaking upstairs. Magdalena's mother was setting the table for breakfast and she gave a little shriek, surprised to see a seven-year-old in her garlic plants. Her mother brought Lina inside and asked her what in God's name was going on up there and didn't she know she could be killed climbing between floors like that? Her mother was sending a message, Lina had said. Something like that. And it was hard to imagine that the radar of even the dullest of men wouldn't pick up on the fact that Lina's mother was just then shattering every bit of glass in the apartment upstairs.

Until then, all that Magdalena and her mother had known about the Valentukas family who lived above them was that their illegal washing machine leaked, leaving an orange stain on their kitchen ceiling. When Magdalena and her mother first moved in the stain was just a tiny spot, shaped like a rabbit. A sign of springtime, no bigger than Magdalena's hand. "A rabbit means a new life," Magdalena's mother had said, standing in the kitchen looking up at the stain, and they would make one. It was not long after Magdalena's father had died.

The stain grew steadily, week after week, changing shape each time Mrs. Valentukienė did the laundry. It reflected Magdalena's mother's moods. When times were good she saw good omens there—a loaf of bread, brown at the edges, that meant a happy home, or a curl like a woman's hair, foretelling money—and when times were bad just the sight of it could make her cry. When Magdalena's mother was a little bit drunk she would tell their fortunes in it. "You see? A mushroom wearing a hat. Ah, and see? He is shooting an arrow. That means that somewhere a nice man is waiting to fall in love with me, only he is like a mushroom, we will have to look very hard to find him."

"In the forest?" Magdalena would ask.

"Maybe," her mother would say, and they would both look up at the stain, which really did look like a mushroom shooting an arrow, and would change again on Saturday when Mrs. Valentukienė did the wash. After another drink or two Magdalena's mother would start to get sentimental and tell Magdalena to go up and ask Mrs. Valentukienė to please never do the laundry again so that Magdalena and her mother wouldn't lose their friend the mushroom who promised so much. Then Magdalena knew it was time to help her mother into bed, to turn out the lights and lock the door and draw the blinds against the moonlight that was surely right that minute streaming over little mushroom men shooting all variety of arrows in all variety of forests, waiting to be found.

Magdalena's phone rang. *Unidentified caller*, it said. She was glad she hadn't been the first to call. She let it ring four times, then said hello.

"Hey," Ivan said.

"Hey," she said.

"Look, I'm sorry I've been a bit out of it lately." Ivan spoke English without an accent, at least according to him. Magdalena was no expert at accents. Maybe it was only his way of trailing off at the end of his sentences, as if he was always deciding that what he was saying wasn't worth the effort before he'd even finished saying it, that reminded Magdalena of the Russian guys she knew back home.

"Uh-huh," Magdalena said. "Is okay." He had been ignoring her at work, going off to do the inventory when her shift started. Lina wouldn't have picked up the phone. But Lina always got called back.

"Look, when can I see you?" Ivan asked. He made the schedule, so he knew what time she worked.

"I don't know," Magdalena said. "I'm busy."

"Meet me in ten minutes, yeah?" Ivan said. "By the fountain."

The stain from the Valentukas family's washing machine had gone through a particularly violent transformation in the week or so before plates began smashing into the walls of the apartment upstairs and Lina climbed down onto their balcony. This was due, it turned out, to Ruta Valentukienė, Lina's mother, washing every piece of fabric in their house, including the red drapes, which made the orange stain on Magdalena's kitchen ceiling blush pink around the edges. Ruta Valentukienė washed the mattress covers and the lace from the windows. She washed the tablecloths and couch pillows. When she ran out of laundry soap she used shampoo, which made the washing machine explode into a mess of freesia-smelling bubbles. It was the only way Ruta Valentukienė knew of getting rid of the smell of burned hair. Lina's father and his new girlfriend—her hair turned to black goo on the ends, the result of Ruta having dragged her out of their bed and straight to the stove where the girl's pretty blonde hair flared up like dry hay—had left in a hurry. But the stench of that hair remained—the bitch. Cheap dye, no doubt about it, Magdalena's mother told Ruta, sniffing the air when she took Lina back upstairs with Magdalena following behind with a broom to sweep up the glass. Good-quality hair doesn't smell like that, Magdalena's mother said, and took over from Ruta, who was crying into the coffee she was heating for them in an old saucepan—there was nothing else left to make it in. Ruta had opened all the windows, the illegal washing machine was groaning quietly in the corner, and even through the scent of shampoo Magdalena could smell something scorched and bitter.

"Do you want to see my shells?" Lina asked Magdalena. Lina was a class ahead of Magdalena at school; they had never spoken to each other before. Though their mothers said hello when they passed each other on the stairs, Lina was usually out playing with the older kids or, when she wasn't, Magdalena was too shy to do more than smile from behind her mother's packages and scuff her shoe against a step.

Lina had her own room, unlike Magdalena, who slept on the foldout couch. Her father was a truck driver and she had shells from all over the world, pink and yellow and white and one giant one, the prize, that curled into itself like a bony ear. "Listen," Lina said. "You can hear the ocean."

"Magdute?" her mother called from the kitchen. "Run downstairs and get us some coffee cups."

"Okay," Magdalena said. But she didn't have to take the stairs. Lina showed her the magic combination: left foot cross right foot, big step to the side and down, change hands and down again, and Magdalena landed with a little thump next to the garlic her mother was growing on their balcony.

After Lina's father left, Lina and Ruta had to move out of the apartment upstairs. Ruta wanted to give Magdalena and her mother the illegal washing machine, but Magdalena's mother insisted on paying for it, which surprised Magdalena because her mother worked in the laundry at the hospital and she could wash their clothes for free.

They carried the washing machine in a procession down the stairs, the four of them, Ruta and Magdalena's mother each straining under one end while Lina directed them from the front and Magdalena followed along behind to keep the cords and hoses from dragging on the ground.

"Like a bride," Lina said.

"Like a bride without her own feet," Magdalena's mother said, out of breath from the weight. They lowered the washing machine down to rest for a moment. Lina's mother started laughing, then Magdalena's mother laughed too, both of them like crazy schoolgirls with a washing machine between them teetering on the steps, and their daughters, looking at them bewildered, then starting to laugh too, not knowing why. That was the beginning of a new kind of laughter, which ever since Magdalena thought of as belonging to moments involving men and disaster, and at the same time an absence of loneliness. When they finally stopped and got the washing machine the rest of the way downstairs, it took the four of them pushing to get it through the doorway of Magdalena and her mother's apartment. They put it in the middle of the living room—there was no other place—and Ruta said she knew somebody who could help them hook up the hoses. Before Ruta and Lina left to stay with Lina's grandmother they had a party, with a cake and dandelion wine, and they used the illegal washing machine as a table. With a crown of flowers and a bit of lace for a tablecloth, it did look like a bride.

Magdalena had gone the wrong way. The shape she'd thought belonged to the yellow church now looked more like the primary school, which meant that the park was in the opposite direction. Now she was sure to be late to meet Ivan. She turned to go back, but there ahead of her was something she didn't recognize, a jumble of shapes and something sticking up out of them into the air. A construction site. What had been there before? She squinted, and the more she squinted, the less certain she was that she was heading toward the school after all. Time was passing. Ivan would be waiting. She had to find out where she was. Magdalena felt around for her glasses at the bottom of her bag. She cleaned the lenses on her sleeve and unfolded the frames. There was hardly anybody on the street.

She put her glasses on and the world took on sharp edges. It was a church, but across from it was a shopping center Magdalena didn't remember ever having seen before. She turned around looking for the

were fixed. Sometimes her mother would still look up at the kitchen ceiling after she'd come home from a night out with her boyfriend, but she stopped telling Magdalena what she saw there. It was easy to see that the news was not good.

"It's a wolf," Magdalena said.

"You're imagining things," her mother said, which was a lie. No matter what angle you looked at it from, the stain was unmistakably a wolf with a long mean snout, and the snout was tinted pink with the blood of Ruta Valentukienė's red curtains.

Not long after Magdalena's mother got rid of the washing machine, Lina's mother got sick and had to go away, and because her grandmother was so old, Lina came to stay with Magdalena and her mother. A cold wind blew all winter long. Magdalena's mother baked cakes to warm the apartment and then left the oven open while the three of them huddled under the wolf and warmed their hands over the pan. It snowed and the wind blew straight from Sweden. Freedom wind, the newspapers called it, and that was the year the Russians left, they became Lithuanians again and people sang in the streets. There were flowers everywhere and Magdalena's mother came home from the store with a banana. She cut it into three parts and they ate it with a knife and fork. Magdalena's mother picked out all the tiny seeds and Lina tried to eat the rind—that was how little they knew about bananas. Magdalena and Lina shared the fold-out couch and they made angels in the snow on the way to school.

It was the year that Magdalena learned to read.

"What's *ap-ree-tsots*?" Magdalena asked Lina one day. They were walking to school.

"I don't know," Lina said. "Stop looking at me like that."

"Why don't you know what it means?" Magdalena said.

"What what means?"

"*Ap-ree-tsots,*" Magdalena said, pronouncing the sound of each letter carefully.

"Why should I know what it means?" Lina said.

"I don't know," Magdalena said. "Why is it on your face if you don't know what it means?"

"It isn't on my face."

"Yes it is," Magdalena said. "Right there." She spelled it. The letters came down from Lina's hairline and ended over her eye.

"*A-P-* what?" Lina said.

It was a strange-looking word, and when Magdalena put the sounds together what came out didn't make any sense. "*Ap-ree-tsots.*"

"I don't think there is a word like that," Lina said, and when they passed a shop window Lina looked in at her reflection. "There's nothing there," she said.

Magdalena's mother's skin also said things that Magdalena didn't understand. She could read the name of her father on her mother's forehead, and the name of her baby brother who died, which was written in the cradle of her mother's arm, but there were also some longer words she'd never heard before. When she asked her mother what they meant her mother told her she was imagining things. "Let me write my name too," Magdalena said one day, holding a pen from her school bag.

"You're imagining things," her mother said again, looking mad when Magdalena said she would only write it very small, next to where *Juozas*, her brother's name, was written on her mother's arm. And then Magdalena understood. The words were something not to be talked about, like the fact that the fortune-telling stain had gotten permanently stuck in the shape of a wolf. After that, Magdalena tried very hard not to let her mother see that she was looking at the words, just like she looked hard at the tablecloth at mealtimes to help her mother forget about the stain on the ceiling, and bit by bit Magdalena learned to read the words in her head without making a sound.

Ivan walked away. Magdalena stood by the fountain and finished her cigarette. She dropped it into the fountain, and—why not?—she made a wish. She wondered what she would do that night, instead of going to work. She kicked the fountain hard enough to hurt her toes, then she started walking. She walked until she was back in front of the yellow church, which Neil had said was beautiful. Magdalena hadn't gone into a church for a long time, but she went in now.

They were supposed to have been best friends for life. They would marry millionaire brothers and connect their houses by an underground tunnel. They would name their daughters after each other and drink coffee together in the afternoons.

It was Lina who decided they should go to London. Magdalena was nineteen and Lina was twenty, and they were looking out over Vilnius from up by the old castle, drinking a bottle of wine and chewing on bits of the cork that had crumbled down into it because as usual they hadn't had anything but their house keys for opening the bottle. They were sharing a set of keys again because Lina's mother had just gone back into the hospital. Magdalena thought about telling Lina that Ruta's skin didn't say she would die there, but she didn't want to get into what it did say, and after all, who knew whether what it said was true. So in the end Magdalena said nothing, and it was Lina who looked out over the city and told Magdalena she was going to London. *London,* the English spelling, was written high across Lina's forehead, and though Magdalena's own skin had nothing to say about it, there was no question that she would go with her.

Actually, Magdalena's skin had nothing to say about anything. Her entire body, from the bottoms of her feet to the bit of her nose she could just barely see if she closed one eye and squinted, was empty of words. Most of the time her own blankness was a relief, though sometimes, when she let herself think about it too much, Magdalena wondered why she alone had been left unmarked, as though the ability to read what it said on the people around her meant she'd have no stories of her own.

Aziz was Lina's first real conquest in London. She met him at the bar where she worked and he took her out on a private boat along the Thames. One night Lina took too much of some pale pink powder Aziz had brought back from Morocco and woke up all alone in a cream-colored limousine with a big dent in its fender and a bump on her head. She was sorry she hadn't told Magdalena where she was going, she said, sitting on the kitchen counter the next morning, opening and closing the silverware drawer with her toes while Magdalena rushed around getting ready for work. She'd be more careful next time, she said, but Magdalena knew it was a lie: Lina had drunk champagne in a long white car, she had heard each bubble rise and break against a crystal glass and she had breathed the air that was trapped inside them. She had watched the city lights flow like a river around her, and she was not going to start being careful now.

Magdalena didn't expect the same things that Lina did, and when they went out together she wasn't surprised to find that the nights in London ended the same way they had in Vilnius: Lina would be gone, Magdalena would find herself kissing some stranger, or sitting in a pub with him and his friends while they bought her drinks. The wall behind their heads would come rushing into focus; she'd see a spider on the wall lift and set each leg with such deliberation that she'd feel she was in a sort of trance watching the spider walk across the wall, while the person in between her and the spider was saying things to her and she was laughing.

In London the men were insurance analysts or bankers rather than the aimless students and guitar players she and Lina had known back home, and sometimes they would ask Magdalena to talk to them in Lithuanian.

"Okay," she would say, keeping her eyes on the spider. "So listen and I will tell you what the two sisters did on the day that God walked by."

The men would laugh like it was going to be something dirty, and Magdalena would tell them in Lithuanian about the first sister, who was too busy spinning wool and stayed indoors, while the other sister left her baking and ran out to greet the stranger without even wiping the dough off her hands. God turned the first sister into a spider and made her sit forever in dark places making thread, while the second sister became a honeybee whose arms are always covered in sweet dough, who rests in a warm hive through the winter and is loved by everyone.

Usually the insurance men would stop her before she got to the end of the story. "Just teach us the bad words," they'd say. Back home people mostly cursed in English or sometimes Russian, so just for fun she'd teach the men the Lithuanian expressions for "bread-and-butter" or "take me to the hospital, I'm about to give birth," writing the words down on a napkin and making them repeat after her, *take me to the hospital, I'm about to give birth.* The insurance men would all imagine they were being very obscene, while the spider on the wall paused, then slid down an invisible string to dangle over somebody's drink.

But the English words across their faces that had looked so unpronounceable at first, hemmed in as they were on either side by consonant sounds, gradually took on meaning, and Magdalena began taking out her contact lenses before she and Lina went out. She'd keep her glasses in her purse, and when she went to the toilet she'd put them on, just to reassure herself that her feet still had edges, that there was a clear place where her body ended and the rest of the world began.

She had stopped wearing her contact lenses altogether when Lina met Tobias Kronen, and so it wasn't until Lina started seeing him regularly that Magdalena really noticed him. He said he was a professional photographer—which Lina laughed at. Men were always telling her they were photographers. But this was true: He showed Lina his card from *National Geographic* and Lina made Magdalena go with her to look for his pictures in the magazines at the library. They were there, iridescent tree snakes and grass huts and street children in Bangkok. He was in London on an extended assignment, and he had a wife and twin babies back in Stockholm, but he liked Lina a lot, he said, and if she wanted to she could go with him to photograph some Neolithic tombs.

So Lina went with Tobias Kronen to a place where a big flat rock buzzed under your hand if the moon was right, and on the drive back Tobias showed her how to use his camera, which was not digital but the old-fashioned kind covered with dials and buttons, the kind real photographers use, Lina told Magdalena, suddenly the expert, as if she weren't always using her phone to take pixilated snapshots of the two of them, the phone held at arm's length so that part of Magdalena was usually missing.

Tobias thought Lina had an eye and he took her to a used camera shop. You'd never know it from the cracked leather strap, but Tobias said the one he got her was the best of the old-time cameras, and for a while Lina walked around taking photographs of street musicians and cracks in the sidewalk, recording the shutter speed and aperture in a little book.

Tobias said that when photography was first invented people believed that each picture peeled off a thin layer of reality. Like a bit of skin removed each time—too many pictures taken of a person, and that person would disappear from life and start existing only in the photographs. So Lina began taking a whole series of portraits of Tobias Kronen—Tobias Kronen eating toast, Tobias Kronen about to cross the street, Tobias Kronen packing his bags, and finally Tobias Kronen at the airport waving good-bye, because apparently she hadn't taken enough to keep him. Lina had the photos blown up big and hung them around the apartment for a couple of days until Magdalena made her take them down. But before she did, Magdalena bought a magnifying glass and when Lina was out she went over each photograph with it, looking for the string of Swedish words that stretched across Tobias Kronen's forehead and down his arms. But in the photographs the words on Tobias Kronen disappeared, leaving his skin as blank as the faces on billboards or the pictures of people in a magazine.

One morning Lina came home with a story about how she'd woken to find a blue-eyed boy—who, the night before, had dropped a pearl into her wine glass and then pushed her into the men's room to do lines of cocaine off the top of the urinal while the pearl dissolved—wrapped up in string. For the first time she thought she really might die right there in that hotel room, she told Magdalena, because the string was more like a flat black cord, the kind that people are strangled with. Especially people who cannot find their clothes in time to run for the door before the person who has wrapped the cord around himself finishes rocking and chanting with his eyes closed.

The story was not so different from other stories Lina told on other mornings in their kitchen, Magdalena in her pajamas, Lina in whatever she'd been wearing the night before, Magdalena doing the dishes and Lina eating the corners off Magdalena's toast or cracking a raw egg into her coffee.

By that time Lina had quit her job at the bar, though somehow she still came up with her share of the rent, and she had the whole night's story to tell now that Magdalena was working two shifts and almost never went out. Sometimes Magdalena listened and sometimes she didn't, scrubbing at a bit of potato burned onto a pan, though she knew it wouldn't come off without soaking.

Really a *boy*, Lina was saying that morning. Exactly her age, his own table at such and such club, took her to one place then another, and so on—Lina was drizzling gin over the yolk floating in her coffee, then rummaging through the fridge for the cream—he was so beautiful, women put their phone numbers into his hand as they walked by, he had done something important for such and such company and they made him a such and such—Lina reached with her fingers into the jar of pickled banana peppers that had been in the fridge since Manny the Argentinean footballer, while Magdalena scraped the potato off the pan with her thumbnail.

At the exact moment Lina had decided to leave her clothes and run for the door of the hotel room just as she was, the boy opened his eyes. He looked at her through the web of black cords he'd made over his face, and asked her to please stay for breakfast. There was a knock at the door, and someone brought in coffee and a platter of star fruit.

The boy's name was Dov Kitrosser, and he was the ninth of ten children born to a family of Orthodox Jews who had left Spain for Russia at the time of the Inquisition, and Russia for England at the time of the pogroms. His grandfather had sold figs beside a newsstand in Piccadilly Circus, and from there he founded Britain's largest fresh fruit dynasty, which supplied London's finest restaurants with champagne grapes, golden watermelons, and raspberries that came packed on cushions of honeysuckle.

According to Lina, Dov Kitrosser had started grafting cherry sprigs onto the branches of his mother's rose bushes almost before he could walk, and by the age of twenty he'd made a name for himself as a botanical engineer, one of the sharpest minds in the field of genetic modification, which, he told Lina as he spritzed a blood orange over the star fruit, would one day feed the world on dryland rice and virus-resistant potatoes. The genes of plants could be combined and remixed to do incredible things. Look, he said, opening a little box attached to the black cords that he'd draped over the back of a chair. Inside was a glass globe the size of a walnut, and in it the world's tiniest apple tree was heavy with pinpoints of fruit.

Lina always talked like this, some of it possible and most of it not, her eyes unnaturally bright, fingers picking at the edges of her dress. But the name reminded Magdalena of something, and the next time Lina took a shower, Magdalena said she had to use the mirror to do her makeup. She put her glasses on and turned for a tissue just as Lina reached for a towel. *Dov Kitrosser*. Like everything else on Lina, she'd seen those words a hundred times before, but they came with no explanation; she hadn't even been sure they were a name. None of the others, not even Tobias Kronen with his cameras, had found their way onto Lina's skin, but Dov somehow was stuck there, the last few letters of his name disappearing into the shadow under her breast.

Still, Magdalena didn't think too much about it, and she'd forgotten all about Dov Kitrosser when several days later a crate of pomegranates was delivered to their flat. Even when he became a fixture in Lina's morning storytelling and the long skirt Magdalena wore to work started disappearing—because all of Dov Kitrosser's sisters wore them below the knee—Magdalena still thought that he would pass. Then one day Lina said that she was leaving. She had found a girl named Roxie to take her room, so the rent would still get paid, and she separated her socks from Magdalena's. Dov Kitrosser came in a car to take her things, leaving Magdalena scouring the enamel off the stove to cover the sound of their footsteps fading on the stairs.

But Lina didn't take the camera with its cracked leather strap that Tobias Kronen had given her; Magdalena found it under her umbrella the next time it rained. Magdalena's glasses had gotten broken when Roxie sat on her purse, and so Magdalena began taking the camera with her when she went out, adjusting a lever on the viewfinder to bring street signs into focus when she needed to. The image through the camera was so sharp that the first few times a face wandered into the frame she clicked the shutter release almost by accident, she was so startled by the crispness of the words across a forehead that suddenly bobbed up to block her view. But when the first roll was finished and she had the film developed, the words were gone, and Magdalena looked through the series of anonymous faces, wondering how anyone decided who was or was not beautiful—to her the lack of words alone made each one perfect.

Lina had been gone for less than a week when Magdalena left the house one morning late for work. She was looking up the street through the camera to see if the bus was coming, when the space in the viewfinder was taken up by Lina getting out of a cab. Magdalena was just about to call out and tell her to hurry over before the bus came if she wanted to use Magdalena's keys to get into their apartment, but she saw that there was someone else in the back seat. He handed Lina a laundry basket full of clothes, and she held his hand till she was all the way out and standing on the curb. Then she let go and the taxi pulled away. The man inside waved but Lina didn't wave back, she just stood in the middle of the street watching it until it turned the corner, with little streaks of makeup running down her face.

It had been years since Magdalena had seen Lina cry, and for a moment she stood watching with the camera to her face. Lina always seemed so capable, like a master puppeteer who, though she might have loved or needed men for certain things, never forgot that they were dolls on strings, and if they danced it was because she made them do it.

Magdalena put the camera away and took out her phone to tell her manager that she'd be late, and she started toward the Lina-size shape that was now waiting in front of their building. Usually Lina's stories of endings came days or weeks after they had happened, but this one she told before they'd even made it up the stairs.

She and Dov had gotten married, a crazy thing, done hastily in the middle of the night when they'd both taken too much of something— Lina wasn't even sure of what—and in the morning Dov regretted everything. He went into convulsions of prayer and by the time he'd calmed down, Lina was so relieved he hadn't torn himself to pieces that she agreed when he said they ought to be apart for a little while, to get their heads straight. So Lina found herself back at the flat, a married woman, leaning against the buzzer with her things in a laundry basket at her feet.

By the time they got up to the fifth floor, Lina wasn't crying anymore. She had a plan, and she hung her head over the sink and made Magdalena cut off all her hair. To make things right, she said. It was part of a ceremony that should have happened on her wedding night. Her hair fell in long blonde sheets into the breakfast dishes. Magdalena pressed the scissors flush against her skin, and as she cut she saw that certain words at Lina's hairline were in fact the beginnings of whole sentences that continued up across her scalp. Lina had more writing under her hair than anywhere else on her body. Some of it Magdalena recognized as history, the stories of things that had happened before Lina was even born. One string of words was in English; others were written in alphabets Magdalena couldn't understand. She had no choice but to look at them. In this state she wouldn't think of letting Lina use the scissors herself. Lina made her get a razor and clear away even the roots, so that no stray hair would float in the ritual bath that was supposed to precede her conversion. "What are you talking about?" Magdalena asked.

"Dov's cousin is a rabbi, I'm going to him," Lina said.

"Why?" Magdalena said.

"I'm going to convert," Lina said. "Dov will change his mind if I'm Jewish." And because Magdalena realized she might be right about that, she didn't tell Lina that she didn't need the rabbi. There had been a whispered conversation years ago, when Ruta was drunk and she came to Magdalena's mother's apartment late one night when Magdalena was supposed to be asleep, about names being changed during the war. But Ruta said a lot of things.

Magdalena made a lather with the dish soap and pressed the razor close. And now she saw that Lina wore her ancestors like a kerchief wrapped tight and hidden under her hair. Her mother was Ruta, born Kazlauskaitė, whose mother was Ona, born Chana Gitelson, whose mother was Rivka, born Fein. When Lina made Magdalena fill the bathtub and said that Magdalena would have to help her because her entire body was supposed to be submerged at the same moment, Magdalena didn't tell her the stories of great- and great-great-grandparents that darkened her scalp or that over one fresh-shaved temple she carried instructions for prayers Magdalena knew Lina had never learned. Instead Magdalena said, "It's not going to work. Your butt will float."

"Please," Lina said. "The rabbi won't do it if I haven't had the bath."

So Lina held her breath and Magdalena pushed her under, trying to make sure that Lina's heels and calves, her bottom and shoulder blades and the back of her naked head all got wet at once. The bathtub was too small and she couldn't quite do it. Just as well, Magdalena said. The whole idea was crazy, and anyway, no rabbi was going to accept an at-home immersion. But Lina wouldn't listen. She gathered her things, wrapped a scarf around her strange pink head, and shouted good-bye from the stairs. For a moment Magdalena thought about calling after her, but Lina was already gone. Magdalena cleared the hair out of the sink by the handful and put it in the bin.

Inside the yellow church it was quiet. Back in Lithuania old women might sit in the last few pews straight through a Sunday afternoon, but in Swindon not so many people went to church and this one was empty except for the smell of flowers left too long in their vases. Magdalena put her glasses on and watched the light filter through the colored glass.

When she was eight or nine years old, after Lina had gone back to live with Ruta in Kaunas, Magdalena's mother got a job cleaning in a church. In the afternoons after school Magdalena would sit in the basement and watch the sisters while they made communion wafers. Sometimes they'd let Magdalena do the mixing, so long as she didn't touch the dough. If she'd been confirmed she could have helped them roll it out and cut it into little squares, but as it was she just watched as the nuns made two cuts for a cross into each square, murmuring *body of Christ*, sprinkled them with holy water, *body of Christ,* and covered them with a white cloth until they could be baked for Sunday morning.

The nuns were old, but they were happy. Magdalena's mother said that this was because the Russians were gone and they didn't have to be nuns in secret anymore. But Magdalena believed she knew the real reason. Now the nuns could wear their old clothes again, with low hoods that covered the words on their foreheads and pinned down over their necks and ears. That was back when Magdalena thought that everybody saw the writing, and she was sure that the nuns were glad not to have to read each other's secrets anymore.

One night a few months after Lina made Magdalena cut her hair, she came to the bar where Magdalena worked on weekends. She was soaking wet—she must have walked all the way from Dov's flat in Stamford Hill to get that wet because it was barely raining. Her hair seemed to have grown back, darker now and unnaturally smooth. Her face was flushed and the things she was saying weren't making a lot of sense. If Magdalena had thought about it she would have known something was wrong. But right then she was worried about her cash drawer, which was coming up short again and again. So she poured Lina a drink and told her to sit at the bar until she was done counting. The register was under by twelve pounds fifty. She counted the drawer again while one of the regulars bought Lina another drink. Twelve pounds fifty short. It was funny how she remembered that. If she'd just paid the difference herself and taken Lina home. If James the day bartender hadn't dropped the petty cash receipt into the ice bin— where Magdalena found it, finally, blotted it dry with a napkin, circled the amount (he'd taken out £12.50 exactly to buy lemons for the bar), and stuck it in the cashbox, then shooed the closing time regulars out and took Lina home. If she hadn't made Lina wait for her, if Lina had had one or two fewer drinks—well, it might not have made any difference, and that was the truth. But what was also the truth was that Magdalena had been glad to make her wait. It had been a long time since she'd heard from Lina, weeks had gone by without even a text, so let her take her turn waiting, and never mind that her head kept dipping up and down.

Lina seemed all right on the bus ride home, except that she was talking too loudly. She and Dov had been living together, there were problems with the family, Dov was spending more and more time away, leaving Lina alone in the big empty flat they had moved to because Dov's mother wouldn't let Lina stay with them. Without his family Dov was losing touch with things, he was going out too much, not caring if Lina was there or not, and so Lina tried to do the things Dov's mother had done, keeping certain fasts and doing things with candles, although Dov hardly noticed. That particular day had been a special one. The women were supposed to go without food or water till sundown when the men would mix honey into wine and tip it to the women's lips to drink. Lina had waited at home all day and into the night for Dov to come. When he did, his eyes were tiny pinpoints, and when Lina asked him if he knew what day it was he said it was probably already Saturday, and he was going out again. When she said that she was hungry he said there was some fruit in the fridge, to help herself, and he was leaving. He had some things he had to do.

So Lina put handful after handful of little orange fruits into the blender until the motor jammed—"Yeah, of course," Magdalena said. "You didn't take out the pits"—and drank them down. And when she'd finished she came to find Magdalena, a little unsteady on her feet and with something bitter on her breath. Magdalena helped her off the bus and down the street and up the stairs to their flat. She cooked some Minute Rice and fed it to Lina with a spoon. Lina fell asleep on the couch and Magdalena got out the camera, wondering what Lina would look like without the writing on her face, and if the blush around her lips would come off too. She wound the camera. Lina was sleeping with Magdalena's jacket balled up underneath her head, and she didn't wake up when the flash went off.

A bird had flown into the yellow church. Magdalena watched it dodge the blue and red streams of light from the stained glass windows, then, seeing the clear glass at the back of the church, the bird turned suddenly. Its wings caught the sun in a flash of white and it slammed against the glass, then fell like a drip of pale ink down onto the floor of the church without making much of a sound. A little lie, to say that life left off like that, like a pause for breath, a little sigh, a tap against the glass.

When they got there the ambulance men told Magdalena to go into the other room. They put Lina on the kitchen floor and started working on her, sticking her with needles and pumping her stomach. Magdalena did not go into the other room, but rather noticed that Lina's body was seven kitchen floor tiles long and three across. Her new hair had gotten knocked to one side and Magdalena saw that it was a wig, like Dov's sisters wore. It was fanned out across the kitchen tiles and Magdalena kept thinking it was going to get dirty. The ambulance men cut open Lina's shirt and pressed paddles against her chest, and Magdalena remembered the story of the girl with beautiful hair. She cut it in hanks and floated them down the river to the man she loved, who wove them into a rope to catch her with.

In Lithuania people said that deaths come stinging like bees, but Magdalena learned that night that this was wrong. Deaths did not strike suddenly; they took time, one had to fill each moment. So Magdalena repeated the prayers she could think of. At some point one of the ambulance men told her there was nothing more they could do. Maybe she'd misheard, because even after he said it they kept trying, and Magdalena began to wish that they would stop, put Lina back on the couch, and go away.

The ambulance man made her sit on the bed and told her again that they were going to stop. She asked him to please try some more. I'm sorry, he said. Is there someone you can call?

Lina's expressions had stayed with Magdalena for a while, stuck in her head like a song. The song faded, the way Lina squinted her eyes a little bit when she was thinking about something faded, but her eyelids, her feet turned out like a ballerina, the way she had looked, just the same and utterly different after the men from the ambulance laid her on Magdalena's bed and went away—that stayed, and Magdalena could run the whole world round, live in her haze, take the pills Barry gave her in a little cup to help her sleep, help them all sleep in that house where the carpets ate up the sound. She could put up her hands, shut her eyes, and still the thing that was Lina but was not anymore would be there in her mind, its eyelids turning gray. No words she'd ever read anywhere had prepared her for that.

"Oh dear," said a woman who had come up beside Magdalena in the church, without Magdalena noticing. She was wearing a little thing on her head that made Magdalena think she was probably a nun, but in a modern, English way. Magdalena took her glasses off and took a step back, keeping the woman's face a blur.

"Oh, the poor thing," the woman said, scooping the bird off the floor and onto a bit of paper. "I've said all along we ought to put something on that glass." She folded the bird into the paper, then she turned to Magdalena. "Are you here for Santiago?"

"Yes?" Magdalena said.

"Hurry now and get into some proper walking shoes—the others left an hour or so ago. You're the last group with a hope of making it by the Feast Day, if you ask me, and even so you'll have to trot. You've got quite a bit of ground to cover before you get to France, and then it's another good five or six weeks, unless you go by sea. The others will be off to Marlborough next, to meet the group coming over from Saint Andrew's in Chippenham. You can probably catch them there if you take the bus," the woman said. "It's a bit of a cheat, but after all, it's quite a long trip. I don't suppose it matters much if you start off here or in Marlborough, does it?"

"I don't know," Magdalena said.

"Let me give you your stamp all the same. Come along," she said, and Magdalena followed her into a little office. "Have you got a book yet?" she asked.

"No," Magdalena said.

"You can pick one up in Marlborough. I'll just put it here for now, shall I? You'll paste it in your book later on." She took out a stamp and ink pad and pressed the stamp down hard on a bit of paper. Magdalena brought it up close to her face to see it.

"What is it?" she asked.

"Scallop shell," the nun said. "After the bones of Saint James had been lost at sea, his body washed ashore covered in shells and perfectly whole, and there's your miracle, see? All the pilgrims buy little badges with the scallop shell on them, you can get one for yourself once you get to France. Don't be shy about going up to anyone who's got one on if you need a bit of help."

"Okay," Magdalena said.

"Off you go," the woman said. "And let me give you something for the way." The woman led her into a little office.

Whole, Magdalena thought. Such an odd word in English. It was the same word Dov Kitrosser's brother had used. "The body must be left whole," he'd said. At the time Magdalena hadn't understood. "In a hole?" she said. "Whole," Dov's brother said. "Like, all in one piece."

Magdalena wished she had been listening more closely to the other things the nun had been saying. Who was this man who had died and then washed ashore whole? There had been a time when Magdalena believed very strongly in miracles. While her mother worked cleaning the church, Magdalena would sometimes follow her and collect the bits of wax she scraped off the floor from under the votive candles, looking for the face of Mother Mary in the drippings. Magdalena wanted to think some more about the little forests of wax that grew underneath the rows of candles, each one all that was left of some certain prayer, and she wanted to know more about the place where dead people washed ashore whole. She might have asked, but the nun was still talking, and in another moment Magdalena forgot all about miracles.

"I made up loads of packages, but the others, you know, they're so weighted down with packs and things they can't bear the extra. But you haven't got much." The woman handed Magdalena a paper bag filled with buns. "The sisters had a bit of fun making bread from the old pilgrim recipes. It'll take your teeth out but it won't go bad. Let me get you some jam to go with it." The woman reached past Magdalena's head and opened a little cabinet behind her. *Lost dog, Bishop's Gate, bone cancer, Joey Dolan's orchard with the apple blossoms out*, it said across her arm. "You'll get hungry, you'll see—I've done the Way twice myself, but the old knees aren't the same anymore." She gave Magdalena a jar of orange-colored jam. "Our tree had such a crop, I've got more preserves than I know what to do with." On the jar was a handwritten label. *Apricot.*

Magdalena had seen that word in typeface along Lina's hairline so often that she had stopped seeing it, but she'd never realized that it was English. It didn't look like an English word somehow, and yet there it was, written neatly in blue ink on the side of the jar.

"It's apricot," the woman said. "I don't remember a year they were so sweet. Come and see the garden—you can pick as many as you like. Eat them as you walk, they'll keep you regular. You'd be surprised how many pilgrims forget that sort of thing."

Magdalena knew she should give the jar back to the woman and leave, bury the sight of the word in the part of her mind she made a habit of not going into. Instead, she let the nun rummage for an empty grocery sack and followed her outside and across the parking lot to a walled garden behind the rectory. "Soaks in the sun," the woman said. "You should have seen our cherries."

She knew she shouldn't, but in another moment Magdalena was taking her glasses out of her bag and putting them on, and yes, there in the garden was a tree with its branches weighted down with little orange fruits. Some had freckles from the sun, and the ground was covered with the ones that had gone brown.

"It breaks my heart to see them spoil," the woman said.

After the ambulance men lifted Lina off the kitchen floor, carried her into Magdalena's room, and were gathering their things to go, one of them spoke to her quietly. For a person so young and with no obvious medical condition, there would have to be an inquest, he said. The body couldn't be left alone. The ambulance men left and a police officer came to stay in the flat until the autopsy people could come in the morning. The policeman was black and his skin was very dark—not one word showed through. He kept offering to wait outside in the hallway, but Magdalena said no. They had left the door to Magdalena's room open a crack, and she didn't want to be alone with the thing that looked like Lina but was not anymore. So she made the policeman cup after cup of tea, even though she knew he didn't want any, and they waited on like that till morning.

After the coroner's people came to take Lina away and the policeman left, thanking her for the tea because he didn't know what else to say, Magdalena could not stay alone in the flat, not just then, when so many things were just exactly the same—Lina's shoes just as she'd left them, one on top of the other with the toes pointed inward like they were ashamed to have been left like that in the middle of the room—while other things, the little sheaths of plastic from the needles they had used on her, did not belong at all.

It seemed important to get the picture on Lina's camera developed, but first Magdalena had to finish the roll of film. She walked to the park down the street. There were children playing. The face of one little girl was darkened by line after line of text. There were little words around her eyes, and bigger ones across her cheeks. Magdalena took a picture. She took a picture of a little boy whose dimples were spoiled by what was written there, and of a middle-aged man reading a newspaper on a park bench, whose nose reminded Magdalena of pictures of her father, but who had big block letters like stains across the rest of him.

The pictures came back to her in the opposite order from how they had been taken, and when Magdalena got to the one of the little girl in the park, her skin empty now in the photograph, she skipped the one that came next, which would be of Lina asleep on the couch. She didn't know why she had thought she wanted to see it.

A few days later, while the inquest was being made, the police department telephoned Magdalena. They had found a policewoman who spoke Lithuanian to tell her what the coroner had found. Lina had eaten the seeds of an entire case of wild Turkish *abrikosai*, apparently by putting the fruits, pits and all, into a high-powered blender—which the police had found unwashed on Dov's kitchen counter, a slush of skin and cracked seeds at the bottom and cyanide residue staining the blades. The policewoman began asking questions. Had Lina meant to do it? Could it have been an accident? Didn't she know that the pits were poisonous? "Poisonous?" Magdalena asked. She'd never heard that before. "Of course," the policewoman said. "Peaches too." Why would Lina have put a whole box of them in the blender? Was she upset? Was she having problems in her life? Magdalena tried to explain that Lina was like that sometimes, that she scratched people's names into her legs with paperclips when she was happy and lit fires in the sink when she got mad. And through all of it, with all the questions and the arrangements that had to be made, the calls to her mother in America and the trouble they had finding the place where Ruta was living, Magdalena never thought to ask what *abrikosai* were in English.

Magdalena took the grocery sack from the nun, who told her to help herself from the tree and be sure to latch the garden gate when she was done. The nun walked back toward the church, pinching dead blossoms as she passed a flowerbed. Magdalena went into the garden and picked one of the fruits. Its skin was soft, a shade lighter than the orange-colored jam the nun had given her. She could feel that the flesh was loose around the pit. She took a bite.

Somehow she hadn't realized that the things written on Lina's skin were happening one by one until there was nothing left for the future. There were no descriptions of marriages or children or disease, and when she'd cut off all of Lina's hair, Magdalena had seen that *acute cyanide-induced respiratory failure after ingesting the seeds of 30–40 wild Turkish* came before that old word visible just below her hairline. *Ap-ree-tsots* was how Magdalena had always thought of it, but the *c* was meant to be pronounced like a *k* and not a *ts* like in Lithuanian because the word was English: *apricots*. And, as Lina stood with her head bowed over the sink and a hundred other things printed across her scalp, Magdalena had tried hard not to understand.

Stupid shitty Lina, to put apricots in the blender without even taking out the pits and then to come home to Magdalena as if she knew Magdalena would never have been able to believe it if she hadn't seen it all the way through. It was the only thing that Magdalena could be grateful for. It was better to be left with the memories of that night pinned up like postcards behind her eyelids than to be like Ruta Valentukienė, who would never really know how to believe that Lina was gone. It was better to have been there, starting with the rosy shadow around Lina's lips, then the chewing sound that woke Magdalena in the middle of the night, and on through the whole thing, the breathing, the thick paste that filled up her mouth, the sound her lungs began making when it was nearly over, the men from the ambulance and the time it took them to come up the stairs, the needles, the plastic gloves, and the little plastic caps they left littered on the floor.

The people doing the inquest questioned Dov Kitrosser again and again, and Magdalena too, asking her if she'd known that Dov had accepted a post with a biotechnology company in Zurich and had bought just one plane ticket there. Had she known about the fights, the threats from his mother, or the Australian businessman that Lina had been seen with the night before?

Tests were run on the blender, showing that the cyanide content of those apricot seeds was particularly high. But, as the policewoman said, it was commonly known that you weren't supposed to eat them. They gave Magdalena an envelope with a copy of the inquest papers, in case she needed documentation when she brought Lina home.

Dov's brother called to say they would pay for the airline company to take Lina's body back to Lithuania. There's no need, Magdalena said. After the autopsy there was nothing to do but cremate her, and she had the ashes double bagged inside a shoebox she could hold on her lap. Something was wrong, but Magdalena didn't understand the silence on the other end of the line until Dov's brother explained that according to Jewish law if Lina's body wasn't buried whole, there would be no way for her and Dov to rise together at the end of time and be reunited in eternity.

Magdalena stood under the tree in the church garden with the bite of apricot still in her mouth, unchewed and getting to be tasteless, like an unwelcome second tongue. She swallowed it.

She'd imagined this moment many times, wondering what would happen to her when she found out for certain whether the words were true or they weren't. If they weren't true, then she was crazy, and if they were, then the whole world was, crazy and cruel to leave little notes like that, as if life was worried it might forget what it had planned. The only thing Magdalena had always been sure of was that not knowing was better than knowing, and so she'd tried hard for a very long time not to look into things too much. The doctor her mother used to go out with did go back to his wife, just like it said under his chin, and her friend Marija did end up marrying somebody called Juras, whose name was written in a band around her ring finger. But Lina's mother was the one who became a drunk, and her skin hadn't said a word about that, while Magdalena's mother had mostly stopped drinking, and still it said *alko-holika* like a brand on the side of her throat. And Marija's baby who was born with a hole in his heart had had whole paragraphs filling up his cheeks.

Well? Magdalena said to herself. The question echoed around inside her head. Then an answer came, not a word but a feeling. A certainty, like a breeze that had found its way into her mind. She thought of the place where *Luck* was written on the inside of her mother's wrist. In the stories Luck was sometimes beautiful and some-times had to be tricked and locked in a basket. But she always got out, she got what she wanted and rode away holding the reins of the horse she shared with Death, who was her kinder sister. There was a drug-store just off Faringdon Road. She would stop there to get what she needed. She would do it today. Magdalena ate the rest of the apricot and spat out the seed.

{RICHARD}

Paris, June

As it turned out, my hotel was only a block or two from the boulevard de Sébastopol, not far from the tower under scaffolding I'd remembered seeing earlier that morning. A statue of a man holding a staff stood on top of one corner of the tower, giving it a distinctly asymmetric look. I made a note that my hotel was on the statue's right-hand side, in case I got lost again.

It was still too early for check-in, so I left my luggage with the lady at the front desk. She insisted on putting an extra piece of tape around Aunt Cat's suitcase before she stowed it in the closet, and then suggested I go out and have some breakfast. There was a bakery nearby. I bought some rolls and looked around for a bench where I could sit and eat them. I stopped at a souvenir stand to buy another city map, and when I saw that my tower had been included in a postcard-size street scene mounted on a tiny easel, I picked that up too. The picture was only a print of a painting that, if you looked at it closely, had been sloppily done in the first place, and there was a sticker on the back saying the whole thing had been made in Vietnam. At ten euros I was sure I was being taken advantage of, but I bought it anyway.

As soon as I'd done it I felt a bit sheepish. I hardly needed another trinket to sit and gather dust, even one brought back from Paris. So I figured I'd send it to my friend Diana. Before Walt died I had her give me a hand sorting through Aunt Cat's old boxes of knickknacks, and I could tell she liked that kind of thing. I'd come in to find her flushed and covered with dust, delighted at a miniature nativity scene set into a walnut shell or a bit of sewing advice—*hide the knot as you would a secret*—stitched onto a pincushion Cat must have made when she was a girl. When I picture Diana now, back home in her own kitchen, I'm certain that the windowsill above her sink is filled with those sorts of little things. The painting on its easel would fit in fine, something to look at while she waits for the water to run warm.

But then I thought that maybe I'd better not. I haven't heard from Diana since she left to go home back in November, and I wasn't sure she'd welcome a souvenir bought on a whim by a man she probably hasn't thought of since. I put the little painting in my pocket, with one leg of the easel still sticking out, thinking that maybe I'd save it as a keepsake after all. It might be nice to look at it now and then and let the picture of the tower with its one corner higher than the rest bring me back to Paris.

The rolls I'd bought from the bakery were still warm, and I found a park with an empty bench where I could eat them. I had to take the painting out of my pocket to sit down. I looked at it again, thinking about life's accumulations. Even my Aunt Cat, who never seemed the type for keepsakes; after she died we found a dozen boxes at the back of her closet filled with roadside souvenirs and baby shoes and bits of cracked china she'd saved over the years, so much stuff that I started having Diana come out every week just to get through it.

My Aunt Cat was not a sentimental woman, but those boxes of knickknacks must have meant something to her because she mentioned them in her will—otherwise we never would have known they were there. They were the one thing she left specifically to me. It became a source of tension between Pearl and me, not because there was anything of real monetary value, but they were family things and I suppose Pearl felt they should have gone to her.

The argument we had about those boxes was part of the reason Pearl was so set against my moving back to the ranch after Aunt Cat died. But somebody had to keep an eye on Walt. Pearl had her kids in school up in Denver and Eddie had his business to run, but I wasn't teaching anymore. My son was about to start high school and there was nothing to keep me in town.

What settled it was Uncle Walt. He broke his hip when he slipped on the ice trying to water the cows in the middle of winter and the doctor said it wouldn't do to move him. He said a broken hip was generally the beginning of the end for old folks like Walt, and when Pearl mentioned selling the ranch and getting him settled in a nursing home, Walt made the kind of racket I don't think any of us had ever heard from him before. So Pearl and Eddie figured they'd let him die there, and they said it was all right if I wanted to stay out at the ranch and keep him company until he did.

We called the farm the ranch and we called the house the ranch too, because even though Pearl and Eddie and I had been just tiny kids when Uncle Walt bought it, it was never the kind of place you could plain call *home*. It had been built as a dude ranch back in the early thirties, and it could have slept a full staff and maybe forty guests if you included the little cabins out back. After knowing my Uncle Walt for nearly sixty years, I still can't imagine why he bought that place. It makes me wonder if maybe there was more to him than any of us kids ever knew. Uncle Walt, who wore the same hat every non-Sunday of his life and outside of the war never went farther than Walsenburg if he didn't have to—I'll never understand what made him so attached to a house with two dining rooms, a chapel out back, and its own dance floor.

Well, I knew Pearl thought I was angling to inherit the place, and so I did my best to make it clear that I wasn't after anything more from Uncle Walt than what we knew he'd already put aside for me. I have my teacher's pension and I get royalty checks from the Beart estate now and then, and it adds up nicely. But Pearl was still mad about the boxes from Aunt Cat, so I told her I'd set aside the china and any jewelry for her, and I promised that when the time came, I'd be sure Walt's Purple Heart got passed on to her boys. When she realized that my moving out there would mean they wouldn't have to hire a home health aide for Walt, Pearl relaxed a little bit.

We had a frank discussion, the three of us in the post office parking lot the day Eddie picked Walt up from the hospital and Pearl and I met him in town to do the paperwork. It was maybe too public a place for all sorts of things to come out, but we put a good forty years of griev-ances in the sun that day, each of us saying what was on our minds. How the money from my mother's estate meant I was the one who got to go to college, though Pearl's grades were just as good; how Eddie had to share his popgun with me; how my getting scarlet fever when I was five practically bankrupted the family; how as kids they always made sure I knew I was somewhere between a nephew and a burden to Aunt Cat and Uncle Walt, but never a son; and on and on, a big wave of past hurts and secret resentments that washed over us standing outside the post office that afternoon while Uncle Walt waited in Eddie's truck for us to figure out what to do with him.

And finally it was decided: I'd stay out at the ranch for as long as it took, and then after Walt we-all-knew-what I'd move back to town, maybe go back to work at the middle school in the fall. But Walt didn't die for another five years, the problem I had with the school board never did blow over, and with hay prices up Pearl and Eddie stopped talking about selling the land.

I often play that conversation over to myself, and though I'd finished my breakfast I sat in the park a while longer, thinking of all the things I might have said to Pearl and Eddie that day. My thoughts vaulted the ocean and brought me right back home, and before I knew it I was calculating acre-feet of irrigation and wondering if I'd left the stove on back at the ranch.

But that couldn't go on all day. I had just over a week to spend in Paris, and thoughts of home weren't going to get me any closer to finding a record of Inga Beart's red shoes. The day was getting warm and I was thirsty, so I got up from my bench and went across the street to a little supermarket.

I found a carton of milk in the canned goods section. It wasn't refrigerated, but I bought it anyway and went back to my bench to drink it. The carton was made of thick paper and it took some doing to unfold one edge into a kind of spout. I took a sip; it was warm and it had a different taste from the milk we have back home. And with that taste came an experience I'm not sure I've ever had before. A brand-new memory came into my mind: my Aunt Cat opening a cardboard container of milk. The cardboard is folded in a sort of a pyramid shape that can't be set down without tipping over, and Aunt Cat is trying to hold the thing upright while digging at one corner with her fingers. When she finally gets it open the paper is frayed and soft.

The memory itself was nothing much, it was just that its newness startled me. It was a strange sensation, to be so many thousands of miles from home, in a foreign city where everything looked and felt so different, and then to suddenly feel the pull of an invisible string as *now* cinched itself tight against *then, here* against *there.*

I was inspecting my new recollection, sort of turning it over in my mind, the way you might examine a piece of a meteorite, when I realized that the memory almost certainly couldn't be real. We always got our milk in glass bottles from the dairy up the road, and when they stopped delivering Aunt Cat used to tape quarters to our jacket pockets for me and Pearl and Eddie to pick up a bottle each on our way home from the school bus.

It worried me. I no longer bother trying to remember where I put my glasses, I just look in all the usual places, and when my son calls me on my birthday I try not to sound surprised. But I didn't think I was to the point of manufacturing memories. Still, there is something calming in a good long drink of milk, albeit funny-tasting. I let the memory be and drank the whole thing, wondering at the strange joke my subconscious must be playing on poor Aunt Cat, to put into her hands a carton of sterilized store-bought milk.

The Beart girls grew up on a dairy farm outside Rye, Colorado, on land better suited to beef. My grandfather broke his health putting in the railroad down around Santa Fe and they moved up to the Front Range with the idea that the Rocky Mountains would catch the good life and funnel it on down. But my grandfather didn't know much about the dairy business, and neither did my grandmother, whose family had run a grocery back east, and in the early thirties when things were just starting to go bad for other folks, the Bearts were already deep in debt. The cows were always getting sick, or else they were being sold off, and after what customers they had were taken care of there was never more than a bit of the skim for the family—or so Eddie, Pearl, and I were told most mealtimes, as Aunt Cat filled our jelly glasses to the bottom lip and waited while we drank them down.

The Beart sisters had the same dark hair and fine features, though only Inga took after Great Aunt Effie, a spinster who, it was said, never left the house because of eyes so light she couldn't stand the sun. Aunt Cat's eyes were bottle-blue, and to hear her tell it, growing up it had been Cat who was considered the prettier of the two. But it was Inga who got married first, at the age of seventeen, to a Hungarian by the name of Laszlo Karpati, a foreigner who was just passing through town. "God knows what she saw in him," Aunt Cat always said. "The man could hardly put two English words together in a way that made any sense." Inga Beart's biographers tell it somewhat differently—the classic escape from a weathered gray house and a neurasthenic mother who wouldn't allow anyone to mention the fact that the high Colorado air had done nothing to change the rattle in her husband's cough.

It was 1936 and the Karpatis were headed for California, but I don't know if they made it there together; a divorce was granted in Nevada later on that year. No one knows much about that period, but Inga Beart apparently took back her own name and found her way to Hollywood, where she was credited for bit parts in several of the "movie musicals" they were making then.

I've seen those films. In one, Inga Beart and a crowd of other young things are made up to look like Egyptians. In another, she dances the cancan. It's terrible stuff, but to my mind it's no coincidence she found her way into the movie business. Whatever it was that got those Hollywood types to give an anonymous girl from the heartland a spot in the chorus was what the literary set discovered some years later: a spark of glamor, a hint of the exotic that was heightened by the unmistakable sense—even when she was just one of the girls doing kicks—that Inga Beart was already far away.

My Aunt Cat, on the other hand, stayed home. She took care of things while my grandfather died of the tuberculosis no one, not even the doctor, was allowed to call by name. She was the one to look after my grandmother in the slow withering that followed her husband's death. The day Grandma Beart passed, Aunt Cat walked out of the gray house forever. She married the Hurley boy from down the road, the one who used to put cherries in his mother's empty milk bottles for the Beart girls to find when they washed and filled them up again.

The war started. My Uncle Walt got his ring finger shot off during the assault on Okinawa and, if one can believe such stories, crawled through the mud to find it so as not to lose the wedding band. "Damn fool thing for a scrap of metal," Aunt Cat liked to say. She spent the war working as a welder in an aviation plant in Colorado Springs, sealing up the bellies of bombers, not knowing or caring that her little sister had made her way to New York City and had just bought a pair of red high heels with the fifteen-dollar second-place prize she'd won for a short story about, as all the biographers point out, a young girl who dreams of going blind.

It was after noon by then, somewhere around four A.M. back home, and I needed a nap. I tossed the empty milk carton in a garbage can and looked around for my lopsided tower. When I saw it sticking up over the rooftops I headed back in that direction, and this time I had no trouble finding my hotel. My room was now available, the lady said, and after some confusion about the key I carried Aunt Cat's suitcase up four flights of stairs, then down a hall and up one flight more. I unlocked my door, set the suitcase on the floor, and lay down in bed without even bothering to shut the blinds.

I closed my eyes, and when I opened them again it was to watch the sun come up. I'd slept into the evening and straight on through the night. The window of my room looked out over clusters of chimneys. They reminded me of the tin cans stuck on sticks Eddie and I used to shoot at when we were kids, and the sun broke apart when it hit their wet metal tops, which meant I must have slept more soundly than I had in years, because I hadn't heard the rain.

I shaved with the door shut so the steam would take the wrinkles out of the pants I'd worn on the plane. When I cut myself on the chin I stuck some toilet paper on it and tried to remember not to forget to take it off. It wouldn't be the first time I'd gone out only to notice in a shop window the reflection of a person with a softer jaw than I remembered and a square of tissue stuck to his face.

After I'd finished getting dressed I made the bed, then made it again, this time with the pillows on the outside. I cleaned around the sink to save the maid the trouble and then I watched the sun light up the tin-can chimney tops.

The fact is, I was nervous, and a little afraid to go out into the day.

Aside from the meeting I'd set up with the lady at the French National Archives, I didn't have much of an idea of where to begin. The archivist had written to me to say that the *"Fonds Labat-Poussin"* Carter Bristol referred to in his book was one of the private collections donated to the National Archives by historically relevant individuals—in this case the Comtesse Lucette Labat-Poussin, whose name Bristol connects so intimately with my mother's. But the archivist hadn't been able to confirm whether any of what Bristol claims to have found in the comtesse's papers was actually there—including the photographs of my mother and some personal correspondence of a very private nature. I'd have to look for those things myself.

Of course, I hadn't come all the way to Paris just to go through a file Carter Bristol had already seen. When I wrote to the archivist that I was also interested in seeing some old medical records, she told me that only a person's own family could access that kind of thing. I wanted to ask her about finding the forms from Inga Beart's admittance to the Hôtel-Dieu hospital on August 10, 1954, so before I left my hotel I gathered up all the documents I might need. I made sure I had the important pages marked in Bristol's book and put my birth certificate inside to save it from getting bent, then I packed my notes into my briefcase and left my key at the front desk.

But as it turned out, I didn't even get the chance to start my research. I followed my map up rue des Archives, but when I got there and told the woman at the reception desk who I needed to see, she shook her head.

"I don't understand," I said.

The woman called a young man over, who explained that the archivist I'd corresponded with was unavailable until later that week.

"But I have an appointment for today," I told him. "We set the date months ago. She has some things to show me. I need to speak with her—I'm only here until next Sunday."

"I'm sorry," he said. "There is a *formation* on the preservation of old texts, and she has been required to attend. It is quite important—in our collections are documents more than one thousand years old, and quite vulnerable to humidity. But, if you will please come back Friday in the morning? She will see you then at half past nine."

I didn't know what to do with myself for the rest of the day, so I made my way back toward my hotel. I'd heard that Inga Beart's books are making something of a comeback in Europe, and as I went I kept seeing them in bookshop windows: It seemed a new translation of the first novel had just come out. I was surprised to see that Carter Bristol's biography has already been translated into French; one store I passed had her book and his displayed together. They'd used a different picture for the cover of the French edition of Bristol's book: a grainy newspaper photograph of a bandaged woman leaning against the railing of a ship. It's a well-known image, taken from the dock in Le Havre by a photographer for the *Herald Tribune*: an American novelist returning home from France with her head wrapped in white gauze. The photograph has been cropped to fit the cover of Bristol's book, but if you have the ability to enlarge the original by two or three hundred percent, and if you can look beyond the dark stains on the dressings wrapped around her face, you will see that her feet, which are nearly hidden in the shadow of a steamer trunk, are bare.

Inside the bookshop a half dozen copies of Bristol's biography had been set out on a display table. Inga Beart's own work was apparently of secondary interest. When I asked about the book of hers I'd seen in the window, the saleswoman pointed me to the *Littérature étrangère* section at the back of the shop, where only the first novel and a short story collection were kept in stock. I thumbed through them, wondering how they fared in translation.

It wasn't until I was in high school that I first read my mother's books. By that time Inga Beart had been dead for nearly a decade. Her novels were popular again and a new generation of scholars and critics were busy rehabilitating her image. I wasn't aware of any of that at the time. I knew, dimly, that my mother was famous, and that mentioning her would set my aunt's jaw tight. If I saw something about her in the paper—having once been a local girl, news items like her candidacy for a postage stamp were covered in-depth—I knew better than to bring it up at supper. But I had never actually seen one of my mother's books, and I remember the quiet chill I felt as I went along the fiction shelf of the school library; *Ba*'s gave way to *Be*'s, *Baldwin, Barnes*, and then *Beart, Beart, Beart*, a whole half-shelf of books, their stiff library dust-jacket covers smudged a little bit, corners blunted enough to show that I was not the first student at Walsenburg Senior High to discover them. I was too shy to check them out; I was afraid the librarian would give me a knowing smile or intrude in some other way on that first meeting between my mother and me. I don't remember which I started with; I may have gone from left to right across the shelf or I may have chosen one because I liked the cover. What I do remember is the afternoons that followed. I'd sit in the stacks, too tall at fifteen for my knees to fold comfortably against me, sneaking bites of my sandwich and reading my mother's books. The sandwich was against the library rules, and the books broke an unspoken covenant of my life in Aunt Cat's house, but I read and chewed with a criminal thrill all through my high school lunch periods.

I imagine that at first I didn't absorb much of the stories. I was more interested in the feel of the pages against my fingers, the weight of the books, paper and spine and thick cardboard covers, the first pieces of my mother I could hold in my hands. But as I made my way across that half-shelf and back again, I found myself drawn into the bounded, bittersweet worlds of my mother's characters. They say she created a new American realism; characters that are by every definition ordinary come alight and blaze briefly—none of her books were long. The critics back then made a scene when it came out that each character was based almost entirely on an actual human being, and it's commonly assumed that Inga Beart's crisis began when she lost her publisher, having been accused of writing *true life stories*—a genre that didn't sell as well then as it does today. Now, of course, she's seen as a pioneer, one of the first to turn the facts of unembellished lives into literature. But even before I knew any of it, I read my mother's books with the sense that I was eavesdropping, the feeling that I ought to turn the pages quietly so the people inside wouldn't know I was there.

Until I went to college, most of what I knew about my mother's own life came from a 1951 *Look* magazine article I found in the periodicals section of the high school library; I'd been through all her books by then and was looking for her short stories. I hadn't realized the extent of my mother's celebrity until I opened the magazine to a full-page photograph of a dark-haired woman who looked a little like Aunt Cat, cigarette holder in one hand, achromatic eyes focused on some distant point. Inga Beart never talked about her childhood, but in between the photographs—*Inga Beart in slacks and a feminine blouse, Inga Beart on New York City's Seventh Avenue*—I read about her brief career in Hollywood and her arrival in New York in 1943, at the age of twenty-four. I learned that the publication of her first novel in 1947 made my mother something of a sensation, and I read with special interest about the years that followed. In '48 she returned to California to work on the film version and later spent some time at an artists' colony in New Mexico. By the spring of 1950 she was back in New York, being seen in all the fashionable places. I remember wondering even then why there was no reference to my birth, which had clearly happened sometime in between.

My birth certificate has me born down in Santa Fe in 1949. Inga Beart's biographers don't have much to say about it. They mention it—me—a little bit, and there's some speculation as to whether my father was an itinerant trumpet player or the Austrian film director who went on to become her third husband—and, of course, they all get around to certain bits of evidence that point to the possibility that maybe Inga Beart was raped and that's the reason she never wanted the reminder of it nearby. For obvious reasons I prefer the former hypotheses, but Inga Beart never did tell.

I nodded to the sales clerk and left the bookshop. I walked on, feeling hungry; I hadn't eaten anything since my breakfast in the park the day before. Church bells tolled in the distance, reminding me of the hours going by. I bought a sandwich, and when I passed a public garden I sat to eat it.

My pant cuffs had ridden up a little when I sat down and I was dusting the crumbs off my lap when I noticed that I had on a pair of Uncle Walt's socks. They were some of his town socks, black with blue thread. They hadn't been worn much and though he probably bought them upward of thirty years ago, they were still in fine shape. Which is what I must have been thinking when I took them out of his drawer. I smiled at myself to see them there on my feet, but it was the smile of a person who finds himself suddenly old. I imagine I am not the first to sit on a park bench with a dead man's socks hanging loose around my ankles, watching the world go by.

I started to have a conversation with him in my head. "You like it there in Paris?" he said to me. "Sure I do," I said. There was something I would have liked to ask him about, but I wanted an answer, and for that the Uncle Walt inside my head just wouldn't do.

In all the time Walt and I lived together, when I was growing up and then in his last years when I moved back to the ranch, neither of us ever said much. In the evenings when I was a kid, after he'd gone out to move the sprinklers—because back then we'd drain the pipes and start the motor up by hand—I'd see him out by the pond, the one that never held water, just standing there. *Having his think*, Aunt Cat said. The sun would be going down and he'd still be there, standing, like he was waiting to catch the leak red-handed. But whatever water was left in the pond always stayed about the same while you were looking at it. After I moved back to the ranch and his leg started getting better I used to drive him down there in the old truck sometimes, and we'd sit, a couple of old guys having our think, not saying much. It was an amiable silence and when Walt passed I missed that silence quite a lot.

It was one of the reasons I finally got around to making the trip to Paris. The ranch took on a new kind of emptiness once Uncle Walt was gone. That, plus I'd gotten a nice note from the lady at the French National Archives saying she'd located the Labat-Poussin file Carter Bristol had looked at. Not that those things were reason enough in themselves. I'd talked myself out of going all the way to Paris plenty of times before; I might have done it again if it hadn't been for what Walt said before he died.

*

I had a home nurse come out for those last few weeks, to help manage the dirty tricks death plays once it's made up its mind. The nurse was a nice girl named Marla and though Walt had held his memory more or less together until the very last, just at the end he started getting confused about who she was. When the pain got bad he'd say, "Damn it, Cat, come along now," and when Marla clicked his morphine drip a couple of times, he'd say, "That a girl, Cat-bird." But in what I believe were his last conscious moments, when the two clicks hadn't been enough and Marla looked over to me and I nodded and she gave him two more, then I nodded again and she gave him two more on top of that, Uncle Walt must have seen someone else entirely in Marla's face, because he looked from her to me like he was glad to find us there together and said, "Now, Ricky, don't be mad at her."

"Mad at who?" I said. "Who are you talking about, Walt? This is Marla here."

But he looked to Marla again and worked his mouth around the words. "You tell him how it was."

"Shh," Marla said.

"Go on and tell him," he said to her.

"It's okay," I said. "You just lie back."

But Walt was trying to pull himself up, holding on to Marla's hand. "Go on," he said to her.

"Shh, now," Marla said. "I'll tell him whatever you need. Of course I will."

"Tell him what you said. You said you didn't want to take him off to Paris."

"I'll tell him," Marla said.

"Paris?" I said. "What's that about Paris?" But Marla shook her head at me, and she helped him onto his side for the coughing. She turned down one of the monitors that was beeping, and told me I could take his other hand if I wanted, and we sat like that until the last breaths came, wracking and terrible, and then, as they say, he was gone.

In the weeks after Walt passed I thought a lot about it, wondering why he'd said the name of a city he didn't have a thing to do with, except that his wife's sister had gone there and lost her mind, and I realized that it must have been my mother that Walt was talking to as he slipped away. Marla said people say all sorts of things that don't make sense at the very end, but I wondered if it might have been for my sake that Walt picked my mother for his final conversation. Maybe after all the years he felt she owed her son an explanation. Maybe he figured I had a right to know. Either way, I'm grateful to my Uncle Walt, who used his last words on this earth to give me the closest thing I've ever had to a confirmation that my mother really did come back to see us. *You said you didn't want to take him off to Paris,* Walt said to her. So her visit had to have been before she made the trip, and she must have come to tell Aunt Cat and Uncle Walt that she was going away to France and leaving me behind.

I don't think Walt ever gave much thought to the fact that his wife's sister was a writer. My Uncle Walt was a star man, the way some people are horse men or Harley-Davidson men; I doubt he ever read two books of fiction in his life. Each year for Christmas my Aunt Cat got him a subscription to *Sky and Telescope*, with the first issue bought off the news rack in town and wrapped up in paper. He bought himself a little telescope, and sometimes when you thought he was out checking on the cows in the evenings he was really up on top of the water tower with it. The water tower was only ten or twelve feet high, but my Uncle Walt took what he could get, and when Aunt Cat said he'd better come down before he broke his neck, he said you never knew but there might be a star ten or twelve feet farther off out there in infinity, and he wasn't going to miss it for lack of standing on the water tower.

Uncle Walt never said much about what he saw up there. But sometimes when I went out with him to do the irrigation he'd give me a little lesson in astronomy. I can picture us, rolling on boots turned to spheres by the mud, Uncle Walt with a shovel over his shoulder, me dragging mine along behind me, making a slick mud trail through the grass while the dogs chased the prairie dogs that had been flooded out of their holes.

Out in the field at dusk when maybe Jupiter was lighting up just

past the hills or Mars was glowing behind a constellation of mosqui-
toes, Uncle Walt would get to talking about black holes and extinct
stars, specks of light out there that took a billion years to make it to our
eyes, and stopped existing in the meantime.

Uncle Walt would set his boot on the shovel and dig up a thick
notch of mud and grass to block the irrigation channel and direct
the water down along to the other field, telling me that every inch of
sky was thick with galaxies hurtling away from each other into a void
whose emptiness you had to bend your mind to get your head around.
And I would listen to him with the eagerness particular to nephews
kept on charity, doing my best to bend my brain, when the truth was,
all I could imagine of the vastness of the Universe was a panel of light
bulbs stuck onto a grid in front of the sky.

I've wondered recently why it was always only him and me who
went out to do the irrigation. Pearl would have been helping Aunt Cat
fix supper, but where was Eddie all those evenings? He might have
been there too, for all I know, off a little way blocking one end of a
prairie dog hole with his shovel while the dogs howled and dug around
the other, while I listened to Uncle Walt's musing on a supernova out
there past Polaris that was bigger and hotter than a million suns and
would one of these eons collapse in on itself and become a black hole
the size of a pinprick with an appetite for all its neighbors. I would have
been listening without understanding much, like a puppy so eager to sit
and stay that it scootches forward on its haunches with the effort, while
my Uncle Walt—who sold his cattle by the pound, his hay by the ton;
who bought his gasoline by the gallon and endured those Sunday
sermons by the minute; for whom volume, mass, and time were such
earthly facts, alterable only by more rain, more fertilizer, or, in the case
of church, by calving season—marveled at the suppleness of the
universe.

But it's possible that Eddie wasn't there, that Uncle Walt took me
alone out to do the irrigating. Eddie was going to get the farm—that is,
if he had wanted it—Pearl would get the house, and they took turns
getting the egg with the double yolk at breakfast. But I used to like to
imagine that Uncle Walt wanted to give me something too, a head full of
facts or a feeling of having been singled out for a bit of conversation.

*

Well, you can imagine my surprise when, not long after I'd had my lunch, I looked up and saw my Universe—or more precisely, I saw that panel of light bulbs. I had gotten lost again, having wandered away from the streets around my hotel and onto a big avenue filled with people and packages. I was going slower than the rest of the crowd, trying to find a good place to stop and take out my map. People kept bumping into me, making little snorts of impatience that needed no translation as they jabbed me with the corners of their shopping bags. At that point I hardly had the will to fight it, and the crowd carried me along, leading me straight for the entrance of a big department store.

Above the entrance was a marquee covered with rows and rows of light bulbs. Some of them were blinking, one or two had burned out. I stopped right there and looked at it, not caring that people were flowing all around me and stepping on my feet. It was not an approximation, but the exact image that always used to pop into my head when Uncle Walt started talking about astronomy. I tried to edge my way over to the side of the crowd to get a better look, but all those bodies kept pushing me along. One stream of people was funneling in through the doors of the department store, while the rest hurried along the sidewalk, and by the time I got my bearings and looked back up again, I must have turned a corner because the light bulb marquee was gone.

That evening I hardly felt like sitting alone in my hotel room. My mind was sure to go around and around the thought of those light bulbs stuck against the sky, and I wasn't sure quite where it would end up. So I took a shower and put on some fresh clothes.

Before I left for Paris I bought myself a rather expensive pair of white slacks, thinking that folks in cities dress differently than we do back home. They're not the kind of thing I'd normally wear; in fact, the color was an accident. I'd taken them to the register, intending to ask if the same style came in brown or gray, when the salesgirl said, "Oh hi, Mr. Beart," and I realized she'd been one of my students. Her name came to me as if I'd just taken roll. "Hi Ashleigh," I said, and asked her how she was. We exchanged some small pleasantries, which for all I know she may have meant, but I was so flustered by the encounter—I had her in class the year my troubles with the school board began and I seem to remember her being friendly with the student the trouble was about. When she said, "Will these be all?" I forgot all about asking for the pants in brown or gray and handed her my credit card.

So, thinking that I might as well get some use out of them, I put them on, and a nice shirt too. I left my hotel key with the lady at the desk, who suggested I try the restaurant next door.

But I didn't feel like eating. I got out my map and chose a direction I hadn't gone in yet. I walked until I was thirsty and then sat down at one of the outside tables of a café. It was hardly busy, but even so the waiter took his time getting to me. I'd looked at the French phrases at the back of my dictionary, but it didn't seem polite to make a mess of his language if I didn't have to. "Do you speak English?" I asked him.

"*Oui,*" the waiter said, looking past me at the people on the sidewalk.

"I'd like a beer, please. Something French, if you have it," I said, thinking it would be interesting to try something new. The waiter said something and when I didn't understand, he tapped a laminated card stuck into a plastic stand advertising Kronenbourg 1664. You can buy that brand in the grocery stores back home, and it didn't sound particularly French, but I told him, "That sounds fine." The waiter may not have understood because he went off to take another order, then stood to the side chatting with a girl on a bicycle for longer than it should have taken to pour my beer. But it was a warm night, the café was on a busy street, and there was plenty to see.

In the time between beginning work on her first book in 1945 and her so-called exile to Paris in 1952, Inga Beart wrote six novels and published two collections of poetry and eighteen short stories—a staggering amount of work, especially considering that she also found the time to marry and divorce two more husbands, get herself addicted to barbiturates, and become a bona fide celebrity, all in the space of about seven years.

That she wrote so much so quickly has always puzzled scholars, especially now that we know that nearly all her characters recreate in detail the lives of chance acquaintances. Even the few critics who still overlook her literary contributions and put her somewhere between hack journalist and outright plagiarist have to admit that it would have required hundreds of hours of interviews to grasp so fully the inner lives of the people that she met. But Inga Beart didn't leave behind any research notes. There are no transcripts of interviews, and many of the real people who appear in her novels recalled only brief conversations; some of them wondered if she'd even been listening.

People who don't know anything about her assume she must have been a kind of genius: She sat with a page and the words just flowed. But the few friends who saw her work said it wasn't like that. None of it came easily. She'd hurl the pages across the room, the typewriter would crash to the floor. She'd slip on a pair of red high heels and go out, surround herself with exiled Russian intellectuals, Europeans with arcane titles of nobility, dissident Chinese, and enough pills and alcohol to allow her to forget the small sad lives of her characters.

Things changed in 1952, when an article in the *New York Post* exposed the undeniable parallels between the life of a young elevator operator and the title character in her most recent novel. The young man claimed he ought to be compensated for the use of his story, and though nothing came of it, Inga Beart's publisher dropped her and she couldn't seem to find another one; none of the big houses wanted the risk of a lawsuit. New exposés were coming out almost by the week, as former landladies, a Brooklyn chiropractor, even my mother's own press agent stepped forward to claim this or that plotline as entirely their own, and Inga Beart found herself in disgrace, accused of exploiting her subjects and cheating her readers.

There was no such fuss in Europe, where Inga Beart's books had sold well from the start, and I suppose Paris was a natural place for her to escape to. I wondered if the waiter might have been a little quicker with my beer if he knew that Marguerite Duras herself had personally extended an invitation to my mother. Inga Beart's elegance, her inscrutable beauty and glittering lifestyle contrasted with the stubbled prairies and calloused hands that populate her novels in a way the French, I think, particularly appreciated. Like Sartre or Duras, she wrote about the half-shadows of modern existence, but she lived in the light.

So, like so many other American writers and artists, Inga Beart received a warm welcome when she arrived in Paris in the spring of 1952. An editorial in *Les Temps modernes* that month predicted that the intellectual ferment of the city would give Inga Beart a new lens through which to see her native land. Other commentators accepted her as the latest addition to a list that included Gertrude Stein, Hemingway, Fitzgerald, and the like, and set about anticipating a seminal work of open-sky Americana inspired by Paris's narrow streets and dark cafés.

But Paris was the end rather than the beginning for Inga Beart, and as I found when I first began my research, only a few photographs from those years made it back to the United States. American magazines reported occasionally on her having been seen with one or another literary personality, but by then the articles had gone from the front pages to the back, where they were stuck in between the ads for nylon stockings and the House and Garden columns, often with titles like "Beart appears disoriented in Paris sighting" or "Reclusive American author refuses French literary honor," and they do not come with pictures.

There is one photograph of Inga Beart in Paris that everyone knows: She is sitting at a little table with a TABAC sign behind her and a small forest of empty glasses in front of her. The picture is dated August 1, 1954—presumably it was the last photograph taken of her before the events of August 10. In it, the ash on her cigarette is nearly as long as the cigarette itself and she is wrapped in some kind of silk. At first glance she looks young, but with a closer look one can see that her skin seems to have taken a deep breath and is holding it just a moment more before the inevitable release. Her pale eyes are looking at something just beyond the camera, so that no matter where you put yourself in relation to that photograph, she will never look at you.

I'd been trying to catch the waiter's eye for some time before I finally put on my hat, stepped inside to say "Thank you anyway" to the bartender, and continued on along the street. Up ahead was a grand-looking arch. I wondered for a moment if it was the Arc de Triomphe, though I knew that one came at the end of the Champs-Élysées, which could hardly be the street I was on—I'd ended up in the kind of neighborhood with sex shops and young men selling DVDs from blankets spread across the sidewalk. A woman in very high heels and a low décolletage stood in a doorway, and it took me a moment to realize that she was there on business. A few doorways up the street was another lady and another. I paused for a moment to watch as a man in an overcoat approached one of them. He and the lady stepped into the shadows to confer, then the man walked away. The woman laughed and called him back. Her eyebrows were painted on at an almost comic angle, as if, though she clearly had been selling her charms for some years now, she was still surprised. The man returned, and in the shadow of the doorway I saw money change hands—I couldn't see how much. The woman pointed to someplace up the street, and the man walked in that direction. The woman took out her compact and looked into it for a moment, then followed in the direction the man had gone.

The lady in the nearest doorway must have noticed I'd been watching because she said something to me in French as I passed. "I'm sorry?" I said, then wished I hadn't; the lady clearly assumed I was after the same thing as the man in the overcoat. "No, no," I said. "No, thank you." Her hand was on my sleeve. I was close enough to see the state of her teeth, the soft puckering of skin between her breasts, a red welt on her arm. She'd covered her arm with makeup, but the skin around her wrist was swollen and shiny, the makeup wouldn't stick. She said something else to me and I could hear laughter coming from the next doorway and the one I had just passed. My face was hot, and feeling like an albino under a full moon in those white pants, I hurried on.

But I couldn't quite shake the sight of the mark on the woman's arm, angry red under flakes of concealer. The tone of whatever it was she'd said to me had been light, an easy joke at the expense of a foreigner. Still, it wasn't hard to imagine the kind of things that might happen to a woman like her in those deep-set doorways. I reminded myself that it was none of my business. For all I knew she might have scalded herself making tea.

It was the way she'd painted her arm with makeup, the trouble she'd gone to—I'd seen that sort of thing before. I walked as quickly as I could, but the memory caught me anyhow: a deep bruise on the inside of a young person's thigh, the way she'd covered it with layers of her mother's foundation, taking such care. I'd tried to help her hide it, one of many mistakes.

I turned off that street, thinking I'd take a quieter route back to my hotel, even at the risk of getting lost. I tried to bring my mind back around to my project, telling myself that my brief encounter with the demimonde had been useful after all. It had reminded me of some research I'd been wanting to do, and I made a plan to go to the Bibliothèque nationale to have a look at the microfilm.

Noir novels were all the rage in France when Inga Beart arrived in Paris in the early 1950s. It was a trend that baffled literary critics, who saw the genre itself as a chalk line drawn around the corpse of French intellectual preeminence. Ghastly crimes were committed on the dark streets of Paris, then solved by cunning detectives with a weakness for unredeemable women; various iterations of the formula came in color-coded series and could be purchased for a franc or two on the platforms of railway stations.

It was this popular preoccupation with macabre plot twists that I hoped might have prompted an ambitious French editor to put more reporters on the Inga Beart story than, say, his counterparts at the Paris bureau of the *Herald Tribune*. Each of the major papers would have surely sent someone to the Hôtel-Dieu hospital on August 10, 1954, to try to get a look at her, but it was possible that *Le Monde* or *Le Figaro* put a second reporter on the job, sending him to Inga Beart's apartment to get some color, as they say. Perhaps a newspaper photographer came along. Knowing his audience's appreciation for the banality of a crime scene, he might have duplicated the shots the police photographer would have taken before him: a coffee cup standing half-full, a slip left hanging on the back of a chair, dark drops like a scattering of buttons across the floor.

And then, perhaps, the photographer would take out a second camera, loaded with color film. The film was expensive, so he'd frame the shot with special care, appreciating with an artist's eye the way a pair of red high-heeled shoes that had been left in a jumble on the mat matched the glossy red of the drops on the floor.

Of course, all this was quite unlikely, and I had a sense that in 1954 the use of color photography in newspapers was still some years off. But I woke up the next morning with the idea still in my head. The Bibliothèque nationale was clearly marked on my map, though it was some distance away, and it was after lunchtime when I finally arrived.

I found myself a little cubby with a microfilm machine that the librarian had to show me twice how to switch on. It was only then that I realized, of course, that the newspapers were all going to be in French. It was more out of embarrassment than anything else that I went ahead and looked through all the articles from that week until I found the ones with her name in them. To my disappointment, only one of them had a picture, the same publicity shot I've seen a thousand times before. The librarian was watching me, so I bent in close to read the story, which is to say I looked at all the words. I didn't understand them, but I already knew what they said.

On the tenth of August 1954, a woman was taken to the Hôtel-Dieu hospital in the center of Paris with severe knife wounds to her eyes. It turned out that this woman was an American author who, despite having lived in one of the more fashionably intellectual quarters of Paris for several years, seemed unable or unwilling to speak a word of French to the authorities to tell them how it had happened, except to insist in English that, really, everything was all right. It was quickly established that the wounds had been self-inflicted and fears of an eye-gouging maniac loose in Montmartre subsided, replaced by horrified gossip when it turned out that the woman was Inga Beart, acclaimed novelist and iconic beauty—although now that her eyes were out the papers tended to put those facts in the opposite order. Why had she done it? Some said it was plain craziness, and there may be some truth to that, for her behavior had become more and more erratic during her time in France, and she'd stopped writing altogether toward the end. The cynics said she'd done it to sell more books, and if so, it worked.

Inga Beart novels became popular again, and upon second reading everyone agreed that, after all, they were terribly dark—and wasn't there something that each of her characters was trying so desperately not to see?

I, of course, knew nothing about my mother's eyes. I would have been five when it happened, and even if I'd been old enough to read about it in the newspapers, I would have missed those headlines altogether, because it was in the late summer of 1954 that I came down with my case of scarlet fever. Inga Beart returned to the States in October 1954 and died soon after in a New York hospital. The cause was complications of an infection of the sinuses—apparently quite common in cases in which the eye socket is punctured through. I was only informed, rather tersely as I remember it, by Aunt Cat that my mother had died, and if any reporters came around I was to holler for her and to keep my mouth shut, instructions I found contradictory even then.

I don't remember wondering why the cause of that sinus infection was never discussed in front of me, or why, when my mother's last days were mentioned at all, it was behind a folded palm or in such low tones that I couldn't catch all the words. It wasn't until I was a freshman in college, trying to impress a girl at a party by telling her that I was Inga Beart's son, that I learned of the circumstances that led to my mother's death.

It was a mixer for the English department, and I think the girl started out believing me—after all Inga Beart and I have the same last name. Then she asked me why she had done it, and of course I didn't know what *it* meant. Then not only did the girl not believe that Inga Beart was my mother, she didn't even believe I had been invited to that party, because how could an English major not know that Inga Beart had dug out her own eyes with a kitchen knife?

I hadn't gone back to the ranch since I left for college, not even for Christmas, but the next morning I skipped my classes and drove a friend's old car down. The car made it all the way to the last turn off the highway—by then it had become the interstate—before it gave out completely, and I ran the rest of the way along the frontage road and up the driveway framed by the Russian olive trees that the dreamer who

95

built the dude ranch had planted all those years before. I remember seeing Aunt Cat down by the ditch, doing something with a roll of chicken wire. Perhaps it was my imagination, but I remember thinking that she didn't look all that surprised to see me there, like she had a pretty good idea of why I'd come. I don't think I'd even said one intelligible word before she was setting down the chicken wire, not minding that it caught and tore her sleeve, saying, "Don't you think it's your fault now, Ricky, don't you think like that," as if the thought had even crossed my mind. I remember I was swearing and crying like a kid and saying some terrible things. Aunt Cat came up and put her hands on my shoulders, like men do when they've got something to explain, and I remember thinking how gray her hair had gotten, how that grim grip to her jaw had relaxed a little in the year I'd been away.

The librarian poked her head in to check on me, and I turned the wheel of the microfilm machine, letting the news of the tenth, eleventh, and twelfth of *août 1954* go by, remembering that day down by the ditch with Aunt Cat and the chicken wire, me eighteen or nineteen years old with all the righteousness of the world behind me, demanding to know why Aunt Cat had never told me the details of my mother's death. And Aunt Cat saying well, she'd decided back then that it was for the best, and so on. Even at the time I remember thinking that she was probably right.

In fact, for the past forty years I've told myself I shouldn't be too hard on Aunt Cat for keeping my mother's injury a secret. I never thought too much about the details of that afternoon or why, as Aunt Cat held me by the shoulders, she took a deep breath, as if what she was going to say was long and saying it would take some doing. But then she hesitated for a moment. She looked at me, she let the breath out slowly.

"You just don't tell that sort of thing to a child," she'd said, and turned back to the chicken wire. And in all the years since, it's only now that it occurs to me to wonder what it was my Aunt Cat might have been about to say.

{MAGDALENA}

Swindon, May

MAGDALENA LEFT THE apricot tree and walked around to the front of the church, where the nun who had given her the jam was digging a hole in a flowerbed for the bird.

"Good-bye," Magdalena said to her.

"Good luck," said the nun.

She stopped at the drugstore on the way home, and kept her glasses on, reading all the words off the face and hands of the woman at the cash register. She learned that the woman had allowed her baby sister to drown in the bathtub, that she believed in God, kept her mother's garden, and would die of something called lymphoma. Magdalena had to stare hard to read the path the lymphoma would take through the woman's organs as it spread, which was written small across her jaw. It made the woman nervous, and she kept running her tongue along her teeth, like she was afraid food might have gotten caught there.

Magdalena let herself into Barry's house and took off her shoes. She stepped into the same prints on the carpet she and Neil had made earlier that afternoon, so Barry wouldn't know she was home if he happened to walk down the hall. She took the razors out of the bag from the drugstore quietly so the plastic wouldn't rustle, but before she opened the package she went to her room and got out the papers from the inquest, just to be sure. They were still sealed in the envelope the policewoman had given her. Magdalena opened it and looked through them until she found the coroner's report. *Cause of death: Acute cyanide-induced respiratory failure after ingesting the seeds of 30–40 wild Turkish apricots.* She'd seen those words exactly when she cut off Lina's hair. Magdalena folded the papers and put them back in the envelope. She went into the bathroom and shut the door without making a sound. Her father had done it just this way, not leaving a mess. Magdalena got into the bathtub. It was easy. She thought about the nun burying the bird. She did not think she was committing a sin; all she was doing was giving God His secrets back. She wished she had gone to Stonehenge to see the people praying on rocks. She opened the pack of razors and took one out. Something pulled at her mind, something she'd wanted to think about, but when she tried all she saw was Lina, marked from the beginning with the text of her autopsy report. On the white inside of Magdalena's wrist was the place where two blue veins ran together, and beside that she could see the faint tug of her pulse. She put the blade across all three and pushed. It hurt, but not too much. She laid her hand flat on the side of the tub and got a better grip on the razor. Was it better to do it across the veins or lengthwise along one of them? She didn't know. She might only have one chance, she'd have to guess. *Luck* it said at just that spot on her mother's wrist. Or was it *Happiness*? Barry laughed at her when she confused those English words. But on Magdalena's wrist the spot was blank. Up the vein, she decided, and realigned the razor. She took a breath. She remembered the woman in the church telling her—what? A body on a beach. A bird hitting glass. An American boy with her name under his eye. What did it mean, that he had the name of a person he would only see once printed on his skin? It must be a mistake, she thought. She wanted to think more about it but she didn't have the time. There was something else, it was important. She thought about putting the razor away and waiting—a day or a week, what could it matter? Give herself time to let the thought come. But there was no point, better to do it now. Imagine she was cutting lemons for her shift at the bar: a quick stroke that was easier the harder she pressed. The razor cut into her skin and a drop of blood came out. She felt a little dizzy and took a breath. She pressed harder. A body washed ashore covered in shells. The picture fixed itself in her mind. *Perfectly whole*, the woman at the church had said. That was important, but she couldn't remember why. She needed time to remember, but she couldn't take it. She readjusted her grip on the razor and pressed down harder.

The door to the bathroom flew open. It banged against the towel rack so hard that the knob on the end of the rack broke a little hole in the door. All of a sudden Barry was scooping Magdalena up and drop-ping her and scooping her again, banging her shins on the faucet and all the time shouting "OH NO OH NO OH NO," patting up Magdalena's arms looking for blood there and accidentally slicing his hand on the razor in the process, so in the end it was Magdalena who had to do the bandaging. And as it was all happening, Magdalena remembered Dov's brother's voice on the phone, saying that if only Lina's body had been left whole, she and Dov might have been together in the end.

For the first few weeks after Lina died, Magdalena had stayed out of the flat as much as she could, leaving with the camera in the mornings and not coming back until the light was gone. So she had no idea how long Dov had been waiting for her when she found him sitting on the stoop outside her building. In the light from the streetlamp Magdalena caught her breath. It was as if something of Lina, the curve of an eyebrow or the tilt of her head, had resisted being pulled out of the world so quickly and had settled, for an instant, on Dov. With the yellow shadows falling just so on his forehead and lips, they might have been siblings. But as Magdalena got closer and Dov looked up, the shadows rearranged themselves and the hints of Lina disappeared, leaving behind the face of a tanned, good-looking boy with raw red lids to his eyes. Lina had said that he was just her age, and he looked even younger. For all his advancement in the world of botanical engineering, Dov couldn't have been more than twenty or twenty-one. He had a paper bag between his feet.

"I'm really sorry," he said. "I tried to call."

Magdalena was surprised how dark his skin was. Except for a shadow who stayed in the hall while Lina packed her things and a silhouette holding Lina's hand inside the cab the day she watched them through the camera, Magdalena had only seen Dov in a picture Lina had on her phone—a pale face framed by dark hair. Lina had said it herself: His skin was like porcelain. On their first night together his heart beat so fast against her that she felt as if she'd trapped some deli-cate wild thing. Like a being from a fairy tale, Lina had said. Like the prince conjured from the body of a white arctic hare. But the skin of the person sitting in a heap on Magdalena's steps was so dark she couldn't make out a single word that was written there.

Magdalena unlocked the door and Dov followed her up the stairs. He didn't say anything else until they were in the flat and he was sitting at Magdalena's kitchen table, crying, hands at his sides, not bothering to wipe the tears away. Magdalena felt suddenly furious at this child, this slack-lipped boy who had been stupid enough to spend some of his family's fortune on a fine Swedish blender with blades capable of pulverizing even the hard pits of the fruit that had made him so rich, Lina couldn't help but fall in love with him. He was wearing jeans that fit like they'd been made especially for him. With his angel face just starting to grow into something firmer, he might have walked out of an advertisement for cologne or flavored vodka if it hadn't been for the soft dark curls at his temples and telltale strings at his sides, like little children wore back home when they dressed up as Jews on the carnival night before Lent began and went house to house, demanding coins and blintzes.

"I brought you her things," Dov said, pushing the paper bag toward her. Inside were a few crumpled dresses, some stockings, and a nightgown.

"I don't want them," Magdalena said.

"Bury them with her," he said.

"I can't," Magdalena said. The funeral home had already delivered Lina's ashes in a plastic bag; they were sitting in a shoebox on the kitchen counter. "I told your brother," she said. "I'm sorry. I haven't known."

She would have explained to Dov how, when the people from the coroner's office finally got Ruta on the phone, she hadn't been able to understand what they were asking and it was left to Magdalena to tell the funeral home to go ahead and cremate what was left of Lina after the autopsy. But she realized Dov's brother hadn't told him about the ashes, or Dov hadn't listened, because before Magdalena could say anything more he put the bag of clothes in her hands and said, "Please. They have her smell." He dug in his pocket and brought out a toothbrush in a plastic bag. "And this, put it with her body."

"Why?" Magdalena said. What did she want with Lina's toothbrush?

"The inside of the mouth, each time you brush your teeth millions of cells come off."

"What are you talking about?" Magdalena said.

"I need her back," Dov said. "I need every part of her back." He was crying again, and it made Magdalena want to scar his smooth face, rake the tan off his skin with her fingernails. Dov kept talking, about a day of judgment and the garden he would make for Lina when they both rose up from the ground at the end of time.

Magdalena did her best not to listen to him. What could have made Lina choose this boy, who now had a thin string of mucus hanging from the end of his nose, over all the others? What did it mean that he had been the one to have his name planted—like a curse—under her heart?

"I think you should go," Magdalena said, breaking into what Dov was saying. She walked to the door and opened it for him, but he didn't move.

Dov had been there all along. When, as skinny kids, she and Lina poured an entire bottle of Magdalena's mother's bubble bath into the tub and painted bikinis on themselves with the bubbles, he was there, his name curled like a snake under the foam that kept running down Lina's chest before they could scoop enough up to make a proper bosom. Dov's name was there when they took off their clothes and jumped into the river on the night of Magdalena's high school graduation, feeling the icy shock of the water give way to a rush of warmth as every bit of blood they had coursed through their bodies.

"Why are you buying just one ticket to Zurich?" she asked him, remembering what the policewoman had told her.

His family wanted him to take the job. He and Lina had argued, he'd bought the ticket, but he wouldn't have gone, he said. They couldn't bear a single day away from each other. What about the fights the neighbors said they had heard? Stupid things, Dov said. Things that didn't mean anything, now. And that night? Magdalena asked. Why had he gone out and left Lina alone like that? What kind of husband was he to leave her in a house without any food, except for fruits with poisoned seeds?

"I couldn't have known," Dov said. "How could I have known?"

Suddenly Dov was kneeling on the floor at her feet, his head in her lap like a child. "I love her," he said, and now Magdalena saw that this, at least, was true. Up close the dusky color of Dov's skin was not his skin at all; it was caused by hundreds—thousands—of tiny letters, as if his entire body had been caught in a fine black web. Magdalena leaned in, and she could see that the letters did not make sentences, like they did on other people. They did not tell stories or record important dates. All over Dov's body, on the back of his neck and on his cheeks and his hands, even darkening his lips and the skin under his fingernails, four letters were repeated again and again. *Lina Lina Lina Lina.*

When Barry asked Magdalena why she'd tried to do it, as they sat on the floor of the bathroom and she wiped the cut on his hand with alcohol then wrapped it up tight to help stop the bleeding, she looked to where Barry's blood and not her own was washing pink down the bathtub drain and she read what was written along the edges of the gash in Barry's palm. *Tell him,* it said. The dot in the *i* had been sliced through by the razor. And Magdalena did. She told Barry about Lina dying and the words she'd seen since before she could even read them, and Dov, who had asked her *how can I go on?* and how she had had to say, honestly, that she didn't know. She'd never seen such singleness of purpose across a person's skin. And how her own skin was blank, as if her existence was an oversight or an accident, and no record had been made. She told Barry about the apricot tree in the church parking lot and what it said on the coroner's report, how she knew now that the words she saw were true, and how she'd cost Lina and Dov their chance at eternity.

But she could tell that Barry thought she was making it all up, because from that day on he started asking her why she wouldn't read out loud what was written on his skin.

Magdalena had met Barry in London, on one of the days when she was out with Lina's camera. By that point she'd lost both her jobs. Roxie had gotten spooked about living in a place where someone had so recently died and moved out, leaving Magdalena to pay the rent. Dov had promised to help, but there was no answer at the number he'd given her, and when she called his office they said he was unavailable and would be for some time.

She was in Regent's Park, taking pictures. By then she'd used up three more rolls of film and was most of the way through a fourth. She didn't know how she'd pay to have them developed, but she didn't care. The important thing was the snap and click of the shutter, the stiff advance of the film. There were bills from the funeral home and the police inspector in charge of the inquest had been leaving her increasingly curt messages, insisting that she go to the station house to fill out the last forms. But it seemed more important just then to peel layers off the faces of strangers like the skin of an onion, too translucent to capture what was written there, so thin as to never be missed. If Tobias Kronen had been right and each photograph robbed a person of a tiny layer of themselves, then each photograph that Magdalena took might dim the words a little, eating away the dot of an *i*, changing an *e* to a *c*. Eventually, if only someone would stand still long enough for her to take a hundred pictures or a thousand or a million, Magdalena thought it was just possible that she could erase the words altogether. But people moved around too much, and the rolls of film were short, so Magdalena had to hope that other photographers would come along to strip the last layers away.

In the meantime, there was the problem of her English. It had improved so much in the months she'd been in London that she read without meaning to as she focused the camera.

West London Chess Club Champion, 1978
Chief comptroller Mackay & Singh (embezzler)
Born with a caul
When we come back the flowers have bloomed take off my clothes
    I think it is for the best
Homosexual
£43,880 a year
Broke Hamida Grigoryan's collarbone in two places
Asks for the children, they say there never were any

Automobile accident, 17 November 2019, 06:59
Simon's hands
The baby's feet

But it would all disappear, along with the diseases, addictions, loves, and debts, when she got the little envelope with the photographs back from the drugstore.

She thought she was taking pictures of all kinds of people, until she heard a voice behind her say, "Oh yeah, she's your best yet." Magdalena turned around and saw a man sitting on a bench with a camera of his own. "Go on, take it before she moves," the man said, motioning for her to turn back to the girl who was standing a few yards away, talking on the phone, making circles with her toe in the sand.

"You've got an eye for the girls, eh?" the man said.

"What do you mean?" Magdalena asked.

"Ah, not from here," he said, hearing her accent.

Magdalena started walking away.

"Don't go away," he said in Lithuanian. Magdalena turned around.

"What did you say?" she said in Lithuanian.

"A good guess," he said, back to English now. Magdalena didn't say anything, but she also didn't go away.

"I've been watching you," he said. "You like taking pictures of pretty girls, yeah?"

"I'm just taking pictures. Not just of girls." Even as she said this she realized he was right, she had been taking pictures only of girls, and only, really, of girls who looked a little like Lina.

"Hey, *labas*," the man said. "Maybe you'll let me see the pictures when you're done?"

"I don't think so," Magdalena said.

"I like taking pictures too."

Magdalena didn't say anything.

"That's a nice camera. Where'd you get it?"

"It was my friend's," she said.

He looked at her for a second. "Hey, are you alright?"

"Yeah," Magdalena said. But she'd started to cry. The camera hung around her neck, with the lens cap dangling on its string. The girl on the phone looked up and moved a little farther away.

"Hey," Barry said. "Now don't do that."

In the end, it was Barry who paid the rent that was due on her flat, and he said she could stay with him in Swindon if she promised to teach him Lithuanian. It seemed like the kind of situation Magdalena would have tried to keep Lina from getting into. But she couldn't stay in the flat in London anymore and she couldn't face the thought of going home to Vilnius where their apartment was empty because her mother was in America, and where everyone had pale skin filled with words she had no hope of not understanding.

At least on Barry's skin most of the words were unfamiliar. What she did understand, she didn't like, but those things had happened in such faraway places that it was easy to imagine they didn't belong to Barry at all. Even when he told her that he was also a foreigner, born in a city that was now called Harare, which, when Magdalena found it on a map, was not so far from the places mentioned on his face and arms, she let herself believe that he'd somehow gotten wrapped in other people's crimes. So she packed Lina's old suitcase, which was the better of the two, and took the bus from London to Swindon, with Lina's ashes still in their plastic bag inside the shoebox.

A month passed after the day in the bathroom when Magdalena told Barry about the words. Now it was June, and she was leaving Swindon the same way she'd come, on the bus back to London with the shoebox in her lap. The bus windows were open and Magdalena could hear the music from an ice cream van outside. She wished she'd made Barry give her enough money for the trip home to Vilnius before she read him anything. She wished that at least she'd had time to buy something to eat. As it was, there had been a scene and Barry had thrown every bit of Magdalena's clothing out onto the street. Veronika had called the police, the new girl had been screaming, and Magdalena had run all the way to the bus station in the center of town with Lina's old suitcase wobbling like a sick dog behind her.

The bus rolled through the outskirts of Swindon. Magdalena knew she should call her mother to tell her she was coming, but she had hardly any credit left on her phone. She looked through her purse again, just in case there was a top-up card in there that hadn't been used. If she called her mother, then her mother could call Ruta Valentukienė, to let her know that Magdalena was finally bringing Lina home. But Ruta had been in and out of hospitals and rest homes, and now she could be anywhere. Magdalena might have called one of their old school friends, but so much time had gone by, she wasn't even sure who knew about Lina and who didn't. It was one thing to tell people in the rush of disbelief right after it happened, the way she'd called her mother during the long night of making tea for the policeman, hardly hearing her mother's voice on the other end of the line as they both said again and again, *Lina is dead*, using the words like shovels to hollow out a place for the empty space to live. The sound of the words dug a little grave for Lina in each of their minds that first night, when the world itself had not yet made room for the lack of her.

The bus was going faster now. The blur outside her window changed from brown and gray to green. Magdalena put her glasses on and watched the countryside.

She hadn't planned on calling Neil, but as the bus got closer to London, Magdalena realized she didn't have much of a choice. There would be no taking Lina home at all if she couldn't come up with the money for the ticket. She'd thought of asking one of the girls she'd worked with in London, but she knew that those kinds of friendships didn't go much past sharing a cab or a cigarette. This is what men are for, Lina would have said, with a dozen possible sources of the price of a ticket to Vilnius programmed into her phone. If there had been time, Magdalena might have asked her old boss at the bar in Swindon, or even Ivan, but now it was too late. She had thirty-eight pence left on her phone—enough for one call to someone who, when her credit ran out, would be sure to call her back. Someone who would be too polite to ask why she was leaving Swindon with her suitcase half-full. She dialed Neil's number, but he didn't pick up.

*

When she got to London, Magdalena stood in Victoria Station, reading the outbound timetable and thinking about the meat pies fogging the glass of the pastry stand next to the ticket counter. She counted the money she had left from the catering work she'd done after she lost her job at the bar, calculating how many meat pies it would buy, because it was not enough to get her even one quarter of the way to Vilnius.

The tops of the meat pies were beaded with grease, their crusts gone limp under the hot lights of the pastry counter. Magdalena settled on beef and onion. She was taking out her wallet when her phone rang. It was Neil. He'd gotten her message about stopping in London on her way home to Vilnius, he said, but he wasn't there anymore. There was something artificial in his voice.

"Well, it's okay," Magdalena said. "It's no problem really, you are busy." She would sleep in the station, buy another top-up card, call her mother and ask her to wire the money.

"No, it's not that, it's just that I'm in Paris right now," Neil said, sounding more normal.

"Oh, you are in Paris?" she said.

"Yep, till August," Neil said. Something about a professor.

She wondered if it was possible that her name had been written under his eye as a kind of receipt. If he'd gotten a haircut since she'd seen him last she might see that her name came at the end of a sentence: *lends bus fare to Vilnius to Magdalena Bikauskaitė*. She'd seen plenty of people covered with little things like that. She was still holding the timetable. London to Paris: the cheapest bus left late that night. She had just enough for the ticket, counting her change.

"I'm really sorry," Neil was saying. "It would have been fun to get a coffee and all."

Magdalena shook her head at the girl behind the pastry counter, who had come up to ask what she wanted.

"Actually this is perfect," she said. "I am changing my bus in Paris."

She looked at the timetable and told Neil the time the bus would arrive. Then she bought her ticket. The man behind the window said something under his breath as she dug in her purse for the last of her coins. She tried not to look at him as he gave her the ticket, but she couldn't help seeing that debts were wrapped tight around his wrists.

"To Paris Gare du Nord, departing tonight, eleven o'clock," he said.

Magdalena looked around the station until she found a bench that was fairly clean. She had hours to wait, and she was too hungry to spend them awake. She put the ticket and her passport and the papers from the inquest inside her blouse. She rested her head on the shoebox, closed her eyes, and listened to the sounds of her stomach until she fell asleep.

{NEIL}

Paris, June

THE DAY FINAL exams finished in London, Neil took the Eurostar
to Paris with Professor Piot and the other research assistants.
Professor Piot made them squeeze in around a little table in the
family section and sent someone to the café car for champagne, and
pretty soon they knew all about the Chunnel as an illustration of free-
market versus socialized political economy. ("Imagine the embarrassment of the queen, who is on board, when this train doubles its speed
as it arrives in France on its maiden voyage, suggesting that Britain's
private investors cannot be relied upon to fix the tracks . . .") They heard
grim stories of the World War One battlefields they passed. ("The mud
was so permeated with human fragments that during the great rains of
1915 whole arms and legs would sometimes slide out of the walls of
the trenches . . .") Professor Piot promised dinner at Maxim's to anyone
who could name the genius whose idea was behind the fast-moving
panzer tank divisions that crossed the Belgian border into France in
May 1940. ("Himmler?" somebody guessed. "Göring?" "Aha!" Professor
Piot said. "While the French generals built their Maginot line, Hitler
read a pamphlet by a certain young colonel named *Charles de Gaulle*
and used these ideas to plan the Blitzkrieg!")

As they got nearer to Paris, Professor Piot opened a second bottle
and told them about the project they'd be working on, which had been
pretty vague up until that point because he was still ironing out the
details with the Musée du Patrimoine. They would be preparing an
exhibition on the old church of Saint-Jacques-de-la-Boucherie. Built by
butchers and torn down by revolutionaries, only its sixteenth-century
bell tower was still intact, "a fine example of the flamboyant Gothic
style," Professor Piot said. The tower was being restored, and the work
was costing the City of Paris a lot of money. Professor Piot had been
hired to help prove that it was worth it. "We must make a good story for
the schoolchildren," he said.

"Perhaps we begin with the Paris of ancient times—" Professor Piot was a hand talker and there were five of them in four seats, which meant he hit either Neil or Loren, the other American, each time he made a point. "It is the dawn of the Christian faith in France, the city takes up only the space of Île de la Cité. Today this is where the tourists go for ice cream. But then we are in Roman times. There are barbarian invasions, the city is behind stone walls. And already economic life is outgrowing them. The dirty professions, the *infected trades*, they call them—the tanners, the furriers, the butchers—are kept outside. And so on the banks opposite the city a great market grows up—you have heard of Les Halles? Now it is an empty shopping mall, a catastrophe of urban planning, but for centuries it is the larder, the very pungent *ventre*, the gut, we can say, of the city—the history of Paris begins some seventeen centuries before refrigeration. And the butchers of this quarter, these men in bloodstained aprons, must rise very early each day, must work through the night even, but at dusk the gates to the city are locked. They cannot attend Mass, you see? Performing each day the most biblical, perhaps, of professions—this butchering of meat—they cannot even pray. And so these men set out to build their own church outside the city walls—" Professor Piot poured a little more into each of their glasses. "From its first days, this is a church of *Paris*. In this church the basins of holy water must be refreshed each hour because so many hands are dipping in covered with the blood of the slaughterhouse, the lye from the tanning shops, the soot and filth of the life of the city—" The train shot through a tunnel, the pressure made everyone's ears pop.

It was in medieval times that the butchers named their church for Saint Jacques, patron saint of laborers and pilgrims, who brought the Christian faith to Spain, was beheaded by Herod, and, so the story went, assisted posthumously in the Crusades. The journey to his burial place in Spain had been one of the most important pilgrimages of the Middle Ages, Professor Piot said. The old pilgrim maps looked like nets spanning the length of the known world, with the butchers' church as the pilgrims' Paris starting point. "In this churchyard penitents from all over Europe are swapping boots, coughing on one another and spreading disease. Monks from Lille are speaking in Latin to friars from Cork. Rumors are spread of miracles, philosophies are interchanged, as well as recipes of poultices for blisters . . ." Neil tried to find a more comfortable way to be sitting on the armrest. Beth was taking notes and didn't notice that Jean-Claude was drinking out of her glass.

The church had been destroyed in the spasms of anticlericalism that followed the French Revolution: "Torn stone from stone in the name of the new Republic and used—who knows? To pave the streets? To replace the cobblestones that had themselves been hurled from barricades?" Professor Piot loved that kind of thing, and his hands were flying all over the place. Neil pressed his head flat against the back of the seat, but still he got hit in the nose. Today, all that was left of the church was its bell tower, from which Pascal had supposedly studied the impossibility of a vacuum and quantified the weight of air, and where, even to this day, meteorological equipment monitored pollution levels at the corner of rue Saint-Martin and rue de Rivoli.

Professor Piot sent Jean-Claude to get another bottle and then with a flourish—Neil and Loren ducked—he gave them their research assignments. Jean-Claude, whose French was, obviously, the best, would be the liaison to the reconstruction crew, making sure that details of archaeological and architectural relevance were preserved. ("The very dirt on the walls is of interest to us," Professor Piot said. "If the walls are clean then we must ask why there is no dirt, and that too is of interest.") Professor Piot himself would concentrate on the medieval era, Loren would cover the Revolution, and Beth, who was getting a Ph.D. in architectural history, would be responsible for the renovations that had been made since Baron Haussmann decided to spare the church's remaining belfry—now called the Tour Saint-Jacques—as he went about razing and reshaping Paris into a modern city. Neil's job would be to track down anything that linked the church to the pilgrimage to Spain. "Okay, so *bonne chasse*," Professor Piot said, raising his glass. "And remember—a church of the butchers. Find for me a history a little bit *au jus*, okay?"

By the time they got to Paris, Neil and the others were so dizzy from all that champagne that they barely made it off the train, but Professor Piot did a little soft shoe to the "Marseillaise" as soon as he touched the marble floors of the station. "We meet tomorrow at the Archives nationales, nine o'clock," he said.

*

In London it had been sticky early summer, but in Paris, somehow, it was spring. On his first day off from work at the archives, Neil sat in a café and watched the reflections of glass windows slide across the old stones of a church. Cigarette ash blew onto him from the next table and he had to stop himself from sticking out his tongue to catch the flakes and let them melt like snow. He watched the little bits of ash floating in the foam of his beer and he thought that it was wonderful. Music was playing. Neil read a book by a French historian in French, looking up every word he didn't know, and a pigeon hopped around his foot with a bit of string looped around one of its toes, as if it had something important to remember.

That summer Neil almost never got phone calls. He didn't know anyone in Paris, except for Loren, Jean-Claude, and Beth, who were all in grad school and barely even spoke to him, and when his mom called with the weekly update on what mail he'd gotten and who from his high school was getting married, she did it on Skype. Not that many people had called Neil in London either, except Veejay sometimes to tell him to hurry home, zebras were having sex on the BBC. So when his phone rang during one of Professor Piot's seminars, he didn't even realize it was his.

It was Neil's third week in Paris. He was supposed to be auditing the seminar as a way to ameliorate his French in between trips to the archives, but so far it had only messed up his English. His thoughts had taken on an incredibly stilted tone—*ameliorate*, for instance—and Professor Piot's lecture that day wasn't much more than a collection of separate words. Taken all together, they had something to do with the Vichy regime's co-opting of the Joan of Arc mythology, which was one of Professor Piot's favorite topics, although it was possible that Neil was mishearing and *Jeanne d'Arc* was really *gendarmes* and they were talking about Pétain's special police. Possibly both.

So as Professor Piot paused while Neil's phone rang and rang, Neil kept scribbling in his notes—a lot of unconnected phrases that trailed off into nothing when they got to the verb—while the rest of the class wondered what moron had "Frère Jacques" for his ringtone. When he finally realized that it was his phone that was ringing and started fumbling around with it to try to turn it off—in an excess of optimism he'd switched the settings to French—he silently cursed Veejay, whose idea of a going-away present had been to secretly download some boys' choir trilling "*sonnez les matines*" to Neil's phone.

At the break, while the class smoked and drank their little coffees out of plastic cups, Neil tried to check his voicemail, only he couldn't remember the new code. He tried to look cool, like he was just texting somebody a really long message, and finally he got the number right. "*One ... new ... message ...*" a voice sang out. Neil had accidentally put the phone on speaker. He pushed a bunch of buttons and missed hearing the person say her name, but right away he figured out that it was the girl he'd met in Swindon. "*So, I am coming to London for taking the bus to Vilnius and I am wanting to ask you do you want to meet for a coffee, because I am going to be there for some hours? So, okay, that's all. Maybe you can call me when you have some moment. Okay, good-bye.*"

Neil only rarely had the opportunity to return girls' phone calls, and when he did, he liked to spend some time rehearsing a casual tone and working up a joke or two. But he had a sudden desire to speak his own language in front of all the Sorbonne kids milling around outside the classroom, flopping their hair in their eyes and discussing existentialism in Fascist literature without saying the second halves of their words, that French university dialect designed to exclude American research assistants.

Neil pushed the buttons on his phone until he figured out how to call the number back.

"Hello?" she said.

"Hey, it's Neil," Neil said.

"Oh, yes."

"I got your message and, gosh, I mean I'd love to meet up, but actually I'm not in London right now." He liked the sound of his own voice, casually speaking a language the Sorbonne kids had to learn from books.

"Well, it's okay," she said. "It's no problem, really, you are busy."

"No, it's not that, it's just that I'm in Paris for the summer."

"Oh you are in Paris?" she said.

"Yep, till August," Neil said. "I'm doing some work for my professor." There was a pause. "Shoot, I mean I'm really sorry. It would have been fun to get a coffee and all."

"Actually this is perfect," she said. "I am changing my bus in Paris."

"Wow, really?" Neil said.

"Yes, for this I have gotten the most cheap ticket." There was another pause. "I will come tomorrow in the morning at six o'clock into the station Gare du Nord. This is Paris?"

"Yeah," Neil said. The class was filing back into the classroom and Professor Piot was already writing a list of dates on the board. "Wow, that's great."

"Yes, so we can meet there tomorrow," she said.

"Cool," Neil said. Six o'clock seemed awfully early. "We can have some croissants."

It was frankly a surprise to hear from her again. Neil had called her up the day after he got back from Swindon to tell her about the camera in the medicine cabinet, and instead of being grateful to him for telling her and pissed at Barry for being such a creep, she had sounded almost amused, leaving Neil wondering, as usual, what he'd done wrong.

He'd worked up the nerve to call her after talking it over with Veejay, who wasn't helpful at all, suggesting that Neil try to blackmail Barry into letting him see the videos and maybe getting a cut of the profits if he were, like, selling them on the Internet or something. "Don't be an asshole," Neil told Veejay, and Veejay did finally call his cousin who was a solicitor in Sheffield, and found out that yes, it was totally illegal to film people in the shower without them knowing it, and even though Barry could try to make the case that it was all in his own house, that argument almost never stood up.

So Neil had called Magdute to tell her that he was really sorry he hadn't said anything right away, but that he had found a hidden camera behind a double mirror in the downstairs bathroom. He'd even gotten Veejay's cousin to say he'd do a three-way call and talk to her about taking Barry to court, but she said she didn't want to. Neil had planned a whole speech about how he felt like such a jerk for having waited a full twenty-four hours to tell her about it, but in the end he didn't have to use it, because Magdute only said "Mmm" when he started back at the beginning and told her about the padlock on the medicine cabinet and the Altoids box with the hole in its side and that weird note. "So this camera is looking at the bath?" she asked, and when Neil said yes, Magdute said, "Ahh, okay," and that was it. When he asked if she was still there she said, "Oh, yes," and something in her voice made him think she was trying not to laugh. He wondered if maybe he was getting worked up over nothing, or if it was all a big joke on him. But as soon as he hung up the phone he told himself that he'd done the right thing. You couldn't know that there was a secret camera in somebody's bathroom and not say anything. And it really couldn't have been some kind of twisted practical joke. The hole drilled through the Altoids box had had rust around it and the box was stuck to the shelf as if it had been there for a long time. Finally he decided that if it was a joke, it would have fooled someone way less gullible, and if it wasn't, well Magdute was a grown-up. Now she knew, and she could do what she wanted.

So it wasn't that Neil was unhappy that Magdute was coming to Paris, it just seemed like it might be sort of awkward. And it wasn't very convenient. There was no good way to take the metro from Gare du Nord to the archives, and he'd have to carry all his books and papers with him if he was going to go straight there after she left. And it wasn't like he and Magdute were friends. Neil thought about calling her back and telling her he couldn't make it. But on the other hand, it wasn't like Neil had girls calling him up every day, asking if he wanted to have a coffee.

Her call reminded him that he'd never sent his father the Christmas presents from her mother. The shopping bag Magdute had given him at the bus stop in Swindon only had a packet of Euro-style coffee in it, along with some woolen socks and a couple of sort of unflattering photos of a woman in front of a Christmas tree. Pretty crappy presents, and they showed that Neil's father and Magdute's mother didn't know each other very well because Neil's father didn't even drink coffee.

The problem was that whenever Neil thought about sending the presents—and he really had thought about it, several times—he ended up thinking about Barry's house and the girl in the party dress he'd seen behind the door. Her particular expression made things complicated. Obviously she hadn't wanted to be seen, and the noise Neil made opening the bathroom door had startled her. But the look on her face, the way her eyes had gone wide and she pressed two fingers to her lips—Neil still wasn't sure if she'd been warning him to keep quiet or asking him for some kind of help. Each time Neil started to look for a box to mail the presents home in, he would get to thinking about the last time he'd been looked at like that, and he'd end up deciding all over again that he couldn't let his father know he'd ever been to Swindon. It was better for his dad to think that Neil had flaked and never made the trip than to have to tell him about the house with the pictures of naked girls and the camera in the medicine cabinet.

Old guys doing weird, probably illegal things involving young women was a subject Neil was never in a million years going to voluntarily bring up in a conversation with his father, who had practically been fired from his job as an English teacher for some stuff that had happened with a student. It had been a pretty big deal in their really small town, on the front page of the local paper for weeks during Neil's eighth-grade year. The girl was also in eighth grade, which made the whole thing worse, and after one single, horrible confrontation, when Neil had said ugly things to his father and his father had cried, neither of them had ever mentioned the thing again.

The girl's name was Becca Gallegos and she and Neil had known each other since they were kids. When Neil's parents got divorced, he and his mom moved into the trailer park where Becca's family lived and she and Neil would ride bikes together and dig for treasure in Neil's backyard. Becca started out a grade ahead of Neil, so they weren't in class together until middle school, when she got held back. It wasn't that she was slow or anything, she just had a lousy home life and missed a lot of class. Which, Neil's father said, was why she needed extra encouragement.

By the time Becca got to eighth grade she was a mess. She wore a bunch of eye shadow and went around looking spooked and scribbling things in a little notebook. It was that notebook that was Neil's dad's undoing, because he offered to read some of her writing and began having her stay after class to discuss it. At some point Becca started telling people that Neil's dad had done some inappropriate stuff and her father threatened to sue the school district.

Things got pretty ugly for a while. Neil's dad didn't do himself any favors by comparing the school board to the Inquisition and ranting about how the language arts department and the entire education system didn't know the first thing about nurturing literary talent. He said he'd never touched her and she said he had. There was a hearing in front of members of the school board, but apparently there wasn't much evidence of anything because Becca never pressed charges and they let Neil's dad resign and keep his pension.

Neil would have dealt with the whole thing a lot better if he hadn't known for a fact that his father was lying. As it was, when kids on the bus would say, "Hey, Beart, how's your dirty old man?" and laugh like that was hilarious, he'd feel all the blood go to his face, but there was nothing really for him to say. He'd hunch down farther in his seat and draw designs in the mist his breath left on the school bus window.

Neil had taken Professor Piot's "Methods of Historical Analysis" class while he was in London, and they'd talked about the theory of *path dependence*, in which events happened in a chain reaction, like a domino effect. One event caused a second, which caused a third, which made it all but impossible that a fourth could be avoided, which led, by necessity, to a fifth, and so on, history hurtling toward a foregone conclusion. It was a way of looking at things that Professor Piot, and, one gathered, all serious historians, looked down on, because a path-dependent explanation of, say, why the Fourth Crusade ended up sacking Constantinople rather than reclaiming the Holy Land didn't take into account the thousand unpredictable nuances of how, why, and when, much less the decision-making role of individuals involved. The schism between the Orthodox and Roman Catholic churches may have set the stage for a confrontation between East and West, but who was to say that the Crusaders would have plundered their fellow Christians if their leader hadn't been charmed at a dinner party by a pretender to the Byzantine throne? "Doubt all claims of the inevitable," Professor Piot liked to say.

Neil, of course, agreed. But path dependence was the only way to explain how things had happened with Becca Gallegos. If Neil's mother hadn't insisted on having NPR on in the car in the mornings as she drove him to school, then he never would have heard about an effort to require House of Commons–style elections for Britain's House of Lords. If he'd never heard the story, he wouldn't have known the answer to the question "The British parliament includes which two bodies of legislators?" which allowed Neil's team to win the district-wide Knowledge Bowl competition and go on to the state finals. If they hadn't qualified for state, Neil wouldn't have had to get parental permission to go on an overnight trip to Colorado Springs. And if he hadn't had to get that permission form signed, he wouldn't have gone to his father's classroom after school one afternoon. He wouldn't have found the door shut, and when he opened it a crack to see if his father was in there, he wouldn't have seen his dad and Becca Gallegos, Becca sitting at one of the classroom desks and his father with his back to the door, bending over her like he was correcting her paper. Neil had been about to ask if he could interrupt for just a second to get his form signed when he heard his father say something like "There's nothing to be afraid of," and he smoothed his hand over Becca's hair, then squatted down next to her and rolled down the cuff of her shorts to cover an inch more of her thigh, as if he were personally enforcing the school dress code. Just as he did, the door handle that Neil was holding onto made a noise. Becca looked up, and for what could only have been a fraction of a second but felt much longer she stared straight at Neil in the doorway. Until the girl behind the door in Swindon, Neil had only seen a look like that one other time, when he was a kid and he found a deer with its leg caught in a fence. Eyes frantic, calculating the chance of escape but coming up short, flicking away. Neil closed the classroom door as quietly as possible, and he almost missed going to the Knowledge Bowl finals because he had to wait until his mom got back from a conference she was attending to get his permission form signed. Because he did not want his father to ever, ever know what he'd seen.

None of it was necessarily all that bad in its own right, but it was a whole lot more than what Neil's father said had happened. There had been no physical contact between them, absolutely none, Neil's father said. And as for the things Becca said, about how he'd told her she was a beautiful young girl with talents he was going to help her realize, it was all a big misunderstanding. He'd meant to be encouraging, to give her a bit of self-esteem, and she'd taken it the wrong way.

Neil never told his father that he didn't believe him. He didn't want to admit to knowing anything more than what people were saying in the halls at school, but the look on Becca's face had made it obvious that things had been happening that shouldn't be, and his dad had had no good reason to be messing with her shorts.

Things ended even worse for Becca than for his father, with the very same people who wrote letters to the editor calling Neil's dad a letch and a predator saying that she was an opportunist and her father was using the whole thing as an excuse to get money out of the school district. It might have been true, because pretty soon after the school board hearing, social services got involved and put Becca and her sisters in foster care. "Couldn't have happened too soon," Neil's mother said. Neil's mom wasn't inclined to take his father's side on anything, but she worked as a domestic violence counselor, and though she was pretty strict about patient confidentiality, it didn't take a genius to figure out that the Gallegos kids had it rough.

Only Neil knew that Becca wasn't lying, at least not entirely, and he kept waiting for Becca to tell the school board that Neil had seen her and his father together in the classroom that afternoon. Neil spent whole days not hearing a word of what was said in class, waiting for an announcement to summon him to the principal's office. But even though Becca could have used a witness on her side, she never told. That made the whole thing even worse, thinking of Becca *protecting* him, as if they were kids again and she was answering Neil's mom's questions about where all the boxes of cherry Jell-O had gone so Neil wouldn't have to open his bright red mouth. Neil stood outside the principal's office one afternoon after it had become a big scandal, trying to convince himself to go in and tell what he'd seen. But in the end he couldn't do it—not out of loyalty to his father so much as out of eighth-grade embarrassment at the thought of having to tell Ms. Schisler that he'd seen his father's hand on Becca's leg.

It was all really stressful, Neil's stomach was in knots for weeks, and when she noticed he wasn't eating, Neil's mom tried to get him to go see one of her therapist friends. She even offered to let him change schools mid-year, which would have meant driving him to Pueblo each day, because she figured that being Mr. Beart's son was making things tough. But Neil said no. He wasn't about to talk to some hippie therapist, and changing schools wouldn't make his dad any less of a liar or Neil any less of a coward. Plus, Becca Gallegos had transferred to Pueblo after someone wrote a big S-L-U-T all over her locker. The last thing Neil wanted was to have to avoid making eye contact with a reminder of his lack of personal heroism each time he passed her in the hall.

Looking back, it shouldn't have been such a surprise to hear his father deny something that had so clearly happened. His dad did that kind of thing. He selected from a range of plausible realities the version of events he preferred to believe in. He did it with Neil's mother when he said she left him because she fell in love with Carl, her Jazzercise instructor, as if he'd forgotten that they'd been fighting like crazy since before the town even had a gym. He did it when he had a fight with the Bureau of Land Management people over whose land the trees at the end of Pop's back pasture were on, and he did it in a big way when it came to certain facts about Neil's grandmother. Neil's dad made such a habit of choosing what to believe, of course he'd found just the right story for himself when it came to Becca Gallegos.

So Neil knew exactly what Professor Piot was talking about when he warned Neil and the other research assistants against getting personally attached to a particular version of history. Too much emotional involvement could lead even a conscientious historian to bias, or worse. It was something they ran into a lot with the documents about Saint-Jacques-de-la-Boucherie. The official histories were often written by people overly invested in the church, and they included all kinds of inaccuracies: The church was said to have been originally founded as the first in the name of Saint Anne long before her cult even appeared in France, for example. It was perfectly understandable that a priest or a monk who had devoted his whole life to serving in that particular church might embellish its importance, but it did not make good history. "Fall too much in love with your subject, and you'll find only the answers you already know," Professor Piot said.

It sounded better in French, but it fit Neil's father perfectly. The last time he and his father had talked, back in January, Neil had tried to point this out, and the conversation had not gone well. They hadn't been talking about Becca Gallegos or anything like that—at least, not directly. The subject had been Neil's grandmother, and though that particular topic always made Neil uncomfortable, it might have been anything.

It had been Neil's birthday, and he was honestly surprised to get a call from his father. Neil's mom had sent him a package of brownies and an e-card to see first thing when he woke up, but his dad wasn't the type to remember birthdays, and he usually sent Neil a check a week or two late. It wasn't that his father didn't care, he just wasn't very good with dates.

But as it turned out, his father *hadn't* remembered Neil's birthday. His dad said hello and started right in on small talk in a way that made Neil sure there was something else he was waiting to bring up. He asked Neil about the weather there in London—which was *cold*, it was January, it had just stopped raining and Neil was trying to avoid the half-frozen puddles as he walked to class. It was cold back home too, his father said. The pipes in the old well-house had frozen, the forecast called for more snow. His father asked about school; Neil said it was fine. His father wondered whether Neil had had a chance to pick up the Christmas presents from his friend's daughter in Swindon; Neil said not yet, but definitely next weekend.

Neil kept waiting for his dad to ask him if he had any plans for his birthday, which in fact he did—Veejay had bought a bottle of something green that was supposed to be absinthe and the girls across the hall were coming over to watch the match against Chelsea. But instead his father said, "So. There's a new book out about Grandma," and Neil realized that this was the real reason for his father's call. *Grandma* was not Nan, but Neil's biological grandmother, Inga. As in Inga Beart, *that*

Inga Beart, whose books were an unavoidable obstacle to passing tenth grade English. Though his father had never met her, he insisted on calling her *Grandma* when he talked to Neil, as if she had been somebody he and Neil actually knew.

"Oh yeah?" Neil said. The book had gotten a good review in the *Guardian*, but Neil decided not to mention it.

"By a fellow named Bristol," his father said. "A real hack job. You wouldn't believe some of the things they write these days."

"Uh-huh," Neil said. He knew what part of the book his father didn't like. It said what all the others said: Inga Beart had a baby, left it, and never gave Neil's dad a second thought.

Neil's father cleared his throat. "And, well, I was thinking. If I could finally find some proof—"

Since they were talking on the phone, Neil was free to roll his eyes. Having a famous grandmother was embarrassing, and Neil had started lying on the first day of each new class when the professor called his name and then said, "Don't suppose you're related to . . .?" But he hadn't meant to start an argument when he pointed out that his father sounded a little obsessive, that the guy who'd written the book was actually a well-regarded professor at Oxford, and that maybe now was the time for his father to deal with his abandonment issues in ways that didn't involve trying to poke holes in the research of real scholars, who ought to have a pretty good idea of what had and had not happened in the life of a woman his father had never even met.

In retrospect, it was kind of a shitty thing to say. Neil had never challenged his father on his Inga Beart theories before. But it was his birthday, and his father was too caught up in rewriting the details of fifty years ago to remember that today Neil was twenty years old.

So maybe that was why, when his father started talking about how as a baby he'd somehow seen and remembered a certain pair of shoes Inga Beart wore—the same story Neil had heard a thousand times before—Neil pointed out how it obviously couldn't be true. Neil's dad was silent for a little while and then said, "Well. I guess I shouldn't have brought it up," sounding like he'd had his feelings hurt.

"Be reasonable, Dad," Neil said. He felt bad, but his father was trying to twist the facts of his mother's life in a way that would make him feel better, and that was exactly the kind of thing Professor Piot warned against.

"I am being reasonable. She came to see us out at the ranch. I was under the table, all I could see was her feet. How could I have seen her feet if she wasn't there?"

"Maybe you didn't really see them," Neil said. "Memories are wrong all the time. People believe what they want to believe. I mean, it can happen." He was pretty sure neither of them wanted to get into the issue of truths and untruths and which ones his father chose to tell.

"I was there, wasn't I? For Christ's sake. I *remember*." Neil could tell by his voice that his father was getting worked up, and he wished he'd just let him leave a message. He had some reading he needed to get done before class.

But today was his birthday. He was twenty years old, a grown-up, and, as Professor Piot said, sometimes one has to stick up for the facts.

"The dates don't work, Dad," Neil said. "You were, like, two when she left the States, right? Even if you had seen her, you couldn't have remembered it." He'd never said anything quite like that to his father before, and he was a little impressed with himself.

"That's not true—at two or three years old, kids remember. There are studies—"

"But you're the only one who thinks it could have happened," Neil said. "Everyone else says she never came back."

"Well, son, sometimes everyone gets it wrong," his father said, and the way he said it made Neil pretty sure that they weren't just talking about Inga Beart and whether she'd made a secret and totally unrecorded visit to Nan and Pop's ranch that Nan and Pop and everyone else had managed to forget.

There was another long silence on the phone. Neil stepped ankle-deep into a puddle hidden under dead leaves and almost forgot to look right instead of left as he crossed Oxford Street, accidentally letting himself remember how his father had said *believe me* that day back in eighth grade when Neil had come right out and asked him about Becca Gallegos. He had called Neil *son* then too, as in *Son, you've just got to believe me*.

"Okay, well, whatever, Dad," Neil said, which came out sounding less nice than he'd intended. His phone beeped to say he was getting another call. He said, "Oops, just a second," and when he tried to put his father on hold he accidentally hung up on him. It turned out it wasn't another call, just a text telling him his credit was low. Neil would have called his father back, except that he didn't have enough for an international number. He could have stopped on the way to class to buy more minutes, but he didn't feel like it; one shoe was soaked through and now his foot was freezing. Neil kept expecting his father to call back and say he was sorry he hadn't said happy birthday, but he never did, and a week or so later Neil got a birthday card and a check in the mail.

But that was back in January. Now it was June, and after Magdute's call, Neil spent the rest of Professor Piot's lecture feeling seriously bad about not having sent his dad her mother's Christmas package. So much time had passed, his father had probably forgotten all about their last conversation. When he got the package he might not even think to ask about Neil's trip to Swindon, and if he did, Neil could always lie and say that Magdute was living with friends. He didn't know why he hadn't thought of it before. The shopping bag Magdute had given him was in his suitcase, along with the jacket and dress pants he'd brought to Paris but hadn't had any reason to unpack. When he got home from class he put the presents in his backpack, planning to mail them on his way home from the archives that afternoon. He figured that if he left a little early, he could get to the post office at Hôtel de Ville before it closed, and next to it was a kiosk with flowers. If he could find some that hadn't quite bloomed and if he remembered to put them in a vase, they would still be fresh enough to give to Magdute the next morning at the station.

But that afternoon Neil didn't end up leaving the archives until quarter to six, which meant that the post office and the flower kiosk would be closed. He'd requested some documents from the abbey of Saint-Jean-d'Angély, where medieval pilgrims on their way to Spain had stopped to see the head of John the Baptist. A choir of a hundred monks was said to have surrounded the relic, singing to it day and night. Neil thought it said something useful about the medieval worldview that so many sleepless voices had been raised perpetually in praise of a decapitated head, and he was trying to figure out if it had been the actual head with flesh still attached or just the skull—the relic itself went missing during the wars of religion in 1500s—when he found a thin bundle of vellum that contained what seemed to be an account written in the thirteenth century by a monk from Rouen who was making the Saint Jacques pilgrimage to Spain.

Neil was interested to see if the monk mentioned stopping at the church of Saint-Jacques-de-la-Boucherie on his way through Paris. At the end of the document was what Professor Piot called a *colophon*, a description of the manuscript that had been added centuries later by an abbey historian, and Neil started his translation there. If what the colophon said was true and it really was a first-person account of the pilgrimage, it could be a real discovery. A famous guide to the Saint Jacques pilgrimage had been written in the twelfth century, and in the fourteenth century a number of wealthy or important pilgrims had recorded their impressions, but there was a gap in information from the thirteenth century, when the roads were particularly dangerous and church authorities began to be concerned about so many penitents and adventurers roaming the continent. Neil thought, with a quick silvery shiver, that just possibly he had come across something new in the dusty carton of records from Saint-Jean-d'Angély.

But before he'd had a chance to look past the spidery Latin of the abbey historian to the monk's own words, it was far past the time he should have been leaving if he was going to make it to the post office, and the archives staff were beginning to turn out the lights. He was the last in line to return the documents to the stern men in gray smocks at the requests counter. He tried to explain that they could just set the Saint-Jean-d'Angély papers aside somewhere, that he would be back first thing in the morning and there was no need to send them back down into the recesses of the National Archives, which Neil of course had never seen, but which he imagined to be the very innards of Paris itself, filled not only with crumbling cartons bound with strings, but with abandoned metro cars and extra guillotines, statues of various Napoleons, flying buttresses, and spare dauphins.

One of the men in the smocks listened to Neil's explanation, then told him that, in fact, he would have to officially request the documents all over again. The box disappeared below the counter. He would have to fill out the yellow form and the green form and get the stamp from the chief archivist again if he was ever going to find out if the monk from Rouen had stopped in Paris at the old church of Saint-Jacques-de-la-Boucherie.

The next morning Neil snoozed his alarm four times, then woke in a panic and had to shower so quickly that the water never got warm. He'd meant to get to the station a little early so he'd have a chance to buy Magdute some flowers, but by the time he got off the metro at Gare du Nord it was already after six.

Neil would have skipped the flowers altogether—now that he thought about it, he wasn't sure they were appropriate—except that he'd been in such a rush, he'd forgotten to brush his teeth. He needed gum. A man walked past pushing a newspaper cart with one hand, holding a bucket of roses in the other, each wrapped in plastic. Neil waved for him to stop. He bought a rose, thinking that white was probably better than red, but when he asked for gum the man rustled through the candy bars and bags of chips on his cart and shook his head. There was a real newsstand at the other end of the station, but before Neil could get there he saw Magdute standing near the information booth with an old gray suitcase and a box under her arm, a stationary point in the flow of travelers. She raised her hand and waved to him.

"Hi," he said when he made it through the crowd. He leaned in to do the cheek kiss thing. She leaned in too, and at the last instant Neil panicked, not knowing which way she was going. He tried to switch sides, which meant they almost ended up kissing each other on the lips, and so they abandoned the whole thing.

"*Bienvenue*," he said and handed her the flower. It was already starting to be too heavy for its stem.

"Okay, so nice," she said.

"I like your glasses," Neil said. Starting off conversations with girls by complimenting them was a nervous tic Neil had. As usual, it just made him look like a jerk, because Magdute took her glasses off right away and put them back into a case in her purse, saying, "I only wear them sometimes."

"Oh, well they look good," Neil said. "I mean, they suit you."

"Well, this is nice for you to say," Magdute said.

"So how long till your bus?" Neil asked. "Should we get some breakfast?"

"Yes, I will have time for that," Magdute said.

Her suitcase flipped over when he tried to roll it, so Neil picked it up and carried it back toward the trains, where there was a little café right on the platform. Magdute sat with her bag and Neil got them each a coffee and a couple of pastries. He didn't know how Magdute liked her coffee, so he got a whole handful of sugar packets.

When he got back to the table, Magdute had her glasses on again, but she took them off as soon as she saw him. It was funny to think that she was shy about something like that.

"I wasn't sure how hungry you were," Neil said, putting down the pastries. "They have sandwiches too."

"No, this is great, really," Magdute said.

They took the first sips of their coffee, which tasted like it had been scraped right off the train tracks, and reached for the sugar packets at the same time. "I hope I got enough," Neil said.

Sunlight filtered in through the yellow glass of the vaulted ceiling, making a web of shadows on the floor. Birds flew around and pecked at an old brioche. A German family at the table next to them was playing cards. Brakes hissed and musical chimes sounded as trains arrived, sliding into their slots at the platform like trained snakes. When Neil looked up, Magdute's pain au chocolat was gone and she was licking her finger to pick up the crumbs. Neil wished he'd bought her a chausson aux pommes too.

"So you're headed home?" Neil asked.

"Yeah," she said. "Actually I have been losing my job in Swindon, and it is not so easy to find another one, so, you know, I am thinking I will go home."

"Gosh, that's too bad," Neil said.

"No, it's okay, really, I think I am a little bit finished in England. My living situation is not so good there, and actually at home in Vilnius my mother is opening one pizza restaurant, so maybe I can help her for running it."

"Oh yeah," Neil said, since she brought it up. "Yeah, that Australian guy, that was definitely weird."

"Which Australian?"

"That guy, Barry," Neil said.

"No, he is not from there."

"Oh, he sounded Australian," Neil said.

"He is from Africa."

"Really?" Neil asked.

"Yeah. You know, Rhodesia?"

"Sort of," Neil said. "But he is weird, right?"

"Yeah," Magdute said.

Neil wanted to ask her more about it, like what had happened after he told her about the camera, but he knew it wasn't his business.

"So how long is it going to take you to get home?" Neil asked.

"Maybe one day and half, something like this," she said.

"Boy, that's a long bus ride," Neil said, and they were both quiet for a little while. Magdute was still picking pastry crumbs off her napkin, even though there weren't any left.

"I'm starving," Neil said. "I'm going to get some sandwiches. What kind do you want? I think they have ham."

"No really, it's okay," Magdute said.

Neil got a ham sandwich and one with egg and cheese and a chausson aux pommes and brought them back to the table.

"Look," he said. "I really hope nothing I said about that thing, you know, that I found, made things too weird for you with that guy. I mean, obviously, it was weird, but I hope it didn't, like, freak you out too much."

"Well, no," Magdute said. It didn't look like she was planning on saying anything else.

"So did you find another place?" he asked.

"What other place?"

"To live—you know."

"No, I am staying all time at Barry's house," Magdute said.

At the table next to them, the German mother won the card game. Three army guards with assault rifles paced in synchronized steps along the platform. Neil thought of the archives with its long tables and the lamps with their little green shades, the cartons of yellowed papers tied up with strings and the old men sneezing quietly into their handkerchiefs, and wished he were there.

"Actually the camera isn't working like you said," Magdute said. Her sandwich was almost gone. Neil hadn't started his yet. He pushed it toward her. He wasn't really hungry.

"What do you mean?" Neil said. "Of course it was working."

"Is working, yeah, but not for recording. I am checking, and the wires are going totally wrong. Barry is shit for installing electronics, he will even have to ask me how to turn on the TV."

"Yeah, but he can still see you, right?" Neil said.

"Only if he is looking just at the moment."

"Still, that's illegal, what he did. It's an invasion of privacy, did you tell him that?"

Magdute shrugged.

"Magdute, I'm serious," Neil said. "He should be in jail."

"Well, no, not for this."

"Yeah," Neil said. "For this."

"It's complicated," Magdute said.

"No it's not. He could have other ones. He could be making videos and, like, selling them on the Internet." Magdute had finished the sandwich and the chausson aux pommes and was folding her napkin into the shape of a boat.

"This is the only thing what I know for making," she said, creasing the bow. "I am one time making good roses, but I'm forgetting for how to start."

"Look," Neil said. "My mom's a therapist and she deals with this kind of stuff all the time. You think it's your fault or something. It's not your fault. He probably has cameras and stuff like that all over his house. You need to tell the police. I mean, there are still other people living with him, right? Other, like, girls?" He was probably talking louder than he should have been, but he was getting worked up. He lowered his voice, remembering how his mom talked to clients when they called her at home with an emergency. "Magdute," he said, "this is not your fault."

"This is funny that you keep calling me Magdute. My name actually is Magdalena," she said. "Magdute—this is, like, name for some little girl."

Normally Neil would have been embarrassed, but he wasn't going to let this go.

"I'm sorry," he said. "Magdalena. I think you should call the police. If you don't, then I will, because I really think it's sick that he's, you know, filming in the bathroom."

"I told you, this is not for Internet. I am really checking this good."

"That's not the point," Neil said, taking out his phone as if he had the number for the Swindon vice squad programmed in.

"Don't call the police," Magdalena said.

"I think it's my responsibility," he said.

"Okay, Neil, that is not a good idea," she said. "Calling police will really not help anyone and it will make a lot of trouble for Barry. Actually he is pretty okay guy sometimes and he have helped me a lot, so don't do this, okay?"

They looked at each other for a minute.

"That doesn't make any sense," Neil said.

"Yeah," Magdalena said. "There are really a lot of things that doesn't make any sense."

After that the conversation was pretty awkward, especially when it turned out that Magdalena didn't even have a ticket to Vilnius yet, and needed to borrow money from Neil to buy one. The ticket cost sixty euros, which was most of his weekly stipend from Professor Piot, and Neil knew there was, like, zero chance she'd pay him back. He was honestly pretty pissed. He felt like he was being taken advantage of, but he knew that, as usual, he'd be nice, say no problem, and it would ruin his day. So it might have been with a little more force than was necessary that he scooted his chair out from the table, not really caring if it made a big screech across the floor, saying he'd have to go find an ATM. As he did, he accidentally knocked over the chair next to him, where Magdalena had put the shoebox she was carrying. Neil tried to catch it as it fell, and ended up batting the box into a table leg. The top flew off, and a Ziploc bag tumbled out. Magdalena gave a little gasp and when Neil picked it up, the seam of the bag broke and powder started pouring out.

"Shit, I'm really sorry," Neil said, cupping his hand under the leak.

"Oh my God," Magdalena said. She dove under the table and started scooping up what had fallen down there. Neil dumped his handful back into the shoebox and ducked down to help her. He sneezed as a puff of fine white dust rose up.

Then the realization of what was happening hit him with all the weight of a cell door slamming shut: Magdalena suddenly leaving Britain with bags full of some kind of powder. Had Barry put her up to this? The powder was dirty white, it had a slight yellowish tint. Jesus, Neil thought. Words he didn't know the precise meanings of, like *horse* and *flake* and *dust* and *snow*, started running through his head. Little cracks appeared in what had been his entire life up until that moment. The cracks grew and Neil's future, all his hard work, his *potential*, the scholarships he'd won and his dreams of thick books with his name on them, all of it crumbled around him as he crouched under the café table with the cigarette butts and paper cups and pale dust all over his clothes.

Not realizing there was a hole in the bottom, Magdalena was frantically scooping the stuff back into the bag—which, by the way, was one of those gallon-size freezer bags, it was not small, and it was mostly full. The German mother grabbed her nearest child and pulled it away. A guy with a laptop next to them was standing to get a better view. Magdalena was crying and Neil realized for the first time in his life how quickly the tables could turn, how somebody who took honors seminars and was extremely conscientious about not bringing so much as a ball point pen into the archives could become, *tout à coup*, a fugitive from the law. He found himself scooting backward. He banged his head on the underside of the table. Dust puffed off his shirt when he stood up. The guards in their pincer formation hadn't noticed yet, but they were headed in Neil's direction, their gaze sweeping across the station like a pendulum with each step they took. In a moment they would see. Every instinct in Neil's body was tensed to run.

Magdalena, on the other hand, seemed totally unconcerned by the fact that the whole world was watching her scoop up a shoebox's worth of the stuff. She had stopped her frenzied sweeping and was kneeling under the table with her face in her hands, sobbing. There were smudges of it in her hair. A crowd was gathering, and the three guards with their giant guns were coming toward them, now at a quicker pace. Neil, as usual, was totally fucked.

"Magdalena," he hissed. "Magdalena, get up," but she was crying, *keening*, with her feet bent under her at funny angles and a string of spit hanging out of her mouth.

"What's happening here?" one of the guards said in French.

"I don't know," Neil said. "She had this box and it fell." The guard looked at him oddly, and Neil realized he'd said "helmet" instead of "box." The guard squatted down and asked Magdalena what was going on. She just went on crying.

"Does she speak French?" he asked Neil.

"I don't think so," Neil said. And he had an idea. "I just met her," he said. "I've never seen her before."

"Lina, Lina, Lina, Lina," Magdalena was saying. Another guard came over. His finger rested on the trigger of his gun.

"What's this?" the second guard asked. The first guard dipped his finger in the powder, the way they did on TV.

"*Cendres*," said the first guard.

"Oh là là," said the second. "A member of the family?" he asked Neil.

By the time Neil remembered what *cendres* meant, the first guard was giving Magdalena some napkins and helping her scoop up the last bits, including one or two largish fragments of what looked like soup bones.

When they had gotten most of it, the first guard said something to the second, who went and got a trash bag from a janitor's cart that was standing by. He wrapped the torn Ziploc bag in the trash bag and knotted it tight, then put it back in the shoebox and helped her up.

"Apology and condolence," he said to her in English, with a little bow, and he and the other guards went on their way.

Magdalena wiped her face. Neil wanted to die.

"It was my fault," Neil said.

"No, is totally okay." Magdalena had gray smudges around her eyes. Neil hoped it was makeup. "I am hearing her in my head right now saying, 'Magdalena you are big fucking idiot for not making the box closed better than that.'"

"Mm," Neil said, not exactly sure who she was talking about.

Maybe Magdalena realized he was confused because she looked toward the shoebox, whose top didn't fit right anymore because of the garbage bag inside, and said, "She is my friend who is dying last year." Neil felt himself inclining his head a little toward the box, as if saying hello.

"I'm so sorry," Neil said. "I just had no idea."

"Well, I am not really wanting to tell you, it is a little bit not-so-happy, you know?"

"Yeah, I know," Neil said. "It was last year?"

"Like over one year ago," Magdalena said. "We are living in London together and then she have some problems with one man, and well, with some other things also, but she accidentally deathed herself on some apricots."

"What?" Neil said.

"Here you want to see?" Magdalena took some papers out of the shoebox and handed them to Neil. It was an autopsy report. *Presence of cyanmethaemoglobin. Marked dark cyanotic hypostasis, petechial haemorrhages, pink mucosa.* "There," she said, pointing to where it said *Cause of death.* "She gets one big juice machine and like totally stupid person she puts in all those fruits with still having the seeds."

"Oh my God," Neil said.

"Yeah, is fucking one in the million, they are telling me," she said.

"That's awful," Neil said.

"Yeah. She is my best friend," Magdalena said. "I am thinking now it's time already I should bring her home."

*

133

Obviously, after that he gave her the money for the bus ticket. She asked for his address, saying she'd send it back to him when she got home, and Neil said, "Okay, but really, whenever," because he was pretty sure they both knew she never would. But he wrote it down on a napkin anyway and gave it to her.

She lifted the napkin up close to her face. "This is your name?" she asked.

"Yeah," he said. "Usually you say it 'Neil,' like, *to kneel*, but I like the way you say it too."

"No, I mean this. This is also name of your father?" she said, pointing to Neil's last name.

"Yeah, didn't you know?" Neil said, then realized there was no reason a person from Lithuania who wasn't some kind of book freak would have heard of Inga Beart. "My dad usually makes it seem like a big deal, so I figured your mom would have heard all about—"

"And your father's other name is Richard?"

"Yeah. Or Rick," Neil said. "It's funny he'd tell your mom Richard. Pretty much he just goes by Rick." But he could tell Magdalena wasn't listening. She was tracing her finger through a bit of sugar that had spilled as if she were trying to think of how to spell it.

"R-I-C-H-A-R-D," Neil said.

"Oh, yes, I know," she said.

They had another coffee, and Magdalena asked him about Paris and what he was doing there, which was nice of her. Neil could tell she didn't feel like talking. Her eyes were still wet, and she kept taking her glasses out of her bag and unfolding them, then putting them away without putting them on. But she had a way of looking at him so intently, with her lips tensed a little, as if something important was going on behind them, that Neil started believing she was actually interested in the Roman-era origins of the Châtelet butchers' quarter.

In his notebook Neil had a postcard of the Tour Saint-Jacques and he showed Magdalena. It was an old one he'd found at the flea market in front of Les Halles, probably from the 1950s or '6os, back when people kept getting killed by chunks of mortar falling off the sides, it was in such bad shape. In the photograph the tower looked sort of corroded, studded with half-dissolved gargoyles. It was going to look a lot better than that when they were done with the reconstruction, Neil told her. The tower had been under scaffolding for almost eight years now, and Neil wouldn't have even recognized it in the postcard except for the unmistakable asymmetry caused by the statue of Saint Jacques himself, who stood perched on one corner, walking stick in hand, pointing pilgrims on their way.

Magdalena flipped the postcard over to read what was on the back.

"It says 'Leaving tomorrow,'" Neil said. "I think it could have been written by someone who was going on a pilgrimage, which is, you know, like a religious trip, because this was the starting point for the Saint Jacques pilgrimage. And see the date? Right around this time of year. Which makes sense because people who wanted to make it by the Feast of Saint Jacques, which is July 25, would have had to leave Paris in June. See, they had to go all the way down to a place in Spain called Santiago de Compostela and also another place, Finisterre—you know, 'the end of the earth.' That was where this guy, Saint Jacques, suppos-edly washed up on the beach. And he should have been all rotten and dead but instead he was perfectly preserved with scallop shells stuck to him, and so it was, you know, a miracle."

Something he'd said had caught Magdalena's attention. She looked up from the postcard, waiting for him to go on. "I mean that's one story. There are lots of others. And of course it's pretty unlikely it was actually him. To have floated all the way from Jerusalem? It's basi-cally impossible. But in medieval times people wanted to worship something they could see for themselves, like an actual *body*. So churches started saying that they had, you know, *relics*, which were usually parts of holy people, their heads or a bone from their arm or even—" The cathedral at Conques had claimed possession of Jesus's *prepuce*, which was a word Neil had had to look up. "Well, some of the stuff they had was pretty gross. But Saint Jacques, he was one of the few whose relics stayed intact. Sorry, *intact*, it's like *all together*. That was part of the miracle. People traveled huge distances because they believed that the saint was so powerful he wouldn't let his body be broken up."

Magdalena was leaning toward him a little bit, like it was important that she hear every word.

"And it's interesting, the reasons people had for traveling all that way, hundreds of miles sometimes. Like, look, I think I've got it here—" Neil went through the papers in his backpack until he found a photocopy of a record from the mid-1300s. "I found this in the archives—see, isn't the script beautiful? What it says is actually pretty sad. It's a dispensation for a woman who'd promised to make the pilgrimage if her baby recovered from some sickness. And it did recover, but then it died of something else, and she was, you know, so heartbroken that she couldn't make the trip. It's not important, historically, except that these kinds of documents are all we have to piece together what it was like for people back then. I mean, you get a sense that life was hard, you know, and short. People lived closer to death than we do today. And that's why religion was so important in every aspect of people's lives." Magdalena was nodding. "Like, instead of going to jail, a pilgrimage would be used as punishment. Criminals or people convicted of heresy—which was basically disagreeing with the church—they'd be forced to walk barefoot, sometimes even with chains locked around them, so that everyone would know what they'd done. I found a list of people from a certain parish who were made to go—people caught sleeping with other people's wives, priests who were, you know, stealing or having affairs. I think I have a copy of it here somewhere— yeah, this is it. See, it says the reason right there: adultery, adultery, lechery, et cetera. Of course sometimes people just did it to get away. You know, get out of town, see the world—in the Middle Ages going on a pilgrimage was almost the only way a regular person could travel. And who knows, when they came to the place where the saint's body was kept they might witness a miracle. People really believed in that stuff back then. Sight restored to the blind, cripples made to walk—"

Now Neil was the one who was leaning in over the table. He suddenly had a terrible thought. Did he have bad breath? He couldn't smell it, but that was no guarantee.

"You want a piece of gum?" he asked.

"Okay," Magdalena said. Neil searched around in his pockets and remembered he hadn't bought any. Then, speaking of miracles, he found a single stick of Wrigley's Doublemint at the bottom of his backpack. He absolutely had to have some for himself, so he broke it in half. "Sorry," he said. "I thought I had a whole pack."

"And where is it happening, these bodies all together like life coming up on the beach?" Magdalena asked.

"It's down in Spain," Neil said.

"And it's a miracle?"

"Well, I mean, it's a story. It's not like bodies are washing up all the time," Neil said.

"But sometimes?" she asked.

"Well, yeah, that's the idea."

As if this had answered a question she'd been thinking about for some time, Magdalena smiled. Then she changed the subject to the thing they'd spent the last half hour being careful not to talk about.

"I've been making one big mistake having her burned after death," Magdalena said, pressing down the lid of the shoebox. One corner was bashed in and the box didn't look like it would make it all the way to Lithuania.

"Why?" Neil asked.

"Well, some people are saying that the body must be—like you say. *In-tact*. For her religion."

"Oh," Neil said.

"If she is not whole, then at the end she doesn't go up with God, something like this," Magdalena said. "So, I have really fucked up."

"Well, I guess," Neil said, which wasn't what he'd meant to say at all. "But, I mean, you didn't know?"

"Not this, about the body. Some person was telling me later on. She have to be having all parts, nothing missing."

"I think I'd rather be cremated," Neil said. "Otherwise you just rot, you know?"

"Not this Saint Jack on the beach," Magdalena said.

"Yeah," Neil said. "But like I said, it's just a story."

Magdalena was quiet for a little while, and then she said, "You know something, Ni-yell? Maybe this is pretty good thing to be dropping those burned parts all on the floor, because until this time, for the last entire year actually, I'm not so much knowing what to do with her, and I'm really wanting to do right, you know?" Somehow with that tiny piece of gum Magdalena blew a bubble big enough to pop and she smiled at Neil again, her one grayish tooth like an exclamation point at the end, all of it at odds with her eyes, which were so light and clear that airplanes might have flown across them. Taken altogether she was the most perfect person Neil had ever seen.

And then something happened that was not a big deal in itself, but was so open to romantic interpretation that it made Neil feel as if the chemical balance of his entire body had been rearranged. Looking at him in that funny way of hers, Magdalena brought her hand up to his face and with a quick movement she traced her fingers along his temple. "You are having one small insect there, is nothing," she said, and smiled again. But Neil hadn't felt any little legs, only the soft touch of her hand brushing back a bit of his hair.

He was still a little woozy as he helped her buy the ticket and left her on the street outside the station, where people with piles of luggage waited for buses bound for Warsaw and Kiev. Then Neil walked back to the archives on rue du Faubourg-Saint-Denis, even though it wasn't the most direct route, because that was the path Saint Denis was said to have taken out of Paris carrying his head under his arm after the Romans chopped it off around the third century A.D. It seemed fitting somehow to be walking in the footsteps of the patron saint of Paris, who had personally delivered his own head to his tomb in a feat of *cephalophoric ambulation*—literally, walking while carrying one's own head—the most ridiculous of miracles.

The gate of the old walled city was in front of him, an arbitrary arch rising out of the streets now that the wall itself was gone. There were shops selling vegetables he'd never seen before, where people bought unfamiliar melons and green tomatoes in papery husks. The windows of a Pakistani sweetshop were packed with sticky orange balls and honeyed bricks of colored paste.

At the Saint-Denis gate, rue du Faubourg-Saint-Denis became rue Saint-Denis and the shops changed. Professor Piot was right, Neil thought. A city trails its past along behind it. Merchants had been required to pay a tax to enter the old city, and the imprint of that fact had lasted through the centuries, so that even now the shops inside where the wall used to be sold different things than those beyond it.

Inside the Saint-Denis gate the vegetable stalls were gone and the stores were filled with rhinestone belts and wholesale lace, fur and wedding dresses, *vente en gros*. Shopkeepers smoked outside with their sleeves rolled up, a begging gypsy girl kneaded an orange between her hands, and a prostitute stood in a doorway, her breasts like brown balloons pushed up against her neck. Long passages cut between buildings ended improbably in sunlight, and it occurred to Neil that he was entering the portion of his life when one began to accumulate regrets. Before, somehow, no decision had seemed too permanent. But now that he was in college, wading straight into whatever it was that would turn out to be his life, suddenly each thing he did or didn't do was tangled up in consequences. And with this thought, as if he'd gotten a look at his own life's ledger of missed opportunities, Neil realized that he shouldn't have let Magdalena get on the bus to Vilnius.

{MAGDALENA}

Paris, June

PEOPLE PRESSED IN around Magdalena, jostling each other to get on the bus. All around her words in Lithuanian sprouted on the backs of hands and across foreheads and chins. Taking off her glasses didn't help. The people were so close and the words were so familiar that Magdalena knew their meanings without even realizing she'd read them.

The line was moving. People were getting on the bus. She looked over her shoulder at Neil, who was now just an orange-headed blur. She waved. Part of the blur waved back. An old woman in front of her was telling her husband to check and double-check their passports. *Stazinis širdies nepakankamumas*, which meant *congestive heart failure*, looped like a noose around her neck.

The patch of color that was Neil waved again. Then it turned and got smaller and smaller among the other shapes. The old woman in front of her was stepping onto the bus. PARIS-WARSZAWA-VILNIUS said the sign in the window. Magdalena looked again for the orange-topped shape, but it was gone.

She got out of line. She took her bag out from under the bus, ignoring the bus driver who shouted after her in Lithuanian and then in Polish that she wasn't allowed to do that, and she walked with her head down across the street and back toward the station. She didn't look up again until she was far away from the bus and the words on the skin of the people around her didn't mean anything to her at all. She put her glasses on and looked around for the ticket counter.

She returned the ticket for half its value, hoping thirty euros would be enough for a ticket to the place where bodies washed ashore whole. She tried to remember exactly what Neil had said. In English she asked several people how to take the bus to Spain. They told her to go to the Montparnasse Station. Was there a bus to a place called the End of the Earth? They didn't know.

The people in Paris looked different. They seemed to have been collected from all over the world. She wished she still had Lina's camera, so she could see the exact shapes of their noses and cheeks. She felt like she had when she and Lina had first arrived in London and she let herself stare and stare at people, trying to see their features underneath foreign words, not worrying that she would read them.

The Montparnasse station was far away, but Magdalena didn't want to use any of her money to take the metro there, so she got a map from the man at the information desk and, feeling a little dizzy because she wasn't used to wearing her glasses, she walked out of the station with the shoebox under her arm, pulling Lina's bag behind her on its shaky wheel. She felt so happy that she blew a bubble with the gum that Neil had given her, even though it was not the bubble-blowing kind.

After Barry had dumped her clothes out of the upstairs window, he'd hurled the camera after her into the street. It had bounced, then shattered its lens against the curb, and in all the confusion with the police and the new girl and Veronika screaming, Magdalena never had a chance to take out the film. She wasn't sorry to leave Barry's house, but she was sorry about that camera.

Barry had been very nice to Magdalena for a few weeks after the day in the bathroom when she told him about the words while his cut from the razor blade was bleeding all over her jeans. But once he stopped being afraid that Magdalena was going to try to cut herself up again when he wasn't looking, he started treating the whole thing as a big joke.

"C'mon Magdute, tell my future," he'd say to her. But most of the things that were written on Barry were in the past. Magdalena didn't understand a lot of what it said, but there were quite a few dates, most of them before she was born, as if Barry had fallen face-first into a history book while the ink was still wet. She kept her mouth shut.

Before she found out the meaning of *apricots*, Magdalena had felt almost comforted by the nonsense on Barry's face. Ugly things were written there, but they were interspersed with words that were still meaningless after more than two years in England, and she found them easy to ignore. But after that day in the churchyard, Magdalena started paying more attention to Barry's skin, knowing the things it said were probably true. He caught her studying him once or twice. "Oh, give us a hint," he would say. Or he'd try to give her a kiss and say, "What's it got to say there about you and me?" But when Magdalena finally did read him what was written there, she did it not because he kept asking her to, but to shut him up about the numbers.

Barry had a whole library of books on World War Two, and his favorite, the one he had tabbed with sticky notes, one with the name of each girl living in his house, was called *The Holocaust of the Jews in Eastern Europe.* When he got mad about something, he'd start yelling at Magdalena and the other girls about the things that had happened during the war as if they had personally been the perpetrators and he was the victim, which was really something, considering what it said on his chin and the back of his neck. They could tell when he was really mad because he replaced their names with death tolls.

To Zosia from Poland he'd say, "Two Point Nine Million, who the fuck is this guy hanging around across the street? Get out there and tell him to push off," or to Veronika, who was Czech, he'd say, "Two Hundred Seventy-Seven Thousand, your goddamn orange hair is stopping up my drains."

But it was Magdalena who got the worst of it, not because her number was highest, not because Barry's family had even come from Lithuania, but because he had read in that book that the Lithuanians hadn't just handed over the Jews, but in fact had done most of the killing themselves.

When he got worked up, even if it had nothing to do with her at all, he'd call her down and ask her how many Jews she knew. Not so many, Magdalena would say, knowing what was coming. How many synagogues were there in Vilnius? Maybe a few, Magdalena would say. "Nope, not maybe a few. Fucking two. How many were there in 1939?" He'd open the book with the sticky notes and point to a page. "Fifty. It was forty percent Jewish, how about that? And how many pits in the forest did it take, would you say? For all of them?"

"I don't know," Magdalena would say.

"But if you had to guess."

"I really don't know."

Once, when she had just moved in and before she'd learned to keep quiet, Magdalena told Barry he'd better be careful of what he said, that a lot of people had died in Rhodesia too. She didn't know what she was saying at the time, but Barry got very quiet after that, and he looked at Magdalena in a way she didn't like at all. It said a lot more than that across his chin and his arms, and even though Magdalena didn't understand exactly what it meant, she knew better than to get into it. From then on she let Barry say what he wanted.

"How many bullets did it take for the babies?" he'd ask.

"I don't know."

"Sure you do. Bullets aren't cheap. Think about it."

"I don't know."

"One? Two? For the little ones, the really tinys. Give up?"

"Yeah, I give up."

"It's a trick question."

"I don't know."

"One half of one bullet. Guess how."

"I don't know."

"Don't know much. Ask Granddaddy. Go on, use the phone. Call old Grandpop up long distance." And Barry would say in Lithuanian in a singsong voice, "Make mama hold baby close. One half for mama, one half for—"

"Okay, it's enough," Magdalena would say, but Barry was just getting started.

"Did you ever go hunting for bones in the forest? You ever go off to take a piss in the forest and poke your cunny on a Jew bone sticking out of the ground?"

"No, I never did this."

And it would go on like that until Barry got tired and said, "But cheer up kiddo. Nobody knew a thing about anything, did they?"

But the truth was, she did know some things about those places in the forest.

*

Sometimes after school Lina and Magdalena would take the bus to Lina's grandmother's house. Magdalena didn't have any grandmothers, and knowing this, and because she was grateful to Magdalena's mother for taking Lina to live with them, Lina's grandmother let Magdalena call her Baba like Lina did, and she stitched both of them tiny dolls that she turned inside out to hide the seams.

Lina's grandmother lived just outside the city in an old wooden house painted blue. She didn't like to go out because she was Polish and she didn't want people to hear her accent, so Lina and Magdalena did her shopping, going to the butcher's and the vegetable market and the pharmacy all by themselves, almost too shy to say what they wanted and then running home with their bags of cabbages and bread and medicines as if they'd stolen them.

Lina always took care of the money, because she was older and it was her grandmother, but Magdalena held on to the list that Baba had written out for them in her old-fashioned handwriting with the spelling all wrong, because Magdalena was the better reader. And when they came home, poppy seed cakes would be warm on the oven and Baba would be stitching yarn onto the heads of the dolls, yellow for Lina and brown for Magdalena.

Baba's skin hung like tissue paper over her bones, and if it hadn't been for her white gold hair anchoring it to her skull it would have slipped off a long time ago. There were hollows under her ears and in her collarbones and her hair was so thin she could hold it all in a child's barrette. From time to time Baba patted her hair and brushed the fine bits back behind her ears in a way that showed that Baba had once been so beautiful that Lina's grandfather had taken a great risk during the war and married her, to save her from being sent away.

But Baba's hands were like the hands of another person. The older and tinier Baba got, the bigger her hands became. They looked to Magdalena like pieces of driftwood that had been soaked and rounded and sanded and smoothed by the sea for hundreds of years.

Baba had been a seamstress, and though her hands looked like blocks of wood they could do anything. If Lina or Magdalena had brought a bit of shiny cloth or a piece of lace with them, Baba would turn it into a dress or a long winter coat for their dolls, with cuffs that turned up on the ends of the sleeves and bits of thread knotted to look like buttons.

Magdalena liked to watch Lina's grandmother work, because when she used the old sewing machine she pushed up her sleeves and Magdalena would get to see the paintings on her skin. Baba had letters on her face and hands and in the gap between her stockings and her skirt like other people, but on her arms the words were written in another kind of alphabet, with letters that looked like tiny paintings, each one shaped almost like so many things but not exactly like anything, and Magdalena would lean in close, pretending she was watching Baba as she finished off a tiny hem, trying to understand what they said.

Baba's skin was so thin and she was so covered in writing that from far away she looked blue. Most of the words on her face and neck must have been Polish because they were much harder to stack one sound on top of another than the words they learned in school, or the words on Magdalena's teacher's face or Lina's or anyone else's. Sometimes Baba would catch Magdalena looking at her, trying to make sense of the line of letters that started at her ear and ran all the way down to the collar of her dress.

"Don't move your lips like this," Baba would say, and Magdalena would try as hard as she could to keep all the sounds in her head without saying anything. But she always lost the first part by the time she got to the end, and without meaning to she'd be back to shaping the letters with her lips. "Stop this," Baba would say again, more sharply. "Someone will see."

One day when they went to visit Lina's grandmother, Ruta was there. Baba stood in front of the door and said to them, "Please, you must not come in today," but they could see Ruta behind her wrapped in a blanket. Ruta started calling for Lina, and Lina ducked under her grandmother's arms. But Ruta was sick and her hands weren't steady. Baba tried to get Ruta to sit down, but she didn't want to. Ruta ripped Baba's dress at the shoulder and Magdalena saw that all across Baba's body there were words, some of them in the language of paintings, written over and across each other as if they were meant for a person with twice as much skin. Ruta's face had changed, there was something slack in her mouth and as soon as Lina saw it she pulled away. Ruta tried to make Lina come back to her, but Lina didn't want to. There were two red points at the tops of Ruta's cheeks. When Baba tried again to make her sit down, Ruta slapped her. Suddenly Lina was crying, and it was as if her crying had no beginning, she started right in the middle with big sobs. Ruta yelled at her to stop it, but Lina only cried louder. It was a screaming, hysterical cry like Magdalena had never heard, and Ruta put her hands over her ears and ran toward the door. She stumbled and got up again, only taking her hands off her ears to take Baba's purse off of the hook by the door, and then she left.

As soon as Ruta was gone Lina stopped screaming. She stood for a moment, then she ran after her mother. Baba called to her, but Lina was already halfway down the street, running after Ruta who was just then disappearing around the corner with Baba's purse dangling from its broken strap.

Baba started down the steps after them, but she nearly lost her balance, and it was only Magdalena being there that kept her from falling. Baba wanted to stay right there on the steps, but Magdalena led her back inside to the sofa. Baba's big hands were tented over her face as if she were reading them, and she sat there shaking her head slowly, not saying anything.

So Magdalena did what she thought her mother would have done. She shut the door. She pulled the torn sleeve back over Baba's shoulder as best she could. She patted Baba's hair and brought a wet rag from the kitchen for the place on her cheek where Ruta had hit her. Then, because she didn't know what else to do, she started singing to Baba as if she were a little child, and by the time she ran out of words to the songs she knew it was getting dark. Baba was still looking at the palms of her hands, and so in the last light Magdalena read to her what was written there, spreading Baba's hand on top of her own and tracing the letters like a gypsy telling the future, except that when she put the sounds together, what came out was all in the past, and she sang it to Baba like the continuation of a lullaby.

In the forest past the station Paneriai they stop the train. First Lidya Kamiemiecki, Jakob and Jacha Gornowski, Solomon Marmorsztejn and his mother Gita, Lejba Byk and Ester Kowarska. Malka who never waited. Smuel, Boris and Ilja. Varvaza brought the children with her. Anna Litvinova and the baby Misha. Irina Kac and the man on the train. Josef Lewin's fiancée Rivka. Mira and Luba Erlich. Jakub, Mama and Anucia at once. Professor Ginzbergas who wore his shirts one for each day. Chana Bir, then Mr. Izakov, the man who sells buttons . . .

"Where is Anucia?" Baba asked, and Magdalena showed her. "And Misha?" There on her thumb. "Jakub and my mother?" There and there.

Then Baba said, "You have to pretend you don't see such things. If you tell like this again they will take me away."

Right before Baba died she lost her caution and asked Ruta to bury her in the old Jewish cemetery, where the gravestones were covered with the same kinds of letters that Baba was. Ruta didn't have the heart to tell her that the cemetery had been dug up years ago when the Russians built the Sports Palace. Magdalena didn't know about any of it at the time, because Lina and Ruta had moved away to Kaunas and it was while they were living there that Baba died. It was only when they came back to Vilnius that Magdalena heard, and only then because Ruta came to their door drunk one night and told Magdalena's mother everything, how Baba's whole family had been killed in a pit in the forest, and how Baba would have been killed too if it hadn't been for an old man, a sage of the community who had always frightened the children by reading from books that weren't there. He looked to where Baba stood with the others beside the train tracks and told her she would run, and she did. She ran through the forest until she was found by Ruta's father, who it seemed very likely had been doing some of the killing. He was a peasant man who lived nearby and he saved her because of her beautiful blonde hair. He hid her for a time in his chicken coop and then when the war was nearly over he married her.

Magdalena's mother had been the one to tell Ruta the night that Lina died. "If I had known," Ruta kept saying over and over on the phone, never finishing the sentence. Magdalena's mother didn't understand what she meant, but Magdalena did. How could Lina's mother have looked at her daughter each day, fed her and taken her to school and sometimes slapped her and left for days without saying why, bought her dresses and held her hand across streets, if she had known that Lina would be gone at twenty-one?

With Dov Kitrosser it was the same. He'd pressed his wet face into Magdalena's shoulder and said, "I never would have left her alone if I had known." And when the policewoman called to explain the results of the inquest, she'd said, "We believe Ms. Valentukaitė ingested the seeds without knowing their toxicity."

But Magdalena had known. If she'd locked Lina in the bathroom the moment she shaved away the last bits of her hair and saw the words *cause of death* underneath, if she'd made up some lie to keep her there long enough to look up *ingesting* and *acute*, to make sure *respiratory failure* meant what she thought it did and then—with Lina probably threatening to pour her lotions down the drain if Magdalena didn't unlock the door—if she'd flipped back to the A's in her high school English dictionary and seen that *apricots* were a fruit and that was Dov's specialty—well, everything might have been different. Lina and Dov might at that moment be together sampling a shipment of pineapples grown without any skins. Or things with Dov might have ended as they usually did and Lina would be back in their flat in London, sitting in front of the open fridge, cooling her feet in the vegetable bin.

It had been a mistake not to believe what it said on Lina's skin, and she didn't want to make that mistake again. So for a little while after Neil called to tell her about the camera and Magdalena realized why Barry happened to bang open the bathroom door just when he did, she thought about taking Neil's advice and reporting Barry to the police. Not for what he'd put in the cabinet—somehow that didn't seem right. After she cut the lock on the medicine cabinet with Barry's hedge clippers she pulled the camera out of the wall and held it up in front of Barry, dangling wires. But Barry just laughed and wagged the finger that was still wrapped in cotton from where he'd cut himself trying to grab the razor from Magdalena, saying, "Guess you're not in much of a position to complain." And it was true. She didn't know why, exactly, but she was glad Barry had come in when he did.

It was the other things she wondered about. Barry had guilt written all over him, and it seemed that someone ought to know. He'd been a young man when he did what he did, and, like the Lithuanian peasants drunk on country brandy and the unfamiliar power to remove whole families from the history of the world, he may have believed that what he did was necessary or found a way to close his mind to the worst of it. But if he had an explanation, it wasn't written down. All that Magdalena saw on Barry's skin were facts and dates.

Still, for a while after the day Magdalena told Barry about the words, she was careful not to say anything more. When Barry yelled to her from the living room one afternoon because somebody had spilled something on his keyboard, calling her Two Hundred Twenty Thousand instead of by name, Magdalena answered. But when he made her take the book with the sticky notes off the shelf and told her to start reading the chapter on Lithuania, marked *Magdalena*, she told him, "You are some sick fuck, you know that, Barry?"

"Read," he said.

"I don't want to," she said.

"It's for your own good. You should know these things."

"No," Magdalena said.

"Then get out. Pack your bags," Barry said.

Magdalena put on her glasses and then, instead of looking down at the book, she looked at him, pretending to stumble a bit over the names, so he would know she was reading.

"Mount Darwin, 2 September 1975. Chained the feet of Erasmus Chiutsi made it look like he hung himself," she said.

"What?" Barry said.

"Burned and beat his brother Amos," she said. "Number 5 Rest Camp, Chilimanzi, 25 September 1975. Beat Mariya Mandiuraya with a stick, set dogs at her breasts. Covered Grace Mandirova's head with a white cloth poured water on her face six times gave her tablets and cotton wool."

"Get out," Barry said. "What the fuck is this? Get out."

He knocked her glasses off, but Magdalena picked them up again and held them to her face—not because she needed them; she'd known it all by heart for months.

"Pokwe Rest Camp, 28 September 1975. Told Mushandi Kurwara the children he has will be the last ones. A bag with wires coming out. Three shocks. Chiweshe Protected Village No. 12, 2 August 1975—"

"I'm going to kill you," Barry said.

After that there was a lot of shouting. Barry chased her out of the house and threw her things after her. The new girl started screaming; there was the sound of police sirens and Lina's camera crashing onto the pavement. Barry ran out after Magdalena with a piece of pipe from the basement, and to stop him from using it Magdalena told him what he'd wanted to know, which was his future. Little words, written small across his eyelids: *blood cancer, metastatic.* He set the pipe down on the pavement, where it rolled a little until Magdalena stopped it with her foot. When she looked at him again Barry had slumped like an old man down onto the curb. She put the pipe in the bushes where the police wouldn't see it, and told the new girl to be quiet. Beginning with the things that Barry had thrown out onto the street, Magdalena started packing her bag.

"'Saves the life of Magdalena Bikauskaitė in the bathtub,' you have this written too," she told Barry as she left. But it was a lie, it didn't say that on him anywhere, and Barry just sat, not looking up.

She'd been walking for a long time. The sidewalks in Paris were uneven; her arms felt like they were tearing out of her shoulders from the effort of pulling the suitcase while trying to keep it balanced on its one wheel, and she still hadn't found the street that would take her to the Montparnasse station. Two women passed by, their faces lined with French words that might have meant anything. A man in a doorway smoked a pipe with his sleeves rolled up; she could see columns of text running down his arms.

Magdalena was beginning to have serious doubts about what she was doing, and she was starting to think she was really crazy for not getting on the bus to Vilnius. The street she was on wasn't on the map she'd gotten at the station and she was trying to read the name on the street sign at the next corner and at the same time thinking that maybe she ought to go back to the station and ask please if it were possible to buy back her canceled ticket—when she nearly bumped into a man who was standing still in the middle of the sidewalk.

He was bending down to look in the window of a shop. Magdalena stepped off the curb to go around him and lost her grip on the handle of Lina's suitcase, which rolled over into the street. The man turned to help her and Magdalena hurried to take off her glasses, because it seemed that out of all the millions of people in Paris, this man was also Lithuanian; the meaning of a string of words in her own language jumped from the man's face into Magdalena's head before she even knew she was reading them.

She had gotten out of the habit a long time ago of reading out loud the words she saw, but the particular phrase on the man's skin was so familiar that she heard her own voice saying it before she could help herself. "*Akys nemato, širdies nesopa.*" It was something Magdalena's mother said all the time. *If the eyes don't see, the heart doesn't hurt.* Something like that. It was one of Magdalena's mother's favorite expressions. She said it when she bought a bottle of high-quality shampoo, taking it off the shelf with a laugh, not looking at the price. She said it, quietly, to Magdalena when they passed a young woman swaying over a bottle on an empty street, and if a friend's thieving ex-husband drove past in a new car, Magdalena's mother would narrow her eyes and say it as loudly as she liked. It was an old-fashioned saying, so well used it hardly meant anything, and the man on the street looked at Magdalena strangely. She was about to hurry past before he could ask her why she'd said something like that out of nowhere in a language she couldn't possibly have known he'd understand, but as it turned out she didn't have to explain, because it seemed he hadn't understood her after all.

"I'm sorry," the man said in English, "I don't speak—"

Magdalena put her glasses back on, just for a moment, and she saw that the man couldn't be from Lithuania; all the other words on him were English. She scanned his face quickly. There were details of his retirement accounts and a life insurance policy: She could see its payout date printed below his ear. At the corner of the man's eye were descriptions of things from his childhood: a matchstick castle, a secret, a time the gate of the chicken coop was not shut tight. On his jaw a marriage, mentioned briefly. Magdalena didn't want to be caught looking too closely, so she took her glasses off.

The man was bending over her suitcase. "I'm afraid you've lost a wheel," he said. He lifted it back onto the sidewalk, and she had to explain that it wasn't his fault, the wheel had been lost a long time ago and that suitcase was always flipping over.

The man turned back to the shop window. Magdalena wondered if maybe her mind was playing tricks and she had imagined seeing words in Lithuanian.

"Do you know what street is for the station Montparnasse?" she asked. He turned to say he was sorry but he didn't know, he was only visiting; she put her glasses on and read again, high on his cheek, *Akys nemato, širdies nesopa*. Magdalena could hear her mother's voice saying it, and it even looked a little like her mother's handwriting on the man's skin. *If the eyes don't see, the heart doesn't hurt.* It was her mother's all-purpose answer to everything, her way of explaining the things one couldn't know and might not want to understand.

The man said something about the shop he was looking in. There were little figures in the window and the man started telling her about his son, who liked that kind of thing. When he bent to point inside the shop she read that he'd come to Paris for a reunion with his family; it was written on his cheek just below her mother's words.

"So you are here together?" Magdalena said.

"My son? No, no he's not here with me," the man said.

It was a risk to ask him anything more. But she could see that the *k* in the word *akys* on his face was made like a Russian character. Magdalena's mother still made her *k*'s like that, the way she had been taught in school. Magdalena suddenly missed her mother—the sound of her voice and the spot of perfect comfort between her mother's chin and her collarbone, where Magdalena's head could still fit when it needed to.

"So, you come for—*reunion*?" she said. She wasn't quite sure how the word was supposed to be pronounced, but she wanted the man to keep talking.

He looked at her strangely, and Magdalena knew she'd made a mistake.

"A reunion? No, did I say that?"

She shrugged as if he had, and though the man looked uneasy he seemed to believe her. He went back to talking about his son, and she nodded, reading the words again. She was tired, her arms and legs were tired, her feet hurt, and it was restful to see letters arranged in familiar patterns. *Akys nemato, širdies nesopa.* That old phrase uncluttered by articles and prepositions, so that four Lithuanian words did the work of nine in English. *If the eyes don't see, the heart doesn't hurt.*

"But you know, those things," the man was saying. "Sometimes they don't work out."

Magdalena nodded again, though she hadn't really been listening. "Things usually can be like this," she said.

The man cleared his throat and picked up his luggage as if he'd suddenly remembered he was in a hurry. She would have liked to keep him standing there a few minutes more. Next to her was the shop window he had been so interested in, and she looked inside. But before she could come up with a polite way of making him turn his cheek to her again so she could get another look at her mother's words, the man was picking up his suitcase and turning to go. He'd been carrying a city map, better than the one she had, and he gave it to her, saying, "Here, maybe you can ask someone else about the station."

"For me?" she said. "Okay, thanks."

The man tilted his head to say good-bye and Magdalena stood looking in the window of the shop. The gum Neil had given her was hard and tasteless. She blew a tiny bubble.

Inside the window the shopkeeper was hanging up his apron. He sat to put on a pair of leather boots. When he was done he turned to the window, nodding to Magdalena when he saw her standing outside, and started clearing a place among the dusty figurines on the display shelf. After a moment he got a box out from behind the counter. He took something out of it and set it in the space he'd made on the shelf. It was a tiny saint, its features pressed into leather so soft it looked almost alive. Magdalena turned to see if the man on the sidewalk was watching too, but he was already gone. She looked back in the window and noticed that the saint's body was covered with tiny shells. The shopkeeper took out a note written in French and taped it to the glass.

The shopkeeper went into a back room and Magdalena stood looking at the little saint. She blew another bubble with her gum. Then the lights in the shop went out. The window display got dark and she had to lean in closer and cup her hands around her face to see inside. They were real shells on the body, each no bigger than a fingernail. Underneath the little saint the shopkeeper had sprinkled a bit of sand. She got too close. The bubble popped against the shop's window and stuck to the glass. The door opened and the shopkeeper came out.

She thought he would be mad about the gum, but he didn't seem to have noticed it. He said something to her in French and began to lock the door behind him. He lifted an old knapsack onto his back and nodded again to Magdalena, then started walking up the street.

Magdalena looked back at the window. She couldn't read the words on the note the shopkeeper had left, but at the bottom he'd drawn a shell shaped like a Chinese fan. The shopkeeper was only a few steps away. He was old, but the boots he was wearing were strong and he had a long staff to lean on as he walked. Magdalena remembered what Neil had said about the pilgrims leaving Paris around that time of year.

"Excuse me," she called after him. "Please tell me—what is this saint from the window?" The shopkeeper stopped and looked at her, not understanding.

"Very sorry, but English, not," he said.

Magdalena tried again. "This little man," she said, pointing back at the window. "With shells?" She cupped her hand along her arms. She tried to remember the name Neil had told her. "Saint Jack?" she asked.

"Ah *oui*. But no for sale," the man said.

"Okay," Magdalena said. "But where? Where is this happening?"

"No for sale," the man said.

"I want to go there," Magdalena said.

The man shrugged. "Very sorry," he said.

In Magdalena's wallet, behind the thirty euros and some expired top-up cards, was the piece of paper the woman at the yellow church in Swindon had given her, with the outline of a scallop shell stamped in pink ink. She took it out and showed it to the man.

"Ah, Compostelle," he said.

"Yes?" Magdalena said.

"Okay," the man said, and he pointed down the street. "*Venez.*" He motioned for Magdalena to follow him, and seeing her heavy suitcase with its one wheel he shook his head.

"*C'est mieux comme ça,*" he said, pointing to the old sack on his back and tapping his walking stick against the boots he was wearing. He looked at Magdalena's sandals and shook his head again. He turned back to the shop, unlocked the door, and went in. He came back out in a moment with a package of rubber insoles and a roll of tape. He handed them to Magdalena, nodding toward her feet. "You come," he said. She adjusted the shoebox under her arm and followed him down the street.

After only a block or two they stopped next to a construction site. "Okay," the man said. He looked around. A group of people had formed around a backhoe at one corner of the lot. As they got closer Magdalena saw five or six nuns in hiking boots filling water bottles from a big jug, and several older couples with backpacks and matching parkas. "To Compostelle," the old man said. "*Pèlerins.*" He held out his arm and walked his first two fingers through the air.

"We go by feet?" Magdalena asked. The old man didn't say anything, but his fingers were still walking. He held up six fingers, shrugged, then held up seven.

"Weeks," he said.

"Okay," Magdalena said.

She took the miniature bow and arrow from Neil's father out of Lina's suitcase and put them in her purse, along with the rubber soles the man had given her and anything else that would fit. She tied a jacket around her waist, then shoved the suitcase under the fence, next to a shed full of construction equipment. She was so used to life without her glasses that it was only then that she thought to look up. It might have been Neil's tower above them, or it might have been another place covered over with white boards and scaffolding. She used some of the tape from the shopkeeper to close the shoebox tight and tied a pair of shoelaces together to make a loop so she could carry it over her shoulder. The nuns looked at their watches, and church bells chimed.

"Okay," the old man said to her. "We go."

{RICHARD}

Paris, June

WHEN I'D FINISHED with the microfilm, satisfied that the French newspapers hadn't covered Inga Beart's loss of her eyes in any greater detail than the papers had back home, I left the library and walked back along the river. It would be evening soon and all up and down the banks of the Seine young people were sitting in groups, tearing off pieces of bread, and passing bottles of wine because no one had thought of bringing paper cups. I might have felt disappointed at what I hadn't found except that I'd never seen a crowd so lovely, clinging like that to the edges of the river, dangling their bare feet out over the water and stretching their toes toward the night.

I imagined my son in with all those young people, leaning on the shoulder of a girl with a ring in her lip or tossing a bit of bread to the ducks. He has the kind of courage I never had, going off to school half a world away. When I was his age there were unspoken boundaries; people didn't think to do those sorts of things. But the rules that were unspoken by my generation went unheard by his, and it turns out that a boy from our little town can go off to college anywhere he likes and learn the things that would make him fit right in among the city kids toasting the sunset in London or New York or Hong Kong or Paris.

I could see my church tower wrapped in scaffolding on the other side of the river and I walked toward it, knowing my hotel was just behind and to the right. According to my map, there was Notre Dame in front of me, and I thought I might go in and have a look, but music drew me back along behind it. I listened to an accordion player, and when the song was done I gave him some money and walked on. At one end of the bridge a man was making a puppet dance while he played the harmonica without any hands, and at the other end a little group had gathered around a young fellow singing "Bye Bye Miss American Pie." When he didn't know the words he filled them in with "wa wa wa-wa wa wa wa-wa whiskey and rye . . ." and the crowd just loved it.

As a little boy Neil and his cousins used to like to jump off the haystack in the barn down at the ranch. Pearl's kids would hurl themselves off, so certain that I'd catch them. And I'd brace myself, calling out, "Ready! Set!" with more confidence than I really had, watching their little bodies fly over the edge and praying to God I would. Neil always faltered for a moment. He would start to jump, my heart would tumble, then he'd stop and start all over. But he always jumped, hollering all the way down, then he'd race Carly and the twins up the ladder to do it again. I ought to give his mother a call, I thought, find out where I can reach him now that his classes are finished for the summer. I don't like to be a bother, but I was remembering Neil as a child, a tiny missile hurtling off the haystack and into my arms back when things were no more complicated than that. I imagined how surprised he'd be to hear from me. "You're in Paris??" he would say, not believing. "Sure," I'd say. "Beautiful city." I would have done it too—they sell prepaid calling cards in the tourist shops—but I remembered our last conversation. I figured I'd wait until I had something to show for my being there.

My landmark disappeared as I went down one street, then re-appeared not exactly in the direction I'd expected. The sunset lit up the windows of the buildings around me with such an orange that each one looked like it was burning on the inside.

I was nearly back to my hotel when I found myself on the same narrow street I'd taken my first morning in Paris. I went along until I came to the shoe repair shop again, and I half-expected to see the girl with the suitcase still standing out in front. But this time the street was empty.

I stopped for a moment to take a closer look at the miniatures in the window. The owner was clearly a religious man: There were little saints and scenes from Scripture along with the crusading knights I'd noticed earlier, all of it made out of scraps of shoe leather and bits of old tools. Sharp tacks found use in a crucifixion scene, and beside the workbench I recognized the guests at the Last Supper, carved out of blocks of saddle soap. The fellow was quite a craftsman; he'd managed delicate expressions with a few twists of an awl in soft wax. *Good hands*, my Aunt Cat would have said. She had them too, fingers that understood pressure and give and suited their strength to the task. She could wring the neck of an old chicken with a quick snap of her wrist or splice the tiny wires of a toy locomotive, and a pinch on the ear hurt just exactly as much as she meant it to.

I got my share of spankings from those hands, but I have my fond memories too, and these came back to me with unusual clarity as I stood in front of the cobbler's window. I remembered how my Aunt Cat used to scoop finger-fulls of something called Chap-Chap Balm for Irritated Udders out of a giant jar she'd brought from the old Beart family dairy, its label gone translucent with grease. Each night before bed she'd coat her hands with it, wrap them up in dishcloths, and sleep like that, and for all they did, my Aunt Cat's hands stayed smooth. I remembered when that case of scarlet fever landed me in a big city hospital, how all through the days or weeks of quarantine in a tiny room that seemed to list from side to side, its round little windows looking at me like animal eyes, the only points of solidness as the whole world tilted and lurched were my Aunt Cat's cool hands cupping my cheeks.

I wasn't the only one who noticed those hands. I recognized them the first time I came across the character of Verna in Inga Beart's last novel. A dairyman's daughter with braids down her back and fine-work hands; she takes a cactus spine out of the barn cat's paw and wins a yellow ribbon for her needlework. She appears later in the novel, briefly, as the mother of a boy and girl, a hardworking rancher's wife who takes care of her hands, as if she's saving them for something.

The biographers say Inga Beart never came back to see her sister or anyone else after she left home at the age of seventeen. But the portrait of Verna, fingers still quick and supple as she grows into a woman of steely middle age, so resembles my Aunt Cat that even if I didn't have my own memory of that day under the table I'd still be certain Inga Beart visited her sister later in life. And in any case, there is a needle-work ribbon—yellow for grand champion, going yellower with age— hanging above the telephone back home, in the frame it's been in since my Aunt Cat won it at the county fair in 1939, three years after Inga Beart left her parents' home for good and ran off with her Hungarian.

Next to the apostles in the window a little Madonna held the baby Jesus wrapped in moleskin in her arms. After all the walking I'd done that day I could feel the heat of a blister-to-be on my foot. A square of moleskin was exactly what I needed. But by then it was getting late and the shop was dark. I leaned in to see if anyone was still inside, and when I cupped my hands against the window to block the glare my palm stuck to the glass. Someone had left their chewing gum. The gum had gone stringy in the heat of the afternoon and when I pulled my hand away a sticky thread stretched between my palm and the shop window, then broke and reattached itself to the glass. Having taught the middle grades for so many years I've found plenty of chewing gum in unwanted places. I got out my handkerchief and cleaned it off as best I could.

It took some doing, and I may have only made things worse. A man had come out of a shop across the street and was standing in the doorway, watching me while he filled his pipe. In another moment he started toward me.

"The proprietor is away," he said, nodding to the shoe repair shop. I shouldn't have been surprised that he spoke to me in English; I must have looked like Yankee Doodle in my old sun hat and the gym shoes I'd brought for walking in.

"I see," I said.

The man didn't seem concerned by the smudges on the window, because he said, "If you have left something to be repaired, I have the possibility to go into the shop and take it for you. I keep a key."

"Oh, well thank you," I said. "I was only going to ask about something for a blister."

"Ah, then perhaps they will help you at the pharmacy. The owner, it will be some weeks until he returns."

"Is he a friend of yours?" I asked.

"Well, we are here day by day, the same street, which is not so full of people, as you see, and so we talk to one another. I watch his shop while he takes his lunch, and sometimes he watches mine." And then, as if he had just noticed that my handkerchief was stuck to my fingers and there was still a gob of gum on the glass, he said, "Ah, this again. I find it happens on my windows too. The children, they pass just here on their way to school."

"A bit of some kind of oil would do the trick," I said. "I used to teach school, and I always kept a bottle of oil soap in my desk. It takes chewing gum right off."

"Mm, yes, I may have something," the man said. "One moment." He crossed the street and went into a small art gallery I hadn't noticed before. After a minute he came back out, carrying a box filled with tubes of paint.

"You're an artist?" I asked.

"No, no," he said. He shrugged in the direction of the gallery and gave a little laugh. "I hope you will say nothing to my clients, but these days it is very difficult to find at once an artist and a master of technique. And so I keep a few things—" He dug around in the box until he found a can of painter's oil and handed it to me. "This I use for fattening the paints. One never knows when one will be required to adjust the perspective, to add a spot of color that must be there."

My handkerchief was ruined anyway, so I used it to daub some oil on the window. I let it sit for a moment. The man gave me a palette knife and I scraped the glass as gently as I could. The oil did the trick, the gum came off. I did my best to wipe the window clean.

"Bravo," the man said. "I will try this myself the next time. You say you are a schoolteacher?"

"Retired," I said. I didn't want to discuss it, so I said, "I was admiring these little figures in the window."

"Ah yes. Well, the owner, he is a funny sort. Every year he makes a *pèlerinage*, a trip for the purposes of religious devotion, to visit the bones of, I believe, this one here—" The man pointed inside to one of the little figures. "He has to walk to the very end of land, as they call it, which is in the north of Spain."

"My goodness," I said.

"Yes, he does this every year in June, and every year I would say it takes some weeks. And when he comes back he has got sore feet and he has missed the customers like yourself. But he has been going now for many years. He tells me there was a time when all the men of his profession were quite devoted to this saint, who made such business for the shoemakers. People would walk great distances to make a visit to his tomb, and when they did, they must have boots. For many centuries the travelers to this site, they have left from just there—" he pointed over the rooftops to the same tower I'd been using as a landmark. "It is the tower of Saint Jacques. Saint James, I believe you say in English."

"I can see why they chose that tower," I said. "I noticed it the first morning I was here. It's been keeping me from getting lost, my hotel is just on the other side."

"Yes, but they are making improvements now, it is covered over. I think you must return when they have finished, they say it will look very nice."

"I'd sure like to see it," I said.

"Yes, and this is important, I think, for it was in a bad state since years and years. Pieces of it would come crashing onto the street, and there were several deaths among the people below. In fact, I have a very personal link to this reconstruction, because my own mother was hit by a stone that fell from this tower, and it is a true miracle that she was not killed instantly on the place where she stood."

"When was that?" I asked.

"Long ago. It is already quite some years since they began to cover it to protect the pedestrians."

I'm afraid I was smiling. It hardly suited the story I was being told, but I couldn't help it. In a flash I saw myself rapping on the door of Carter Bristol's window office at the university where he teaches, saying, "Well, Carter, you got it wrong." I imagined myself personally supervising the sewing of the addendum he would have to write into the spine of each of my mother's biographies. But I was getting ahead of myself.

"Do you remember what year it happened in?" I asked.

"I think it was '99, though perhaps before, when they put a sort of net around it. But if you are interested the city has put a sign saying the length of these renovations."

"I mean your mother's accident," I said.

"Ah," he said. "Well, it would have had to be many years earlier. Yes, I was just a child. My father was always agitating for the *mairie* to do something about this tower."

"As early as 1953 or '54?" I said.

"It is possible," he said. "I'm afraid I cannot ask her. My mother passed away not long ago."

"I'm sorry," I said. "I'm very sorry to hear that."

"Yes, well, it had been expected. And still it is not the same. When your parents are gone—and my father died some years before—when both of them are gone, then you feel differently. Who is left to remember the first time I clapped my hands or stood *tout seul*? One begins to think about such things."

"Yes," I said, but I was thinking of the bricks falling from the tower of Saint Jacques.

"But we are of that age," he said.

"Yes," I said again, and thanked him for his help.

With the exception of a few short stories and a little bit of poetry, once Inga Beart got to Paris all she wrote were letters, mostly to a few close friends back in New York. Several of those letters are available in archival collections, and it's clear from reading them that in the months leading up to August 1954 Inga Beart was losing her grip on reality. She spent whole pages listing mundane events in the lives of unnamed characters, as if the letters served as a reservoir for an excess of words she no longer had the strength to organize into novels.

But when Carter Bristol was writing his biography of my mother, he apparently discovered in the files of that Parisian comtesse several letters that scholars hadn't seen before. In one, Inga Beart seems to be sketching the outline for a character based on her neighborhood druggist. According to Bristol's book, the letter went like this: *"Have been studying the apothecary's assistant, seems he'll be crushed by rocks falling out of the sky. So you see? The French is coming along. Must admit I had to take him home with me for a glass of pernod . . ."*

The letter is dated July 18, 1954, placing it among the last things she ever wrote. The tone is rushed, as if she'd dashed it off without stopping to think, and none of it makes much sense.

But Carter Bristol claims that this letter and others like it exhibit the same emotional detachment one finds in the writing samples of the criminally insane. He tells us that Inga Beart had come to believe she had the ability to actually shape the lives—and deaths—of the people she used for her characters. It was a grandiose delusion typical of the sociopathic personality: She thought she could make the sky itself fall in on the unfortunate druggist, just by power of suggestion.

In fact, Inga Beart's entire body of work was coercive, Bristol says. He has a whole chapter on a divorcée named Mary Hamlin whom Inga Beart met in New York. She is said to have been the model for the character of Anna-Lee: a woman who once worked at her father's roadside diner and who, years after the book was published, actually did end up swallowing a bottle of sleeping pills, just like Anna-Lee. What most people see as a tragic coincidence, Bristol takes as proof of my mother's power over her subjects: After reading her own life's story all the way through and watching Bette Davis play her in the movie version, the poor woman went ahead and lived it, just as Inga Beart had written.

Of course, I never knew most of the people who appeared as characters in my mother's books; the similarity between my Aunt Cat and Verna, the rancher's wife, is the only example I can speak to personally. But that one relatively minor character is enough to convince me that Bristol has got it all wrong. Inga Beart didn't prescribe events; she took her cues from what was already there. While I hid under the table absorbing the image of my mother's shoes, my mother would have had the chance to catalog a whole range of spot-on details about the life of the woman her older sister had become.

When I try to imagine things as they must have appeared to her as she sat in Aunt Cat's kitchen in 1951 or '52, I can see how my mother might have come up with a life for Verna that ended up being similar, in some ways, to Aunt Cat's. She would only have had to look out the window at the sloping pastures that were always hard to irrigate, the weeds just waiting for an opportunity along the edges of the field, to figure that, with the price of beef falling as the big cattle operations got bigger, the ranch wasn't going to be able to support the five of us for long—the natural conclusion being that Aunt Cat, like her neighbors, like Verna, would have to get a job in town. In my mother's book there's a mention of Verna having found work at a dental surgery; my Aunt Cat began cleaning teeth for Dr. Braun in Walsenburg around the time I was finishing junior high. But there's nothing too odd about that; dental assistant was one of the few professions open to women of that era. When you take into account their shared manual dexterity, it seems logical enough that both the fictional Verna and my Aunt Cat wound up with their steady fingers effectively, if not always gently, scraping and polishing away the residue of so many Sunday candied hams, black coffee, chewing tobacco, and other enemies of rural tooth enamel. In any event, it's ridiculous to think of my Aunt Cat even subconsciously mimicking the life choices of a character in an Inga Beart novel; as far as I know, she never read a single published word her sister wrote.

But Bristol brushes these sorts of particulars aside and spends the rest of his book analyzing my mother's interviews, her relationships with men, even the things her teachers wrote about her in grade school, to come up with the idea that she had a near-complete inability to feel emotions of empathy, which run from pity all the way to love. She was unable to imagine the emotional lives of her characters, and so she borrowed—some say stole—the most intimate experiences of the people around her. It never troubled her that those details had been given in confidence; even the act of betrayal left her numb. And Carter Bristol knows all this because he has a Ph.D. in literature and another in abnormal psychology, because in her wedding pictures Inga Beart's eyes are looking just beyond each husband's head, because none of those husbands could even speak English very well, which, Bristol says, helped her put off a little longer their discovery that she could not feel, just like some people have no ear for music and others can't tell the difference between red and green.

He also dissects in a very scientific way Inga Beart's supposed lesbianism, and at the same time her penchant for men from far off places. He makes various guesses at my own paternity, and goes into all the other nasty details that keep a book like his on the bestseller list. He's even done some interviews on the morning television talk shows, and he always gives the same rueful chuckle, as if he wished it were not his duty to inform the public of the most shocking aspects of my mother's private life, then launches into the kind of head-shrink mumbo jumbo that puts one off one's breakfast.

Unfortunately, people watch those shows, and Bristol's book really has changed the way the world sees Inga Beart. I suppose I shouldn't mind so much, because her book sales have actually increased since his biography was published, and I get a one-eighth share. It comes to quite a sum now that it seems everybody wants to reread her novels, looking for signs of a sociopathic personality.

But I do mind. For all she wasn't, Inga Beart was my mother. I might be able to dismiss Carter Bristol's interpretation of her life as just another fad the professor types have to make up to keep themselves relevant, if he hadn't been so smug and short with me the time we spoke. Bristol never once tried to contact me himself, which is surprising, considering that his book mentions me more than any of the other biographies. But unlike the other recent biographers, who called me up for at least a cursory spell check of Aunt Cat's married name and so on, I didn't even know Bristol was writing the book until I saw it on the New Arrivals shelf at our local library. And by then of course it was too late.

It wasn't the scandalous bits I objected to. For what it's worth, I think Bristol may be right when he says it's time to do away with the cult that sprang up around Inga Beart after she ended the way she did. And while most of us would prefer that the more intimate details of our mothers' private lives not be splashed around like that, I can understand and even appreciate the public's curiosity. After all, Inga Beart wasn't always considered a hallowed figure by the literary world. During her lifetime she was just another public personality, whose exploits were more often than not discussed in the tabloids in unflattering terms. No matter how I feel about it personally, I can accept that it is time to make her human once again.

What I cannot accept is inaccuracies, particularly where I am concerned. I played only a small role in Inga Beart's life, and no one, least of all me, is trying to deny that. But I was there. Why else would she have come back to see me, however briefly, before she went to France? Whatever was on her mind when she walked out of that Santa Fe hospital where I was born, she did not intend to leave me altogether, and this is crucial to disproving Bristol's theory that my mother lacked the normal spectrum of emotion, that she felt none of the shades of love, regret, and loneliness so familiar to her characters.

But when I called Bristol up to tell him the short list of what his book got wrong, he wouldn't even talk to me. I tried to be reasonable. I told him, "You know best about the New York years, and you know best about Paris. I'm no psychologist," I said, "but I thought you'd like to know that she did visit me once, so it's not like you said."

I wanted to tell him about the shoes, how I remember them, but he cut me off with something like, "Well, you're on your own on that one." And then, as if he were trying to spare my feelings, he said, "She never went back to Colorado, alright? She never set foot there again. It's a fact."

"You're a shrink," I said. "What do you know about facts?"

"I know this is hard for you," he said.

"What about Verna and the needlework ribbon?" I said. "My aunt, Catherine Hurley, really won one of those, did you know that?— Huerfano County Fair Grand Champion, 1939—and my mother left home in '36. She must have seen it when she visited—how else could she have known?" I would have told him about the smoothness of my Aunt Cat's hands, how her fingers were delicate and cool, like Verna's.

"I'm not interested in arguing with you," Bristol said. "I think I've made it clear that there are some unanswered questions. No denying that. But Inga never went back to see the family—your aunt said so herself in her interview with the PEN Foundation. I believe you'll find the exact citation in my book."

I tried again to tell him. "Her red shoes," I said. "I saw them, I promise you, when I was just a kid. She came to visit, it must have been in '51 or '52, before she went to Paris. I was under the table, I saw them right up close. They had a double strap that fastened at the ankle, a second crease on the strap at the third hole." The call was costing me a fortune, he's off in England after all, but I hardly cared. "How could I remember those shoes if she hadn't come to see me?"

"Look, I really don't have time for this," he said. "If you have concerns about the book, you can address them to my publisher, and otherwise I'll thank you not to call my office again."

I didn't stand a chance with the publisher and he knew it. A high school language arts teacher on early retirement, against Dr. Carter Bristol, professor of literary psychology at one of those schools where they wear the hoods. But. That was before I knew that Inga Beart's letter about the druggist was not necessarily the product of a depraved imagination that Bristol made it out to be; that Parisians in the 1950s sometimes did get hit by falling rocks. Just that little hole in Bristol's theory made me feel that I was onto something. I pictured my Aunt Cat, holding up a hand-knit mitten, looking for the place where one of us kids had snagged it on barbed wire. In my mind she was wetting the frayed ends of the yarn between her lips, knotting them together again, reminding me or Pearl or Eddie that the whole thing's just one thread and a little tear unravels everything.

{NEIL}

Paris, June

I T WAS THE final hour before the archives closed for the day. Everyone was bent at a sharper angle over their *fiches* and *dossiers* and old books supported on rolls of green velvet like frail kings, all of them leaning into the last minutes of the day. Usually Neil was one of them, waiting until the third announcement of closing time to put the documents back in their cartons and return them to the cross-eyed man in the gray smock at the counter. But that day, after seeing Magdalena off at Gare du Nord, Neil hadn't been able to get much done. He'd arranged his notes around him and put in his request for the monk's papers from the Saint-Jean-d'Angély abbey again, then started paging through a carton of documents about monastic communities in Rouen.

The problem was that Neil still had a little bit of Magdalena's friend's ashes under his fingernails, and it was making it hard to concentrate. The things he usually loved about the archives—like the way two old papers might be stuck together with a pin that was shaped differently from the pins of nowadays, or how a document might be dated according to the Revolutionary calendar, the fifth day of the month of Brumaire in the year III, for example—weren't holding his attention.

Neil looked through a bundle of papers and found a reference to a twelfth- or thirteenth-century document by the abbot of Vendôme, forbidding monks to go on pilgrimages and citing a decree by the pope that said the same thing. That was interesting, because it meant that the monk from Rouen was violating the pope's edict—or maybe he had a special dispensation—when he set off on the road to Spain. It was something to bring up at the next project meeting with Professor Piot. The personal motivations of medieval pilgrims was one of the themes they were considering for the Tour Saint-Jacques exhibition, and Professor Piot might like the idea of a rebellious monk, wriggling free of monastic life and setting off on an unsanctioned adventure. Neil turned to a new page of his notebook and wrote *Monk from Rouen— why?* And underneath it, *adventure?*

Neil had been a little sloppy in what he'd said to Magdalena at the station. The pilgrimage that left Paris from the Tour Saint-Jacques technically ended in the town of Santiago de Compostela, which meant "field of stars" and didn't sound as interesting as going all the way to Finisterre, the "end of the earth," like he'd told Magdalena—though there were some scholars who said that Finisterre, which was a bit farther west on the Spanish coast, had been the original destination. According to them, the symbol of the scallop came from the shells pilgrims collected there as a way to prove that they'd really been to the edge of the world. And the legend of the body of the saint washing ashore at Finisterre covered with scallop shells and surprisingly preserved was only one of the miracles associated with Saint Jacques— or James, as he was called in English. But it was an image Neil particularly liked because it seemed like the kind of miracle one could almost believe in. There were hundreds of miracle stories dating as far back as the tenth century, and Saint Jacques was generally credited with bringing people back from the dead and doing other things that, in Neil's opinion, only saddled the faithful with impossible hopes. But in that particular miracle story the saint's divinity served simply to keep his skin and eyeballs intact for the arrival at his burial place, and that was enough.

In fact, it was Neil's theory that stories like the one about the body covered in seashells—as opposed to the more standard miracles—had helped to make Saint Jacques's the most popular medieval pilgrimage after the ones to the holy cities of Rome and Jerusalem. Neil didn't have enough evidence yet to present his idea, but it seemed like the kind of thing Professor Piot himself might come up with. Neil could almost hear him describing to his students how the world might have looked to a pilgrim like the monk from Rouen, who couldn't raise his eyes to heaven as the church demanded without first seeing that the world around him was full to the pores with rot and disease. The image of a body held together in defiance of decomposition had attracted wanderers from all over Europe; it might have been enough to draw a monk away from his prayers. Neil opened his notebook and added *looking for miracles?* under *Monk from Rouen.*

He had just enough time to look up the actual edict from the Vendôme abbot forbidding pilgrimages in the *Patrologia Latina,* a collection of medieval texts that the archives staff kept in the reference room. But he could still remember the feeling of Magdalena's fingers brushing his forehead as they sat at the café table, and he was afraid that if he thought about anything else for too long the memory would fade. And when it did he would lose forever the exact sensation of her fingertips, the way she'd looked at him and smiled so that he'd felt his whole body change temperature, but hadn't been sure if it was to hot or cold. Neil put the papers back in their carton and gathered his notes.

Most days after he finished work, Neil liked to walk through the old streets near the archives where the buildings leaned in overhead on either side as if they had important things to say to one another that they didn't want the passersby to overhear. Then he usually got a beer and a bucket of peanuts at his *zinc,* which was the same divey bar with duct tape on the bar stools that Professor Piot had gone to when he was a research assistant at the National Archives, and where Neil and the bartender discussed, of all things, the shifting fortunes of the New York Yankees. The bartender, whose name was Émile, watched every single Yankees game when it came on at one in the morning while he was closing down the bar, which meant that Neil had to do actual research to keep up his end of the conversation. Neil's team was really the Rockies, but he couldn't bring himself to tell this to Émile, who thought that all Americans were from New York. They usually talked in French, and Neil, whose brain was already in knots after hours of translating administrative documents with archaic past tenses, had to contort his mind still further to figure out how you'd say *grounded out* and *deep fly ball.* Still, it was nice to talk to a real person after a day spent looking at bits of old parchment that no one else had bothered with for centuries.

But today Neil didn't feel like discussing Joba Chamberlain's string of perfect seventh innings, even though he'd read the AP story on his computer for just that purpose. He started walking toward the river, thinking he'd just go home, but the afternoon was so bright and his little apartment was so dark—it was student housing, literally in the shadow of the Sorbonne—and he hated the feeling of being shut up inside, having to turn on the light to read while the rest of the world was out in the sun.

He crossed the river behind Notre Dame and stopped to listen as a man with a beat-up guitar sang "Summer of '69" for a group of tourists. Radio stations were required to play a certain percentage of songs in French, but Neil had noticed that the street musicians in Paris generally stuck to the American classics, the same songs that were probably right then being played with half the right lyrics on sidewalks all over the world. *Wa-wa wa wa-wa-wa, I knew that wa-wa now or never, those were the best days of my life.* Professor Piot would have drawn some lesson from that about gaps in the historical record, pointing out that Radio France archived every single broadcast, but the buskers working for coins gave a much more accurate indication of popular tastes, and they were never recorded.

Neil turned around and went back across the river. The last thing he wanted to do was go home and sit around eating Pim's while his imagination followed Magdalena's bus as it got farther and farther away, wondering if the best days of his life were somehow already happening without him really noticing.

He walked down rue de Rivoli and decided he might as well have a look at the Tour Saint-Jacques. It was something he did less often than one might expect, considering he was spending his entire summer researching it. The restoration wouldn't be done for a month or two and the park around it was fenced off. Along the tower's southeast side a group of bums slept on the warmth of the metro grates at night and moved into the shade of a chestnut tree in the afternoons. They drank jugs of wine and read old paperbacks, rewrapped their swollen feet and fought each other, and Neil found them more interesting than the tower itself, which, still covered in scaffolding with its gargoyles poking out the top, reminded Neil of an old man with the sheets pulled up to his chin. Neil imagined making friends with the Saint-Jacques bums, finding out the things they knew about that spot that no one else did, like what happened underneath the grates, which dropped down at least three or four stories into the heart of the Châtelet metro station, or whether they thought it was ironic that Nicolas Flamel, a fourteenth-century alchemist famous for having discovered the secret to immortality, had been buried in their churchyard.

That day the bums were busy unpacking. A few of them were gathered around an old suitcase, taking out shirts and underwear that clearly did not belong to them. One tried to trade his socks for better ones, but they were too small. Another had found a rose in one of those plastic sheaths and was emptying a can of beer to use as a vase.

Neil walked around the fenced-off tower, looking up. At the top of each of the four corners of the belfry were statues of the *Tétramorphe*, the Four Evangelists as beasts: an angel for Saint Matthew, a lion for Mark, an eagle for John, and what was supposed to be a cow for Saint Luke but looked more like a dog—and in front of the eagle was Saint Jacques himself, a relatively modern addition to the tower. He held a pilgrim's staff and scallop shell, but his back was turned to Spain, as if he had already gotten what he'd gone there for and was on his way home.

It occurred to Neil that the Rouen monk's account of the pilgrimage was dated 1259, right around the time the cathedral of Saint Jacques in Compostela had begun granting indulgences, which were holy remits of sin written out on slips of paper excusing a pilgrim from some portion of the suffering he or she could expect in Purgatory.

It meant the monk had been traveling at a particularly interesting moment in the history of medieval Christianity. The age of miracles was nearly over. Religious authorities were recording fewer acts of divine intervention on earth and busying themselves instead with what lay beyond. By the mid-1200s they would have been developing the system of indulgences that led to a major increase in pilgrim traffic, as even the poorest peasants gathered what offerings they had and set out for far-off shrines, believing they could buy a lesser stay in Purgatory. Neil got out his notebook and made a note to check the date indulgences were first granted to pilgrims at Santiago de Compostela. Under *Monk from Rouen* he added *indulgences?* next to *looking for miracles?*

*

Back on the metro grate the bums were laughing. One of them had found a bra in the suitcase and was trying to put it on, but he was having trouble with the clasp. A jug of wine was in danger of being spilled. Neil headed toward them, wondering if he should use *tu* or *vous*. He decided the familiar sounded friendlier.

"Not your size?" he said.

"Go fuck yourself," the bum said, and down went the wine. Neil decided it was best to cross the street.

{RICHARD}

Paris, June

"AH, YES, YOU wrote some months ago," the archivist said as we sat down in her office at the appointed time. "Your mother was a friend of the Comtesse Lucette Labat-Poussin?"

"Well, no, not a friend," I said. I wondered how much the archivist knew about the comtesse. "An acquaintance, if that. She and my mother may have known each other socially."

The archivist looked at the page I'd marked in Bristol's book and typed something into her computer. "I see," she said, and if one of her eyebrows lifted higher than the other, it was very slight.

Lucette Labat-Poussin, heir to a copper fortune and comtesse by marriage, was something of a personality in her day. She was a generous patron and unpredictable lover, usually to the same people, and she openly preferred members of her own sex long before such things were done. Her attentions and her money went to dancers and actresses mostly, and though she took an interest in writers too, no one aside from Carter Bristol has ever suggested that one of them was Inga Beart.

I suppose Bristol is only taking his theory of my mother's psychosis to its logical conclusion when he claims that Inga Beart's final act of self-destruction was in fact aimed at destroying someone else. He's done quite a job of gumming up history to make the comtesse play the part, claiming that what Inga Beart did to herself was meant to hurt the comtesse most of all. In my view, there is little evidence to support the idea that Lucette Labat-Poussin and Inga Beart even knew each other very well, let alone that they had the kind of passionate clandestine affair Bristol describes. In all my research I've found their names mentioned together just a handful of times, usually as guests at the same party, and Inga Beart didn't seem to benefit from the kind of financial support that generally accompanied the comtesse's affections. No other biography of Inga Beart contains more than a passing reference to Labat-Poussin, but this hardly troubled Bristol. According to him, if their relationship was more successfully kept secret than the comtesse's other exploits, it was only because she was at that time entangled with at least two other younger women and took some pains not to offend a sense of propriety among her society friends.

The archivist handed Bristol's book back to me and wrote out a card with the call number for the comtesse's papers. Before I'd had a chance to ask about the medical records from the Hôtel-Dieu hospital, she was motioning for me to follow her out of her office. Clearly our meeting was over.

The archivist pointed me to the main reading room, where I gave my form to the man at the requests counter, then waited until he called my number. The comtesse's papers were in a cardboard box tied up with strings; almost certainly Carter Bristol had been the last to knot them in a little bow. Inside there was a pile of typewritten papers, some handwritten letters of odd sizes, and a stack of photographs. Naturally I looked at the photographs first. Many were of the Comtesse Labat-Poussin as a young woman.

In his book Bristol explains the supposed relationship between them as one of nostalgia on the part of the comtesse, who saw in Inga Beart a measure of the loveliness she herself had nearly attained in her youth. I had to agree with Bristol that in some of the pictures Lucette Labat-Poussin kept of her young self she does look a bit like my mother, though the resemblance is mostly superficial, in the hairline and the shape of the face. Her light eyes, though similar, are flat and direct, nothing like my mother's, which from her earliest school pictures appear as twin wells reflecting a colorless sky at their depths.

The comtesse apparently told someone that they had been mistaken for sisters, and it was because of this physical resemblance, Bristol says, that Lucette took an interest in Inga Beart when she arrived in Paris. As a sort of vanity project she tried to stem the psychological as well as physical damage Inga Beart seemed intent on doing to herself with a combination of morphine, barbiturates, and bacchanalian soirées. But, according to Bristol, by the summer of 1954 Inga Beart's mania had progressed to the paranoiac stage. She was afraid that the comtesse was getting too close, and so she ended the affair in the most effective way she could. By blinding herself she destroyed the very likeness the older woman was trying to preserve.

Of course these are only Bristol's conjectures. Nowhere in all of Inga Beart's correspondence, in gossip columns, or in the memoirs of their contemporaries is there a single mention of the two of them being seen together outside of social settings. Even on August 10, 1954, no one ever swore to anything. In essence, Bristol has based his entire claim on a bystander's account that a dark-haired woman who matched the comtesse's general description was seen bringing Inga Beart to the Hôtel-Dieu hospital the day she lost her eyes.

Still, I'd assumed that Bristol was telling the truth when he wrote in his book that he'd found pictures of my mother among the Labat-Poussin papers, and I was honestly surprised when I got to the end of the comtesse's stack of photographs without so much as a glimpse of Inga Beart. Most of the rest of the carton was taken up with drafts of the same type-written document—all in French—which seemed to be the comtesse's memoirs. I looked through it all carefully, scanning each page for my mother's name, but I never found it. There were no love letters, no mention of the druggist, the falling bricks, or the glass of Pernod. Dispirited, but madder than ever at Bristol for having so clearly fabricated a relationship between the two of them, I packed the carton up again and returned it to the counter, where a man in a heavy apron took it and scanned my card. I thanked him and turned to go, but he said something to me and, seeing that I didn't understand, he motioned for me to wait. So I waited and he came back with another carton.

"That's not for me," I said. "I only had the one." But the man didn't understand. He pushed the carton toward me and pointed to the card the archivist had given me.

"*Vingt-trois*," he said.

I shook my head. "No, I think you already gave me the right box," I said.

"*Vingt-trois*," he said again. He pointed to the carton I'd just returned. "*Un*," he said. He pointed to the new carton on the counter.

"*Deux.*" He pointed to the shelf behind the desk where more cartons were waiting. "*Trois, quatre, cinq, six, sept*, da, da, da, *vingt-deux, vingt-trois*," he said, and showed me a list of numbers on the card.

So I took the next carton of the Comtesse Labat-Poussin's papers. It was similar to the first; I couldn't find my mother anywhere. The third and fourth were just the same.

It was clear that the comtesse had been a much more prolific patron of the arts and letters than I had gathered from Bristol's book or from the research I'd been able to do on my own back home. There were dozens of folders labeled with the name of this or that project, and with the help of my little dictionary I got the sense that the comtesse had dabbled in all manner of things, from financing operettas to the rehabilitation of historic sites that had been destroyed during the war. She seemed to have saved everything—train tickets, programs from amateur theaters, letters written in smudged ink on hotel stationary, all of them in little packets bundled together and labeled in the same tilting script. Of course I couldn't understand most of it. I looked closely at all the photographs and the *to* and *from* lines on the letters, but there was no sign of Inga Beart.

I'd promised myself I would make it through carton number ten before I stopped for the day, but by the time I got to the sixth my eyes were having a hard time focusing. I still wanted to see the medical records, but the archivist I'd talked to that morning seemed to have gone home. It was just as well, I thought. I was tired and though I hadn't eaten anything since breakfast what should have been hunger was replaced by a kind of spinning feeling, the same mild vertigo I've experienced from time to time ever since that childhood case of scarlet fever locked me in a rocking delirium that the doctors said I was lucky to survive.

On my walk back to my hotel I turned again down the street with the shoe repair shop on it. The shop was still closed, but the man who had helped me clean the chewing gum was standing in front of his gallery, wiping his hands on a rag. I was hardly in the mood to talk, but I couldn't just walk by without saying hello. I remembered that

I'd made a note to find out more about his mother's injury; I wondered if there might be old newspaper reports about people being hit by bricks falling from the tower. It was hardly a subject to begin a conversation with, but he seemed to be in a talkative mood, asking me about my trip and what I thought of Paris, and it was easy enough to bring the subject around to family history, since after all that was the reason for my visit.

He seemed politely interested in my project, but before I could find out about the newspaper clippings he was telling me that he too made a hobby of historical research. He had collected a number of pieces of memorabilia from the SS *Hirondelle*, which, I soon learned, was a luxury ocean liner built in 1914, with a mural by Marc Chagall painted on the ceiling of the dining room and a resident ballet.

"It was not the biggest of the great ships, or the fastest, but for style, it was something incredible," he said. "There are stories—during the First World War it was made into a hospital ship. The dining room itself was used for this, and you can imagine the soldiers looking up from their cots to the chandelier—the Chagall, of course, was put in later, but the original chandelier was made with some six thousand pieces of crystal brought from Vienna. And these young men—from *Provence*, from the *Massif Central*—who would have seen nothing like it before or after, opened their eyes to this sight and believed they had passed over, you see, to heaven."

"Goodness," I said.

"Oh yes. The nurses had some trouble to convince them otherwise."

We were standing outside the gallery. "Come in, come in," he said. "Perhaps you would like some tea?"

"Thank you," I said.

He took me through to a little room at the back of the shop, where he quickly arranged a bit of plastic sheeting to cover a canvas in the corner, then cleared a small table for us. "Sit, sit," he said. He put water on to boil in an electric kettle and served me on an original *Hirondelle* tea service.

"Yes, a terrific vessel," he said. "A reinforced hull quite advanced for its time—it survived several U-boat attacks and was taken for use by the British navy during the Second World War. And then, after all this, one day in 1959 while the sun is shining and the sea is calm, it sank not far from the port of Southampton. The reasons are not entirely understood, even to this day. Sugar?" he said, offering me a spoon shaped like the forked tail of a songbird. "*Hirondelle*," he said. "I have forgotten this word in English. A delicate bird, she makes her nests in the eaves with bits of earth."

"Might be a swallow," I said. "I have them in my barn back home."

"Yes, yes," he said. "She has the weight of a handkerchief but she flies each autumn some ten thousand kilometers and returns with the spring. Lemon?" he asked. "I'm afraid I have no cream."

"I'm fine, thank you," I said.

There was paint underneath his fingernails and the room smelled faintly of turpentine. "I hope I'm not interrupting your work," I said.

The man gave a little laugh in the direction of the canvas in the corner. "No, no, this is nothing. Some small adjustments to the current exposition." He touched the corner of the plastic sheeting. "I try to be discreet."

"Of course," I said.

"A matter of perfecting the balance. The fellow I'm showing now, he has got such a very nice way with the light. But the subject, it slips from the eye." He nodded to the canvas. "This one here has been hanging for months. Such potential, and yet I watch the customers—they look to the frame, then to the ticket with the price, then to their watches. Then they are gone."

"So you're repainting it?" I asked.

"Repainting, no, never this. I allow to be seen what was there before. Minimal rearrangements, nothing beyond the small correction of a line." When I didn't say anything he said, "You will understand, I'm sure. In our professions—you say you are a schoolteacher? What material do you teach?"

"English," I said. "The middle grades."

"Yes, yes, of course. So you will understand exactly. When one sees such possibility, hasn't one a duty?"

"I'm not sure what you mean," I said.

"To develop the potential. Of a painting, a student. One must give what one has."

I had to smile at that. "I'm not sure my former employers would agree," I said.

"Oh?"

"I'm retired," I said. "The circumstances were, well, they were not what I'd expected. It was that," I said, nodding toward the plastic sheeting. "Developing potential. But the school board didn't see it that way."

"Oh?" he said again.

I shrugged, wishing I hadn't said anything at all. "That sort of thing can be misunderstood."

He nodded. "Well, yes, for a schoolteacher there are always difficulties, I'm sure. An underappreciated profession. And the children now, one hears they can be quite difficult to manage."

"Oh, no, not really," I said. "I enjoyed teaching. Kids that age, like you say—there's so much potential. There was one student in particular, I took an interest. We got to be quite close."

The man took a sip of tea. "Ah," he said, and he looked at me closely. "A young lady?"

"I'm sorry?"

"Well, certainly, these things can happen. And between a teacher and a student, quite common I'm sure."

"No, no," I said. "It was nothing like that."

"No, of course," the man said.

He took another sip of tea. I took one too and burned my mouth. More than anything I wanted to stand up and walk out of his shop, hurry back to my hotel room and close the blinds, put my mind on my files and documents and a cold glass of milk, maybe a ham sandwich too. But the gallery owner was refilling my cup, edging a bowl of sugar cubes politely in my direction. His interest was familiar—I got plenty of that sort of thing during the school board hearing: the curiosity of people who've already made up their minds. I set my tea cup down hard on its saucer, then remembered that I was his guest, that he'd been awfully nice to invite me in. "I'm sorry," I said. I ran my finger around the underside of the cup, afraid I'd chipped it.

The man waved his hand. "Very high quality ceramic, made to endure the storms at sea."

"It's just that everyone thought the same thing. About the girl."

The man set his own cup down. "I apologize. These things, it isn't necessary to discuss."

"No, it's all right," I said. "To be honest, no one even asks about it anymore."

The man and I sat without saying anything. He looked down at his cup, and I remembered the ugliest stretch of that conversation with Pearl and Eddie out behind the post office. "You're an embarrassment to us," Pearl had said. "Eddie's lost business because of you, did you know that?"

"Jesus, Pearl," Eddie said.

"Jerry Deitch got someone else to do his deck, you told me that," Pearl said. When Eddie didn't say anything she turned to me. "His daughters were in your class. He said if he'd known he would have pulled them out of school."

It's not what you think, I might have said. *There's been a mistake.* But it was all still so fresh—it wasn't even clear, at the time of that conversation, that I wouldn't be teaching again the next fall, and I had my reasons for keeping quiet. The gallery owner put more water on to boil, and I thought about how many times in the years since then I've told the whole thing through to a sympathetic audience all in my own head—the flesh-and-blood people who might have been interested having long ago stopped asking.

"It was five or six years ago now," I told the man. "At the end of the semester I used to have my classes do a bit of fiction writing. And that year I had a very bright student. She'd shown some interest in my mother's work. My mother, like I said, was a writer. And so I assigned one of her short stories to the class—it wasn't what I usually did. What my mother wrote was always based on real people and actual events, and I told my students that I wanted them to do the same, write about something they knew, something they really understood, but give it the guise of fiction. Let those lines blur, I said, for the sake of a good story. In any case, when this particular student turned in her assignment, well, there were problems at home and she turned in a story about a girl who was being mistreated. You know. By a very close relative."

"I see," the man said.

"It was clear she wasn't making it up. It had to be taken seriously. I told her to come see me after class. It was the father, a very bad situation. I should have sensed it before. Maybe I did, but not to the extent."

"Mm, yes," the man said. "What does one do?"

"Well, I was in a difficult position," I said. "I handled it poorly."

I would have liked to have left it at that, but the man poured the rest of the tea into my cup and asked me to go on. So I did my best to explain. I told him I should have known that what this student needed most just then was someone she could trust to keep a secret. But after all those years of working with young people, I was still naive. "There are rules," I said to her. "I can't let this go."

I thought she was just upset when she threatened to bring me into it. "How come you like me so much, anyway?" she said. "You could get in trouble for that." I should have taken her seriously when she reminded me of how I'd patted her hand, given her a ride home once or twice, written something friendly in an old copy of *Mrs. Dalloway* I'd given her. "You're not supposed to do things like that," she said.

"I'm sorry," I said. "I didn't mean to make you uncomfortable. But that is not what we're talking about. I need you to see someone about what's been happening to you."

In the end she agreed to go to the school nurse. There were bruises on her arms. "And other places too," she said, and she showed me one on the inside of her leg. I knew the nurse would recognize right off what was happening. In return I promised that her family would never see what she'd written—a promise I have kept, despite it all.

A little bell sounded at the front of the gallery and the door chimed open and closed. "One moment," the gallery owner said. He went into the front room, saying something in French. "Tourists," he said when he sat down again. "They will not buy. Go on. The nurse."

"Well, I assumed things were being handled," I told him. "And then—it was strange. People started to stop talking when I walked into the room. At school, in the teachers' lounge. I didn't understand. But what she'd told the nurse—somehow the facts got rearranged. It was me, she said, *I* had done it. Of course at that point the school board got involved. I told them what she'd said to me, but by then it was too late. They said, 'Why didn't you report it immediately?' and I tried to explain, but the girl denied everything. And no wonder—they had a hearing, and the rules said the parents had to be present when she gave her side."

The man leaned back in his chair and puffed out a breath in an understanding kind of way, so I went on. I told him how the committee figured out pretty quickly that there were problems with her story, but by the time the family issues fully came to light, the school board had it in for me. There was talk of sexual improprieties and accusations of the kind of clumsy innuendo that, as a teacher of the language arts, especially offended me. They didn't like that I'd met with her outside of class or that we'd had a relationship based, I'd thought, on real affinity. I explained that I'd tried to be a friend, that I thought she needed one in a system that didn't know how to nurture a kid like her, but they couldn't understand that. All they cared about was whether I'd sat too close or touched her hair, imposing the school system's code of conduct like a grid over a simple human relationship. I was tired of having the things I'd thought were real and good turned rotten in the eyes of other people, and I told them so. And when I'd finished they looked at me coolly, and said, "You seem very upset." So I stopped trying to explain. "I didn't put a hand on her," I said, and for their purposes it was true enough. I finished out the semester and then I left without a fuss.

Through it all, I did my best to make sure no one outside of the old battle-axes on the school board found out that the girl had confessed to me, unbidden, the afternoon it all began. I've wondered since if it was the right decision, but at the time I had genuine concerns about her safety if the truth came out. Once our local paper got hold of the story I could have done myself some good if I'd shown a reporter a copy of what she'd written in her homework assignment. And it would have been easier for me to get a teaching job in another district if the gossip they printed up like it was news wasn't always followed by "*Richard*

Beart declined to be interviewed for this article." But there's nothing like the combined effect of a school board investigatory committee and a small-town newspaper to make a person feel like he's shouting at the wind. Whatever it cost me, keeping my end of our bargain seemed the least I could do to help protect that child from all that she was up against. And it was too bad. I'd taken an interest in her in the first place because I truly believed she had a gift. "You could be a great writer someday," I'd said to her, never guessing that her first successful work of fiction would be at my expense.

The gallery owner was quiet, and I sat for a moment, knowing my face was red and that I'd been talking too long. I remembered the ladies on the school board, listening with lips closed tight, sure that if they kept me talking long enough they'd catch me in a lie. And perhaps they had. I've learned by now that the truth is full of angles and refractions—and though everything I'd just told the man was true, it was also true that the school board hearing had left me with a kind of shame that was harder to bear than the public humiliation because it was entirely my own. I'd known from the beginning that the girl was troubled and I'd done nothing about it; I'd thought those troubles would be useful to her later on. I told her what they used to say about my mother, that she wrote to ease a sadness she could never quite explain.

The man drained his teacup and stood up. I wasn't sure from his expression what he thought of it all, and I half-expected him to tell me to get out of his shop. So I was surprised when he took a bottle down from the shelf and asked if I'd like a glass. I shook my head. "I really should be going," I said.

"Yes of course," the man said. He took my cup and saucer and nodded to my notebook, which I'd set on the table. "Best of luck with your research," he said.

"Thank you," I said. "And thank you for the tea."

"Not at all. I hope you will stop by again while you are here in Paris." He nodded toward the canvas in the corner. "Perhaps when the paint has dried. You can tell me what you think."

I thanked him again, saying I'd be sure to do that. I knew I ought to ask him to tell me more about his mother's accident, but I hardly wanted to prolong our conversation. As I left the shop I told myself I'd just have to live without the knowledge, because I was not going to make the mistake of going down that street again. I'd told the man more than I've ever told anyone back home. I wondered if every traveler had the same experience—if there was something about being a stranger to a place that made things better left inside one's own head want to heave themselves, uninvited, into the light.

{NEIL}

Paris, June

NEIL BALANCED HIS saucer on his knee, then thought better of it and set it on the table. He let Madame Piot carve him off a thick slice of foie gras. It came from the Piot family farm in Dordogne; Professor Piot's sister-in-law had tube-fed the goose by hand, which was something Neil would rather not have known. Madame Piot sniffed the foie gras, frowned, and laid the slice across a piece of bread on Neil's plate.

"Eat," she said. "It's going to go bad by tomorrow."

It was forbidden to discuss work at the Piots' Sunday afternoon teas. Something had given Professor Piot the idea to try to assimilate his research assistants into normal society by having them over to his house to speak French and eat unfamiliar foods off of china so thin it was nearly translucent and exposed each gap in conversation with a chorus of little clinks. Aside from Neil and Beth and Loren—Jean-Claude had made up some excuse about visiting a grandmother in Lyon—there were two rheumy-eyed Sorbonne kids who were doing the actual layout and text for the museum display on the Tour Saint-Jacques, and a German archaeology student who worked on the site. Madame Piot fluttered around them with an eagle eye for an empty plate or an emptyish glass, and everyone searched their brains for conversation topics that did not include the tower of the old church of Saint Jacques. "If it was written on calfskin or you found it under a rock, save it for Monday," Professor Piot announced at the beginning of each Sunday afternoon, laughing as if it were the first time he'd said it. So they bit their lips and wracked their brains, trying to think of some normal everyday thing to talk about, while all anyone was really interested in were the pearls they'd pried out of that week's research.

They ended up talking about whether the falafel was better in the fourth arrondissement or the fifth, and the relative merits of the Châtelet movie theater versus the one up by school, while Madame Piot quizzed them about cultural activities: Had they seen the light show at Saint-Paul? Wouldn't they like to see the absurdist play about nothing that had been playing in the same little theater for thirty years? Oh, definitely, they all agreed, all of them anxious for Monday, when they would cram themselves into Professor Piot's office and sift through their notes on the past week's discoveries, tacking and flattening time like a butterfly under glass. Historians are grave robbers, opening coffins and looking for jewels, Professor Piot had told them more than once, looking jolly and clapping his hands a little with delight at the thought of it. It was endearing until you realized that he was not necessarily speaking metaphorically. During Neil's first week in Paris Professor Piot had taken the team to the catacombs to see the bones that had originally been buried in the graveyard of the old church of Saint-Jacques-de-la-Boucherie. He'd been right in the middle of telling them all about how it had taken so many hundreds of midnight processions of carts draped in black to collect the thousands of bones from all over Paris, and everyone had been feeling eerie, imagining the noise all those carts of skeletons would have made across deserted cobbled streets. Priests had led the way, chanting the mass of the dead and swinging incense to cover the smell. Neil had been trying very hard not to step in the little puddles of water that had collected between the stacks of thigh bones and skulls, when all of a sudden Professor Piot paused, dug a tibia right out of the pile, and turned to them saying "*voilà!*"—to make some obscure point about nutrition during the Hundred Years' War.

But while Neil dreaded Sunday tea *chez Piot* as much as anyone else, it was a sign of how incurably uncool the whole group was that, for the first time in any social setting ever in his life, Neil found himself doing a lot of talking. This was his third Sunday at the Piots', and he was still the only one who'd ever had anything to say when Professor Piot asked them what *besides* research they had been up to that week. Even when he hadn't done something, Neil could think of an embarrassing personal experience to relate, if only to avoid one of Professor Piot's lengthy dissections of French politics—which he usually gave while his mouth was filled with some kind of jellied meat. Neil thought about telling the story of spilling Magdalena's friend's ashes in the train station, but he didn't feel up to it. He'd forgotten again what the word for ashes was, and it wasn't even all that funny. So he kept quiet and ate another slab of foie gras, trying his best to pretend it was cheese.

In the days since Tuesday, when Neil had seen Magdalena off at the station, he'd been feeling particularly distracted. He'd even skipped work at the archives, ostensibly to organize his notes, and ended up spending most of Friday wandering around the city. He kept replaying the meeting with Magdalena in his mind and giving it different endings. As often happened when Neil let his imagination go, the scene that he'd originally created as the most impossible of all had become his favorite, and his imagining of it had become so real that he could hardly believe that reality had failed to let it happen. A few days of intense daydreaming had closed the gap between fact and fantasy, not to the point that he believed it *had* happened, but that he believed it *might have* just as easily.

In Neil's reimagining the ashes still spilled, but in a way that was entirely not his fault—perhaps the feral offspring of the German tourists had done it. In this version Neil helped Magdalena sweep them up, delicately lifting bone fragments out from the cracks in the floor and comforting Magdalena with a tactful little joke about how her friend obviously wanted to spend some time in Paris.

Then, as they talked, and Magdalena looked at him with that intensity in her eyes, the really important part would happen. She would be looking at him, and then when she lifted her hand up to his temple she would leave it there a moment, maybe letting her fingers brush down along his jaw, and she would say, "Ni-yell, I am just really wanting to kiss you right now, okay?" It seemed so entirely possible it might have happened that way that Neil was having a hard time thinking of anything else. Her lips would be moist from all that crying and her mouth would taste like gum—as would his, thankfully—and they'd probably end it sort of laughing at themselves, not an awkward laugh at all, but a laugh that transcended all the obvious differences between them, like the fact that she was perfect and Neil had baby fat, that they thought thoughts in separate languages and had only moments before been strangers to one another.

Madame Piot interrupted Neil's dream, and Gare du Nord dissolved into the Piots' living room again.

"Neil, why so quiet?" Madame Piot said. "Have some Camembert."

"Okay," Neil said.

The problem was that he would never, ever see her again. She had gone back to Lithuania, and unless she actually sent him those sixty euros, which he was now feeling like a real jerk for not having just given to her outright, he would never hear from her again. He didn't even know her last name. He could ask his father, but that would mean he'd have to call his father, which would mean explaining about the Christmas presents, and that was definitely out. Why hadn't he asked for her e-mail? Her mother was opening a pizza shop, she'd said. How many pizza shops could there be in Lithuania? Neil let Madame Piot refill his glass. He saw how it would happen. The place would be filled—maybe it would be the grand opening. She'd be running around taking orders, her hair sort of messy around her face. He'd stand off to the side, having a drink at the bar until she had a spare moment. Then as she went by he would say, "Hi Magdalena." He would smile shyly but in a charming way, and she'd know right away that he'd come all this way to see her, just to make sure she'd made it on the bus okay. She'd push her hair up out of her eyes, worrying that she was sweaty or that there was tomato sauce on her shirt, but of course Neil wouldn't care at all. And she'd look at him just for an instant in that way she had. What would happen next wasn't very clear, but it hardly seemed to matter, and Neil was already refining the scene that hadn't happened at the train station to make it happen in the pizza restaurant, when he realized that all the others were carefully transferring the crumbs from their knees to the saucers of their teacups, Madame Piot was thanking them for saving the foie gras from being thrown away, and it was time to go.

The next day Neil presented his findings on thirteenth-century monastic pilgrims, but he had to stop in the middle of his sentence because he'd totally forgotten to finish his research. He hadn't checked the *Patrologia Latina* or found out when exactly the pope had forbidden monks to go on pilgrimages. He hadn't even gotten very far in his translation of the Rouen monk's own account, which was written in a strange Latin script that wasn't like anything Neil had studied in his paleography class. Afterward Professor Piot took him aside and asked Neil to meet him for a beer that afternoon after he finished work at the archives.

Neil was pretty sure Professor Piot was going to give him a lecture on how a historian must do a complete review of his sources before making any kind of statement of fact. This had happened to him once before, when he improperly cited something in his final paper for Professor Piot's Methods class in London. Neil knew he was being paranoid, but he also knew that Professor Piot wouldn't hesitate to replace a sloppy researcher, even right in the middle of a project.

"So?" Professor Piot said as Neil carefully slid over the duct-taped part of the seat at the bar across the street from the archives.

"I'm sorry about the meeting. I don't know what I was thinking," Neil said.

"No, no," Professor Piot said. "The meeting, who cares? But you? Everything is okay?"

Usually Professor Piot talked to Neil in French, working in a lot of nonintuitive colloquial expressions. The fact that he was using English now could mean any number of things, including that he no longer considered Neil worth the effort.

"I'm fine," Neil said. "I'm just, I don't know. There's this girl and— things could have turned out better. It's really not a big deal."

"Hm," Professor Piot said. "Maybe you're spending too much time in the archives?"

"No, really, not at all," Neil said. Before Professor Piot could say anything else Neil took out his notebook. "There's a lot more I want to find out about that monk—he started out in Rouen, but he's writing from Saint-Jean-d'Angély, so I think he's pretty sure to have gone through Paris. And if so, he might have stopped at the church of Saint-Jacques.

It's 1259, and, you know, there just aren't many first-person pilgrimage narratives from the mid-1200s."

Professor Piot didn't say anything, so Neil kept going. "I was even thinking we could feature him in the display, maybe talk about what motivated him to make the trip? It might be interesting because there was that decree forbidding monks from going on pilgrimages—I think it was Pope Urban II. I'm trying to figure out if the Rouen monk mentions getting any kind of special permission in his account. It's just the handwriting, I mean, the translation is taking me forever."

"Mmm, yes," Professor Piot said. "Look into all of it, very interesting. But take some time for yourself too. Call up this girl. Take her to the Bois de Vincennes."

"Okay," Neil said.

"You can rent rowboats there."

"Yeah, that sounds nice," Neil said. "Only, she's in Lithuania now. I mean, she took a bus. We got a coffee at the station and, I—I don't know. I think I kind of blew it."

"Oh?" Professor Piot said.

Neil didn't want to explain about the ashes, so he said, "You know. I sort of said all the wrong things."

"Ah," said Professor Piot. "Well, yes, this can happen."

They talked some more about the monk's papers. The problem wasn't the ink—in fact, the text from the 1200s was darker than the 1680 date on the colophon at the end, which explained that the papers had been salvaged after the Huguenots burned most of the Saint-Jean-d'Angély archives in 1568. The monk's manuscript itself was vellum, eight folio pages covered in tight Latin script. Neil couldn't read any of it. The penmanship was so perfectly uniform and the letters all finished with an odd downward stroke, so that nearly every one of them looked like a *q*. Professor Piot promised to get him a script key that might help. But the trick, he told Neil, was to forget everything he'd ever learned about the act of writing.

"Imagine instead how you would make your letters if you are writing with a piece of a feather on a very expensive parchment, and if you are a holy man, taught to write by holy men, and so on, you see?"

"Sort of," Neil said.

"You say the date is 1259? So this monk is writing in a Gothic hand I think, yes?"

"That's what it looks like," Neil said. "But there's something funny about the characters. There are these little, I don't know, *tails* trailing off at the bottoms of the letters. I'm not sure it was ornamental. It's more like he wasn't lifting his pen all the way up."

"Well, if you're right and he was on his way to Santiago, perhaps his arm was tired. These old manuscripts, so much is said inadvertently, if we know to see it."

"Well, the script is pretty formal," Neil said. He didn't want Professor Piot to think he was just being lazy. "It's basically a book hand, so I think he must have been trained as a scribe. But Gothic normally finishes with little upturned feet on the letters, right? And his keep flicking downward. I'm sure I'll figure it out. It's just, you know, finding how to start."

"It is often a question of changing one's perspective," Professor Piot said.

"Right," Neil said. He took a sip of his beer and thought about the eight pages of tiny loops and hooks that would be waiting for him again tomorrow at the archives. "Actually, sorry. I'm not really sure what you mean."

"When you yourself write, perhaps you think of making the letters to look distinct from one another, like they do in the newspaper. But this monk, it is some two hundred years before he will see a sheet from a printer's press. For him the page must be harmonious first, only then does he think of clarity for his reader."

Professor Piot dipped his finger in his beer and began to trace the alphabet across the table. "You live in the age of free will, you imagine that each of us may do what we like, independent of our circumstances. But this monk, he is a believer in the great narration. For him each act, each stroke on the page is part of a continuum. So? It is natural for him that a letter may be distorted by the letter next to it. A *t* for example, or very often an *r*, may change its shape depending on where it falls inside a word. This is true especially in the Gothic scripts, where the text was made to resemble the weaving of a tapestry. And a tapestry— it is not made of individual stitches, but of a single thread, you see?

Look at the page from this perspective and the meaning may become more clear."

Professor Piot ordered them each another beer.

"So this girl, she lives where, in Vilnius?" he asked, as if they'd been talking about her all along.

"Yeah, I guess," Neil said.

"This is a very beautiful city, very rich, historically, you know. Napoleon passed through Vilnius on the way to his great defeat. There is a small monument there. On the side you see when you are facing east, it says, 'Napoleon Bonaparte passed this way in 1812 with 400,000 men.' From the other direction it says, 'Napoleon passed this way in 1812 with 9,000 men.' In fact, many of them froze to death just outside the city gates. A terrible winter, 1812. But this time of year the climate in Vilnius is very nice."

"Have you been there?" Neil asked.

"Oh yes. I have one very good friend there, a professor at the university. Kazys Uzdavinys." Professor Piot signaled the bartender for the check. "He wrote a lovely paper on the dental findings from the bodies of the Napoleonic conscripts. I'm sure you can stay with him for a few days."

"In Vilnius?" Neil asked.

"Of course. Perhaps you would like to go and tell this girl what it was you wanted to say."

"Mm," Neil said, and he was going to explain how actually he didn't really know her very well, he didn't know where in Vilnius she lived, and that even if he did know, there was a major difference between imagining how things would go if he were to show up on her doorstep unannounced and actually doing it. But Professor Piot had got hold of one of his favorite subjects, which was advising his students to live lives of impractical adventure, and it was hard to get a word in.

"One must do such things, you know," Professor Piot was saying. "I myself once made such a completely crazy trip when I was about your age, to a far off wilderness called *Chicago*. And in the end it all was shit, but you know, if I had not done it, well, it wouldn't be a life, and that's the way it is. For the sake of those historians of the future we must live our lives today."

"I know, I know," Neil said.

"And we must make them interesting."

"I know," Neil said. Professor Piot said this a lot.

"You need some money for the ticket?"

"No, no," Neil said. "I mean, I'm not sure—"

"Take this," Professor Piot said, pushing more than several twenty-euro bills across the table. "You can give them back in August. In fact, while you are there I have one small errand in Vilnius for you to do."

So Neil found himself walking back to Professor Piot's office to check the departure times for the all-night bus to Vilnius, because Professor Piot insisted that if Neil waited until morning he would never go. Neil was trying to think of some way to get out of the whole thing without disappointing Professor Piot, when he remembered about the pizza restaurant. He could find her that way. Professor Piot took out his phone and started dialing, and before Neil could tell him it really wasn't necessary, Professor Piot was saying, "Kazys, old man!" and making all the arrangements. And while Professor Piot was talking, Neil remembered the light brush of Magdalena's fingers along the side of his face, the way she kept taking her glasses off when he looked at her.

Professor Piot hung up the phone. "Okay, so they will expect you," he said. "Fine people, Kazys and his wife, and as I remember they have a fold-out couch." He wrote down their address and told Neil he was giving him three days off work in exchange for tracking down a certain file at the Lithuanian archives.

"Something about the Tour Saint-Jacques?" Neil asked while Professor Piot searched through the sticky notes on his desk, looking for the number of the file.

"No, no," Professor Piot said. "This is a new project, one that came to me by way of a Jewish group here in Paris. They would like to learn more about a certain cemetery in Vilnius. An apartment complex is going up, and it appears that the spot was once an important burial place from the time when Vilnius was a great center for Jewish learning."

"What do you want me to look for?" Neil asked.

"A little thing. I'll go myself in the autumn, but while you are there you can get this—" he gave Neil a sticky note with numbers written on it "—at the Lithuanian State Historical Archives. I believe this is the founding document of the cemetery, a charter from the Polish king allowing the Jews the right to burials outside the city walls, but there has been some confusion about the date. Kazys has been promising for months he will check this for me, but then he goes abroad, and this and that. Frankly, I think there may be some politics involved. And Kazys—well, it can be a delicate subject. He may prefer to keep himself removed. Make sure you get photocopies."

"Of course," Neil said.

"Okay, so, give Kazys my regards," Professor Piot said. "And have a good time." He gave a big wink that Neil pretended not to see. Neil remembered too late that Professor Piot was not the most discreet person. By the next morning all the research assistants would probably have been told that Neil was off visiting his *petite amie* in Lithuania. But—who knew? By then it might be true.

{MAGDALENA}

Between Orléans and
Meung-sur-Loire, June

I T WAS SIX days since they'd left Paris. Already nearly all of
Magdalena's euros were gone, the shoelaces she'd been using to
carry the box with Lina's ashes had broken, and most of the skin on
her feet had been replaced by Band-Aids. Sometimes she and the others
walked from town to town on little paths through fields of vegetables
or in between planned forests of strange geometry, straight white
poplars and birch planted neatly row on row with vines strung drunk-
enly between them. Other times they walked single file along the
shoulder of the highway, where signs showed the towns still had French
names for considerable distances ahead. She tried to ask the old man
with the walking stick how far they were from Spain, but he couldn't
understand her, and neither could the nuns, who had started tearing off
the ends of their sandwiches and giving them to Magdalena when they
stopped for lunch.

Up till then Magdalena had kept her distance from the English
speakers in their group, preferring not to get too close to the familiar
words on arms and elbows and sunburned knees. But realizing that she
would need someone to split the price of a bunk with her at the next
hostel—either that or sleep outside—Magdalena let herself fall back
behind the group a bit to walk with Rachel, who, Magdalena had
noticed, also slipped pieces of bread into her pockets when they stayed
the night at a place with free breakfast.

Rachel had been born and would die in Clapham and, though she
claimed to be one of the pagans, she told anyone who would listen that
she was counting on the saint at the end of the road to wipe away the
particular sin of having started a son out in life with a heroin habit.

"What's the box for?" Rachel asked her as they walked.

"My friend," Magdalena said.

"Like a present?" Rachel said.

"No," Magdalena said.

"Yeah, all right," Rachel said, and for a while neither of them said anything.

Rachel seemed to have twice as much skin as everyone else. It swelled the space between the top of her shorts and the bottom of her tank top and stretched the leather cords of the pendants around her neck. All that skin had a number of sad things written on it, some of which Rachel told her in not quite the same versions as they walked, Rachel panting a little and wiping the sweat from her forehead with the loose insides of her arms, where Magdalena read *starving* on the left and *broken by Colin* with a date a year in the future on the right.

"Are you walking for penitence?" Rachel asked.

"I don't know," Magdalena said, because she didn't understand the word.

"I'm doing a cleansing," Rachel said. Rachel didn't believe in guilt, she said, or negative thinking. Magdalena nodded. They walked for a little while and then Rachel said, "And also for penitence, yeah. You know." Magdalena didn't say anything, but pretty soon Rachel was repeating the story that everyone, even the French nuns who couldn't understand, had already heard, about falling pregnant and how they'd taken her son away when he was born and put him in care. "He was in a bad way, shakes, you know, and problems with his lungs. You know?" She kept asking Magdalena if she knew. Magdalena nodded. He'd been born too small, too early, with a long list of poisons in his little veins that Rachel wore, in alphabetical order, down her arm. "I don't even know if he made out alright. They told me, you know, maybe he wouldn't." Still Magdalena didn't say anything, though she did know, the answer was set out clearly along Rachel's hairline, almost exactly where on Lina's face the word *apricots* had been.

That night she and Rachel split the cost of a bed at the hostel. The nuns brushed their teeth and Magdalena eased her feet out of her sandals and ran a needle and thread through each of her blisters, like her mother used to do when she got home from work, cutting the thread after every stitch so that the ends stuck out of the blister on either side. "What are you doing that for?" Rachel said.

"For letting the water out," Magdalena said. "So they don't get big. I can do for you too."

"Fuck no," Rachel said. "Trying to stay away from needles, yeah?"

Rachel watched Magdalena for a little while, then said, "Want me to read your Tarot?" Magdalena didn't know what she was talking about, but she said okay, and Rachel took a small wooden box wrapped in a blue silk scarf out of her backpack. "Blue is my aura," she said, and opened the box. She spread the scarf out on the bed and shuffled a deck of fortune-telling cards.

Some of the markets in Vilnius had gypsies or old Russian women who read fortunes, and once Lina and Magdalena had paid to have theirs told from a deck of cards with the corners all gone. Magdalena couldn't remember whose idea it had been, probably Lina's. They'd taken the money out of what Magdalena's mother had given them to buy vegetables, and her mother must have known what they'd done when they came home empty-handed except for a few cucumbers, flushed with conspiracy and awed by the images of blindfolded men with swords, lovers, the Hanged Man, and the Fool.

Rachel shuffled the cards and told Magdalena to cut them, then dealt a few face down in a semicircle on the blue scarf. She flipped them over one by one. Magdalena only half-listened, wondering why people who had a choice would want to know what was coming. She remembered the cards the gypsy woman had used, thick and oily from so many years of being stroked by dark fingers.

Magdalena and Lina had been too young then to care much about the future; they'd only wanted to find out if the boys they would marry were in their class at school, and Lina had asked the gypsy woman when her mother would be coming home. The woman caressed the cards with her fingertips as if she were coaxing Time to give the answer up, then said that for a question like that they would need to pay extra. Magdalena said no, but Lina made her give what was left of the vegetable money to the woman, who closed her eyes, turned over a final card, and let her fingers play across it. "She will come by this time next month," the woman said. Lina was so happy she ran all the way home, leaving Magdalena to hunt for a few spotted cucumbers that had been thrown away, so she'd have something to give her mother. But a month passed, then two and three, and still Ruta didn't come.

When Rachel had finished explaining Magdalena's cards to her, telling her she would find love and warning her to stay away from Virgos, Magdalena put her glasses on and asked if she could try. She shuffled the cards as Rachel had done and laid them out across the scarf.

Magdalena knew that Rachel had probably asked the cards a thousand times for news about her son, and she needed to make sure that this time Rachel believed them. So, as she turned the cards over, Magdalena scanned Rachel's face and neck for dates, picking out the ones that had already passed and looking for bits of information that Rachel would recognize. "You have one young sister I think," Magdalena said.

"It says that?" Rachel said.

"It's here," Magdalena said. "This card with the woman by the gate means sister. You have been taking care of her, I think, when you are a child."

"Yeah," Rachel said. "What else does it say?"

"You have some hard things in your life. You have some problems with health when you are young. Things with the heart."

"Where does it say that?" Rachel said.

"Oh, just there," Magdalena said, and when Rachel pressed her for how she knew how to read the cards so well, Magdalena told her a story about a grandmother who was a gypsy and had taught her all the old ways.

Magdalena turned over more cards until she found some that looked like they could mean what she wanted to say.

"And here and here in the pieces of money and this with the child on the horse, this is about your son."

"What does it say?" Rachel said.

"He is doing okay," Magdalena said.

"Yeah?" Rachel said.

"He will have brown eyes and draw you a picture."

"Yeah?" Rachel said again. "You're sure?"

"This is for sure," Magdalena said. "He lives with some nice people, you will see him some day." She didn't want to say too much more, so she turned over another card.

"But what about that?" Rachel said. The next card was the Devil.

"This one says only you have one not-so-good man in your life," Magdalena said.

"Is that supposed to be Andy, does it say?" Rachel asked, squinting at the figure on the card.

"Colin," Magdalena said, not thinking. Rachel looked at her strangely.

"How do you know about Colin?" she said.

Magdalena remembered the way the gypsy woman had spread her fingers over the cards, as if she were pulling meanings out through the paper. She had talked in a singing voice and wore a silver shawl over her clothes to hide the fact that she was just a poor woman selling stories. "All in the pictures," Magdalena said.

"Nobody knows about Colin," Rachel said, very quietly.

Magdalena laughed. "This is just for playing, okay?" But Rachel didn't laugh, so Magdalena said, "I am hearing you say this name Colin when you are dreaming or something in the night."

"That fuck," Rachel said. "I hope I didn't say too much."

"No, it's okay, no one else is even hearing I think," Magdalena said, and turned over a card with a picture of a woman kneeling at a stream, filling pots of water under the stars. She didn't dare read anything else off of Rachel, so she made one up. "You will be very lucky with business," she said. "You are going to make money like water."

The next morning the woman who'd slept in the bunk above theirs came over as Magdalena was making a replacement strap for her sandal out of a piece of Sellotape that Brit and Olaf, retirees from Norway, had given her. "I hear you give Tarot readings," the woman said.

"It was only for a game," Magdalena said.

"Your friend said you learned from your grandmother."

"Just some little things," Magdalena said.

"Do you have time?" the woman asked. "There's something I really need to know." Then she said, "Your friend said ten euros, right?" and Magdalena nodded. Rachel cleared them a place on a bench outside and spread the blue scarf out in front of Magdalena, then stood a little way back to watch. Magdalena set the cards out in the pattern Rachel had used the night before and flipped them face up one by one for the woman who, it turned out, was following the pilgrimage not to where the remains of the saint were buried, but to get to the shrine of a pre-Christian fertility goddess. The man she was traveling with had turned back, she told Magdalena. Should she go on without him? Magdalena had no idea. She could see no names or birthdates of children on the woman's face or shoulders or arms, but there was a wedding in the future, to a man whose name could only be Spanish, and on the woman's calf was a ledger of mortgage payments to be made on an apartment in Madrid.

Magdalena turned over more cards and pretended to study them. "I think you will find something new in Spain to make you happy," Magdalena said. The woman nodded but she didn't look like she believed it. "You will find love," Magdalena said.

"Mmm," the woman said. Dates of another marriage and a divorce from a man named Jim were written on her cheek. Along her jaw it said *A courthouse wedding, no white dress. He said the beach would be too expensive but really, he never liked the sand.*

"You are married before, but this is not working."

"That's right," the woman said, looking more interested.

"You have the dream of a marriage by the sea."

"Well, yes," the woman said. "A long time ago."

Magdalena tilted her head as if she were thinking and read *Level A2 instructor, Instituto Cervantes.* A list of verb conjugations wrapped around the woman's elbow. "You are a teacher for Spanish, right?"

"That's right," the woman said. Magdalena traced her finger across a card with a picture of a hand coming out of the sky, and leaned closer to read what was written along the woman's shoulder.

"And you have wanted to come to Spain to work, but this couldn't happen." The first husband had something to do with it, Magdalena read, but what exactly was buried in the woman's armpit.

"Yes, yes," the woman said.

"There is a new marriage for you, by the sea, and you will live in Spain, I think, with a man who is better than the first," Magdalena said, and gathered up the cards quickly, wondering if the woman would press her for details. But the woman was already taking some bills out of the pocket of her shorts. She added an extra five euros. "For the good news," she said.

That afternoon Rachel caught up with Magdalena as they walked and suggested that now might be the time to fulfill the money-making prophecy Magdalena had seen in Rachel's cards. Rachel would bring the customers and Magdalena would use what her gypsy grandmother had taught her to pay their way to Spain. Magdalena laughed at her at first, but that night when they stopped at an abbey where anyone with a stamp of a scallop shell from the previous town could stay for free, Rachel found her three more customers, all from a Swedish back-packing group, and told them the price was fifteen euros each. The words on their skin were all in Swedish, but Magdalena could pick out a few names and dates, and as it turned out, she didn't need to do much more than mention the name of a person or a place to make the back-packers look at each other and laugh, a little nervously. Then whatever Magdalena told them next—generalities about luck or love or a phrase she remembered from the gypsy woman in the market—would strike the person listening as truth, decoded from the pictures on the cards as if they were precise hieroglyphics only Magdalena could understand.

And so, after spending all her literate life trying to avoid seeing the things written on the people around her, Magdalena became, almost by accident, a professional fortune-teller. As they made their way toward Spain she started wearing her glasses all the time, not only because they let her walk faster but because she might pass someone resting along the way with their sleeves rolled up and certain details about their life exposed, and then meet that person at a pilgrims' hostel later on, when it was cool and everyone was wearing sweaters, and be asked to tell their fortune. She learned to mix stock fortune-telling phrases into her readings, finding that saying a thing like *"There is a man in your life, you aren't sure of his commitment"* or *"You are not quite satisfied in your profession"*—things that were always true—put her customers at ease, and more often than not, despite pressing her for details of the future, it was really the vaguer warnings and assurances they wanted to hear.

She made mistakes sometimes, or accidentally revealed information that even the cards weren't supposed to know. Once or twice in the beginning people made her put the deck away before she was finished and hurried off, looking at Magdalena oddly and crossing themselves. But as they went along she developed the techniques of a confidence man or a sideshow illusionist, deciding first what she was going to reveal to her customers and then asking them questions that came just close enough to the answers she wanted that they left impressed, not knowing how, exactly, but assuming that Magdalena was using some sort of subtle hypnosis or psychological sleight-of-hand.

Sometimes as she walked Magdalena wondered if any of the gypsy women in the markets had the problem of knowing more than was profitable. She'd tried for such a long time not to think too much about why she saw words where she did or if she was the only one. Knowing madness or worse might be hiding underneath questions that went too deep, Magdalena had always tiptoed through her own mind when she had to, and stayed out when she could. But maybe it was the way the road to Spain stretched in front of her until it narrowed to a pinprick and disappeared into blue, or the way fields and hills rose and fell for as far as she could see. Surrounded by so much space and sky Magdalena began letting go of her old habit of pinching off her thoughts before they could get away from her, and for the first time in a long time she let them roll all the way to their ends.

She thought about the things that made no sense: the Scottish nun they'd met whose skin was taken up entirely with the names of wild birds. Or a teacher she'd had in high school who had a recipe for buckwheat soup on her forehead. There was someone else, she couldn't remember who, whose skin was covered with a list of library books a lifetime long, and the dates that they were due. She remembered the man she'd met on the street in Paris, who'd sounded like an American but had an old saying that her mother liked written in Lithuanian across his face.

She thought about the words on her mother's skin, as familiar to Magdalena as the sound of her voice. Her mother had *Juozas*, the name of Magdalena's baby brother, on her arm, and *Rimantas*, the name of Magdalena's father, on her forehead—that was where, her mother had told her, her father had gotten flustered and kissed her, instead of on the lips, as they stood at the altar. The details of a gall bladder operation that her mother had had as a girl circled a scar on her stomach, and a patch of skin without a scar described a hysterectomy with minor complications. On the back of her mother's wrist was her favorite joke about the priest and the tailor, which made her laugh so much when she told it that she always skipped the best part, and her mother's thighs were wrapped in superstitions—*if you drop a comb be sure to step on it, never sleep in moonlight, a dream of brown bread means a happy home, a rabbit means life, a barking dog means death, the devil dances at weddings, never whistle indoors*—things she'd learned from Magdalena's great-grandmother, who, as an old woman, had saved her fingernail clippings in little bags, knowing she would need them to climb the icy mountain that in the old Lithuanian stories was the only way to Paradise.

But as they walked toward Spain there were days when the only thing that could take Magdalena's mind off her feet was to think about her father. Her mother hardly ever talked about him, and they'd never had anything to do with Magdalena's aunts and uncles and cousins on his side, who blamed Magdalena's mother for the things that had gone wrong. "You have his eyes," her mother sometimes said to her, and when Magdalena was young and her mother was sad, sometimes Magdalena would feel her way around the house, keeping them closed so her mother wouldn't be reminded of the man in the photographs, who had strong hands and a tired face and eyes as clear as glass.

"He thought about things too much," her mother said once. "He went around in circles in his mind, and after Juozas was born he couldn't take it anymore." Magdalena remembered that her mother had said "after Juozas was born," not "after Juozas died." The two things had happened on the same day, and it was possible that Magdalena's mother thought of the two events as one, or that she said it like that because she couldn't bring herself, still, after all the years, to say it the other way. But as she walked, Magdalena let herself wonder, out loud inside her own head for the first time, if it was possible that her father had stopped wanting to go on living when his son was born and he saw that there was just one date written on the baby's skin.

They walked through fields dense with tiny flowers that left streaks of pollen across their ankles. Rachel had fits of rasping sneezes— *hay fever* it said across the bridge of her nose—and Magdalena wondered if her father had ever guessed that there might be others like him. In London it had happened to her twice. Magdalena had seen them, or she might have—both times she'd tried so hard not to believe it that now she couldn't be sure. There had been a man with no shoes in a tube station who'd looked at her with eyes like mirrors in an empty room and smiled in recognition. The other time it was a child, a little boy she'd seen at an outdoor market in Islington whose pale gaze was all the more noticeable because his skin was dark. He'd been holding his mother's hand, watching the people pass by, mouthing the words.

They passed a market on the outskirts of a little town. The nuns bought a bucket of tomatoes and Rachel and Magdalena ate them like apples as they walked. Magdalena thought about how her father had died right around the time she learned the alphabet. She wondered if he'd ever taken her to a place crowded with people and watched to see if she moved her lips.

She thought about the list that began at the nape of her mother's neck and continued in small print all down her back, recording each drink she'd had in the days and weeks and months after Magdalena's father died. The last entry came just above her mother's pants line—it sometimes showed when she bent over and her shirt rode up—saying *3.2 liters Stumbras Vodka under birches*. Out of the whole world only Magdalena could possibly know it was a reference to the day when, having lost a baby and a husband, and then, if the log was right, 152 nights to Stumbras, Magdalena's mother had bundled Magdalena, age four, into her snowsuit, collected the bottles under her arm, and together they'd gone into the woods behind their old apartment building, where they unscrewed and dumped each one, holding their noses and watching the liquid burn little holes in the snow under a stand of birch trees, which, Magdalena's great-grandmother used to say, house the spirits of men who die too soon.

The roads were getting steeper. The Pyrenees, Olaf said. Brit told them to be sure they were drinking plenty of water. As they hiked up hillsides covered with olive groves, Magdalena listened to Rachel talk about her days doing junk, sleeping in doorways and robbing her mum, and it occurred to Magdalena that the things she'd gotten used to reading as her mother reached for a pan or changed her skirt or stretched out her toes to let the polish dry had something in common. They were stories Magdalena had heard as a little girl, or they were hints of stories her mother might someday decide to tell her, and a number included phrases in the imperative tense—*don't pick the thin-stemmed mushrooms, check that the butcher's scale is zero to begin with*—as if her mother had made notes across her skin of the things that Magdalena ought to know.

But Magdalena's mother's body did not say *Magdalena* anywhere, and as they walked and she listened to Rachel cycle through the stories of her life, Magdalena let herself wonder why. Maybe, like Lina, her mother had things written under her hair. Maybe Magdalena's name had gotten lost in her ear or covered over by the birthmark behind her mother's knee. There had been no *Magdalena* on Lina either, or on Ivan or Andrius, Magdalena's boyfriend in high school, or on Marija or Ruta or even Rachel, but it couldn't be that Magdalena was meant to come and go without leaving so much as her name; she had seen herself on Neil: *Magdalena Bikauskaitė* unmistakable in the hollow of his eye. In the station in Paris, when she'd lifted the bit of hair that stuck out over Neil's ear, she hadn't seen any words of explanation. Her name was a fact on his face, like his blood type and the dates his children would be born and the place he went to high school, and she thought about this too as the languages on the other pilgrims became more varied, leaving her understanding only the names—Marias, Paolos, Gottfrieds, Kristofers, Josés, and Adriennes—on strangers' cheeks and hands and dusty legs. When she told the fortune of somebody covered in a language she couldn't understand she learned to choose a name and say it carefully, and often she was able to tell from the look on the customer's face whether Paolo or Kristofer was that person's father or their son, a lost love, ex-husband, or favorite saint. She wondered what Neil would say if a stranger on the road looked into a crystal or fussed with a deck of cards and then said *"Magdalena Bikauskaitė"* to him. Would he look confused? Or would he recognize a logic to that name that no one else would understand?

They crossed the border into Spain. The roads were busy with pilgrims hurrying to finish in time for the saint's feast day and every time they stopped to rest, Rachel found someone who wanted a fortune told. They could buy sandwiches now, and they had their own bunks at the pilgrims' hostels. Calluses formed around the threads in Magdalena's feet. Rachel said it was disgusting, but she had to admit that Magdalena had been right, it stopped the blisters.

By then Magdalena had enough money for a decent pair of boots. Brit offered to take her shopping for the kind that breathed, but when they came to a town that had all the big outlet stores, Magdalena told Brit that she'd decided to use the money for something else. Of all the things written on her mother's skin, there was one story that Magdalena knew the beginning to, but not the end—and besides, she'd spent her childhood reading *pay your debts* off the inside of her mother's elbow whenever she rolled up her sleeves. When they stopped for the night, Magdalena asked at the desk for paper and an envelope and she got out the napkin where Neil had written his address. His last name struck her as a familiar fact. She'd seen those letters all her life on the soft skin below her mother's collarbone, where the name Neil had said was his father's had been given Lithuanian grammatical endings—*Richardui Beartui*—the dative form looking clumsy on those foreign words. It meant *to Richard Beart* or *for* him, turning Neil's father into a noun whose meaning was incomplete standing alone like that, as if her mother had hugged the letters of the alphabet to her chest and come away with an unfinished sentence about a man in America claiming her heart.

Magdalena looked at the piece of blank paper the clerk had given her. *Hello my dear Neil* she wrote at the top, and stopped to think. She didn't know quite how to make him understand, or where to begin. Rachel had met a group of German Wiccans and gone off to have a beer, so Magdalena had to ask one of the French nuns who taught school to help her with the English.

When she was finished she wrapped the letter around Neil's sixty euros. She sealed the envelope and took it to the post office on their way out of town the next morning—though she knew from the warning across the back of her mother's left knee that one should never send cash through the mail.

{NEIL}

Vilnius, June

JUST LIKE MAGDALENA had said, the bus ride to Vilnius took thirty-three hours. Sometime during the night they stopped beside a field, men went in front of the bus, women behind, and Neil woke the next morning as they crossed the German-Polish border wondering if he'd dreamed the sight of all those bare white bottoms twinkling in the moonlight. They stopped again in Warsaw, where everyone stood at a counter to eat potatoes and cold beet soup, then back on the bus. Fields and forests and little wooden farmhouses with thatched roofs went by, and Neil went in and out of dreams, waking to re-plan in his head for the hundredth time just how everything would happen. The bus rolled through pine forests and finally through hundreds of Soviet apartment buildings on the outskirts of Vilnius—some of them without glass in the windows, some with laundry hanging from cement balconies that seemed ready to chip off. Cracks ran like ivy along the seams of the buildings and Neil imagined again the scene in the pizza restaurant, preparing a little speech for himself, wishing Magdalena had left something so he could return it to her the way they did in movies. *Madam, I believe this handkerchief is yours.* He thought about lying. *Magdalena? Is that you? I'm here to do some research and, I mean, what are the odds?* But he settled on honesty. *I just thought it would be nice to, like, see you again.*

His first miscalculation was the pizza. He realized it before he even got off the bus. What an idiot he was to think that Magdalena's mother would be opening Vilnius' first pizza restaurant, as if Lithuanians were still standing in bread lines behind the iron curtain. He saw twelve pizza places before the bus got to the station. While he was looking for the city bus that would take him to Professor Uzdavinys' house, he saw three more. In fact, he had never seen so many pizza restaurants in his life. They were everywhere, with big color photos outside advertising the spicy chicken pizza, the egg and pickle pizza, the chunky chili pizza.

Professor Uzdavinys' house was actually near enough to the station that he walked rather than trying to find the bus. Professor Uzdavinys' wife, Renate, was there, just getting ready to go out. She was a professor too, and in perfect English she told Neil to make himself at home and go right ahead and take a nap, he was sure to need it after that long bus ride.

But Neil had no intention of sleeping, when there were so many pizza restaurants to search, looking for a particular person with her light eyes and her one gray tooth. He started by going from pizza place to pizza place, peering inside.

But that couldn't go on forever. After an hour or so he was getting really hungry, so he went into one of them. Just for kicks he ordered the American pizza—it came covered in barbecue sauce—and purposely looked the other way until the waitress was right there at his table, still holding out hope that it might be her. It wasn't.

After the pizza his head was clearer, and he realized how ridiculous it all was. He also thought of something he couldn't believe he hadn't thought of before. He still had Magdalena's number in his phone, on his missed-calls list from when she'd left the message about meeting him in Paris. He could call her, just to ask if she'd arrived okay, and then he could say, sort of casually, "Actually I'm here in Vilnius, maybe we should meet up." It wasn't quite the scene he'd pictured, but it would have to do.

But when he called the number it went straight to voicemail, as if her phone had been turned off. *"Hello and please to leave a message,"* it said. "Hey, Magdalena, it's Neil. I just wanted to—sorry, this is Neil from the train station, in case you know, like, several. I just wanted to make sure you got home okay and everything and actually, well, ah, just call me back when you get this, yeah, so I know you're okay. I mean if you want to. Call me. So yeah. Okay, um, bye." In a lifetime of sounding like a loser on the phone it was the worst message he had ever left.

He called her again a little later, and then, not wanting her to have a list of missed calls from the same number, he bought a phone card at the post office and called from a pay phone. He wondered if maybe her phone didn't work in Lithuania. If he knew her last name, he could try to look her up in the phone book. He called his mom, thinking that maybe she could google *grand opening pizza Vilnius* for him, which might at least narrow things down. But he'd forgotten that she was away on a yoga retreat in Utah. Finally he called his father, which was what he should have done in the first place. His dad would know Magdalena's mother's last name, and he might even know the name of her restaurant. Next to the possibility of a completely wasted trip to Lithuania, all the reasons he'd had for not calling seemed less important. But his dad didn't pick up.

Maybe it was because he couldn't reach him, but the thought of his father's phone ringing in the big empty house made Neil sad. Even though he'd gone months without thinking too much about it, he started to miss his dad, wishing he could at least say hi and give him ten tries to guess where he was calling from.

His father had never changed the answering machine, and it still had Nan's voice pronouncing each word slowly and clearly as if she were talking to someone on the moon. *"You have reached Walter and Catherine Hurley. We probably couldn't make it to the phone in time, or else we're out in the yard."* And then, because she hadn't known how to stop the tape, Neil heard Pop's voice, saying, *"That oughta do,"* and Nan saying *"Well, if they've got something to tell us, they can go ahead and say it,"* and the sound of water running in the sink.

Hearing their voices just about did Neil in. He hung up without leaving a message and stood for a while in the telephone booth, which someone had peed in pretty recently, thinking about Pop, who could do the fly-away-birdie trick with a bit of newspaper so that it fooled Neil and his cousins every time, and Nan, who once showed him a fish brain that looked like a piece of chewed bubblegum. He was sad for his dad, all alone in that big house, and for himself, all alone in a telephone booth in Lithuania. Naturally he wound up wondering what had made him think he ought to come all this way to stand in pee and broken glass and hear the telephones of the people that he loved just ring and ring. He used up the last of the money on the phone card calling the cell phone his father kept in the car for emergencies, but his dad had probably forgotten to charge it, and it rang straight to a message saying the voicemail had never been set up.

Then, because it was starting to rain and he'd never been so lonely in his life, he called Veejay. He had to use his mobile, but he didn't even bother leaving the phone booth. He was getting used to the smell, that's how depressed he was.

"Yo yo, wassup," Veejay said.

"Hey," Neil said.

"Hey."

"So guess where I am."

"In jail."

"No," Neil said.

"In bed with Amanda."

"What? No," Neil said. "What are you talking about?"

"Dude, you love her," Veejay said.

"No I don't," Neil said.

"Hang on a sec," Veejay said, then, "'*Her fingers chase the shadows, leave her shoulders bare. Her hands brush imagined breezes from her hair—*'"

"Jesus, is that my *notebook*?" It had been missing since before Neil left for Paris. "Where did you find that? I was looking everywhere."

"Wait, it gets really good. '*Her fingertips against her pasted lips—*'"

"*Parted* lips. Come on Veejay, what the fuck?"

"It really looks like pasted here. Man, you have terrible handwriting."

"You are such an asshole."

"Well she loved it. She thought it was really sweet."

"What?" Neil said. "You showed her?"

"She thinks you have a gift."

"I'm going to kill you," Neil said.

"Okay, dude, I'm joking," Veejay said. "She went home for the summer, remember? Chill."

"I can't believe you stole my notebook," Neil said.

"I didn't steal it. I found it in the couch."

"Whatever," Neil said. Then he had an idea. "Hey wait a second,

Veejay," he said. "Will you look a few pages back? I think I wrote this girl's name down there."

"What girl?"

"That girl from Swindon."

"The one in the pornos?"

"They weren't pornos. She said he wasn't even recording."

"Uh-huh," Veejay said. "Okay, is it Magdalena, like, Bike-o-skatie or something?"

"Yeah, exactly. How's it spelled?"

"M-A—"

"The last name," Neil said. "Just spell the last name."

"B-I-K-A-U-S-K-A-I-T-E," Veejay said. "And there's a dot over the *E*. Or it might be soup. I'm kind of eating right now. No, it's definitely a dot."

Neil wrote it down, *Bikauskaitė*. He didn't know how to pronounce it and Veejay said it sounded like a rash you'd get on, like, the fifteenth day of the Tour de France, but Neil found a spot of white marble in his brain and carved it in. *Magdalena Bikauskaitė.*

Then he didn't feel like telling Veejay about the phone booth or how it was raining and he had no idea where he was, or about the egg and pickle pizzas. When Veejay asked him how he was liking Paris, he said it was pretty great. And when Veejay asked him how many hot French girls he could see at just that moment, Neil took a second to look at the empty street where two old women in babushkas were waiting out the rain under the awning of what was, of course, a pizza restaurant, and said four or five, but one had armpit hair.

"Man," Veejay said. "You really are in France."

There weren't any Bikauskaitės listed in the phone book. There were a few people named Bikauskas, and then it went to Bikauskienė. Neil wondered if he'd written the name down wrong when his father first called to ask him to deliver the Christmas presents. He tried to remember his father's friend's first name. Had it started with a *D*? He wasn't even sure he'd ever heard it. There was a Dijana Bikauskienė, but that didn't sound right. And there was a Nellija Bikauskienė, but that wasn't it either.

He called Dijana first. No answer. Then he called Nellija. Nothing. Then, not knowing what else to do, he flipped through the phone book, waiting for the rain to stop.

The Vilnius phone book was attached to the pay phone by a little wire. Someone had torn out everything after *R*, but even in the space from *A* to *Q* Neil noticed a number of new letters: the *E* with a dot over it, a *C* with an upside-down *circonflexe*. It reminded him of a joke he and his dad had had when he was a little kid.

It was basically a nonsense world that they'd invented—either his mother never knew about it or she was never invited in. It started when Neil was learning the alphabet, so he must have been kindergarten age or even younger. At school they were taught to sing *Ay, Bee, Cee, Dee, Ee, Ef, Gee, Aych, Eye, Jay, Kay, Ellameno, Pee* ... And like all parents probably did with their kids, especially parents who were also English teachers, Neil and his father would play the alphabet game. *Starts with Cee,* his father would say as they stood in the checkout line at the grocery store. *Candy,* Neil would say. *Cash register,* his father would say. *Candy bar,* Neil would say. *Coupons,* his father would say. *Kellogg's,* Neil would say. *Not exactly,* his father would say. *Corn on the cob,* Neil would say. *Cole slaw. Cans. Corned beef hash. Crocodiles.* And on and on. *Starts with Ess. Soup. String beans. Spider-Man. Soda pop.*

Starts with Ellameno, Neil said once when it was his turn to choose a letter, and his dad thought that was so funny that they started making up a whole world populated with made-up fantastical things: the ellamenopede who liked to eat ellamenoghetti twirled around forks held in each of its ellamillion hands. There was the ellamenopotomus who lived under Neil's bed and had to be lulled to sleep, as he remembered, by bedtime songs rewritten. *There was an ellamen-old lady who swallowed a fly* had been one of them. *I don't ellamen-know why she swallowed that fly.* Neil's father had liked Ellamenoland so much that every year as part of the vocab unit he gave his language arts students extra credit if they could make up and define a word that started with ellameno—something Neil had to live down, painfully, when he got to middle school.

That got him thinking about the other things he and his father had done together before his parents split up. When Neil begged for a mail-order town for his train set and his mother said absolutely not, it was too expensive, he and his father set out to build one out of match-sticks. Together they made cabins, then manor houses, railroad stations, castles, pagodas out of matchsticks, even a supertanker that came apart in the bathtub when the glue dissolved. His father sliced the heads off the matches with a razor blade so that the stick was all that was left and Neil dipped them long-ways into a pool of wood glue and laid them one on top of the other for rafters and walls. Neil's mother would go around sweeping up the little rolling match heads they forgot to throw away. She said they were a fire hazard. Neil's fingers were clumsy and he spread the glue too thick or made the walls all crooked, but his father's matchstick houses were perfect, tiny chinks cut for windows, a red Twist-Em for a flag waving from the ramparts of a matchstick fortress.

After his parents got divorced Neil would spend weekends at his father's house, and sometimes they would work silently, building wooden cities. Neil's father would be absorbed in the project while Neil cracked stick after stick in mute frustration, trying to make the rounded sides of a space station. Later they switched to sugar cubes, which had the same problem, but which allowed Neil's father ever more elaborate creations, variegated palaces tinged with Easter egg dye, castles with turrets and double-thick walls.

Then Neil went to middle school and he and his father stopped building things. Neil had speech and debate practice on the weekends, and his father started spending most of his time doing research. When Neil did stay with his father he played Tetris while his dad looked through old books, and during long summer afternoons wasps would eat the sugar cube castles his father had never bothered to throw away.

It was still raining, but Neil was tired of thinking about his childhood. He was almost guaranteed to get lost trying to find his way back to the Uzdavinys' apartment, and Renate was expecting him for dinner. So he zipped up his sweatshirt, put his phone in his pants pocket, where it had the best chance of staying dry, and dug around in his backpack for the map of Vilnius that Renate had given him. But he must have left it at the pizza place, because he got all the way down to the bottom of his pack without finding it. He did find that he'd accidentally brought his Latin dictionary with him from Paris, which explained why his backpack was so heavy, and underneath it was the bag of Magdalena's mother's Christmas presents for his father. He'd forgotten all about sending them after he left Magdalena at the bus station. The wool socks were going to get wet and the photos of Magdalena's mother were already a little bent, though the coffee in its vacuum pack was fine. Neil thought of his dad waiting for those presents since way back in December, checking the mail, maybe even calling the post office to see if a package had come that was too big to fit in the mailbox, and felt awful. He needed to buy a new map anyway, so he put the shopping bag under his shirt to keep dry and went out into the rain, heading back toward the post office where he'd bought the phone card.

The post office was farther from the phone booth than he'd realized, and by the time Neil got there he was soaked. He found a map of Vilnius, but the clerk just stared at him when he asked if she spoke English and kept staring as he mimed putting the things for his father in a box. Finally she got up and went into the back. Neil waited a long time. He heard a kettle boil. The woman came back sipping a cup of tea and holding a box that was way too big. Neil put the presents in and then, because he had to have something to keep them from sliding around, he ripped out most of the blank pages from his notebook and crumpled them up for padding. Since he didn't know whether Magdalena's mother was Dijana, Nellija, or someone else, he didn't know how to say who the presents were from, or how to explain why they were coming with a Lithuanian postmark. He used another notebook page to write *Hi Dad—Here are those Xmas presents from your friend. Sorry it took me so long.* He threw the note away and wrote it a couple more times, trying out a few different explanations for why he was in Lithuania, but it all seemed too complicated. He didn't know which would make his father feel worse, not getting anything or getting a big box in the mail and then opening it to find only coffee and socks and a crappy note. So he scrapped the whole thing. He'd send the presents when he got back to Paris. The lady made him pay for the box anyway; she gave him his change and went off to find the sugar. Neil said thank you, though she was already gone, put the presents back in his backpack, and walked out into the rain.

*

The next morning Kazys Uzdavinys told Neil how to get to the Lithuanian State Historical Archives, and he took the trolley bus to the outskirts of the city, past markets where old ladies set handfuls of tiny strawberries out for sale. He got off the trolley and followed Kazys's directions until he came to a medium-size building with thick curtains drawn across the windows.

The reading room of the Lithuanian archives looked like an orderly classroom, with rows of school desks facing front. He had a reference number and a note from Kazys; he gave them to one of the archivists, and she took him to a section of the indexes.

"Polish?" she said.

"No, American," Neil said.

"But you speak Polish?" she said.

"No," Neil said.

The archivist shrugged, and she flipped through the index to the number Professor Piot had written down.

"This?" she asked. The description of the documents meant nothing to Neil.

"I guess," he said. "I don't know Lithuanian. I'm just supposed to get this file."

"This is Polish," the archivist said. "If it is before 1795 it is Polish."

"Oh, right," Neil said. "What does it say?"

The archivist shrugged again. "I don't speak Polish." Then she said, "So you come tomorrow?"

"Well, I'm leaving tomorrow," Neil said.

"The documents are ready only tomorrow."

"Oh," Neil said. "Well, okay."

There wasn't really anything else for him to do, so he asked the archivist if she had a phone book. She gave him a newer one than he'd seen in the phone booth, but still no Bikauskaitės. "Is there anything like a registry for phone numbers?" he asked when he went to return it.

"If it is public, it is in the book," she said, not looking up.

"Just, there's someone I know who lives here, but I can't find the name," Neil said.

The archivist looked at the paper where Neil had written down the spelling of Magdalena's last name, and then at the page in the *B* section of the phone book.

"Here," she said. "*Bikauskas* is father. *Bikauskaitė* is just for unmarried girl."

"Oh," Neil said. "I'm looking for her mother actually. Her father isn't around. I don't think." What if his father's friend was married? He hadn't asked Magdalena, he'd just assumed her parents were divorced or something. It could be pretty awkward if her mom had a husband Neil's dad didn't know about.

"So it will be *Bikauskienė* for the mother," the archivist said, pointing to *Dijana* and *Nellija*, the same numbers Neil had called from the phone booth, and pronouncing them slowly as if she were talking to someone very stupid—which was a good thing, because Neil hadn't realized the *j*'s were pronounced like *y*'s.

"That's great," he said. "That's really great. Thanks."

The archivist gave him something that was almost like a smile.

The next morning he was going to call both Dijana and Nellija again, but he never got to Nellija, because when he called Dijana Bikauskienė's number, a woman answered.

"Hello, Dijana?" Neil said. He was a little nervous and his throat was dry. His voice sounded like it belonged to someone else.

There was a pause, then, "Yes?" she said in English.

"Hi, my name is, I'm Rick Beart's—Richard's—" Neil had forgotten to practice what he was going to say beforehand. But it didn't seem to matter, because Dijana made a sound like she was happily surprised.

"Ah, hello!" Dijana said. "This is great to hear you."

"Thanks, it's really nice to talk to you too," Neil said. He cleared his throat and wished he had some water.

"How are you?"

"Good," Neil said. "Actually, the crazy thing is, I'm here in Lithuania. I had to come here for, ah, work stuff, and so I'm in the neighborhood and I was just wondering if—"

"You are here? You are in Vilnius?"

"Yeah," Neil said.

"Great, this is great! So you will come to see me?"

"Well, sure, that would be nice," Neil said, amazed it had been so easy.

"I am almost not believing this. Really, you are here?"

"Yep. Yeah, it's a little crazy."

"No, not crazy. I am—ah, I forget English."

"It's okay," Neil said.

She invited him to come for dinner that night and gave him the address, saying again, "I am really not believing."

Neil couldn't believe it either. Magdalena must have said some pretty nice things about him because her mom seemed genuinely excited he'd called. Neil had been expecting Dijana to pass the phone to Magdalena, but it was probably just as well that she hadn't, because Neil had no idea what he would have said. Or maybe her mother wanted Neil's visit to be a surprise. That was okay by him. In his mind he started rewriting the scene in the pizza restaurant, changing the setting one more time to Magdalena's mother's apartment, but keeping all the most important details the same. He called Professor Piot to tell him he would be staying in Vilnius an extra day, and then he took the trolley bus back to the archives to look at the documents.

The file Neil had requested was actually a very old book, centuries older than the century-old carton holding it together. The carton was covered with archival stamps and crossed-out notations; it was confusing, and Neil had to look at it for a few minutes before he realized that what he was seeing was the history of Lithuania, more or less, stamped and restamped across the carton. It seemed that as the country changed hands, the archives did too, because next to the faded Polish label was an archival notation in darker ink, which Neil, who was normally pretty good at deciphering old handwriting, studied for a long time before he realized that he was looking at the cursive form of another alphabet, with loops and swirls in unfamiliar places. It must be Cyrillic, Neil thought, but it had clearly been made by a much older Russian administration than the heavy block letters of the Soviet archival stamp next to it. That in turn had been crossed out and replaced with a much newer-looking stamp, with its own reference numbers added in thick permanent marker, as if the *Lietuvos Valstybės Istorijos Archyvas* intended to have the last word.

The book itself had once been bound with thick leather covers held together by strings. Neil could see the weave of the paper; it crumbled when he accidentally touched an edge, leaving fine dust on his fingers. On the first page there was an official-looking invocation of the monarch, *Sigismundus Rex*, dated 1623. He turned the pages carefully. It seemed to be a collection of administrative documents—charters, registries, and acts, the daily business of an empire recorded in ornate Polish script. Neil had spent a lot of time looking at those sorts of documents, but he still felt a thrill at the thought that someone like him, a college kid who was basically nobody, could find himself holding pieces of paper that had been signed by kings.

Neil often wondered if other people felt like this, and he looked up, wanting suddenly to find a stranger to smile at, some old man with a stack of notes and a magnifying glass who would understand exactly how Neil felt. But the other people in the reading room were all hunched over their documents. Microfilm machines whirred and clicked. Behind the glass window of her office the archivist arranged white and purple flowers in a vase. She wiped her desk with a rag, then arranged the flowers again so that the white ones were surrounded by purple.

Neil found the document that matched the reference number Professor Piot had given him. He made a note of the title of the document, and that it came under the year *MDCXXIX*.

It was getting late, and Neil wanted to be sure he'd be able to take a shower and still have plenty of time in case he got lost on the way to Magdalena's mother's apartment. He started sweating just thinking about it, and he wiped his hands on his jeans before carefully closing the book. He put it back in the carton and stood in the doorway of the archivist's office, watching as she pinched a dead blossom and found a better angle for the vase, waiting for the right moment to ask how to get copies.

{RICHARD}

Paris, June

I WASN'T THE ONLY one who'd forgotten that the French National Archives opened late on Saturdays. I waited outside the gate with one or two others until a guard came and unlocked it for us, then I went upstairs to the office of the woman I'd spoken to the day before. She seemed slightly put out to see me there and reminded me that the staff were available for consultation from Monday to Friday only, and that such meetings had to be scheduled in advance.

"Well?" she said when she'd finished. "What is it you want to know?"

I told her I was interested in seeing my mother's medical files. "No, we have nothing like this here," she said. The records from Inga Beart's stay at the Hôtel-Dieu hospital, if they existed, would be located some blocks away, where the archives of the Assistance Publique-Hôpitaux de Paris were kept.

She wrote down the address. "It isn't far. You know the Place des Vosges? The street is just beyond. But I think you will have to wait. I don't think you will find anyone there to help you on a Saturday."

"Thank you very much," I said, and wished her a good weekend. I still had the rest of the comtesse's twenty-three cartons of playbills and memoirs to look through, and so I went back to the documents counter and asked for carton number seven.

I settled down at one of the long reading tables and spent the morning and most of the afternoon on cartons seven, eight, and nine: receipts from various dressmakers, old rail tickets, the sorts of things most people have the sense to throw away. I checked all the files that had dates from the early fifties, but none of them connected the comtesse to my mother.

The funny thing is, I might never have discovered anything at all if the man from the art gallery hadn't offered me a cup of tea the night before. I only opened the folder labeled *"Hirondelle"* thinking that maybe the comtesse had financed one of those murals he'd talked about—and I only knew that *Hirondelle* was spelled the way it was because it had been traced in gold script across the rim of my saucer.

The folder contained just two sheets, printed out on heavy paper with the name of a transatlantic steamship company at the top. They were in French and I thought that it was too bad the gallery owner wasn't there to see them, because it seemed that the comtesse herself had taken a trip onboard the SS *Hirondelle* sometime during the 1950s. I'd scanned most of the first paper without thinking much about what I was doing when it occurred to me that in fact the voyage had been made in 1954, which might give the lie to Carter Bristol's claim that the comtesse was present when Inga Beart did what she did. But I double-checked the dates: Inga Beart was taken to the Hôtel-Dieu hospital on August 10, and the *Hirondelle* arrived at Le Havre, France, on August 8, 1954, which would have given the comtesse just enough time, I suppose, to be back in Paris in time to witness Inga Beart's disaster.

That is when I realized something odd. The paper I was looking at was an embarkation schedule for a round-trip ticket with New Orleans as the city of origin rather than Le Havre. After arriving from the United States on August 8, the comtesse was set to leave France again on August 20. And it seemed she wasn't traveling alone. The price was given in francs for two tickets, tourist class, which the comtesse had apparently paid for in June of the same year.

The second piece of paper was a receipt from the steamship company. In just the way one hears one's name above the din of a crowded room, the one familiar word on the page jumped out at me. My hands were shaking as I got out my notebook and copied down "*deux billets pour passager Beart et gardienne, classe touriste . . .*"

I'd never quite imagined that Carter Bristol might have been right, although, as I told myself without really believing it, this was among the least important of details. So what if my mother had had an affair with the comtesse? It hardly proved Bristol's theory as to why she put her eyes out, and certainly the trip was never made, since it's well established that Inga Beart was in Paris the whole time. The *Hirondelle* left New Orleans on July 28, 1954; Inga Beart sat at the *tabac* on August 1, and after her injury on August 10 she did not leave France until October

1954, when they transferred her to a psychiatric hospital back in New York. I looked up the word *gardienne* in my dictionary, and found it meant *guardian* or *caretaker*, just as I'd thought. So it seemed clear the comtesse understood that Inga Beart was in a bad way, even when she bought those tickets in June 1954.

After that, as you can imagine, I set out to look at every bit of paper in every one of the sixteen remaining cartons. In carton number fourteen I found what I'd come for: a file nearly an inch thick, labeled "*Inky*"—a nickname my mother must have picked up sometime after she left home, because I never heard Aunt Cat or any of the cousins refer to her that way. They say she had the habit of biting down on the tip of her pen while she was thinking, leaving a bit of blue on her lips.

There was no doubt it was the file Carter Bristol had seen. I really can't be sure of all of what was inside, but there were letters from the comtesse to various doctors and psychiatrists on my mother's behalf, and handwritten drafts of what could only be love letters from the comtesse to my mother. There were letters from my mother too, written in French, specifying dates and times to meet. There did seem to be a great deal of secrecy surrounding their relationship. I did as best I could translating word for word with my pocket dictionary, and though much of what I came up with made no sense at all, I did learn that they chose to meet in "unknown places with enough darkness," and that the comtesse had called my mother "*chérie.*"

I copied everything down, going carefully page by page and putting in all the accents. Toward the end of the file I came to a thick waxed-paper envelope. It was marked "*juin 1954.*" Just as Carter Bristol had said, inside were a half dozen photographs printed on small squares of paper with scalloped edges. In one picture Inga Beart stands in front of a dressing room mirror, her face mostly in shadow; in another her bare shoulders are reflected in that same mirror. I looked through them slowly, hoping as I turned over each one that it would show her feet. But the angles of the photographs were intimate; the person who took them had been standing close. Only one included anything of my mother below the waist. She and several others are seated on a sofa with an ornate mantle behind them. Two light-haired women smile up at the photographer, a man in evening dress raises a glass, but my mother has turned away. Her legs are crossed in the parallel slant that women seemed to favor then and her feet are hidden, as if by design, by an elaborate tea service placed on a low table in front of her.

If there's one thing I've found in the time I've spent doing this kind of research, it's that every so often one gets slammed up flat against the limits of our modern ability to get our hands on information. Here I was, having traveled halfway across the world to look at a photograph that a complex bureaucracy had managed to preserve behind cardboard and string. And what a fantastic achievement, what a scientific wonder the invention of the snapshot was, because there in front of me I had an image of my mother just as she'd looked in an unguarded moment half a century ago. But even with all that luck and preservation, all it took to keep me from knowing what she'd been wearing on her feet was a china teapot that I would never in a thousand years of technological advancement have the power to move five inches to the left.

I made notes on all of it in as much detail as I could, and I hardly noticed how much time had passed until the archivist, the same one I'd spoken to that morning, tapped me on the shoulder to say that they were closing for the day. And sure enough, everyone else in the big reading room had put away their things and was standing in a long line to have their bags checked before they went out the door. I packed the carton up in a hurry, though as carefully as I could because I could feel the archivist watching me with arms crossed a few feet back, making sure I didn't fold over any corners.

I ought to have felt as hungry and dispirited as I had the day before. The lunch I'd brought had sat all day forgotten in the locker and the information I'd found seemed only to reinforce Carter Bristol's version of events. But just the fact that I had found anything at all made the details seem unimportant. I forgot my resolution not to pass the art gallery again and I hurried in that direction, hoping that the owner would be standing outside. And when I turned down the little street, sure enough, he was.

Now, I didn't want to be a nuisance, and I wasn't sure he'd feel like translating the pages of notes I'd copied down. But he seemed glad enough to see me, and I had the *Hirondelle* to tell him about. I started off with that, saying that during my research I had, by chance, stumbled on the very subject we had been discussing the day before.

"Ah-ha, she was having money difficulties, this comtesse," he said when I showed him the notes from the *Hirondelle* file.

"I don't think so," I said. "I think she was quite wealthy."

"*Classe touriste*, this is the second class," he said. "On the *Hirondelle* in the second class they had a swimming pool and there are some fine pieces left from the dining room, but for the wealthy it must be *classe cabine* I think."

"But the ticket wasn't for her," I said. "The ticket was for my mother, she was a friend of hers," and I showed him what I'd copied down from the steamship company's receipt. "Here—it says '*Passenger Beart and a guardian*'—I'm assuming a caretaker, maybe a nurse," I said. "She wasn't well."

He took the notebook from me and looked at it a moment, as if he couldn't quite read my handwriting.

"*Gardienne*, yes, this is one who would be responsible for her," he said. "And here, *passager Beart*, this is your mother? So I think it must be the feminine, a small mistake of the *e*. And also here, there will be an accent." He took out a pen and fixed the spelling to *passagère*.

"Sorry about that," I said. "I was writing quickly."

I showed him the other notes I had, from letters back and forth between the comtesse and Inga Beart, and the comtesse's letters to the doctors. I didn't want to come right out and tell him my mother had been having a romantic relationship with this woman, but he seemed to figure it out, because he laughed a little to himself and said, "Well!"

"Can you make anything out?" I asked.

"This Lucette, your mother's friend, she is saying she knows what will be best for your mother, your mother must trust her and on like this, but also that the husband—or perhaps it is another woman?— must not find out. And then, if you'll excuse me, there are some details which are more—"

"Oh, well yes," I said, remembering certain parts of Bristol's book. "I think I've already heard those. Just, if you can, what does it say there, where it talks about a voyage?"

"Ah, here this Lucette is referring to something that must have been said before. She is asking this person, which will be your mother, not to leave Paris, that in fact there will be something important to happen for her here. Important for her benefit. It seems your mother has been talking of some trip, yes, about leaving for some time. Lucette is writing, '*You are always running looking for peace*' and—is this an *r* that you have written here?—yes, '*you are always running looking for peace, but I will make you happy here,*' and so on. Something like this."

"Thank you, really, thanks so much," I said.

"But it is strange that you found this in the files of this comtesse," he said. "Perhaps the letter was never sent."

"Either that or she kept a draft, it was hard to tell exactly."

He turned to the next page of my notebook. "Ah, and this too is interesting," he said. "This you found in the same place?"

"Yes," I said. "I think it's a letter from a doctor."

"Mm, it must be. He is telling madame that her friend is suffering with a certain alienation—there is a void, he says, in her relations. He is recommending that this friend must put her face to certain unhappy realities, and so on."

"Unhappy realities?" I asked.

"Something like this. She must look to certain facts which can be difficult to bear. This doctor is telling madame that she may help her friend to do this if she wishes." He studied the page a moment more. "Ah, but come in," he said. We were still standing on the sidewalk in front of his shop. "Perhaps you would like another cup of tea?"

Throughout her life Inga Beart seemed to have a need to defy the domesticity expected of women in those days—leaving a rural childhood behind for the glitter of first Los Angeles and then New York and Paris, marrying exotic men and leaving them, never able to stay long in one place. The comtesse was not the first to suggest that she had something to outrun. It gave her an air of tragic adventure that the critics appreciated and the artistic set couldn't get enough of. Something in her suggested an exhilarating proximity to the edge of an abyss, and people—certain kinds of people—were drawn to her because of it, as if by getting close to her they would be able to see what lay beyond.

But according to the biographers, a change took place around 1949, which, coincidentally or not, was the year of my birth. Though she continued to produce novels at the rate of about one a year until 1952, by the end of the forties most scholars agree that Inga Beart's best work was behind her. She developed a well-known appetite for opiates and became a frequent guest at gin-soaked dinner parties where her drinking took on a kind of savagery that friends and acquaintances hadn't seen before. Whether this in fact had anything to do with me, or whether it was the inevitable disintegration of a psyche held together somewhat tenuously in the first place, is a matter of debate.

In any case, the Comtesse Labat-Poussin wasn't the first to try to cure Inga Beart. Before my mother left for France she'd spent time in several high-priced sanatoriums and spas, probably similar to the luxury rehab centers one hears about for celebrities today. She underwent electric shock treatments at Bellevue Hospital in New York and, at the urging of her publishers, who were concerned with the decline in the quality of her work, she saw several well-respected analysts. I've often wondered if it was one of them who convinced her to come back home, if it was at the behest of a New York doctor that my mother sat down at Aunt Cat's kitchen table, hands with a bit of a tremor, perhaps, one foot tapping against the table leg. In my memory of her feet I can see a tension there; the delicate muscles from ankle to toe are stretched tight. Perhaps I hid from her on purpose, crawling under the table because I was afraid of this strange woman. She would still have looked the part of the glamorous lady novelist, "*a woman of quick wit and exquisite eyebrows*" as *Vogue* described her once. But in my child's way I might have sensed that she was tensed to run.

The gallery owner and I sat down in the back room and he poured our tea into a different set of *Hirondelle* cups. Breakfast dishes from the upper dining room, he told me, recently purchased at an excellent price from a dealer in Marseille.

"What do you think, it is possible?" he asked, holding his teacup up to the light. "Perhaps your mother on her voyage drank from this very cup. On the *Hirondelle* fine Arabic coffee was served all day on the upper decks—they say it was better than anything you could find in Paris."

I started to explain about the dates and my mother's injury and how it wasn't possible she'd actually used the ticket, but I stopped, letting myself believe for a moment that Inga Beart's life had gone a different way. I pictured her on board the *Hirondelle*, steaming back across the ocean toward a little boy, a sunburned child whose days were spent thigh-high in alfalfa, who fell asleep each night to the memory of his mother's shoes. I imagined her looking out over the ocean, raising a cup to her lips, leaving a mark on the china from the lipstick she painted on thick to cover stray stains of ink.

"My goodness," I said, and I held my cup up too. "Now wouldn't that be something?"

{NEIL}

Vilnius, June

D IJANA BIKAUSKIENĖ LIVED in a big block apartment building in the suburbs of Vilnius, and it took Neil longer to get there than he'd expected. He got lost and had to show the address to several people before an old man, looking at him suspiciously, pointed toward the third in a row of identical buildings. In between them lines of laundry had been hung out to dry, and though it was after eight o'clock the summer sun wasn't close to setting. White sheets and baby clothes, a little girl's dress, men's undershirts, the blouse and skirt of an airline stewardess, some hipster jeans, large cotton underpants, and a checkered tablecloth waved in the breeze. Neil tried to remember what Magdalena had been wearing at the train station in Paris, but he didn't see anything that looked her size.

The stairs up to the apartment were dark, and there was a row of mailboxes with Russian letters on them. That was the kind of artifact Professor Piot especially loved. The Soviet Union might be dead, but Lithuanian postmen still had to read Cyrillic to deliver the mail. Neil climbed the stairs. Someone had spray-painted *BROOKLYN* in big letters on the wall.

He found the door and double-checked the number, then remembered to swallow his gum. He knocked. A woman opened the door with a big smile on her face that went away as soon as she saw him. She said something in Lithuanian.

"Hi," Neil said, "I'm Neil. We spoke on the phone yesterday, and I—Sorry, do you speak English? Is this number thirty-four?"

"Yes," she said. "You are who?"

"Neil," Neil said. "Neil Beart. I'm Rick's son. We spoke on the phone—"

"Ah," she said. Then, "Ah, *Ni-yell*! Hello! And very welcome!" She said his name just like Magdalena did. "Yah, I'm sorry, I am not even understanding you will be here. Ah, this is great. Your father is arriving, yes?"

"Oh, no, actually. My dad's still back in the States. I'm here on my own." Dijana seemed surprised to hear that. "Sorry, I guess I didn't really make that clear on the phone."

"This is you on the phone?" Dijana said.

"Yeah," Neil said.

Dijana stared at him a moment, then she started laughing in a way that left her steadying herself against the wall. Neil stood in the hall uncomfortably, wondering what the neighbors would think. Magdalena couldn't possibly have missed all the commotion; he wondered why she hadn't come to the door. It was then that he noticed that Dijana was awfully dressed up. She had on a red checkered skirt and matching high heels and a flower in her hair.

"I am thinking all the time this is Rick who is calling."

"Gosh, I'm really sorry," Neil said. "I should have explained better."

"Come in, come in. I am making you stay in the door. Ah, the famous Ni-yell. No, this is great. On phone you have really voice like your father is all."

The apartment smelled like something good was cooking slowly. The furniture inside was covered in lace. "I brought you these," Neil said. He hadn't been able to decide between flowers and wine, so in the end he bought both.

"Wow, so nice," Dijana said.

She led him into the living room, which was small and doubled as a pantry. There were neat rows of pickles in jars and some containers of cooking oil under the TV. Porcelain dishes lined a glass case, and the lace curtains were drawn, diffusing the sunlight outside. There were plates of cold fish and mushrooms covered in plastic wrap on the table. Neil wondered if Magdalena was still at work. Dijana brought beet soup in on a tray.

"Oh, let me help you with that," Neil said. There were only two bowls.

"No, no, sit. Eat." She uncovered the plates of fish and poured them each some wine.

"Is Magdalena around?" Neil asked.

"Magdalena? No, she is in Swindon still," Dijana said. "To health and thank you for visiting." She touched her glass to his. "And also to your father."

"Cheers," Neil said. He accidentally banged his glass into Dijana's. Had he misunderstood? Wasn't Magdalena home to help her mother with the pizza restaurant?

"So you are liking Vilnius?" Dijana said.

"Oh yeah. Such a beautiful city," Neil said. He'd gone with Magdalena to the counter and he'd bought her the bus ticket himself— Paris through Warsaw to Vilnius—so it wasn't like the whole thing had been a story made up to get his sixty euros. She should have gotten there by last Thursday at the latest. Why didn't her mother know she was home?

"Oh, yah, is very beautiful city, especially in center," Dijana said. She brought a spoonful of soup to her mouth, then started laughing again and put it down. "Ah, Ni-yell. You must think so funny of me, all the time thinking it is your father coming visiting."

"No, it was my fault," he said. "I guess I didn't really introduce myself." Had something happened to Magdalena on the way home from Paris?

"Actually this day when you called, I am just thinking to your father, and thinking how nice if he is phoning me sometime. And then I'm hearing him on telephone, and wow, so amazing! And he is here in Vilnius, such nice surprise! But it is you are here now and—ah! You must think I am some funny person, how I look. You see, I have worn these things special."

"You look really nice," Neil said.

"Yah, your father is giving me these things, they are from his aunt."

"Really?" Neil said. What exactly had Magdalena said at the train station? She was going home to Vilnius, she'd said that for sure. She'd lost her job in Swindon. She hadn't had money for the bus ticket, so she probably didn't have enough to be buying food for the last—what? Eight days? She'd seemed awfully hungry at the station. Was eight days long enough to starve? Good thing she wasn't super skinny. God, he was such an idiot. Why hadn't he insisted on giving her some extra cash for the trip?

"Well, he is giving me the skirt, yah, and the shoes also are from this aunt to your father. I think they are really old things. Really good value."

"Gosh, yeah, I guess so," Neil said. He took a deep breath and tried not to freak out. Magdalena was probably staying with friends. Maybe she wanted a little vacation before her mother put her to work making pizzas. But something wasn't right. Wouldn't she have told her mother she was planning to come home?

"She have some good style, this aunt to your father," Dijana was saying. "I'm finding everything what I wear tonight in her closets. Your father, he's asking me to clean them and saying to keep all what I want. It is cool, yah?" Neil nodded and smiled as if what she was saying were really interesting. The skirt Dijana was wearing looked like it was meant for square dancing and had a silver Navajo belt to go with it. Neil could almost remember that skirt from a dress-up raid on Nan's closet when he and his cousins were kids. But he couldn't imagine that Nan had ever worn the shoes—red and witchy-looking with heels that left gashes in the carpet.

"Oh, yeah. Retro," Neil said. It was surreal. He was having dinner with Magdalena's mother, discussing the things in his great-aunt's closet. It wasn't the way he'd expected to spend the evening. He didn't want to cause Dijana a lot of worry, but the more he thought about it, only half-listening as she went on about Nan's old clothes, the more likely it seemed that Magdalena hadn't been telling either of them exactly the truth. Obviously she wasn't still in Swindon, but something must have happened between Paris and Vilnius, because she hadn't come home either.

"So, have you heard from Magdalena recently?" Neil asked, doing his best to sound casual while Dijana filled his plate with the last of the fish.

"This is only for beginning," Dijana said. "Eat, eat, the chickens will be cold."

"Mmmm, wow, this is really good," Neil said, swallowing whole a large piece of salmon. "So, Magdalena. Have you heard from her?"

"Oh, yes, she is sending me one phone text on Wednesday, saying she is very loving England."

"Really?" Neil said. At least she was alive.

"Yes, and she is going with her boyfriend to be sleeping in tents, how do you say?"

"Camping?"

"Yes, this. So now her phone is not working anymore."

Neil began chewing each bite carefully, fifteen times on one side of his mouth and fifteen times on the other before swallowing, like Nan used to say would save him from developing esophageal problems later in life. He noticed that Dijana was sort of watching him out of the corner of her eye as she said the thing about Magdalena having a boyfriend, and after a moment she jumped up to get the chicken.

"Your father, you know, he is always speaking about you. You are very famous to him," Dijana said from the kitchen.

"That's nice," Neil said. He had no idea what he was chewing, but he kept going, *thirteen, fourteen, fifteen*. A boyfriend. Of course.

"He is always speaking to me about the things you are doing when child, all the things you liked, and how you were so funny child and smart. He will say to me, 'My son, he knows to read *Latin*.'"

"Oh, well, yeah," Neil said. He wondered if his father had told Dijana that Neil chose to live with his mother after the divorce. He tried to swallow, but he'd chewed all the moisture out of whatever it was in his mouth and it wouldn't go down.

"He is alonesome, your father I think."

"Yeah, that's true," Neil said. "But he has his things he does, you know. He has his research." He washed the mouthful down with some wine. Magdalena hadn't been dressed like she was going camping when he saw her at the station.

"Well, but these are not real things," Dijana said.

She scooped most of a chicken onto Neil's plate and added potatoes and another kind of mushroom. As they ate Neil tried to find out more about what had happened to Magdalena. What exactly had she said in her message? Was it like her to keep her phone turned off? But Dijana kept giving him little sympathetic smiles and steering the conversation back to Neil's father and the old house, and finally Neil got the hint and let it go. Magdalena had a boyfriend. Or something. He let Dijana serve him the rest of the mushrooms.

"I am really loving this place of your father, is really like something from Hollywood movie, with so much countryside and horses."

"Oh, does he have horses out there now?" Neil asked. His father wasn't much of a rancher. His aunt Pearl always said he was crap at running the place and the land was going to seed.

"Yah, not horses, but is this kind of thing, you know. Like John's Vein."

"What?" Neil said.

"Like Hollywood movie. John's Vein. You know, this country-western man who is shooting?"

"John Wayne?" Neil said.

"Yah. I am really liking this, is like John's Vein movie this house of your father. And so much interesting things inside." She heaped another helping of potatoes onto Neil's plate and poured them both more wine.

"I guess so," Neil said. When he was a kid he used to have to pull goathead thorns the size of thumbtacks out of his feet when he walked around barefoot in Nan and Pop's house.

"Has kitchen like for a restaurant," Dijana said.

"Well, it was built to be something like a hotel. Only, you know, it's so out in the middle of nowhere. I think whoever built it lost a lot of money."

"Yah, me and your father, we are finding one machine to mix paste for cooking—so big like for factory and not even used. And such nice thing, when I leave, your father is sending to me for making pizzas," Dijana said. "Is like real antique but working pretty okay."

Neil managed to fit the final potato into his stomach and finished his wine. Dijana cleared the dishes and came back with cake. She got a bottle of cherry brandy down from a shelf filled with little glass animals and photographs in souvenir frames: There was a moon-faced baby Magdalena, a little girl Magdalena, a high school–age Magdalena and another girl posing with purple streaks in their hair. "Cool figurines," Neil said when Dijana caught him looking at them.

Dijana poured some brandy into each of their wine glasses and lifted hers a little toward the photos on the shelf. "Actually, it is all because of Magdalena that I am meeting your father."

"Oh yeah?" Neil said.

"Yah, it is because of her I go to Colorado. Your father, he tells you how this is?"

"I don't think so," Neil said.

"Well it is one funny thing. When Magdalena is child she will like to do this thing, she will, how do you say? Tickle with fingers like this to my feet, to make me laugh, and she will say this funny word. *Puebolo*, something like this. She says, 'Yah, *mamyte*, your feet will take you there.' This is like some big joke between us. And when I first come to U.S. I am living—you know New Jersey? Well, this is not so nice, and my friend, one Polish lady what I meet, she tells there is some place where is job like in casino. With Indian people. And she tells me name to this place and it is just like that: Puebolo."

"Pueblo?" Neil asked.

"She tells me this is real country-western town."

"Well, sort of," Neil said.

Dijana was pouring them each another glass. "So I am like, wow, I will tell Magdute this funny story how I go to this town name of Puebolo! And actually this casino, this is not happening, but okay, I am there already, I must to find some job, so I clean houses—this I always know for doing. And so I meet your father, and when he's driving me one time for work he asks to me to tell him how do I come there. Because, really, in this place there are not so many Europeans. So I tell him this long story, and he listens and he is so nice, he says like, 'Someday I will meet this daughter and I will tell her big thanks you are here!' And I tell him, 'Okay, for this you must to come to Lithuania!'"

"Well, I'm sure he'd really love to visit," Neil said. "It's just, you know. He's not much of a traveler."

"Yah, this is true," Dijana said.

She started telling Neil more about her time in America, and about the pizza restaurant, which wasn't doing as well as it might because construction on the big shopping center across the street had been postponed. But, Dijana said, there were rumors that a group of German investors was taking over the project, and as soon as the shops opened her pizza place would be able to double its output with help from the old dough machine.

After another cherry brandy she started looking sad. She put her hand on Neil's and her eyes got wet. "Your father is some great man," she said.

"Yeah, that's pretty cool of him to send the mixer," Neil said. Actually, he thought it was a little weird that his father had given away part of Nan's kitchen like that. And it must have cost a fortune to ship something so heavy halfway across the world.

"And for so much other things also." Dijana told Neil how his father had helped her wire money home, he'd helped her with dentist bills, he'd even driven her all the way to the immigration office in Denver to see if they could get her a proper work permit.

"And you know, while I am in U.S. there is one really terrible thing happening. This daughter to my friend, she died, but out of country, yah? And your father, he is helping me so much to find where is my friend because actually she is very sick, in hospital, but I am not even knowing which one." Neil's father had called up somebody at the Lithuanian consulate in Washington and got them to track down the girl's mother. "When it is happening Magdalena is calling me and crying, telling me her friend is died, and me I know I must find the mother and tell her, so horrible, you know? But I have no number for her. And your father he was coming to drive me for cleaning, and he sees me like this, so crying everywhere, and he finds for me how to call her. She is in really bad place this friend, in hospital for crazy people. But I make them let me talk to her—she's not so crazy, just all the time drinking—and better it is me who tells her this thing, not people of hospital."

It must have been the girl in the box, Neil thought, and his toes curled under at the memory of the puff of white dust as the ashes poured onto the floor of Gare du Nord.

Dijana refilled her glass and added to Neil's too, though it wasn't empty. The things she was saying didn't sound at all like Neil's father, who was always so caught up in the past that he was barely able to navigate the present, who had forgotten Neil's birthday, and who hadn't gotten around to changing the answering machine message with Nan's voice on it in the five years she'd been dead. Neil could hardly imagine him on the phone with foreign bureaucrats, tracking a dead girl's mother through a warren of Lithuanian mental institutions. He wondered through a haze of wine and cherry brandy if it really was his father they were talking about, or if Dijana had gotten confused and was telling him about some other man she'd met in America.

"So do you and my dad still talk much?" Neil asked, then realized that maybe he shouldn't have. It might hurt her feelings that his father hadn't mentioned her more. "I mean, it's been a while since I've spoken to him."

"No," Dijana said. "I think he is so sad when Walter have died, he isn't calling me anymore and now I have left America. But I have always telled him please to visit me some day."

"Well, the ranch, you know, it's a lot for him," Neil said. "But I think it's great he had you to help with the house. I mean, the place is a mess."

"Yah, this is for sure," she said. "You know I have found also one entire—how do you say? For making alcohols like they do in country? I have found this too not even used and I am remembering when I am little girl in country and my uncles are making *schnapps*, you know? From apples. So much old things in this house. But with really good quality, and I am telling your father he must sell, not just give away." She leaned in, as if she were going to tell Neil a secret. "Actually, Ni-yell, pizza, this is not my greatest dream. What I am really loving is having someday one shop where is filled with old beautiful things, all very fashion and antique. So I am all the time looking for old things with big value. Like these things what I'm wearing. Such beautiful belt, yah? Is all silver. And for shoes, these I'm finding in back of aunt's closets and I can see she is not wearing for so long time. They are all the time folded in newspapers, like so old I have never seen."

"How old?" Neil asked. The thing for making alcohol must have been some kind of still. He tried to remember if the dude ranch had been built during Prohibition—that would be interesting—and he wondered why his father had never mentioned he was cleaning out the place.

"Well, this is how I know they are really big value," she said. "These shoes are in newspapers all from before even I am born. And I am some old lady, so, you know, they are for real antique! I am thinking I could sell them, but see, they are, how do you say? With repairs."

Dijana hefted her foot up for Neil to see the restitching along the sole of one shoe, nearly spilling her wine and giggling "oh-pah!" when she flashed Neil a bit of veiny thigh. "And when I am thinking it is your father coming tonight, I'm glad I haven't selled, so he can see these things what I find, how it looks. He is always saying to me, so many old things, they are too long going not used."

Neil had clearly had more to drink than he'd realized, because as soon as he saw the shoe up close, he started giggling too. It all seemed very funny, though when he tried to share the joke with Dijana, his tongue was a little too thick and his thoughts were a little too slow to make much sense. *"Double stitch below the anklebone. Straps cross left over right on the right foot, right over left on the other."* He'd heard his father say it a million times.

"Yah!" Dijana said. "Exactly. The working is so nice."

"Does my dad know?" Neil asked.

"What?" Dijana said.

"Does he know you have these? Does he know where you found them?"

"He is telling me I can take all what I like," she said.

"No, totally, I didn't mean—"

"He is all the time saying this."

"Of course," Neil said. "I just meant, did you show them to him or anything?"

"I am telling you I wear only tonight like for surprise."

"Wow, this is crazy," Neil said. His father really had remembered them. The shoes on Dijana's feet looked exactly like the ones his father always talked about. Neil was surprised at how well he knew them himself, just from his father's description.

"Oh man," Neil said. "My dad is going to have a fit."

"He won't like?" Dijana said, and suddenly Neil forgot what was funny. The room, which had begun to tilt a little from the brandy, righted itself. Inga Beart's red shoes had been lost in Paris—it was one thing Neil's father and all the historians agreed on. So how was it possible they'd ended up at Nan and Pop's ranch?

"They must have been Nan's," Neil said.

"What?" Dijana asked, but this time Neil didn't even try to explain. The red high heels with the crisscross straps that his father remembered seeing—there was no other way. They'd probably been there for years, wrapped up in newspapers at the back of Nan's closet, a place Neil's father never would have thought of looking, because he knew that Inga Beart had left her red shoes in France. *These* red shoes, which Dijana had now taken off and was holding up to the light, and which Neil could see really did have creases on the straps just like his father remembered, couldn't have been Inga Beart's. They must have been Nan's all along.

"Neil? Is okay?"

"Yeah," Neil said. He looked for a tissue in his pocket. "I think I have allergies."

He could imagine how it might have happened: his dad as a little kid, so used to seeing his Aunt Cat in farm boots that the one time she got dressed up for a party he got confused and thought she was his mother finally coming home.

"For this you should take honey," Dijana was saying. "Honey from farm, this is the best thing. You want some?"

"No thanks," Neil said.

"I have some in kitchen. Really good. Really organic."

"I'm fine, thanks," Neil said.

Dijana cleared the glasses, and Neil dabbed with his napkin at a wine spot he'd made on her tablecloth. This had been some evening for the Beart men, he thought. Magdalena was off camping with her boyfriend, and the shoes Neil's dad was sure were his mother's had really belonged to his aunt—however impossible it was to imagine Nan putting her foot into something that did not keep her heel planted firmly on the ground.

As Neil was leaving, stuffed full of cake and drunker than he'd intended, Dijana said, "So your father, he is not liking these presents I am sending for Christmas?"

"Oh, gosh, I forgot to tell you. He loved them. Wow, I'm really sorry. He told me to tell you," Neil said. He wondered if Dijana had somehow sensed that her Christmas presents were right there in Neil's backpack, still a little damp from the rain.

But she was smiling. "Yah, your father is telling me he is really needing for socks, and these I have made with hands."

"He said they fit great," Neil said.

"Well, you must give him thanks for me also. Magdalena tells me the things he sends are very beautiful."

"I'll tell him," Neil said.

"She tells that they are Indianish things, but she will not tell me more than this. I must to wait, she says, but now you are here before she is coming home."

"Yeah, that's true. Crazy thing."

"She tells me I will be very happy when I see these things. So you must to tell your father thank you very much."

"I'll tell him," Neil said, but he was pretty sure he never would. He wasn't thinking all that well as he left Dijana's building, but his mind was clear enough to recognize something new: a feeling of responsibility, like he was the parent and his dad was the child and it was up to Neil to head off hurtful and unnecessary truths. When his father found out about the shoes in Nan's closet he would finally have to admit to himself that Inga Beart never came back, not even for a visit. And with that thought came a realization, as if Neil had stepped off one of the invisible edges of childhood and found to his surprise that everything was simpler on the other side: His father didn't have to know.

It was well past ten o'clock as Neil walked to the tram stop, but the sun had only just then fully set behind the buildings and the sky was turning from pink to red. Neil felt sad and wise and sort of dizzy. He hadn't been able to stop his mom from running off with the Jazzercize guy, he couldn't fix his father's lousy childhood, and he obviously hadn't been able to keep his dad from getting into trouble with Becca and the school board. Now it was happening again. Life had set his father up for a major disappointment. But this time there was something Neil could do about it. And as he waited in the late-night dusk, hoping the tram was still running, Neil made up his mind not to tell his father about seeing Dijana and her old red shoes.

*

The next morning Neil picked up the photocopies of the file for Professor Piot at the Lithuanian archives, then spent the first few hours of the bus ride back to Paris worrying about Magdalena, who, it seemed, was either seriously unreliable or in real trouble, stuck with no money on a broken-down bus or kidnapped by human traffickers who might at that moment be securing her to the wheel well of an airplane bound for Abu Dhabi. At absolute best, the text she'd sent her mother was the truth and she was off toasting marshmallows with some guy who didn't deserve her. And then there were his father's Christmas presents, still balled up in their shopping bag at the bottom of his backpack. Neil had been planning to mail them first thing when he got back to Paris, but now that didn't seem like such a good idea. When his father got the package he would probably call Dijana up right away to say thank you, and when he did, she'd be sure to tell him about how she'd worn the things from Nan's closet when she thought he was coming to dinner. She'd mention the red shoes, and while a normal person wouldn't think anything of it, Neil's dad would be sure to ask, just out of habit, exactly what they looked like, and the whole story would come out. Neil pushed the bag down deeper in his backpack, and felt awful.

By the time they crossed the border into Poland Neil had decided that he would toss the bag into the first garbage can he saw when he got back to Paris, maybe even drop it in the river so there would be no changing his mind if he started thinking about how Dijana had knit the socks herself. He would feel bad about it for a day or two, but there was no other way. Getting rid of those presents might be the nicest thing he'd ever done for his father.

"Well?" said Professor Piot. He was outside smoking his before-lunch cigarette when Neil got to the archives.

"Here's the file," Neil said, giving him the copies. They had gotten kind of wrinkled because the guy who'd been sitting next to Neil on the bus kept putting his feet all over Neil's bag.

"Very good, very good," Professor Piot said, flipping through the papers. "So you had a good time?"

"It was great," Neil said. "It was really nice to see her again."

"Ah?" Professor Piot said, looking at Neil sideways.

"So, you can read Polish?" Neil asked. He didn't want to talk about the trip.

"Oh yes," Professor Piot said. "My father was born Piotrowski in Bialystok. You'd be surprised how often it comes in handy. Quite an important force in European history, the great Polish empires. Ah, this is interesting," he said, looking closely at the documents. "It would seem that the Jews of Vilnius are being granted the continued use of a cemetery that has already existed. Very interesting. And the date? 1629? Yes, this is excellent."

"What else does it say?" Neil asked. The document was several pages long.

"Well, it is an official act, so a number of issues are addressed. Questions of whether the community will be allowed to keep their butchers' shops, make use of the public bathhouse, hm, yes, and so on. The spelling is really quite antique. Ah, which reminds me." Professor Piot took out a packet of papers. "Here—the script key for Gothic Minuscule, not entirely complete. Take this one too, it is a secretary hand from around the time your monk was writing at Saint-Jean-d'Angély, and one that originated, I believe, in the monasteries of northern France. Notice the similarities between the *b* and the *v* if it comes at the beginning of a word."

"Great, thanks," Neil said.

"A number of letters are joined together, you will see. And also the simplified *r*, which comes only after an *o*."

"Right," Neil said, looking through the pages. It would be a relief to get back to the monk from Rouen.

"Ah, and there is one more thing," Professor Piot said. "Something came for you at the office address." Professor Piot dug through his briefcase, which was filled with books and papers and chunks of masonry he'd found at the site. "Here," he said, handing Neil an envelope addressed in round handwriting with the 1's made European-style, like upside-down *V*'s. It was stamped with *Albergue Municipal de Peregrinos,* and the name of a town in Spain as the return address.

"Who's it from?" Neil said.

"*J'en ai aucune idée,*" Professor Piot said, with a smile that Neil didn't understand until he turned over the envelope and saw *Thanks also for nice coffees at station, M,* written across the back as if it had been an afterthought.

"Wow, oh my gosh, wow, thanks," Neil said. He held the envelope by the edges, not caring that Professor Piot was sort of chuckling as he ground out his cigarette and arranged some pieces of gargoyle in his briefcase until he could get it to close.

"If you see Beth, tell her I have gotten hold of some early drawings of the *clocherie,*" he said.

"I will," Neil said.

Professor Piot said good-bye. Neil tucked the script key into his backpack and opened the envelope.

A sheet of paper was wrapped around a small stack of euro notes. The letter started out in blue, then there were several blots of ink and the writing became purple. Neil read it, then read it again. Some of the spelling was unusual, and she seemed to have picked up a little French.

Hello my dear Neil. I am writhing to You from the road which lots of other pelerins are on. Funny to say I am pelerin too, on the Way of Saint Jack just like You describe. Aktualy I am not taking this bus for Vilnius like we said, reason is long and very complicated histoire. You are telling to me about people of old times, remember? How they are going to Saint Jack always with so much problems in life? Aktualy I think still it is like this, people carrying weigths upon them, so much heavy and penitent things. And when You tell how this body comes on the beach, with Saint Jack looking like not even deathed and covered with scalped shells of all ocean and these shells are putting back his skin like the life, then I am thinking really to my friend, how I am making cinders with her when in fact it is important for her to be completed when deathed. So I will take her to End of the Earth where these pelerin nuns say Saint Jack, he has miracle for all (even those not quite believing!) But I writ You now for one other reason, is this: You are saying me name of Your father, yes? You know how I am knowing already

his name, RICHARD? My mother isn't calling him this. I know
RICHARD BEART because this name my mother is all the time
carrying, it is close on her heart. I do not meet Your father but
maybe for him it is same? They are for each other? Do not
worry so much for why, only please tell to father to call my
mother for saying hello. I think she is really waiting him all
life. Okay, I am going to tell You so long. Thanks also for kind
help of euros 60.00. I have some small job now so I inclose the
return of these euros here.
 Sincerely regards,
 Your Magdalena

There was something scratched out at the bottom, as if she'd
started to write a P.S., then changed her mind. Neil read it a third time.
It was pretty crazy of her to go off on the pilgrimage like that, and he
didn't know what she meant about his father's name, or what it was her
mother was carrying. But she'd asked him to tell his dad to call her
mom, and that, at least, was clear.

Neil took out his phone to call his father, then remembered what
he'd decided after he left Dijana's apartment. He had to keep his dad
from finding out about the shoes.

Neil put his phone away and read the letter again. It was interesting how much pilgrim vocabulary Magdalena had picked up—
calling the pilgrimage the *Way of Saint Jacques* and using words like
penitent. An example of how the old customs were passed on from
pilgrim to pilgrim; Neil hoped it was a sign that Magdalena was traveling with people who knew what they were doing. He skimmed past
the confusing parts. Something struck him about the particular words
she'd used: *people carrying weigths upon them* . . . Neil tried to remember
exactly what they'd been talking about at the train station when
she'd asked about his research. He had mentioned the woman with the
baby, the criminal priests and chronic adulterers. *So much heavy and*
penitent things. Neil took out the script key from Professor Piot. He
thought of the little tails on the monk's letters, the way the strokes of
the pen seemed to trail off the page. He looked back at the letter. There
was the part about Magdalena's mother, something she was *all the time*

carrying, something *close on her heart.* Neil remembered what Professor Piot had said about the monk's handwriting: Perhaps his arm was tired. Neil shoved Magdalena's letter into his notebook, grabbed his backpack, and hurried into the archives.

He read Magdalena's letter a few more times while he waited for the monk's file, telling himself that the idea was crazy, he shouldn't get too worked up. But when the carton from the Saint-Jean-d'Angély archives came and he opened the packet with the monk's eight vellum pages again, Neil felt suddenly weightless as the bottom dropped out of time. For a moment he had the sense that he was looking straight through the monk's parchment and into an afternoon at the Saint-Jean-d'Angély abbey seven hundred years ago. He could see the monk dip the sharpened quill of a goose feather into ink, trying to hold his hand steady as a heavy chain around his wrist dragged each stroke downward. The precise balance of a hollow quill against parchment took decades to achieve; Neil could see the monk struggling to keep his movements even, to recalibrate the pressure of his pen against the page, his wrists bound by by iron shackles, the kind a heretic would be required to wear as he walked toward Santiago de Compostela, dragging his chains.

Neil looked around. Beth must have gone to lunch and Professor Piot had already left for a meeting with the archeology students. There was no one for Neil to tell.

He looked back at the parchment. Now that he had the idea in his head he couldn't see it any other way: The monk had been writing under some impediment. He'd been carrying an actual physical burden, even as he sat with his pen at the abbey of Saint-Jean-d'Angély. The date of the parchment was 1259, which, if Neil was remembering right, was around the time of the Inquisition of Languedoc. Local bishops would have been busy rooting out seditious thoughts among their clergy, especially in France, where the Cathars and other heretical groups had been challenging the church for some time. Neil had read about priests made to walk barefoot across Europe because of minute differences in the interpretation of the liturgy, the placement of the *and* in the naming of the Holy Trinity, things that seemed so laughably trivial now that it was hard to imagine heaven and hell had once hung in the balance.

Magdalena's letter was lying open next to the monk's parchment. *Do not worry so much for why, only please tell to father to call my mother* . . . Neil thought of Dijana and Nan's red shoes. He thought of his father, so weighted down by a made-up memory that he couldn't do much more than inch through life, and he knew what Professor Piot would say: A historian must not hide the facts for the sake of protecting the people or nations or ideas that are close to his heart. Neil checked his watch. It was still early morning in the States, but his father always got up early.

Neil left the monk's documents where they were and went back downstairs to get his phone, thinking about how he would describe to his father the effort it must have taken the monk to form each letter, as every adjustment of the pen made the rough metal bands dig more deeply into the raw places on his wrists. He would tell his father about the trials of the early Inquisitions, and his father would picture the monk sitting silent, holding fast to some unsanctioned detail of faith while the church authorities measured out the weight of his heresy in iron—both of them remembering the thing with the school board and how Neil's father had refused the lawyer the teacher's union offered him and wouldn't talk to the people from the newspaper when they asked if he denied the allegations. How he'd asked Neil to please just believe him, and how that hadn't been enough.

There would be a silence, and then, if his father didn't start talking first, and if the moment seemed right, Neil would tell him about Magdalena's letter and Dijana and the shoes.

Neil got his phone out of the locker, but he hesitated a moment before he dialed the number, imagining his father, a little stunned, probably sitting alone at Nan and Pop's old kitchen table, in the place he'd always thought *she* must have sat, finally knowing for sure that his mother really had abandoned him.

But then Neil thought about Dijana, who obviously really liked his father, and how she'd gotten all dressed up when she thought he was coming to dinner. He dialed the number. He thought about Inga Beart, who'd been too busy being famous to visit her son even once, who'd given his dad so little of herself that he'd had to invent a memory of her just to get by, and he thought about Nan, who must have bought herself a pair of fancy shoes in a moment of extravagance and then kicked them deep into the back of her closet when she found out they gave her blisters, never imagining that in the time she'd had them on, the little kid Neil's dad had been had made an imaginary mother for himself.

The old answering machine chimed. Neil hoped his father wouldn't take it too hard.

"You have reached Walter and Catherine Hurley. We probably couldn't make it to the phone in time, or else we're out in the yard . . ."

"Hey dad," Neil said. "I'm really sorry it's been such a long time, but, ah, that Lithuanian lady, you know, Dijana? I think she'd really like to hear from you. Actually, kind of a crazy thing—she found some shoes in Nan's closet, some red ones, like you always said you—well, she'll tell you all about it. I have her number here . . ." and so on, imagining the sound of his voice slowly turning those tired tapes on the old machine next to Pop's chair, on top of the box where Nan used to keep coupons. He imagined his father coming in to find the little light blinking, rewinding the tape a couple of times to be sure he'd heard right, then picking up the old rotary phone and dialing the string of numbers that would ring to Dijana's apartment with its lace and cooking smells, where, surely, somebody would answer.

Then, though he knew he ought to get back to his documents, Neil left the archives and hurried back to the oyster bar whose dumpster he had chosen to throw his father's Christmas gifts into earlier that morning, when he'd been thinking that no matter how bad he felt about Dijana's homemade socks, that dumpster was the one place where he wouldn't be tempted to retrieve them.

The garbage hadn't been collected yet, and Neil rolled up his sleeves and ignored the looks from people on the sidewalk as he plunged his arm in up to the elbow. He almost passed out when he accidentally grabbed something with legs and long limp antennae, but he kept at it, digging past shells and old lemons until he felt the edge of the shopping bag. Except for the smell and an orange stain on the toe of one of the socks, the Christmas gifts were fine.

Neil couldn't put off sending the presents again, so he went straight to the post office on rue de Moussy, where the clerk wrinkled her nose but gave Neil an airmail envelope and a wet paper towel for his hands.

"Priority or Express?" she asked.

"Express," Neil said. "It's a Christmas present."

The clerk looked at him oddly.

"Last Christmas," Neil said.

"Seventy-four euros."

"Oh," Neil said.

"Priority is twenty-one euros."

"That sounds fine," Neil said. He paid with some of the money from Magdalena, then he ran all the way back to the archives. He knew he should hurry upstairs—the archives staff didn't like it when researchers left documents lying out in the reading room for longer than the time it took to have a very small coffee or use the bathroom. But those eight vellum pages had kept their secrets for centuries; they could wait. Neil had one more thing he had to do. He sat in front of his locker and went through his notes until he found a map of the Camino Francés, the pilgrim route that started out in France. The address Magdalena had written from was one of the first few towns in Spain, which meant she was making good time. He took his computer out and walked around the locker room until he found a place where the wireless signal was strong enough to check the bus fares on the Eurolines site. Neil's debit card got a lousy exchange rate; it would be better to go to the bus terminal and pay in cash. But he didn't trust himself to wait. Magdalena wouldn't get to Finisterre for at least a week or maybe two, and that would give Neil way too much time to change his mind. The ticket was ninety-eight euros. Well, if he spent that much he'd have to go. Neil punched in the number on his debit card and bought the ticket.

{RICHARD}

Paris, June

IT TAKES EIGHT minutes for sunlight to reach the Earth, my Uncle Walt once told me. Just eight minutes for the light to travel all that way, and when the sun goes out, for eight minutes no one down on Earth will know a thing about it.

Uncle Walt must have read that fact in one of his astronomy magazines, and it must have come into his mind on one of the summer dusks we spent digging our shovels into mud, trying to block the irrigation water in the far corner of the field for long enough that the hard ground would be persuaded to let a little in. I remember looking up at the sky bleached by a sunset without any clouds and imagining the sun blinking out and darkness sweeping down through outer space, while for eight strange minutes the trees were still growing and people were still walking around, opening their newspapers and watering their cows in a doomed light, not knowing that the sun was already gone.

That thought has stuck with me all my life. It is less a fear of darkness than it is of those last few minutes of sunlight, of the world still going on normally when in fact the great irreversible event has already taken place, the end has already come and disaster is hurtling down.

One evening a year or two before he died when Walt and I were sitting in the old truck looking out at the half-drained pond, I asked him if he remembered telling me the fact about the eight minutes. He didn't, but I suppose adults and children live in different worlds where words mean different things, and a remark a grown-up person doesn't even remember making can bore right to the core of a child and stay there for the rest of his life.

Well, it's those eight minutes of sunlight that come to mind as I think back over my first few days in Paris, when certain sights or sounds kept tugging on memories the way the shadows might begin to come in at different angles as darkness rounded Venus and rushed toward Earth on the heels of that final sunlight. Which is not to say my world went dark. As I made my way to the archives of the Assistance Publique-Hôpitaux de Paris I felt no subtle warning run down along my spine, no sense at all of what I would find there. And that is probably for the best. I am no Inga Beart, to put out my eyes at the sight of knowledge, however difficult that knowledge may be to bear.

During Uncle Walt's last year I had Diana come out to the ranch every couple of weeks to clean. Walt and I didn't do much picking up after ourselves; still, most of the dust and the clutter in that house was from years past. Diana would fuss over Walt, getting him another pillow and that kind of thing, and I think he liked it. I liked having her there too, and it wasn't only because I knew she needed the money that I started asking her to come every week instead of every two. She washed the windows and cleaned out the back kitchen, where we found an electric mixer the size of a sink still in its crate, unused for all those years.

When she'd finished with that I had her go through Aunt Cat's boxes, though I knew Pearl would be mad if she ever found out. The will hadn't been entirely clear about who they belonged to, saying just *"For Ricky, the boxes in the back closet. There's something of your mother's you might as well have."* Both the lawyer and I interpreted that as meaning *all* the boxes in that closet, even though the only thing that had been my mother's was a little doll trunk with *Inga* stenciled on it. Pearl didn't agree, but though she'd gotten worked up about it right after Aunt Cat passed away, she hadn't so much as set foot in the old bedroom in the years since, let alone looked in the closet, where Aunt Cat's clothes were still on their hangers. So I figured it was as good a job as any for Diana. I set aside the doll trunk and I looked through a few of the other boxes—candlesticks and tablecloths and such from old Grandma Beart. I took what I could find of the silverware, thinking that Pearl's daughter, Carly, might like to have it someday. It made me sad to think of getting rid of the things my Aunt Cat must have thought I'd be the only one with any patience for, but I knew Diana appreciated the work and I was running out of things to ask her to do. I told her to set aside any papers or photo albums, keep what she liked of the rest, and take everything else to Goodwill.

On Tuesdays I'd go to Pueblo to pick her up, and sometimes as I drove her down to the ranch we'd get to talking—me doing most of the listening—about our kids and Uncle Walt's health and those sorts of things. She was not an uncomplicated woman, I could see that, but she had a way of taking a subject that would otherwise fill me with apprehension—Uncle Walt's trouble moving his legs, for example, or the problems a friend was having back home—and she would lift those things up into the daylight and show them for what they were: life's simple, practical calamities, best considered head-on. I'd spend most of each week looking forward to her being there, planning conversations we might have. Then when Tuesday came, I'd find I didn't have a thing to say to her—and be contented in her presence all the same.

One day when I picked Diana up she was complaining of a tooth-ache, and by the time we got to the ranch it was clear the tooth was really troubling her. I got her some aspirin and some ice, and I could see her cheek was puffing up. When Aunt Cat went back to school to be a dental hygienist she learned to assist in root canals. I remember her saying that a bad tooth will only get worse, and so I told Diana that I'd drive her into town to see the dentist. She didn't have any kind of insurance, but I told her not to worry about the cost. As it turned out, they sent her to the emergency dental clinic in Pueblo. There was quite a wait, and though I kept bothering the nurse to get her in as quickly as possible we spent most of the day together in the emergency room waiting area. It might sound like I was unconcerned by the discomfort she was in, but that's not what I mean when I say that I appreciated each moment of that afternoon. The two of us, side by side in our plastic chairs. I felt—for no good reason—that there wasn't a thing more that I wanted from the world.

To help her pass the time I told her about getting scarlet fever as a boy, which was complicated by an allergy to antibiotics and turned into double pneumonia, and how my cousins were always jealous that I got to go away to a big city hospital. I told her about the round windows in the walls that, in my delirium, spun and spun, and how the nurses put on a puppet show for me, with one of their old-fashioned white starched caps as a ship, how even now I can't stand boats because they bring back the rocking feeling of that fever.

I told her about the day my son was born, and how that was the happiest day of my life, and, though she was trying to open her mouth as little as possible, she told me about how her daughter came out more quickly than expected in a big Soviet hospital without enough doctors, where, if it hadn't been for one of the other expectant mothers catching her in time, the baby would have slipped right off the delivery table and onto the floor.

These were the thoughts that were going through my head as I walked to the medical archives, and it's odd to say that as I was approaching what I imagine is as close as I'll ever get to knowing my mother's secrets, I wasn't thinking about her at all. I didn't know where Diana was at just that moment, but I made a plan to find out, and though the story of her daughter being born in that Soviet hospital was awful, in its way, telling it had made her laugh through her toothache— and me too, imagining the whale of a woman in the next bed lunging to catch a slick tiny person as she slid off the edge of the delivery table and into the world.

The medical archives had a slightly antiseptic smell, though that might have been my imagination. The building had been an elementary school once; there was a water fountain sized for six-year-olds in between the bookshelves and over it a display of old-time photographs of nurses and midwives posing gravely with unnerving implements.

A lady at a desk said something to me, then seeing I didn't understand, she asked me in English what I was looking for.

"I'd like to see a hospitalization record from the Hôtel-Dieu hospital," I said.

"What is the name?" she said, and I spelled it for her. She typed some commands into the computer, and I waited, wondering if she had read translations of Inga Beart's books in school, if she would ask me what it was like to be her son, and what I would tell her if she did.

"Ah, yes, okay," she said. She began writing down a file number, then stopped. "Ah, but this is 1954."

"That's right," I said.

"After 1939 these documents can go only to the patient."

"Well, but she was my mother," I said. "Look, it says right here," and I showed her my birth certificate, glad I'd brought it with me for just this kind of thing. I gave her my passport too, so she'd know I was who I said I was.

"Okay," she said. "But these documents can go only to the patient."

"But she's dead," I said. "She died in 1954."

"You have a paper showing this?"

"No," I said. I hadn't thought to get a copy of the death certificate. "She died when I was very young, see, and I didn't know till later—"

"Yes, but we must have this document. Maybe she is still living, so we cannot give her file."

"She is not still living," I said. "My mother was Inga Beart, the writer. She was very famous and she died just a few months after the record was made, in November 1954."

"Okay," she said. "But I will have to see the document of her death."

"It was in all the newspapers," I said. "Everyone knows about it."

"Please, you must be quieter. People are reading."

"Everyone knows," I said, quieter.

The woman typed something else into the computer. "I am looking, and we have no document of death for her. You can see only your own file, you do not have the right to look at what is hers."

It occurred to me that she was right. What claim do I have over the personal information of a woman I never knew? All my life in one way or another, people have been telling me the same thing. I stood there looking at the woman for a moment, and I believe I had every intention of turning to leave. But I saw the blue door framed by the edge of the tablecloth, I watched the cup fall and smash into four pieces, petals of a china flower blooming as it hit the floor. I saw the red shoes, and how a piece of the cup must have flown up and nicked a spot just below her anklebone, where a drop of red blood beaded but didn't run.

"But I'm her son," I said.

I saw the stitches that anchored the strap in place, the scuff across the heel. I saw the way the slim bones adjusted themselves under the skin when she stood up and how veins covered the arch of each foot with bluish lace.

"Look," I said. "I have the paper here. She was my mother." I showed her my birth certificate again.

"Yes, if you want only your file, it's okay," she said.

"I want my mother's file," I said.

"You cannot have this file. Beart, Inga was in hospital in 1954. Files after 1939 can be released only to the patient."

"Yes, I know," I said.

"So you would like to see your documents?"

"What documents?"

"For Beart, Richard."

"No," I said. "You don't understand. I'm an American, I don't have documents here. Only my mother has documents because she lived in Paris for a while, and I—at the time I wasn't with her."

"They must be yours," she said, looking at my birth certificate, then at the screen. "Documents for Beart, Richard at the hospital Hôtel-Dieu. You will have to fill out this form here, with the number of the *fonds* first, like this, okay? I can help you."

"No, no," I said.

"You want the documents or you don't want?"

"They're not mine," I said. "Richard Beart, it's a common name."

The archivist paused a moment and looked back at my birth certificate. "Ah, okay," she said. "Yes, it's a mistake if you say you have not been there, but I see that the day of birth is the same."

"I've never been in France before."

She typed something more into the computer. "And also the day of *inscription* to hospital is the same."

"What day?" I asked.

"It was 10 August 1954 for Beart, Inga also, yes?"

"Yes."

"And it is the same for Beart, Richard. Ah, maybe there was an accident and they went together?"

"No, no accident," I said.

"Oh, yes, you are right."

"How do you know? What does it say there?" I asked. "Would you just read me what it says right there on the screen?"

"It says 'quarantine,' this is all. *Quarantine paediatrique.*"

"Why was she in quarantine?"

"No, this is for Beart, Richard. For Beart, Inga it says nothing more here. But for the quarantine they have a different system for the records, I can see that the file for Beart, Richard comes from a separate collection. In fact, for a time the children's quarantine had its separate administration—"

"What was he quarantined for?" I asked.

"Well, that I cannot say," she said.

I remembered the hospital rocking, Aunt Cat's cool hands on my cheeks and those round little windows like animal eyes—like the portals of a ship—their frames fastened with rivets to the wall. "Let me see the file," I said.

"Well, no, if it is not yours you must not see it."

And when the rocking stopped, the nurses with their starched white caps, a crack in the plaster ceiling, my head thick with fever, not able to understand what they said.

"But I had scarlet fever," I said.

"Yes, but these are records from the hospital Hôtel-Dieu in Paris, and you say you have never been a patient in this place."

"But I had scarlet fever in 1954."

The archivist looked at me a moment, then back at my birth certificate, and then at the computer. She tapped her pen against her lips. "Okay," she said, and she wrote some numbers on the forms she had given me. "Wait here."

She came back a few minutes later with a thin blue file and led me to a private room to look at it. "Please do not photograph the documents," she said. "There are official photocopies only and for this there is a fee."

"Thank you," I said. She went out and shut the door.

The file was labeled in the blocky, almost imperceptibly uneven printing of an old typewriter, the last name all in capitals the way they do in France. For a moment or two I just looked at it, thinking about how one's own name always seems so odd and unfamiliar if one sits right down and stares at it. I'd come a long way, and this was not the person I'd expected to find.

"Hello there," I said to little *BEART, Richard*—though when I opened the file it was my Aunt Cat I recognized first, in the handwriting on the hospital admittance form. She'd been in a rush, and the curving, graceful script that always seemed more feminine than the rest of her had a panicked slant, the end of one word trailing into the first letter of the next as if she couldn't spare the time to lift the pen. But the curl to the *R* in my first name, the looping numbers of my birth date were unmistakably hers. The questions on the form were all in French; she'd left most of them blank and scrawled across the top *FEVER CHILLS RASH TONGUE IS WHITE* and with a double underline *ALLERGIC TO AMOXICILLIN!!* I turned the page.

I'm very grateful to the woman at the medical archives, and I made myself a note to send her a box of chocolates and a card as soon as I get home. I'll be sure not to be too specific in the card—I wouldn't want one of her superiors to get ahold of it and find out she bent the rules. She told me in no uncertain terms when I came back to the desk to ask for her help—because of course the rest of the file was all in French—that the archivists absolutely did not do translations. But maybe I was just insistent enough or else there was something in my face that told her that my world and everything I'd believed up until that point hung ready to pivot on what that file said. She sighed, put a sign out on her desk, and followed me into the little reading room.

When I think of my Aunt Cat a certain memory often comes to mind. It's a story I would have liked to have told at her funeral, except that folks who hardly knew her wouldn't have found it appropriate. One day when we were kids, someone—one of the men who worked around the farm, I think—came in at suppertime to say that there was a hurt dog out on the highway and someone'd better shoot it. It went unspoken in our house that it was Aunt Cat who handled that kind of thing. She put her boots on and gave Eddie a little pat on the shoulder—he'd gone all white thinking it was probably Goodboy, who was always chasing tires. She got Uncle Walt's gun out of the closet and she and the farm hand went out. Eddie started crying all over his supper, but I knew that, things being as they were, the dog had a bit of luck to have Aunt Cat be the one to do it. It may not be much, but it's the thing I'd like to have gotten up and said the day we buried her: Aunt Cat's hands wouldn't shake and she'd get it right on the first try.

It's the steadiness of my Aunt Cat's hands I think of now when I imagine her leading me up to the blue door, and the door opening into a room with a table covered in lace. My hand would have felt hot in hers. She had been checking my temperature, the file said, and told the doctors that I'd been a bit flushed since a few days before we landed at Le Havre—though it seems she thought it was just seasickness that had kept me in bed through most of the voyage. She'd been planning to take me to a doctor as soon as we landed but—I suspect—the comtesse insisted that I be brought straightaway to Paris, where, Aunt Cat told the doctors, I had vomited during a visit to a Parisian department store. The medical file doesn't mention why I was taken shopping, though I imagine the comtesse had something to do with it, perhaps buying me a new outfit in which to meet my mother. It must have been there that I stood under a marquee with a grid of light bulbs stuck up against the sky and, dizzy with the crowd and the fever, looked up and saw my Universe.

From what I pieced together over the next few days from the comtesse's papers and the information in the file, it seems that a number of specialists had agreed that a new psychotherapeutic technique that translates to something like "emotional shock therapy" was just the thing to rid Inga Beart of her most persistent demons. The plan was to jolt her back to health not by electric current, as was the fashion, but by the sight of her living, breathing—and, by that point, flushed and dizzy—child. And so the comtesse, who spared no expense, agreed to pay my passage, and Aunt Cat's too, all the way to Paris.

I wonder if, as she half-carried me up those stairs to her sister's apartment, Aunt Cat hoped that the comtesse and the specialists were right, that my unnaturally pink cheeks, along with a new sailor suit and the pacifying effect of the fever, would help make Inga Beart love me, or keep me. If Aunt Cat stood waiting for the blue door to open, hoping that she'd be boarding the ship back to the States alone, back to a husband and two small kids who were already plenty enough to handle.

Exactly what happened next will probably never be known. Even after I got Inga Beart's estate manager to send me a copy of her death certificate by express mail and had the notes in my mother's own medical file translated by a professional service the archivist referred me to, there are still gaps in the story that may never be filled. Now that Inga Beart, Aunt Cat, and the Comtesse Labat-Poussin are all dead, I'm the only one left who witnessed it, and I don't remember a thing about that afternoon except for the blue door, the falling cup, my mother's shoes, and—was it?—a drop of blood on her ankle.

I don't know if my mother tried to shield her eyes or run into another room, or if the comtesse forced her hands down to her sides or blocked the door to keep her there, though I'm sure it's not fair to credit cruelty like that to a woman who, it seems, had only Inga Beart's best interests at heart. All it says in my mother's file is that Inga Beart begged them not to make her look at the child. There was an argument between her and the comtesse—all of this according to "the sister," who told the story to the receiving doctor. At one point Inga Beart apparently appealed to Aunt Cat, expressing what the doctor called "acute distress" and saying that "she did not want to see what was going to happen"—an indication, perhaps, that she recognized she was on the brink of a dangerous loss of self-control. Then, somehow, she was made to uncover her eyes and turn her face to me.

I assume that Aunt Cat pushed me under the table when Inga Beart went for the knife, probably thinking that she meant to use it on me. According to the medical file, it was a small kitchen knife with a curved blade, the kind used for peeling fruit. Maybe it had been left on the table that morning after my mother had her breakfast; maybe, when the doorbell rang, she was taking the skin off a peach. I know that sometime soon afterward the comtesse fainted, and it was Aunt Cat who clamped a dish towel over her sister's face and, possibly with help from a neighbor, called for an ambulance to take them—and me— to the Hôtel-Dieu hospital, where it didn't take long for someone to notice that my coloring couldn't be due to shock alone. I had a fever of 41.7 degrees Celsius, according to the records, 107 degrees Fahrenheit by my calculation and extremely serious for a child of five. They packed me in ice; no doubt they lectured Aunt Cat about dragging a child brimming with microbes all over the country, and, according to the records, they forbade her from entering my room. But, a nurse noted, she did anyway, and stayed to watch me turn from red to white to blue as the fever eased and they unpacked me from the ice, and then from blue to white to red as it flared back up again.

"Don't you think it's your fault now, Ricky, don't you think like that," Aunt Cat had said, standing at the fence with the jagged end of the chicken wire caught on her sleeve the day I came home from college mad as anything, having learned that my mother's death had been precipitated by an act of self-destruction I'd never known a thing about. I remember her saying that, because later on as I turned the conversation over in my mind I reasoned to myself that Aunt Cat must have been talking about why my mother left me as a baby, all those years ago.

Aunt Cat also said another funny thing that day, that, I confess, I never thought too much about until I stood in the medical archives looking at my own name on a hospital form all in French. I'd said, "Didn't you think I'd find out someday?"—meaning that sooner or later I was sure to learn the cause of my mother's fatal infection of the sinuses. Aunt Cat, who must have misunderstood the question, said something like, "But you were delirious. You had a fever so bad they told me you wouldn't remember a thing." She put her hands on my shoulders and took a breath, but I pulled away from her.

"I'm not delirious," I'd said, misunderstanding in my turn.

And then, perhaps realizing that I didn't know as much as she'd assumed at first, that no fever-locked memory had burst its dam, Aunt Cat let that long breath go and said, "Well, you just don't tell that sort of thing to a child." She set her jaw and went back to the chicken wire, and that may have been the last and longest conversation we ever had about my mother.

*

Of course, what I learned at the medical archives set me to thinking about a lot of things, reinterpreting conversations of thirty and forty years ago, and with the final days of my stay in Paris spent rushing around trying to get documents translated and copies made, it's only now, on the plane back home, that I've thought back to what my Uncle Walt said just before he died.

It might not have come to mind at all, except that I've got the window seat next to a nice young couple from the suburbs of Paris. They told me, in very good English, that this is their first overseas holiday together. They're going to New York to see Rockefeller Center and Niagara Falls. I leaned back in my seat so they could get a better view of their hometown from the air as we circled Paris and banked to the left. Of all the people in the world this young couple might make me think of, the ones that come to mind are Cat and Walt, who were once that age, fingers intertwined without even thinking about it.

By now they've fallen asleep with the armrest uncomfortably between them. The girl's head is on the young man's shoulder, his cheek against her forehead, and it occurs to me that of course it must have been Aunt Cat and not my mother that Uncle Walt was talking to as he slipped away. In those last moments, when the nurse turned down the ping of the monitor and a veil on the hereafter lifted, Cat is the one Walt would have seen.

"Don't you be mad at her," he'd said to me, and I see now how he might have looked to where Aunt Cat was waiting for him just beyond this life and figured there would never be a better time to patch things up between us.

And to her he said, "You didn't want to take him off to Paris." It wasn't abandonment my Uncle Walt was talking about, it was something more like love: Aunt Cat didn't want to give me to my mother. For all the trouble I was to her, my Aunt Cat would just as soon have kept me. And before he left this earth it was the one thing Walt thought I ought to know.

And if I'm right about that, then things begin to fit. My memory of my mother's shoes is clearer than it ought to be because I saw them when

Inga Beart was already in Paris; I was five, not three. It wasn't Aunt Cat's kitchen table I remember hiding under, of course it wasn't: The tablecloth was made of lace. And what Bristol and all the others say is true. My mother never came to see me.

Well, I might be feeling the influence of an especially long dawn as we fly with the sun from east to west, more time than I've ever had before to watch the beginning of a day, or it might be my unfamiliar vantage point above the clouds. It isn't often that one sees the world from way up here. But it seems as good a place as any to let an old idea go.

Instead, I imagine a long-distance telephone call from Paris, the comtesse arguing with Aunt Cat, telling her a boy ought to be with his mother. My Aunt Cat agreeing, in the end, to make the long trip with me to Paris. And when it was all over and we boarded the ship back to America together, I'd like to think that maybe Aunt Cat forgot for a moment that I was one more mouth to feed and felt half-glad that the comtesse's plan had gone so wrong and she hadn't gotten rid of me.

As for the red shoes, I guess I'll never know. It's likely that they were taken off sometime before my mother reached the hospital. Along with the catalog of ocular lacerations that, even without knowing French, I can't manage to read without feeling a little ill, the doctor's notes show that Inga Beart was also treated for an oblique fracture to the fifth metatarsal: a broken little toe. That kind of break most commonly occurs when a toe meets with axial force, for example, when it is stubbed against the corner of a step or a curb. And because it implies that the toe has been wrenched from the foot, it almost always happens barefoot. It's possible that Inga Beart's shoes were removed during the ambulance ride, but it's more likely, to my mind, that Aunt Cat took them off of her before she went about getting her sister down the stairs, and left them there on the floor of the apartment.

Without a bit of evidence to back it up, I imagine the comtesse waking from her faint a few moments later, perhaps with the sound of sirens on the street below. Finding herself alone on the scene of what the police and reporters were sure to recognize was the final act of a bizarre and gruesome drama, I imagine her slipping quietly away. But the comtesse was a woman who saved the drafts of her love letters; she had an eye for posterity. So maybe on her way out she picked up those red shoes from where they lay in a jumble on the floor and kept them— for her records. And yet even as I imagine this—the comtesse hurrying through the courtyard with my mother's shoes clutched in her handbag—I can hardly fault her. I hung on to those shoes as my single memory of Inga Beart, why shouldn't the comtesse have felt she had a right to do the same? Aunt Cat, with her practical tastes and the way she felt about her sister, wouldn't have cared a thing about them, and the gawkers and scavengers who were sure to arrive hardly deserved them. But for the comtesse, and for me too, it was different. We'd come as close as we ever would to something bright and rare. I suppose we both wanted a souvenir.

I haven't made up my mind just yet about what do with the informa- tion in those medical files. I could make quite a splash with an article in the *American Literary Review* or one of the other journals, a brand- new chapter in the life of Inga Beart. The knowledge of her sister's visit, the comtesse's plan, and, of course, who it was she was so desperate not to see would add a new layer to the debate over why she blinded herself. It would certainly prove Carter Bristol's theory wrong; with a scene like the one that must have taken place in Inga Beart's Paris apartment brought to light, Bristol would hardly be able to go on claiming that Inga Beart's child meant nothing to her, that she was pathologically short on emotion.

On the other hand, I'm not sure I want to be in the business of telling my mother's secrets to the world. Bristol and the others will conclude that, whatever my mother felt for me, it was a far cry from maternal affection. A woman who couldn't stand the sight of her own child, that's how Bristol will put it. He'll say she tore her eyes out in a rage after she was forced to look at me. I may just let those documents continue their slow progression into dust in the archives of the Assistance Publique-Hôpitaux de Paris, and keep my mouth shut.

But there is one person I will tell. This was a family affair, after all, and as Inga Beart's grandson, it's Neil's story as much as mine. I'll call him up when I get home and let him know what I've found. He's got a head for this kind of thing, and I'd like to hear what he makes of it. But knowing me, I'll mix up the important points, I'll forget to say how it was that I happened to open that *Hirondelle* file, or that I thought of him as I watched the young kids sitting along the Seine. I've loved words all my life, but when it's mattered most, I've never been too good with them. I'll mess it up when I try to tell him that I hope he never has to piece together old documents and scraps of memory to figure out what he meant to his father.

The captain says we've hit a bumpy patch just over Nova Scotia, and my tomato juice is rippling in its plastic cup. I'll take these notes and type them up when I get home, to give to Neil when I see him next. I've gone on longer than I meant to and let all sorts of extra bits creep in, and when it comes to Inga Beart and what exactly happened that day in August a good half-century ago, he'll have to draw his own conclusions.

But as for me, I believe my mother blinded herself before she ever saw me, because starting in the Santa Fe hospital when she turned her head away as I took my first breath, and ending in that Paris apartment, it seems that was the way she wanted it. And if this is true, and Inga Beart managed to put out her eyes in time to spare herself the sight of me, then I suppose there will come a day in the not so distant future when I will choose to believe she had her own good reasons. Maybe I'll be sitting out in the old truck watching the pond, thinking it over. How my Aunt Cat pushed me, five years old and flushed with fever, under the table when she saw what was about to happen; and my child's mind fixed not on the screams or the blood but on my mother's shoes and a china teacup falling to the floor. Other people will assume that it was shame transformed into a kind of crazed resentment that made Inga Beart blind herself rather than look her child in the eye, or see a face that had her nose or—I've been told—something of her smile. And yet. As I look out at the cattails or walk down to the water's edge, maybe I too will find myself able to choose what not to see.

They say that once her eyes were gone, for her last few months Inga Beart was happy. The experts may someday take a second look at what she said before she died, starting with the interview she gave to a reporter after they'd transferred her to a hospital for the blind in another part of Paris. She was tired of reading, she told him. They may find the account the ship's doctor gave of the voyage back to New York a month or so later, in October 1954, and think again about what he said: Inga Beart had contracted an infection on the boat, and as she lay on fever-soaked sheets, her face still in bandages, she covered the wall beside her with words. According to the doctor, who told a reporter about it later on, she recorded a kind of hallucination. He said it was hard to read exactly—something about bodies marked with ink and how blindness shut out what she'd rather not see. When they got her to New York they realized the infection had gone to her brain and none of it was taken seriously. But it might be time for a young Ph.D. student somewhere to argue that, for Inga Beart, who said once that she'd been trapped into a life as a writer, blindness was an escape.

But there will be other articles to write, and the scholars might never get around to it. I may decide that, as the only witness left to wonder, maybe the puzzle is mine to solve. When I get home I'll walk down to the pond to see how much water has been lost in the time I've been away, and I'll sit a while, turning it over in my head: My mother chose darkness rather than be made to look at me. I'll measure the space at the edge of the pond where the water has receded and the mud is cracked and dry, and a thought will strike me, a perfect explanation. I don't know just yet what it will be, but I have time. The rain will come, the pond will fill on up again, and one of these days I'll find a way to see it as an act of love, the kind no one will believe.

{MAGDALENA}

Santiago de Compostela, July

THE PILGRIMAGE HAD ended but Magdalena was nowhere near the sea. They had come to the town of Santiago de Compostela, finally finishing in front of a big church. Everyone else was hugging or praying or looking for a place to charge their phones, and Magdalena stood in the middle of a ring of souvenir stands selling scallop shells, wondering if she'd misunderstood.

"Where is the place where the bodies come up from the sea?" she asked Rachel, then Brit and Olaf. They didn't know. But a Filipino nun from another group told her that she'd better continue on along the *Camino Fisterra,* the old pilgrim route to the town of Finisterre, if she wanted to see the place where Saint James had washed ashore covered in scallop shells. Some people would be leaving together the next morning.

Rachel stayed in Santiago, praying in the saint's cathedral to have her sins erased. Magdalena didn't have the heart to tell her that, as far as she could tell, they were all still there. Brit and Olaf decided to go with her, and they and Magdalena joined the Filipino nun, a German couple, and Father Malloy, a convict from Londonderry who said that so long as he was violating his parole he might as well make it to the end.

They left just as it was getting light, walking west. Olaf had a compass set into the top of his walking stick, and he called out directions as they went—*west-north-west, west-west-north-west, west.*

As they walked, Father Malloy talked. He wasn't cut out to be a criminal, he said. In another life he might have been the philosophic type, but in those days there was no escaping politics, and he'd been caught running guns for the IRA. In prison he'd been such a model inmate that the guards used to drive him out to the bogs and leave him there, with a bag of crisps and a bit of plastic sheeting in case of rain, to give the dogs some practice. Father Malloy would walk for a while, then find a dry place to sit, maybe read the paper, and wait until they found him. Only Magdalena believed Father Malloy's stories. Most of them were written out verbatim on his arms, in between homemade tattoos.

He had entered the priesthood by way of a correspondence course while he was in prison, and when he first started holding Mass in the exercise yard the attendance was low. But pretty soon other prisoners began coming to him for confession, or anointments, or to have him sprinkle holy water on handwritten appeals.

It was in prison that Father Malloy had learned about the pilgrimage of Saint James, and as Magdalena and the others walked through little towns where thick-legged women stood in doorways and watched them, expressionless, as they passed, and lichen slowly chewed the stones of ruined castles, he told them things from the books he'd requested at the prison library. If the pilgrimage to Finisterre wasn't made during one's lifetime, it was said, then it would have to be made after death, the soul traveling no farther than the length of its coffin each day.

"Look here," he said, pointing to the faint outline of a cross carved into stone. The Crusaders had followed this path, leaving the sign of a cross to mark the way. The pilgrimage even had its mirror in the sky. That band of stars we call the Milky Way was called the Way of Saint James in medieval times, he said, because it guided pilgrims from the north toward Spain, and because those stars themselves were said to pave the path Saint James had taken when he rode down from heaven to help fight the Moors.

Father Malloy talked, Brit and Olaf and the German couple took pictures, and when they stopped to rest, Brit handed out granola bars. As they walked Magdalena picked yellow flowers off the scrubby bushes that grew along the road, rolling the petals between her fingers and counting her steps, as Father Malloy said the medieval travelers had done, using their pilgrim staffs to keep an even stride so they could measure the distance of their journey.

It took three more days to walk from Santiago to Finisterre. The roads were mostly empty and there were fewer pilgrims' hostels. They walked farther each day than they had before, looking for a place to sleep. Father Malloy bought olive oil and anointed each person's aching feet.

On the afternoon of the second day they saw the sea, still far off in the distance. Father Malloy climbed to the top of a rocky ledge and named it Montjoie, as medieval pilgrims had called the hills from which they first caught sight of a holy place.

They walked faster, smelling salt in the air. When they reached the ocean the continent drew itself up. For the last few kilometers the path climbed a narrow peninsula, the land rising to make a last stand against the sea. No one talked as they walked; it was all uphill.

A stone cross marked the spot where the path ended, and all around it were the remains of little fires where pilgrims had burned their boots. Long before the Christians claimed it for their own, Father Malloy said, Finisterre had been a site of pagan worship, the western-most point of all the known world. Past the horizon was the land of eternal youth, the place where the sun turned around. Rumor of it had traveled as far away as Ireland, and when the Romans arrived a century or so before the birth of Christ they stood on that bit of rock and watched the sun fall into the sea and named the place the End of the Earth.

The German couple took pictures of the ocean. Magdalena set down the shoebox and the others took off their packs and climbed down the rocks to a radio tower hung with pieces of clothing. Old shirts and worn-out socks flapped like flags, some of them recent, some of them threadbare from the wind. Brit and Olaf tied their parkas there, Father Malloy left his knee brace, and the Filipino nun took out an old felt hat no one had known she'd been carrying and fastened it around the metal bars with safety pins.

The sea was a long way below them. Waves hit against walls of rock and pieces of things got caught against the cliffs. Whole trees, parts of ships, and plastic drums collected there, wearing themselves to roundedness in water churned the color of milk.

"Where is the place where the bodies wash up?" Magdalena asked Father Malloy. He didn't know exactly, so after everyone had had their picture taken they picked up their packs again and followed the path down toward the town of Finisterre, past the statue of the Virgin that was said to grow real fingernails and, occasionally, perspire. Signs pointed them to the harbor and then along an old pilgrim path until they came to a place where the land seemed to have forgotten its fight against the ocean. It bowed to it instead, creating a stretch of sandy beach.

When they got to the water they all waded right in, not even bothering to take off their shoes and socks. And when their hot swollen feet had been cooled and felt somehow lighter than they had in days, in spite of being waterlogged, they headed toward the snack bar where the Norwegians had promised to buy everyone paella.

Magdalena stayed in the water, waving to say that she'd be along soon. Her feet had calluses like silver coins and nothing had ever felt as good as the ocean on her skin. She held the shoebox over her head to keep it out of the spray, then realized that was stupid—what did it matter now if it got a little wet? She opened the box and tried to untie the plastic bag inside, but the knot was too tight. She tore it open with her fingernails and took out a handful of ashes. The dust stuck to her wet hands and she accidentally tossed the first bit into the wind. Finally she waded in until the water was up to her chest and dumped out the whole bag, including at least one cigarette butt that must have gotten swept up off the floor of the station in Paris. The ashes eddied around her, the heavier pieces sinking while the rest made a skim on the water and stuck to her arms.

A wave came and took the ashes with it. Magdalena held on to her glasses as the water lifted her up, drenching her hair. She had a sudden memory of Lina in the rain, spinning with open arms in the middle of an empty street. Lina with Magdalena's mother's mascara running down her face, shouting for Magdalena to come, then spinning again with her eyes closed, her hands open to the rain. The empty shoebox was soaked through. Magdalena crushed it flat and waded back to shore. She wrung the water out of her shirt and moved the bag with her clothes higher up on the sand, because the tide was coming in.

There was a place where the beach was sandy, and farther along there were rocks. The sea hit against them, spraying up then washing over and down, crashing and receding. Like breathing, Magdalena thought. She looked to see if the ashes had washed up with the waves, but they were gone.

The beach stretched on, a pale line of sand tracing the shore as it curved to the east. Pebbles gathered around Magdalena's feet each time the waves rolled out. In among them was a shell, not a scallop but just an ordinary shell whose edges had been worn away. She tossed it out and it washed back again, settling like a pale toenail on her foot.

Another wave rolled in and Magdalena saw the body. Then the wave went out and it was gone; Magdalena wasn't even sure she'd really seen it. Another wave and it appeared again. A rabbit, made supple like a sack by the pounding of the sea.

With the next wave it was gone, then another and the rabbit washed up again, farther down the beach. Gone and back again, a little farther on. Magdalena followed. The next wave came and lifted the body, fanning its fur. It was so much a part of the movement of the water that it didn't seem dead. It was just a body, after life.

The rabbit rested on the sand for a moment, but as Magdalena came to it another wave washed it away. Gone and back, then gone again, farther down the beach each time until the snack bar was just a tiny dot behind her. The body settled for a moment between some rocks, but before Magdalena could get to it the waves pulled it under again.

A moment later it reappeared at the place where the beach narrowed. Far in the distance now, someone had come out of the snack bar and was calling her name. Probably Brit, telling her not to leave her bag lying on the beach like that. Magdalena pretended not to hear, and watched as the water folded and unfolded the body, tumbling the rabbit until it was sleek and boneless, its fur washed new by the sea.

"Magdute!" her mother had called from the kitchen when they first moved into the new apartment after Magdalena's father died. "Magdute, look!" her mother had said, and with an "Ouf!" she lifted Magdalena up to see the stain on the ceiling in the shape of a rabbit: a sign of springtime, of new life and ordinary things.

"Magdalena!" the person on the beach shouted—it wasn't Brit. It was a man's voice, but the sun was in her eyes, it was hard to see. He wasn't tall enough to be Olaf or round enough to be Father Malloy. A wave crashed, and the rabbit went under again. "Magdalena!" The person was coming toward her.

Another wave came, and another, but the rabbit was gone. Farther down along the beach a crumpled bit of brown washed up, but it was too far away for Magdalena to tell if it was the rabbit again or an old paper bag. The waves were higher now, water and foam and dark pebbles that rolled back into the sea, erasing her footprints and leaving the sand empty and smooth.

Every year on her birthday Magdalena's mother told her the story of the night she was born, how her father had left the hospital and stumbled with a bottle of cognac and a box full of matches into the old church on Saint Mikalojaus Street, where he spent the long night lighting candles by the hundreds until someone called the fire department, seeing the church ablaze. In the morning he came back, looking, Magdalena's mother said, like he'd had an even longer night than she'd had. The nurses put baby Magdalena in his arms, frowning at the smell of him and then trying to take the baby back as he started to unwrap her with clumsy hands, unwinding her blankets and pulling off her diaper, swatting at the nurses who tried to stop him, stinking of alcohol and incense. His hands shook, her mother said, his fingers were burned by hot wax, and by the time he'd gotten the newborn Magdalena entirely undressed and had examined every bit of her she was screaming and the one single doctor assigned for a floor full of mothers had come running. The nurses called her father a drunken pig and said he'd be sorry when his baby daughter caught her death of cold, but he'd held Magdalena to him, hours old, red and howling, and laughed and laughed—so happy, her mother had said, to see all her fingers and toes, her round belly and skinny legs and the wrinkles on her feet.

She thought of the man in Paris with her mother's words on his skin. *If the eyes don't see, the heart doesn't hurt.* It was what her mother would say when Magdalena asked to look at the picture that had been taken of the three of them that day at the hospital, tiny Magdalena in her mother's arms, her father flushed and smiling. *"Akys nemato ..."* her mother would say then, because looking at the picture made her sad. But now Magdalena thought of that old phrase and her own unmarked skin and felt the beginnings of an understanding.

She thought of her father steeling himself to look at words written all across a tiny body—and then laughing with relief to see that actually his baby was covered with nothing at all, just a newborn rash and a faint down of hair. When he danced her around the nurses, singing a nonsense song so that even the oldest and maddest of them had to smile, it was out of joy at the blankness of his daughter's skin. Because for her, at least, nothing was already planned.

Another wave came. Magdalena let the sand wash over her feet and bury them. She looked back toward the snack bar, squinting against the sun. The person on the beach was running now, calling to her and waving his arms. He was close enough for her to see that his hair was orange in the light and he was wearing a sweatshirt she recognized from the train station in Paris. Out of habit she started to take her glasses off. Then she changed her mind, and left them on.

A NOTE ON THE AUTHOR

ADELIA SAUNDERS has a master's degree from Georgetown University's School of Foreign Service and a bachelor's degree from New York University's Tisch School of the Arts. She grew up in Durango, Colorado, and currently lives with her family in New York City. This is her first novel.